# ROSINGS PARK

## JACK CALDWELL

WHITE SOUP PRESS

For information, address Jack Caldwell, 15060 Germany Oaks Blvd, Prairieville, LA 70769.
https://cajuncheesehead.com
http://whitesouppress.com/
http://austenvariations.com/

ISBN: 978-0-9891080-8-9

Layout & design by Ellen Pickels
Cover design by Ellen Pickels
Front cover image: Rebecca Young
Front cover paintings: *Portrait of a Gentleman* (1770–72) by Henry Benbridge
*Lady Elizabeth Stanley, Countess of Derby* (1776–78) by George Romney
*Portrait of a Gentleman* (1805) by François Mulard

# Dedication

To Barbara
my #1 fan

# In Appreciation

To Debbie Styne and Ellen Pickels
for all their hard work.

To Abigail Reynolds and Maria Grace
for all their sound advice.

To all the fans.
This one is for you.

# Author's Note

THIS WORK USES CHARACTERS INVENTED BY MISS JANE AUSTEN in her series of Regency novels. It is intended to honor Miss Austen and the immense pleasure her words continue to bestow upon the world.

This novel is part of my *Jane Austen's Fighting Men Series*. It is a sequel to my earlier works: *The Three Colonels* (Book One), *The Last Adventure of the Scarlet Pimpernel* (Book Two), and *Persuaded to Sail* (Book Three). It features characters from and references to events in those novels.

While *Rosings Park* stands on its own, the reader's enjoyment will be enhanced by reading the earlier books, especially *The Three Colonels*.

— *Jack Caldwell*
*Prairieville, Louisiana*

# Dramatis Personae

## KENT

**The Honorable Sir Richard Fitzwilliam, CB:** Colonel, British Army (retired), owner of Rosings Park, son of Lord and Lady Matlock, veteran of the Peninsular War and Waterloo (awarded the Order of the Bath)

**Anne, Lady Fitzwilliam:** wife of Sir Richard (m. 1815), daughter of Sir Lewis de Bourgh

**Sir Lewis de Bourgh, Bart.:** late owner of Rosings Park (d. 1803)

**The Honorable Lady Catherine de Bourgh:** widow of Sir Lewis, mother of Lady Fitzwilliam, sister to Lord Matlock

**Reginald Kendrick:** owner of Glendale Farm, nephew of Sir Lewis, cousin to Lady Fitzwilliam

**The Rev. William Collins:** rector of Hunsford Parish, heir to Longbourn Manor in Hertfordshire

**Charlotte Collins:** wife of Rev. Collins, friend to Lady Fitzwilliam

**Mrs. Jenkinson:** companion to Lady Fitzwilliam

**Mrs. Parks:** long-time housekeeper of Rosings Park

**Dawson:** Lady Catherine's personal maid

**Troop Sergeant-Major George Gregory:** British Army (retired), serves as majordomo for Sir Richard

**Philip Evans:** recently hired steward of Rosings Park

**Romeo:** an Italian greyhound and Lady Fitzwilliam's pet

**Joseph Clarke:** tenant farmer at Rosings and member of the tenant committee

**Peggy Clarke:** wife of Mr. Clark

**Mrs. Johnson:** a seamstress in Hunsford

**Cork Johnson:** Mrs. Johnson's son

**Adam Shepardson:** footman employed at Rosings Manor, cousin to Mrs. Johnson

**Simon Shepardson:** Adam's ne'er-do-well brother

**Mr. Lionel Hibbert:** magistrate for Hunsford

## DERBYSHIRE

**Fitzwilliam Darcy:** owner of Pemberley Estate, head of the Darcy family, nephew to Lord Matlock and Lady Catherine

**Elizabeth Darcy:** wife of Mr. Darcy, friend to Mrs. Collins

**Bennet Edward George Darcy:** son and heir of Mr. Darcy (b. 1814)

**Anne Frances (Franny) Darcy:** daughter (b. 1816)

**Chloe Wickham:** eldest daughter (b. 1813) of the late Major Wickham, niece and ward of the Darcys

**Mrs. Nivens:** nanny for the Darcy children

**Mr. Thompson:** steward of Pemberley Estate

**The Right Honorable Lord Algernon Woodhouse, third Viscount Llewellyn:** master of Ambervale Lodge, heir to the Wakeford earldom

**The Right Honorable Georgiana Woodhouse, Viscountess Llewellyn:** wife of Lord Llewellyn, sister to Mr. Darcy

**The Right Honorable Lord Hugh Fitzwilliam, fifth Earl of Matlock:** head of the Fitzwilliam family, brother to Lady Catherine

**The Right Honorable Lady Alexandria Fitzwilliam, Countess of Matlock:** wife of Lord Matlock

**The Right Honorable Lord Andrew, Viscount Fitzwilliam of Matlock:** eldest son and heir of Lord Matlock

**The Right Honorable Lady Eugenie, Viscountess Fitzwilliam:** wife of Lord Fitzwilliam

*—continued*

## WALES

**Sir John Buford, CB:** Colonel, British Army (retired), served during the Peninsular War and Waterloo, friend of Sir Richard and Colonel Brandon

**Caroline, Lady Buford:** wife of Sir John, friend to Lady Fitzwilliam

**Beatrice Albertine (Bea) Buford:** daughter of Sir John (b. 1815)

**Abigail Smith:** maid to Lady Buford

**Mrs. Foley:** nanny to Miss Buford

**Corporal Davy Frost:** British Army (retired), Sir John's personal servant, served as Buford's batman (orderly) in the army

## LONDON

**Colonel Christopher Brandon, MP:** British Army (retired), owner of Delaford Manor, magistrate of and Member of Parliament for Delaford, close friend to both Sir Richard and Sir John

**Marianne Brandon:** wife of Colonel Brandon, friend to Lady Fitzwilliam and Lady Buford

**Joy Brandon:** daughter of Colonel Brandon (b. 1814)

**John Richard (Dickie) Brandon:** son (b. 1815)

**Thomas Tucker, Esq.:** solicitor and partner in the firm of Phillips & Tucker of London and Meryton

**Mary Tucker:** wife of Mr. Tucker, sister to Mrs. Darcy, friend to Lady Fitzwilliam and Lady Buford

**Rosanna Wickham:** youngest daughter (b. 1815) of the late Major Wickham, born after his death at Waterloo, niece and ward of the Tuckers

**Major Frederick Tilney:** British Army, an officer in the Twelfth Dragoon Guards, friend to Sir John, married to Violet Blakeney Tilney, daughter of Sir Percy Blakeney

## OTHERS

**Colonel Archibald Denny:** British Army, serving under the East India Company, posted to Calcutta

**Lydia Denny:** wife of Colonel Denny (m. 1816), widow of Major George Wickham (m. 1812–1815), and sister to Mrs. Darcy, traveled to India with Colonel Denny

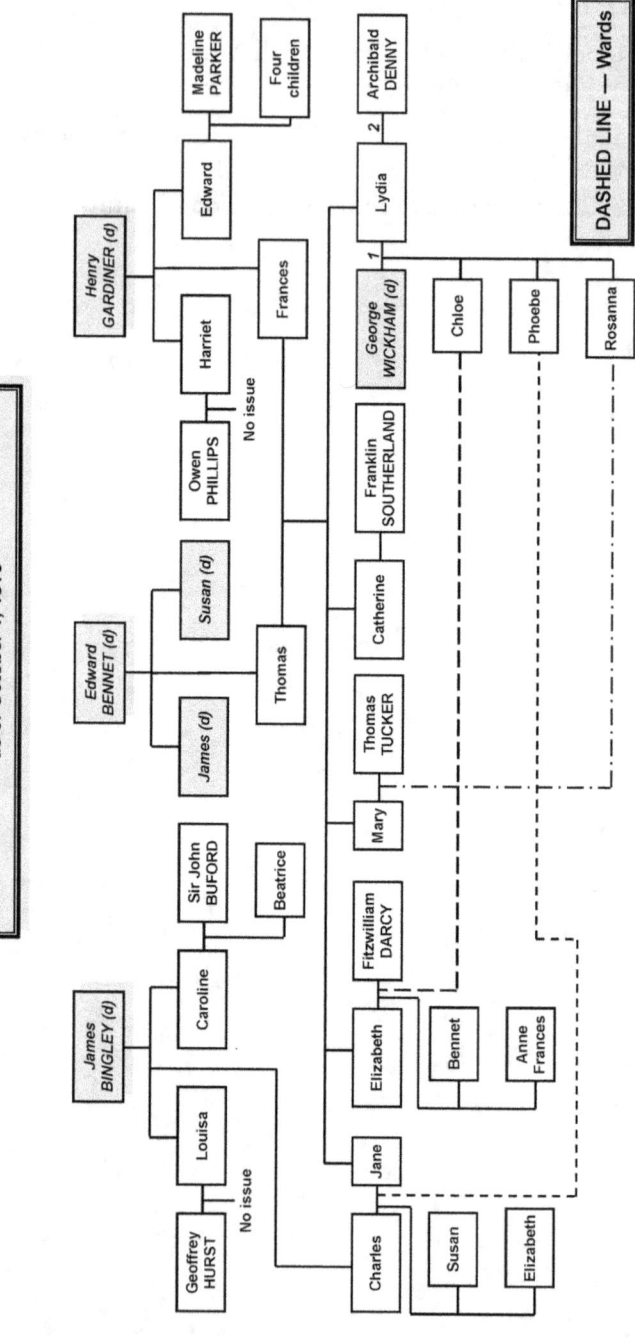

BENNET / BINGLEY / GARDINER FAMILIES
as of October 1, 1816

DASHED LINE — Wards

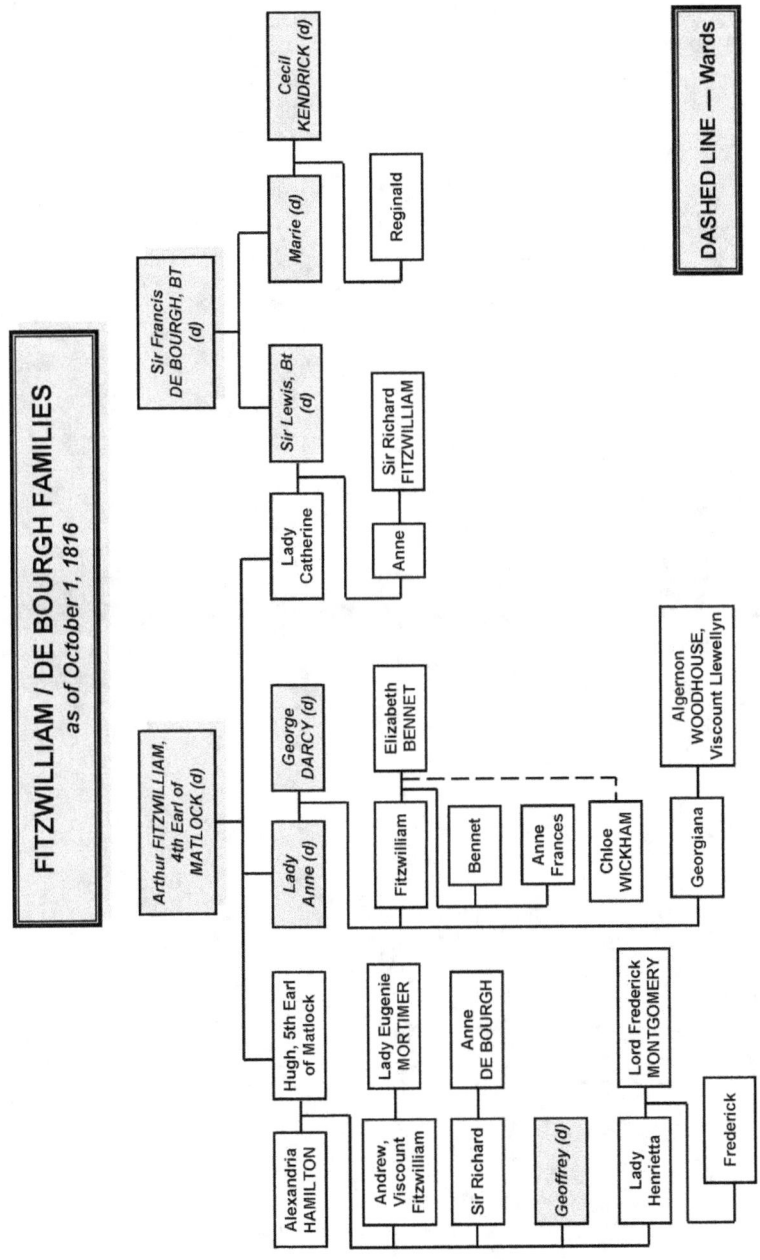

FITZWILLIAM / DE BOURGH FAMILIES
as of October 1, 1816

DASHED LINE — Wards

Sir Francis DE BOURGH, BT (d)

Cecil KENDRICK (d)

Marie (d)

Reginald

Sir Lewis, Bt (d)

Sir Richard FITZWILLIAM

Lady Catherine

Anne

Arthur FITZWILLIAM, 4th Earl of MATLOCK (d)

George DARCY (d)

Elizabeth BENNET

Algernon WOODHOUSE, Viscount Llewellyn

Lady Anne (d)

Fitzwilliam

Bennet

Anne Frances

Chloe WICKHAM

Georgiana

Hugh, 5th Earl of Matlock

Lady Eugenie MORTIMER

Anne DE BOURGH

Lord Frederick MONTGOMERY

Alexandria HAMILTON

Andrew, Viscount Fitzwilliam

Sir Richard

Geoffrey (d)

Lady Henrietta

Frederick

# Prologue

That the magistrate's men came after dark was no surprise, given the methods the Johnson family employed to put bread on their table. What was surprising was that the men chose to break down the door.

One moment, the Johnsons were consuming their meager soup in the dark main room of their rented cottage. The next, Mr. Johnson, beaten and bloody, was pinned to the wall by three brutes, and Mrs. Johnson's arms were firmly held in the grasp of a fourth. The screams and curses had awakened their son, and the boy added his cries to the din. Two other men were in the small room, and while the constable ordered that the house be searched, the other man, the steward of Rosings Park, loudly demanded that the sobbing brat be quiet. Mrs. Johnson screamed as the steward raised his hand to strike the child.

"Here," drawled an aristocratic voice, "none of that, Perkins."

The already crowded space was filled by the newcomer, though not by his physical presence. Indeed, the man was of middling height and very slim. He wore a coat of gold over ivory breeches, a powdered wig under his black tricorne hat, and held a tall, ebony-painted, walnut walking stick adorned with a brass knob in his left hand. It was not his voice, nasal and high-pitched. No, it was the

13

authority the man exuded that lit the dank scene like a lantern in a coal mine.

"Is this the man, Perkins?" asked the gentleman—for dressed as he was, the newcomer could only have been one.

"It is, Sir Lewis," the steward assured him. "This is the thief."

"And have you found what he stole?"

"Aye, master," cried the constable, holding aloft the pilfered treasure.

"Hmm," the master of Rosings Park and magistrate for Hunsford mumbled as he inspected his property. He then walked over to the prisoner, stopping only a foot away. He studied the injured man as one might a troublesome insect. Finally, he spoke.

"You stole from me, Johnson."

The man had to spit out a bloody tooth before answering. "I don't know nothin' 'bout that—" His protests were interrupted by a slap on the face.

"Stop your damned lies!" the constable demanded. "We have the seeds right here!"

"I tell ya, I don't know nothin' 'bout no seeds," Johnson insisted.

Mr. Perkins then spoke. "Things have been disappearing for years, Johnson, and I've had my eye on you. Now here's the proof. It's the noose for you."

That got through Johnson's bravado. "Hangin' just fer seeds?"

"Those are not just seeds," the gentleman said in a cold, dangerous voice. "Those are the future of Rosings Park. How can we have spring planting without seeds? How can we have wheat without seeds? You might as well have taken the money right out of my pocket.

"But hanging may be too severe. Confess, and I shall be merciful. Where is the rest of it?"

Johnson just stared at the gentleman. A violent shake from one of his captors loosened his tongue. "Buried it in th' woods," he admitted in a mumble.

"I wager there's more besides, Sir Lewis," said the steward.

The gentleman nodded in a satisfactory manner. "You will lead my men to the cache. Should all be recovered, I shall recommend transportation to the court." To the constable he said, "Take him away."

"Transportation? Ya might as well kill me!" Johnson screamed as the brutes dragged him out the door. The gentleman seemed to pay him no mind, occupied as he was by glancing about the small, rundown cottage.

"Sir Lewis, what about them?" asked the steward.

Sir Lewis turned to Mrs. Johnson. "You, too, benefited from your...husband?" At her nod, he continued. "You benefited from your husband's crimes. You are as guilty as he."

Mrs. Johnson said nothing. Not only did she know any protest would fall on deaf ears, the bloody rich bastard was right. She knew full well what sort of man Johnson was when she married him. He was just like her father—crooked and careless—big promises of an easy life that never came true. She was the daughter of a thief and the wife of a thief. It was the only life she knew.

"Should we take her in hand?" asked Mr. Perkins.

Sir Lewis shifted his gaze to the young boy, his cries reduced to sniffling. He looked at the lad with an unreadable expression. "Your child?"

Mrs. Johnson nodded.

"He is about the same age as my daughter," Sir Lewis mused. "A boy. You are fortunate."

Mrs. Johnson shrugged. It was neither good nor bad. He was her son.

The gentleman sighed. "Perhaps my next child will be a son." He turned his attention to Mrs. Johnson. "Do you have some honest way to earn your bread?"

Mrs. Johnson spoke for the first time. "I'm a fair seamstress, Sir Lewis."

"Hmm." The gentleman stroked his chin. "You cannot remain

here. This is a cottage for a working family." He turned to the steward. "Have we a cottage available on the estate? One that is out of the way?"

Mr. Perkins scratched his head. "There's an old blacksmith's shack on the other side of the woods, but it's in poor shape."

"Yes, that will do." The gentleman turned again to Mrs. Johnson. "Normally, you would share your husband's fate, but I am a Christian man, and I shall offer you a choice. You can accompany Johnson into exile, or you can move to new quarters on Rosings. You will receive no other charity from me, save what the church decides to do, and you must earn your way in the world with your needle and thread."

Mrs. Johnson eyed him suspiciously. "An' what else?"

Sir Lewis sneered. "Do not flatter yourself, woman, that I would ever soil my hands on you. You must rebuild your reputation by honest effort, or you may go with your husband. I have stated my offer. What is your choice?"

There was no choice as there was no love between Mrs. Johnson and her husband. He was simply there to provide what little he could to the table, and in turn, she shared his bed. She would not risk her life for him. Many died on the voyage to exile. She would be lonely in Hunsford, but so be it. "I'll stay."

"Very well. Perkins, see that her belongings are packed and moved to the shack as soon as may be. Make any repairs to the roof as needed." He turned again to Mrs. Johnson. "You owe my benevolence to your son. Treat him well." The baronet walked over and ruffled the frightened child's hair. "Let it not be said that Sir Lewis de Bourgh is not a generous man."

Obviously pleased with himself, the gentleman left and never saw the look of hate on the face of Mrs. Johnson.

*April 1815, Sumbawa*
*Dutch East Indies*

FOR CENTURIES IN THE SOUTHERN PACIFIC OCEAN, A FOURTEEN thousand-foot mountain stood sentinel on the Indonesian island of Sumbawa. The island was highly productive agriculturally; honey, horses, and sandalwood flourished due to its fertile soil. Dutch invaders a hundred years before introduced coffee to the mountain's western slopes. There was food for the people and for trade with others far away.

As in all things, abundance came with a price. The people who lived on Sumbawa had no idea their bounty was derived from ancient volcanic ash. The mountain, named Tambora, was actually an awakening volcano—a volcano that would change the world.

The eruptions began in early April and grew in intensity over a week. Those who could flee tried, but there was no place to go, no place to hide. On April 10, time ran out. The sound of the final explosions—the largest eruption seen in recorded history—was heard sixteen hundred miles away. A third of the mountain—five thousand feet—utterly disappeared. The volcano ejected thirty-eight cubic miles of pyroclastic igneous rock into the stratosphere. Tsunamis as high as thirty feet raced around the seas. Two centuries later, scientists would rate the blast at eight hundred megatons.

Twelve thousand people immediately perished.

All the ash and debris pumped into the sky by Tambora would take years to fall back to earth. Sunlight was blocked around the world, particularly in the Northern Hemisphere. There would be years without summer and with abnormally cold growing seasons. That meant there would be small or no harvests in Europe and America.

The dying had just begun.

# Chapter 1

The Honorable Sir Richard Fitzwilliam, C.B., former colonel of Dragoons, stood on the front steps of Pemberley on a cloudy, chilly afternoon, watching a carriage as it began its journey back to Nottinghamshire. The grounds, festooned with flowers and flags swaying in the light breeze, pronounced to the world that a grand celebration had occurred that day. A celebration that would change Pemberley and its master forever.

Richard was dressed not in a military uniform but in a fine blue jacket, buff trousers, and an overcoat because of the brisk weather. The only indication of his former occupation was the scarlet sash of the Bath peeking out beneath his jacket. Richard was no more to go a-soldiering. He was now a gentleman farmer tasked with the management of an estate.

He was ill-prepared for his new duties. An adult life of marching, drilling, shooting, and killing did not a farmer make. He had much to learn and needed someone to teach him. Fortunately, his instructor was almost a brother to him.

He glanced at his companion and mentor, tall and dark, standing beside him on those broad steps. "Are you bearing up at all, Cuz?"

Fitzwilliam Darcy, owner of the Pemberley estate, allowed a small sigh to escape his lips. "I am tolerably well, Fitz. And you?"

"I? I have no complaints." Richard's light-blue eyes danced with amusement. "In fact, I am having a splendid time. It was not *my* sister who married today."

"No, but Georgiana was your ward. I know you must feel it."

"All I feel is pride at the lovely lady Georgiana has become. Or should I now say the Viscountess Llewellyn?"

"As you choose."

Richard laughed. "Gad, you are dull today! Have no fears, Darce. Llewellyn is a fine young man. He will treat her like a princess. You should know—you picked him for her!"

A small smile graced Darcy's lips. "I cannot take credit for that. Elizabeth made the match. I was allowed a veto. But you are correct: the viscount is devoted to Georgiana. I am happy they will be living in Derbyshire. Elizabeth would be quite devastated if their Ambervale Lodge estate was further than a day's travel."

Richard did not remind his cousin that Elizabeth would not be the only resident of Pemberley to be distraught at a more distant removal by the former Georgiana Darcy. Instead, he glanced one last time at the retreating carriage. "Speaking of living nearby, do you think the Bingleys and Bennets will reach Mayfield tonight?"

"They should. The roads are in good condition, but there are fine inns along the way, should that become necessary." Darcy shook and slapped his arms. "At least this cold weather is dry! Let us return inside."

The light breeze ruffling his sandy-red hair, Richard nodded, his ruddy face creased in a smile. "You know *she* is still holding court. Would you not prefer the billiard room?"

Darcy did not share his cousin's humor. "I shall not leave Elizabeth alone with her longer than necessary." The two moved through the door to the vestibule where a footman collected the gentlemen's overcoats.

"I think Lizzy is in no danger. And she did promise to be on her best behavior."

"All the same…" Darcy adopted his usual countenance for battle: he stood taller, raised his chin, and assumed a neutral expression. A marble sculpture projected more warmth. The only indication of his anxiety was his slightly longer strides as he walked to the sitting room, Richard at his side. The door was open, and they could hear a woman's voice from halfway down the hall.

"In my day, the union of two august families would have occurred in town," boomed a quarrelsome voice.

Darcy picked up his steps.

"And a service by a country parson! It is insupportable!"

"Of course, Lady Catherine," responded a lady in a far gentler tone, "but brides must have their way, and Georgiana is so attached to Pemberley. Most of her family and friends are nearby and the viscount's too. Nothing else would do. Georgiana and my sister Mrs. Southerland are quite close, and she would not have anyone except Mr. Southerland to bless her union with the viscount, not even her uncle the bishop."

A third lady spoke up. "The wedding was lovely, Mother. There can be no complaint."

The gentlemen arrived at the doorway. Even though she had been there for three days, it still shocked Richard to see Lady Catherine de Bourgh ensconced in a chair in the late Lady Anne Darcy's favorite sitting room.

"I shall speak as I choose, Anne," Lady Catherine said harshly.

Lady Anne Fitzwilliam, lovely but frowning, sat on a couch next to her cousin and hostess, Elizabeth Darcy. Mrs. Jenkinson, Anne's longtime companion, was in a chair nearby. Richard's heart swelled at his wife's fine looks, but the color in Anne's cheeks was heightened by more than her pink gown. He was distressed at the certain cause of her displeasure: Anne was clearly exasperated with her mother. Richard was afraid she would respond with a sharp retort.

"Lady Catherine, I have not had the opportunity to ask your opinion of this room," Elizabeth injected smoothly. "I believe it was your sister's favorite."

Lady Catherine narrowed her eyes. Richard wondered whether she suspected Elizabeth was patronizing her with the change of subject.

"Indeed, it was. We spent many hours in this delightful room, talking of many things." The grand dame's eyes turned to her nephews. "*Many things*. Darcy! I take it your last guests have departed?"

Richard shifted his feet uneasily and saw Darcy's jaw clench for an instant. He suspected Darcy had the same impression he did of Lady Catherine's comment of "many things." She again was referring to her assertion that she and Lady Anne Darcy had planned a marriage between their children.

The old woman was stubborn. Darcy had been married to Elizabeth for four years, and Richard had married Anne de Bourgh ten months prior. What was done was done, and there was nothing she could do about it. Indeed, it seemed by her attendance at Pemberley that Lady Catherine finally accepted the situation.

And she *had*, Richard realized. Lady Catherine knew Anne was happy with her choice and Darcy did not regret his, but the obstinate old woman was insisting again that she was *right*, in spite of all evidence to the contrary. She was a fool.

Darcy nodded. "Yes, they have." He turned to his wife, and the familiar soft look Darcy reserved for Elizabeth and their children graced his face. "Jane, Charles, and the Hursts should be safely back at Mayfield by nightfall."

"It will be an uncomfortable journey. Hurst is larger than ever," Richard could not stop himself from adding.

As he feared, he earned a sharp look from Anne. "Richard…" she said in that dangerous voice that warned of consequences for his impertinence. Lady Fitzwilliam was small and slim with a quiet demeanor, but for all that, she *was* a de Bourgh and was given to expressing her displeasure as only a member of that family could when provoked. At least she reserved her occasional reprimands for the privacy of their rooms—unlike Lady Catherine, whose frankness of character overrode simple courtesy like an avalanche.

Richard shrugged. He must be true to himself, and if the price was the occasional short tongue-lashing from his sweet Annie… well, he knew best how to placate her.

"I am glad to hear it," said Elizabeth to Darcy before turning to her guest. "But, Lady Catherine, as you can see, the years have not been kind to the drapes in this room, and I fear the fabric will be impossible to duplicate. I was wondering, since their replacements will be new, whether there were any improvements to the room that might serve, all while respecting the wonderful taste of my husband's dear mother. Have you any suggestions?"

Richard almost laughed. Elizabeth could not have said anything that would appeal more to Lady Catherine's enormous vanity. *Lord, Cousin Lizzy could manipulate a bloody bone from a starving wolf! Be careful, Darce. If she chooses, she will have you dancing from puppet strings, if she has not done so already!*

A small smile stole across Lady Catherine's usually dour face. "I must give it some thought. You are correct in saying this room is quite lovely as it is, but any space can use some restrained improvement. Restrained, I say! Too many young people these days change things just for change itself, with no thought to economy or tradition. It is always better to seek proper guidance."

Elizabeth nodded. "Thus, my question, milady. My time in town has shown me numerous examples of what you have said. The tradesmen are happy for the work, to be sure, but ostentatious display is a poor exchange for proper understated English elegance."

Lady Catherine raised her chin. "Very true."

"Hah!"

The overbearing widow turned. "What was that?"

Richard covered his mouth. "Forgive me, Aunt. A cough. The weather is so beastly." He glanced at Anne, whose eyes were shooting daggers at him. *Oh, I shall pay for that.*

"You should rest, Richard," said his aunt. "You will be of no use if you fall ill."

"That is excellent advice, milady," said the bespectacled fifth woman in the room, one whom Lady Catherine was laboring mightily to ignore. Not only was Mrs. Tucker the sister of Mrs. Darcy and therefore of little importance, she was married to the lawyer who assisted the Earl of Matlock in overthrowing Lady Catherine and installing Anne as mistress of Rosings Park. What was even more distasteful to the grand lady was that the selfsame solicitor was seated right next to his wife.

"Mary is right, Mama," said Anne. "You should rest before dinner."

Richard saw his aunt's lips tighten. Lady Catherine took great issue with Anne's friends. She had no objection to Georgiana, now Lady Llewellyn, and she could not really object to Elizabeth Darcy, if truth be told. She would like the intelligent and witty lady even better if she could forgive her marriage to Darcy.

But people like Mary Tucker were, to Lady Catherine's sense of entitlement, intolerable, as was Charlotte Collins back in Hunsford. And she disliked Caroline Buford, who remained in London, tending to her wounded husband. There was something of Lady Buford's demeanor and independence that offended the old lady's sensibilities. Caroline was similar to Elizabeth, save that her manner was more pointed and cutting and less witty.

Of course, both Richard and Anne adored all these ladies, which made matters worse.

But instead of resisting, the grand dame rose from her chair. "I think *all* the ladies should retire. It has been a long day, and it would not do to appear at dinner with tired eyes. Come, Anne. Mrs. Darcy, you shall accompany me above stairs. Pray see that tea is brought to my room."

Anne assisted her mother to rise, and Elizabeth assured her that her request would be fulfilled. As the ladies passed the gentlemen,

Richard saw Elizabeth wink at Darcy. Right behind was an unperturbed Mary Tucker, and Richard winked at *her*, which earned a smile.

Now that the gentlemen were left to themselves, Richard turned to Darcy. "We have some time, Cuz, and I admit I am a bit chilled. Do you have any of the excellent Cognac I enjoyed during my last visit?"

"I was able to hide a bottle or two from your clutches," returned Darcy dryly. "What say you, Tucker? Shall I open one in honor of the day?"

"I have never turned down a Cognac in my life, Brother!" cried Thomas Tucker. What the shorter man lacked in height, he made up for in intensity. "Lead on."

Within minutes, the master of Pemberley, the consort of Rosings, and the lawyer for both were sharing a brandy in Darcy's grand study.

"How is the harvest progressing at Rosings?" asked Darcy as he settled down in an armchair, a fire blazing in the hearth.

Richard gestured at the flames. "What harvest? This damned cold has the crops in a terrible way. We had to reestablish the rents this year because there were improvements to drainage that needed to be done, but we shall be fortunate to collect anything from our tenants."

Darcy was grim. "Conditions are bad everywhere. I am thankful we have so much in sheep, but feed costs have risen while wool prices continue to fall."

"Yes, but you have your people, and they are devoted to you. Pemberley is an island of peace in a sea of troubles. That is why the riot in Leicestershire never touched you."

"The Luddites are fanatics and fools," proclaimed Tucker, who had many political connections.

"That is rather harsh," said Darcy.

"Perhaps, but they do their cause no favors by their actions. It will go hard for them. The government is shaken by the poor economy and the unrest from it, and they will want to make examples of the leaders of the mob. Are things unsettled in Kent, Sir Richard?"

Richard sighed. "There is grumbling, to be sure, but nothing serious." He paused. "Caruthers wants to leave me."

Darcy sat up. "Your steward? He has been at Rosings more than sixteen years. Why?"

"He wants to retire, and his only daughter lives in Cornwall. Her husband is steward at an estate there. They want Caruthers to live with them and play with his grandchildren."

Tucker smiled. "A pleasant way to spend one's autumn years. When will he leave?"

"He said he will stay through the harvest, but he wants to remove to Cornwall before Christmas."

"So, you need a new steward and quickly." Darcy put his hand to his chin. "Shall I make some inquiries for you?"

Richard hid a grimace and, he hoped, his annoyance. "I would not refuse you, Darce. A list of names is all I ask. I can take things in hand from there." He should have known his otherwise admirable cousin would try to manage things. "Tucker, would you be so kind as to draw up the required papers?"

"Consider it done, Sir Richard. I shall start working on it upon my return to town."

Richard downed his drink. "Excellent! Gentlemen, what say you to a game of billiards before dinner?"

That evening, a robed Richard left the guest bedroom and crossed the small parlor to the door opposite. He halted, steeled himself for what he was about to receive, and knocked on the door.

"Come in, Richard," said Lady Fitzwilliam.

Richard closed his eyes—he knew well *that* tone of voice—and entered the room.

He saw Anne at the dressing table, her back to him, running a brush through her dark tresses. Her dressing gown hung loosely from her slim frame. Richard noted that the maid had already been dismissed.

He gulped. *It seems she wishes to begin directly.*

"What on earth were you on about this afternoon?" Anne spoke in a low voice and did not bother to turn around. Instead, she stared at his reflection in the mirror. "Were you *trying* to enrage Mother?"

An instant apology would have been expedient, but Richard Fitzwilliam was not always an expedient man.

"Oh, come now, Annie," he said, using an endearment to appease her. "How could I help myself after Lady Catherine's ridiculous pronouncement? Condemning ostentatious display in favor of understated elegance?" He moved farther into the room and leaned next to the fireplace. "Rosings is the very definition of ostentatious display! You and I have discussed this, and I know well your plans to redecorate once this time of economy is past. At least I stopped myself from laughing in her very face." He looked at the flames in the hearth. "Lord, it is warm in here!"

"That is because I am chilled." Anne put her hairbrush down and turned to her husband. "You restrained yourself, and I appreciate that. But you know Mother can be difficult, and this is a very special time for Lizzy. What a triumph for her to have Mother come to Pemberley! Do you not know she has been striving for this since her wedding day?"

Richard was confused. "Why would she want Lady Catherine here after everything that has happened? My aunt's behavior was abhorrent."

"It is Lizzy's nature. She cannot bear strife within the family."

"It was no one's fault but Lady Catherine's!"

"Of course it was. But Lizzy knows how dear family is to Darcy. She would not be easy until he and Mother reconciled."

"She is a better person than I."

"You really should behave yourself. It may not appear so, but Lizzy is exhausted. Not only was she distracted by preparing for

Georgiana's wedding and recovering from Frances's birth two months ago, but she also had to deal with the fact that Mother has not yet made peace with her brother."

Richard smirked. It had been a comedy that morning to keep Lady Catherine and Lord Matlock out of each other's way. Even though they were across the room from each other most of the time, Lady Catherine could still be heard mumbling about her conniving thief of a brother while the earl was harrumphing about his harridan of a sister.

Of course, there was no justice to Lady Catherine's accusations. Lord Matlock's "thievery" was simply the enforcement of Sir Lewis de Bourgh's will, thereby bestowing upon Anne her rightful inheritance.

As for the earl's complaints—well, it was against his father's character not to reply in kind rather than take the high road and pretend his only surviving sibling was not making disparaging remarks about him.

The Fitzwilliams were a quarrelsome family, and no mistake. Thank goodness Richard's parents left for their estate soon after the happy bride and groom departed.

"I am sorry Lizzy is feeling poorly. Should I apologize?"

"No, she would be mortified if she knew what I told you."

"Hah! She is more like Darcy every day." Richard walked over and placed a hand on Anne's shoulder. "I am sorry to have upset you, sweetheart."

Anne placed a hand on his and leaned her head fondly on them. "Thank you."

Richard smiled roguishly as he gently pulled his wife up from her chair and into his arms. "I know a better way of warming you than that fire, my lovely."

For one so small and slim, Anne's lips were exceedingly warm and inviting, and Richard could never quite get enough of them. Slowly, the passion in her kisses matched his, and Richard moved his hands from her waist to her bottom.

Anne broke contact. "No! Not here."

"Annie, I beg you," he whined, trailing kisses on her swan's neck.

"I-I cannot." She stepped away from his embrace. "Not here."

"Sweetheart, I do not understand." Except during their honeymoon tour, Anne showed a distinct aversion to making love anywhere but in her bed at Rosings. In fact, they had yet to make love in *his* bed, Richard recalled.

"I am...uncomfortable," she said, clearly agitated. "This is Lizzy's house."

"Are you concerned that they will know we—?" He raised his eyebrows. "Gad, we are married! What do you suppose they think we do?"

She turned from him, tears welling up. "Pray do not press me. I cannot explain it, but it is impossible." She started to cry in earnest. "I know I have failed you as a wife. I am so silly and foolish, and I lost our baby, and—"

"Never say that!" Richard embraced her from behind, setting her head back against his broad chest. "Things like that cannot be helped. There will be other children. After all, we have not been married a year." He hoped more than believed his assurances, for he did not know whether Anne's mysterious former malady—caused, to his bewilderment, by *cats*—affected her ability to bear a child. "I love you so much, and I want to make you happy."

She turned into him, grasping him tightly. "I love you, too. I *am* happy—I am."

For a few minutes, the couple stood in the middle of the guest bedroom in a tight embrace. Then, noticing Anne's weariness, Richard gently guided his wife to her bed. Once she was comfortable under the sheets, he kissed her one last time.

"Sleep well, sweetheart," he said.

She touched his face, her fingers tracing his features. "We shall be home soon, and all will be as it should be. Goodnight, my dear."

Richard gave her a tight smile, extinguished the candles, and made his way out of the room by the light of the fireplace.

# Chapter 2

The journey from Pemberley to Rosings was uneventful, and Lady Catherine was not particularly overbearing. So it was that Richard and Anne were in good spirits as they stopped at the dower house. Once Lady Catherine was comfortably established within, the carriage continued to the main house. For not the first time, Richard was happy the distance between the two abodes was one that Anne's formidable mother found uncomfortable to walk.

As Richard handed down Anne and Mrs. Jenkinson, they were met on the imposing front steps by Mrs. Parks, the longtime house-keeper, and Troop Sergeant-Major Gregory, a relatively new addition to the household. Mrs. Parks made her curtsy, saying that the butler had taken to his bed again.

Richard shook his head. The butler, Wilkinson, had been at Rosings for as long as Mrs. Parks and Mr. Caruthers. He was loyal, but his health had taken a turn for the worse. The Fitzwilliams would never turn him out, so they elevated Sergeant Gregory, Sir Richard's former aide from the army, from personal servant to majordomo of the household, giving Gregory most of the butler's responsibilities. The change had not caused too much trouble with the staff because the sergeant and Mrs. Parks got along.

It was yet another example of the changes at Rosings. First were

Anne's elevation and Lady Catherine's overthrow, then the new mistress's marriage to Sir Richard, and now, both the butler and steward—all of this in little more than a year. Change was inevitable in life, but so much in so little time made people nervous, especially at Rosings Park.

There was another change as well, and it made its presence known as soon as Anne walked through the front door.

"Romeo! Wherefore art thou, Romeo?" cried Anne.

There was a scampering of nails on polished wood floors as a blur of gray hurtled towards them. In the next instant, Anne's arms were full of wiggling legs, wagging tail, and licking tongue.

"I see your lover has missed you," remarked Richard.

Anne knelt down and held the Italian greyhound's head in her hands while making cooing noises. "And how is my sweetie? Did you miss Momma?" Romeo's response was to lick her face.

"I know he did not miss *me*," said Richard sarcastically. As though on cue, the dog saw him and let out a low growl. "There, you see? Your dog hates me!"

"No, he does not. It is just because you are mean to him."

"Mean to him? Just because I want time alone with my wife?"

"I asked you not to speak so in public."

Richard rolled his eyes. "You know exactly what I am saying."

Anne grumbled. "Perhaps if you had a dog of your own, you would not be so jealous."

"Jealous! You are being ridiculous." Richard truly did not resent the dog's presence. Romeo had comforted Anne in the aftermath of her miscarriage. Richard and Mrs. Jenkinson were also pleased that whatever there was about cats that made Anne ill did not apply to dogs. Richard's main problem with Romeo was that he was the first dog Richard had ever met that did not take to him, and it rankled.

He reached down to help his wife to her feet. "Come, Lady Fitzwilliam, let us retire to our rooms and clean off the dirt of the road. And bring your nasty beast as well."

Anne smirked. "Yes, I suppose you can come as well, Sir Richard."

A FEW DAYS LATER, ANNE HAD JUST STOPPED HER LITTLE phaeton before the Hunsford parsonage when Mrs. Collins came out the door, her arms filled with baskets. Pausing only to greet her friend and patroness, Charlotte placed her burden in the carriage and climbed in.

When asked why there was no servant about to assist her, Charlotte replied, "Oh, it is no bother. I am young and healthy still and certainly need no assistance to hop into your delightful phaeton."

Anne sighed, suspecting the true reason no maid helped Charlotte was that the Collins family had lost another servant. The resignation rate of servants was notable; six months was the average stay, although one man-of-all-work lasted but a week. As Charlotte had managed to retain the housekeeper, the cause of the desertions had to be placed at the feet of the master of the household. Mr. Collins's penchant for contradictory orders and pompous pronouncements was more than the average servant could bear. At least Mr. Collins left their cook to her own devices.

As Anne drove into the village, she again pitied her long-suffering friend. She had suspected the Collins's marriage was one of expediency. Surely, there was some affection on Mr. Collins's part, given his flowery statements that the pair was made for each other and his pleasure in his children. Charlotte was kind enough, and she did nothing to diminish her husband before others in spite of Mr. Collins's often mortifying behavior. The fact that Charlotte was a mother several times over spoke to the fact that her husband was no stranger to her bed.

Anne shivered. *That* sort of thinking was unpleasant indeed!

She reminded herself to be generous. During the crisis the prior year when Anne was at war with her mother over Richard, Mr. Collins had surprised everyone. He had defied his former patroness and thrown in his lot with Anne, risking his family's serenity if not their security. Such loyalty and courage had to be respected and admired.

It was well to remember, too, that Mr. Collins was devoted to his flock. What a shame that his intellect was not equal to either his piety or his intentions! The man was a fool—a well-meaning, good-family-man sort of fool, but a fool nevertheless.

The phaeton stopped at the new home of Mr. Joseph Clarke, a promising farmer to whom Richard had granted a larger tenancy. He had proven himself despite the abysmal weather Rosings had suffered that season. The production on Mr. Clarke's lease had held its own, and he had been vocal in supporting Richard and his plans for modernization. Mr. Clarke was now on the tenants' council, and there were those envious of the rapid rise of "Fitzwilliam's Favorite," regardless of the young man's ability, industry, and shrewdness.

The elevation of Mr. Clarke was shared with his wife, and it was now as the lady of one of the first houses of Hunsford that Peggy Clarke welcomed the patroness of the village and the vicar's wife. Their time in the Clarkes' house was short, for there were calls to make and shopping to be done.

The air was cool for October, and the bundled party made its way into the center of town. Lady Fitzwilliam received the welcome due her station from passersby, and she took pains to share a word with everyone they met. At one time, it would have been Lady Catherine walking the village and spreading her wisdom, but for some reason, she had stopped doing so years ago.

Anne knew her mother's present haughtiness and disdain for the common folk of the village served her ill, and *she* was determined not to make the same mistake. It was hard overcoming her native reserve—in this Anne was much like her cousin Darcy—but she kept in mind the excellent example of her husband and accorded herself much success.

The butcher shop was their first stop. The owner was overly generous in his welcome, to Anne's way of thinking. Unlike her mother, Anne did not enjoy fawning behavior from others.

She withstood his compliments for a short time before asking, "Did you receive Mrs. Parks's order, sir?"

"Oh yes, my lady! See, here is the joint your housekeeper wanted. The flesh is red and the fat white, just as Lady Catherine always desired!"

Anne blinked. "You are very kind. You *do* understand this order is for the great house at Rosings and not the dower house, I hope."

"Indeed, indeed! Lady Catherine made that very clear when she was here."

*Mother was in the village? Why? She had not done that for years!* "Is that so?"

"Yes, madam. It was like old times, her stopping by. Such an important lady! She was kind enough to correct a misapprehension. Somehow, I thought you wanted a guinea fowl for Sunday, but she informed me that a goose was what was intended. I am thankful she caught the mistake."

A lifetime of hiding her feelings when it came to her mother served her well, and it was with no great effort that Anne kept her countenance rather than giving free rein to her outraged spirits.

"A happy chance, to be sure. Should we expect delivery today?" Assured the meat would reach Rosings by the afternoon, Anne nodded. "By the way, we shall have a guinea fowl Sunday next—the largest you can acquire. Thank you, sir. Good day." A tightness about the mouth was the only indication of Anne's annoyance.

As they left the shop, Anne struggled to remain calm. *How dare she?* her mind raged. *By what right does Mother change my menu? I am mistress of the house, yet she countermanded my orders. A goose, indeed! Richard particularly wanted guinea fowl. It is his favorite, but because Mother prefers goose, it must be that all other birds are not worthy for my table! Oh, how angry she makes me!*

Since Anne's marriage, her mother had been a source of continual vexation. Lady Catherine had talents and a certain genius in running other people's lives, Anne had to admit. However, *she* was now mistress of Rosings and patroness of Hunsford—not her mother. The old woman simply would not retire quietly to the dower house.

Anne could not denounce her mother publicly, no matter how richly she deserved it. It was simply not done. Speaking to Lady Catherine did no good, and arguing made things worse. There seemed to be no solution but to bear her mother's behavior as best she could.

A touch to her arm brought Anne back to the present, and Charlotte gave her an affectionate and sympathetic look. It was clear she understood what had happened, comprehended her friend's discontent, and pitied her. Anne was relieved that no one else seemed aware of her unhappiness. It would have been mortifying should the level of animosity that existed between mother and daughter become common knowledge.

"G'day, miss."

Anne's head jerked up at the low voice to see a large person right before her. The greeting gave her enough time to stop and not walk right into him. She recognized the young man in an instant and placed a hand to her breast.

"Oh, Cork, you quite startled me!"

"Cork," scolded Charlotte, "you should not stand blocking the way like that. For shame!"

Cork Johnson was a large young man in his mid-twenties, his six-foot frame holding almost fifteen stone. His arms were like two small trees. He wore workman's clothes: trousers smeared with horse manure, a satchel at his side, and a soft, narrow-brimmed hat upon his enormous head. But for all his power and presence, his round, unlined, open face was blank. A child's face graced a giant's body.

"Sorry, Miss de Bourgh." His head dipped.

"Cork," said Charlotte kindly, "she is Lady Fitzwilliam now."

He looked up. "Oh, yes. Married the colonel—Cork remembers." The man smiled. "Colonel's a nice man."

Anne smiled uneasily at Cork. All of Hunsford knew of the harmless idiot son of the seamstress Mrs. Johnson. The pair lived in a remote cottage on Rosings. No one knew of Mr. Johnson's whereabouts or whether he was even alive.

"Good morning, Cork," Anne said, receiving a wide grin from the fellow.

The young man had some other name Anne could not recall—it was listed in the baptismal records of the church, she supposed—but he went by the nickname Cork. No one knew whether the fellow was aware it was short for "cork-brained," but if he did, he did not seem to mind.

"Morning to you, *Lady Fitzwilliam*." He let out a low laugh.

"Yes." Anne was ashamed that she was unsettled by the giant's presence, but she truly desired to leave. "Pray, excuse us."

"Yes, ma'am." He doffed his hat good-naturedly.

Cork was large enough to work as a farmhand, but his mind was suited only for the most menial of jobs. So, when he was not cleaning out the stables at the post station, he wandered about town or tossed stones at trees. Cork liked to practice his aim, and he was as much a fixture of Hunsford as the tall oak tree in the village common.

The ladies continued down the street, Charlotte leaning over to whisper, "Oh, I wish he would bathe."

Anne agreed but was thankful for the interruption. She had lost her anger at Lady Catherine for a while.

TRUE TO HIS WORD, DARCY HAD SENT A LIST OF CANDIDATES for steward. Richard read over it carefully and unhappily. Several men were apprentices from properties owned by Lord Matlock or Darcy.

Richard had little desire for another steward whose total loyalty might be suspect. Mr. Caruthers had been an excellent steward, to be sure—hardworking, intelligent, and dutiful—but he remained his father's man.

Both Mr. Caruthers and Mrs. Parks had been under the employ of Lord Matlock for fifteen years, an unusual arrangement designed to protect Rosings from Lady Catherine's capricious management. Upon their marriage and Anne's ascension to the ownership of Rosings, the estate shouldered the burden of paying Mr. Caruthers's and Mrs. Parks's salaries. Even so, Richard could never escape the feeling that Mr. Caruthers constantly measured his new master's abilities against the earl's.

Ever self-reliant, Richard wanted to prove himself capable as a gentleman farmer. He felt he could not do that if he hired someone whose fidelity might belong to Pemberley rather than Rosings. It was one thing to ask Darcy for a list of names, quite another to hire a Pemberley man. Sir Richard eliminated from Darcy's list anyone who had worked for the earl or his cousin. That left four names, but after interviewing two, Sir Richard was dissatisfied. The men knew their business—there was no doubt about that—and Fitz expected that the others on the list did as well. Indeed, they all were much like Mr. Caruthers, which was the problem.

The otherwise excellent Caruthers had an infuriating habit of getting his own way. Oh, certainly, he listened attentively to Richard's wishes and plans; no steward could be more courteous. Then, Caruthers would ask for clarification, which would lead to a discussion that would end in critiquing Richard's ideas. Mr. Caruthers was at all times polite and almost fatherly, not quite condescending. Before much time had passed, Richard would inevitably bow to the steward's superior ideas. That Mr. Caruthers was almost always right did not help matters. Rosings was Richard's, and he wanted to run it.

Richard turned his mind to another issue. There had been a case of vandalism on the estate. Broken fence railings allowed sheep to escape while the Fitzwilliams were at Pemberley. It was a minor problem—the sheep were recovered and the fence repaired—but it was troubling that, according to Mr. Caruthers, the damage was intentional.

There was a knock on the door. "Sorry to disturb you, Sir Richard," said Wilkerson, his voice quivering, "but Mr. Collins is here to see you."

Richard stifled a groan.

"Want me to deal with him, Colonel?" asked Sergeant Gregory.

Richard turned to his longtime aide. Troop Sergeant-Major Gregory was a forty-year-old veteran of the Light Dragoons who had served with Fitzwilliam in Italy, Spain, and Belgium during the wars against Napoleon. After Waterloo, he had mustered out along with many of the survivors of that last charge. Fitzwilliam, having spent all of his adult life in the military, wanted an adjutant, so he took on his old comrade. It was a balancing act. Officially, Sergeant Gregory ran the servants and employees of Rosings on behalf of the old butler, but in actuality, he worked in concert with Mrs. Parks, who answered to Lady Fitzwilliam. It was fortunate that the sergeant and the housekeeper were of one mind in most matters.

The best way to describe the stocky former soldier was that he was neither fat nor plump but *wide*—broad of shoulders with large hands and a rather flat face. In a red coat, he was a fearsome sight. In a black coat, he was incongruous.

Richard sighed. He was tempted by Gregory's offer. There were many pleasures attached to Richard's present situation: a loving wife, a loyal staff, and a comfortable house. Unfortunately, there was also a price. Chief among them was the fawning attentions of the Reverend Mr. William Collins. Rare indeed was the day when the vicar did not present himself at Rosings, requesting an audience with him or his wife. Richard sometimes wondered whether Mr. Collins could go to the privy without receiving his employers' opinion on the matter. The man was a nuisance. Yet, Richard was indebted to him for his loyalty to Anne. He could suffer the attentions of a devoted fool.

Richard scowled. "No, no, I shall see him. Show him in."

Moments later, his sanctuary was invaded by a tall, heavyset man of thirty years who had perfected the art of walking quickly while offering a bow. Only his familiarity with Richard's study prevented the man from meeting with misfortune. Standing before the desk, hat in one hand and several papers in the other, the oaf nearly genuflected.

"Sir Richard, I thank you most sincerely for giving me, your humble servant, a few moments of your valuable time! Indeed, I would not trouble you for the world, but as my office calls on me to offer moral guidance to the people of Hunsford, I must keep the wishes and advice of my exalted benefactors in mind lest I fail in my primary duty. A few words of wisdom from you would be of infinite use to more than myself, I am sure."

Richard sighed, dropped his chin into his left hand, and held out his right. "I suppose you wish me to review Sunday's sermon?"

"Your condescension knows no bounds!" Four sheets of paper, closely written, were Richard's reward.

"Pray, be seated," Richard offered, knowing they would be discussing the sermon for at least a half an hour. Straightening, he began perusing the manuscript. "I thought you usually consulted Lady Fitzwilliam with these matters."

"Ah, that is the customary practice, my good sir, as Lady Fitzwilliam has taken over that office from Lady Catherine de Bourgh. But your most excellent lady demurred, her time taken up with my Charlotte. May I say again how fortunate it is for my wife that Lady Fitzwilliam has condescended even to acknowledge her, much less befriend her."

"Think nothing of it," said Richard absently, his attention focused over a passage. Two paragraphs in and Mr. Collins was already repeating himself. He frowned. "There seems to be a little repetition here, sir."

Mr. Collins blanched. "Oh? Forgive me, sir! Lady Catherine always directed that points of particular importance be repeated to emphasize their consequence. Do you disagree?"

Richard looked up. "That is good advice. I have used it on the training grounds many a time. However, we are talking about a church congregation in Hunsford, not raw recruits at Horse Guards." He offered a small grin to lessen any offense. "I believe we may forgo repetition, eh?"

"As you wish, sir! Oh, Lady Fitzwilliam was right. She said a gentleman's opinion is what I should seek!"

Richard was taken aback. "She said that?"

"Indeed, she did, sir," Mr. Collins replied with a smile on his broad, flushed face. "I know with your excellent guidance my sermons will sing to heaven! How fortunate for the people of Hunsford!"

*There goes my Thursdays*, was Richard's wry thought. "Yes, how fortunate."

*Annie was behind this, eh? Well struck, my dear. I believe I shall reward you with an early evening and late morning for this!*

# Chapter 3

Mr. Macmillan, the eminent London physician, bent over the undressed man on the bed and firmly squeezed his left thigh. "Does this cause you any discomfort?"

"No," answered Sir John Buford.

"Good, good," mumbled the man of medicine as he continued his probing examination of a long scar on the outside of the thigh. "The muscles have knit well in the last year. I am pleased with the progress." Mr. Macmillan straightened up. "I have seen enough. You may dress."

There were two others in attendance—a dark-haired lady and a servant. The lady made a gesture and the servant moved to hand Buford a pair of trousers. The physician shrugged on his coat while speaking to the lady.

"It is important for Sir John to exercise that leg, madam. Nothing too strenuous, mind you. A good walk in the park each day would do very well for the present."

"What of riding, sir?" she asked.

"In moderation, I have no objection as long as Sir John gets in his walks. Different muscles, you see." Mr. Macmillan turned back to his patient, who was now sitting up in trousers while his man helped him with his shirt. "We cannot allow the muscles to decline due to lack of use. You must walk, Sir John, and use your cane." A rare smile grew on the older man's face. "We cannot have a knight of the realm falling onto the street, now can we?"

"I suppose not," answered Buford curtly.

Mr. Macmillan ignored his rudeness. "I should like to see him again in a few months."

"Of course. Thank you, sir," said the lady. "I shall see you out."

"Very good," he returned. "Good day, Sir John."

The pair left the bedroom and walked down the stairs. "Mr. Macmillan, is there anything else I need to know?"

The physician glanced at her. "He may experience discomfort in the beginning, but the exercise is vital. Thus, he must use the cane." He paused. "And what of you, Lady Buford?"

Caroline Buford (née Bingley) was surprised at the question. "I have no idea what you mean. I am quite well."

"I have dealt with war wounds before, my lady. Far too often, I am afraid. I speak not of the physical injuries but of the emotional ones. A depression of the spirit is not uncommon in cases like this, and the weight of it often falls to the family." He stopped only a few steps from the bottom of the stairs and looked at her closely. "Has he been cross and angry?"

Caroline's green eyes were focused on her clenched hands. "Only on occasion. It is to be expected with his pain. He has been grievously wounded."

Mr. Macmillan shook his head. "I should not like to disagree with you. I do not have ladies attend my examinations as a rule, but I make an exception for you. You have chosen to be his nursemaid and have been an excellent one. You have followed each of my instructions to the letter. Much of Sir John's present recovery can be attributed to you. It is a very noble thing you have done, but it can drain one's spirit just as completely as any illness. You must take care and see to your own health."

"He is my husband!"

"It would not harm you or Sir John to have assistance. The servant—he is a former soldier, is he not?"

"Corporal Frost was his batman in the army."

"Let him take some of this burden off your shoulders, madam. Surely, your husband would not object to that."

"I shall consider it," Caroline allowed.

Mr. Macmillan gently took her hand. "You must take care, for there are others who depend on you. And how is Miss Beatrice faring?"

"My daughter is very well, I thank you." Caroline smiled. "I see your meaning, sir. You are very insistent."

"Only to those I care for." Mr. Macmillan glanced at the footman at the bottom of the stairs. "I shall see myself out. Do not hesitate to contact me for any reason."

Caroline gave his hand a firm squeeze. "You have been a godsend, sir."

The old man snorted. "Such twaddle! I bid you good day, Lady Buford."

Caroline watched as the distinguished gentleman took his overcoat and hat from the footman and walked out into a cold London morning. For the hundredth time, she blessed Mr. Darcy and his connections; Mr. Macmillan was the Darcy family physician. She turned and ascended, noting that her husband's mother awaited her, wringing her hands.

"The doctor, what did he say, *chérie*?" Albertine Buford asked, her French accent pronounced even after thirty years in England.

"He is pleased with John's recovery, Mother Buford. He wants him to walk out and exercise his leg."

"Then, exercise he shall have!" the widow declared, revealing the steel beneath her motherly façade. "You shall walk out with him, yes? He can deny you nothing," she added with a wink. By then the pair reached Buford's bedroom door. Caroline opened it for both of them.

"Caroline!" cried her husband. "What if I were indecent?" He was not; he sat on the bed wearing his jacket, Corporal Frost tying his cravat.

"And what of it?" was her mischievous reply. "We are your closest relations. You have no secrets from either of us!"

In all the upheaval and drama of her two-year marriage to John Buford, Caroline had found her true character. She was a wife and mother and knew what it was to love and be loved, to depend on others as they depended on her. She discovered a strength she never knew she had and, sometimes, an engulfing serenity. She still owned a sharp tongue, but that she reserved for those who deserved it. Such was the difference between five-and-twenty and seven-and-twenty.

"Leave off, Frost. That will do." Buford struggled slightly to rise to his feet, and Caroline forced herself to hold back rather than help him.

Waterloo had been very hard on Sir John Buford, former colonel of Hussars. Her husband, for all his sterling characteristics, was a prideful man. The scar on his face stood out in white relief against the redness on his cheeks. Caroline knew John hated his scar more than his other injuries—even his missing left arm. It was his vanity, and he feared Caroline would tire of the sight.

Foolish man—thinking she loved only his handsome features! He was still the John Buford she had come to love. His tender lips and bright blue eyes were undamaged, as were his impressive mental faculties. He retained his strong right arm. And he loved her more than she deserved.

In a very even voice, she said, "Mr. Macmillan said you should walk out each day, and I believe now is a capital time to do so." She smiled to soften what was indeed an order.

Buford was not deceived. "I have just suffered being prodded and mishandled for almost an hour without complaint. And you say my reward for my good behavior is to slap on a heavy coat, leave this warm house, and traipse about in the cold? I thought I had left the army!"

Caroline kissed his cheek. "I shall be waiting for you downstairs. Corporal Frost, pray accompany us."

"Frost can stay here," Buford grumbled. "I can manage without him."

"I think he can use the exercise as well. Can you not, Corporal?" she said over her shoulder as she made for the door.

"I'll have him downstairs as soon as may be, ma'am," Frost vowed.

"You are supposed to be on *my* side, Frost!" Buford cried.

"And he is, my dear son," said Mrs. Buford as she reached up to kiss his cheek. "So am I, and so is Caroline. Now go and be a good boy, yes?"

Buford House, on Berkeley Street, was just outside the more fashionable streets of Mayfair. It was Buford's assertion that since he must walk, he ought to have a destination. Caroline's proposal that they call upon the Tuckers was accepted. She kept to herself her concern that the distance might be too much for her husband's first excursion.

It turned out it was, and Corporal Frost was sent back for the carriage while his employers took their ease on a park bench. Within a half an hour, the party was off again and soon arrived at the steps of a smart little dwelling outside of Cheapside. Buford's limp was pronounced, which did nothing to lighten his mood. The maid knew the couple on sight, Lady Buford being a regular visitor, and she escorted them directly to the sitting room.

"Caroline! Sir John!" was Mary Tucker's delighted cry. Instantly the two friends were embracing, sharing kisses on the cheek. Mary gave the same welcome to Buford and led him to a chair near the fire.

"I am not an invalid," Buford complained.

"Of course, you are not," Mary returned, "but it is the most comfortable chair in the house. Caroline and I shall make do on the settee." She turned to the maid and told her to see to Buford's people and ordered tea. "What brings you here today?" she asked as she took her place beside Caroline.

"We went for a walk and decided we had to call on you, my dear," was Lady Buford's reply to the woman she loved like a sister.

"Walk!" Mary cried. "Surely, you did not walk all the way here!"

"No, we took to our carriage after walking partway," Caroline assured her, "but Sir John is much recovered, and Mr. Macmillan requires him to walk."

"He is a hard, old tyrant," grumbled Buford.

Caroline ignored him. "We trust Mr. Tucker is well."

"He is and will be very sorry he missed you. But he must be at his office at this time of day."

"Of course. Pray give him our regards. And is Miss Rosanna in good health?"

Mary's plain features lit up. "She is very well." It was clear she was elated with her baby niece. "We can look in on her later, if you like."

Caroline gave Mary a disapproving look. "What? You will make us wait to see your little angel? You are very cruel, Mary!"

The very serious Mary Bennet had mellowed considerably since her marriage to Thomas Tucker, but she never owned a particularly good sense of humor. Therefore, it took a moment before she realized her friend was teasing her. "Would you like her brought down now?" she asked carefully.

"If it is no bother." Caroline softened her request with a smile.

Mary nodded and excused herself. Meanwhile, Caroline noted the puzzled expression on her husband's face. "I thought the stairs might be too much for you today," she whispered, guessing Buford's question.

"I could have managed."

Stung, Caroline flinched. "John, I do not want you to overdo."

"I know I am a damned cripple, but I am not totally helpless." He stared at the fire.

Caroline bit back a sigh. There was no moving her husband when the Black Dog was upon him. Most of the spells were brief, and his later expressions of regret and apology genuine. Caroline had been advised to disregard any harsh words when those moods appeared.

However, Corporal Frost confided that not all soldiers overcame this melancholy. They sought refuge in drink or opium, falling into lives of depredation and illness before suffering early deaths. Frost saw no evidence of this with Sir John, for the colonel had steadfastly refused laudanum during his recovery.

What was troubling to Caroline was that John's spells were recurring more often lately, paradoxically as he physically improved. She would help her husband if she knew how. All she could do was pray, and she was not convinced it was enough.

At least, Mary had not heard his language.

Caroline brightened when her friend returned, carrying an infant. Rosanna Wickham was a lovely, healthy girl of ten months. Mary beamed as she presented her.

"My, how she has grown!" Caroline exclaimed. "And her hair! I have never seen such beautiful golden hair on so young a babe. It took forever for Bea's hair to grow out."

"And how is Beatrice today?"

Caroline smiled as she spoke of her daughter. "She is very well." Rosanna's response was a strong wiggle. "Goodness, she has strong legs!"

"To the nurses' sorrow!" Mary laughed. "She must run after her. Is Bea walking yet?" She gave over the child to Caroline's embrace. Dark blue eyes studied her green ones before the child gave a giggle.

"She is just starting. My goodness, Miss Rosanna has a great deal to say," Caroline observed. Indeed, the baby babbled incessantly while waving her hands.

Mary bit her lip. "Yes…well, she is my sister's child, and Lydia took after my mother—"

"And her father was George Wickham," Buford pointed out. "Let me see her."

Caroline was more surprised at her husband's request than his brusque manner. Still wary of his mood, she carefully handed over the wiggling Rosanna. Buford settled the child in his lap using his right hand, placing her head against his stump of a left arm. He did it quickly with no assistance, obviously a result of much practice with his own child. Rosanna instantly quieted, to the wonder of the ladies.

Buford's features softened. "She is nothing to Bea, of course, but she is very pretty."

"John!" Caroline was mortified.

"It is quite all right," said Mary. "I would expect a father to favor his own over others."

Buford turned to Mary. "I meant no insult, Mrs. Tucker." He returned his attention to the babe.

"You could be civil about it," Caroline pointed out with a frown.

"I did apologize, my dear," Buford said levelly while he kept his eye fixed on Rosanna, who was clearly captivated. "You will be a sweet girl, yes? You must not give your papa and mama any trouble, for they love you. They *chose* you. That is a special thing."

Caroline turned to Mary. "You may not know this, but John's sister, Lady Suzanne Douglas, is actually his cousin. Her parents fell victim to the influenza when she was a baby. Not only did the Bufords take her in, they adopted her."

"Suzanne is sister to me and daughter to my parents," Buford insisted. "We raised her from infancy. She *is* a Buford, and I will not hear anything differently."

Caroline caressed his shoulder. "And now she is a Douglas."

"Yes, well...I *might* allow that Lord Frederick is good enough for her."

She kissed the top of his head. "You are all generosity."

Buford smiled slightly and cooed at the baby. Meanwhile, the tea service arrived, and the ladies crossed over to the far side of the room and busied themselves with it, talking in low tones.

"Mary, I am so sorry for—"

Mary touched her arm. "Say no more. We have talked of this. We must show Christian charity for those who suffered so grievously while in service to the country. I am not offended. Pray, how is Sir John faring?"

"He recovers more of his strength every day, and Mr. Macmillan is pleased. But the Black Dog is always around the corner."

"Such trying spells! My sympathies, dear. Have you any relief?"

"Relief? What do you mean?"

"Caroline, you have been nursemaid to your husband for over a year. What aid have you received? And I do not speak of servants."

"Mother Buford has been beside us all this time. I hate to think of what may have been if she had not. John's brother and sister, Phillip and Rebecca, have been a great help, but they are not always in town. They have duties to the estate in Wales. After the harvest, we may see them. Corporal Frost has been a godsend."

"And Louisa?"

Caroline shrugged. "She would do more, but she cannot abide a sickroom. She and Hurst are in Scarborough until Twelfth Night when they return for the Season. Charles and Jane have their own family. They will be returning to town from Mayfield in January, as well."

Mary spoke louder. "Lizzy and Darcy are ensconced at Pemberley. Nothing could induce them to leave Derbyshire, I am sure. We shall not see them before the Season, depend upon it!"

"What was that, Mrs. Tucker?" came Buford's voice from across the room.

"I was saying that the Darcys remain in Derbyshire, Sir John."

Buford huffed. "Darcy and Pemberley! Upon my word, I am surprised he has not dug a moat about the place and pulled up the drawbridge!"

"There are few who do not enjoy Pemberley, my dear." Caroline brought him a cup of tea.

"Thank you. Well I, for one, like London better." He placed the cup and saucer on a small table by his elbow. "Living in the country all year would surely drive me mad." He chuckled as he took his first sip.

Caroline laughed, pleased to see that his morose spell had vanished for the time being.

The visit passed in pleasant conversation, taken up mostly by Mary answering Caroline's questions about the Llewellyn wedding. Mary assured her that Georgiana adored their gift of a figurine.

Just then, Mr. Tucker was announced. "Good afternoon, my dear," cried Mary, "but what brings you home so early?"

"I have spent much of the day occupied with some sad business and decided to hurry home to you." He then greeted the Bufords.

"Was it the Elliot business, dear?"

"Yes. Mr. Elliot was buried today." Tucker glanced at Sir John. "Are you familiar with the Elliots of Kellynch Hall?"

Sir John demurred, but Caroline spoke up. "I take it you speak of that terrible attack on Mr. William Elliot. It was in all the papers this summer. When did he pass?" Caroline's one remaining vice from her earlier days was her love of gossip.

"Two days ago. As the funeral was small, a notice will be printed tomorrow."

"And that horrible woman who poisoned him. Does she remain unpunished?"

Tucker nodded. "We learned Mrs. Clay has fled the country in the company of her personal maid. At first, it was thought she sailed to America. It is now believed she is somewhere on the Continent. In any case, she is currently beyond British justice."

"I do not wish to speak ill of the dead, but I have heard some things about this Mr. Elliot," Buford said carefully.

"Say no more, Sir John. The stories about the late Mr. Elliot are all too true. I represent his heir's family—that of Captain Wentworth."

"Captain Wentworth, famous for the *Laconia*?" Assured it was so, Buford turned to the ladies. "He is cousin to George Blakeney's bride. You recall Dorothy Blakeney, do you not, Caroline?"

"You are acquainted with the Blakeneys, Sir John?" asked Tucker.

"Only in passing with the baronet and his lady, but George is a good friend. His sister married another of my comrades, Major Tilney."

"The George Blakeneys called on us this summer," explained Caroline, "and the Tilneys have been regular visitors."

"Fine friends to have," Tucker pronounced significantly. Everyone in London knew the wealthy Blakeneys were very close to the Regent.

"But what do the Wentworths have to do with the late Mr. Elliot?" asked Caroline.

"Mr. William Elliot was heir to Sir Walter Elliot of Kellynch Hall. As Mr. Eliot left no issue, the estate and the title will descend upon Sir Walter's passing to the firstborn son of his eldest daughter. Miss Elliot is yet unmarried, so the heir presumptive is the son of his second daughter, Anne Wentworth, wife of the captain."

"A sad business, to be sure," observed Mary, "but one should be happy for Master Wentworth."

Later, as they prepared to take their leave, Buford surprised his wife while waiting for the carriage by inviting the Tuckers to dinner the week following.

"I am certain we should be happy to do so, Sir John," Mary said carefully, her eye on Caroline.

"It is a wonderful idea," said Caroline smoothly, covering her husband's *faux pas*. "I shall send a note to determine which night would be agreeable to you." The ladies shared a kiss on the cheek, and the Bufords left.

"Well, Corporal Frost," said Caroline, tugging at her gloves as the carriage rolled down the street, "you must make sure Sir John has a suitable coat for next week as we shall have guests for dinner." She would not look up.

Caroline was upset. There were certain duties reserved for the wives of gentlemen, and she jealously guarded them for herself. For Sir John to usurp her role could be considered an insult to her abilities to manage his house. But it would not do to have a disagreement with Corporal Frost in attendance.

Buford was insensitive to it. "Frost knows his business, Caroline."

"You are right, my dear. We shall say no more," she allowed, not meaning a word of it.

THE ARGUMENT STARTED ONCE THEY WERE ALONE IN THEIR private apartments. "What is wrong, Caroline? You are not upset over the invitation, are you?"

"It was my understanding that the lady of the house issued invitations," she snapped at him, "but perhaps things are different in Wales."

Buford harrumphed. "You cannot stand on ceremony with the Tuckers! They are practically family."

"Family or not, it is not done!"

"They will not mind."

"I mind! *I mind!*" With that, Caroline dissolved into tears.

Buford took his wife into his embrace, wrapping her as tightly as he could. At first, Caroline fought his touch but soon gave in.

"Now, now, there is no call for this. It is but a trifling matter."

It was the wrong thing to say. "No, it is not!" she cried, roughly escaping his hold. "You have no appreciation for my position!"

"What is this? Of course, I respect you."

"John, can you not see? A wife should be mistress of her house, but I am not! We live with your mother in Wales! We stay in your brother's house in town! I am mistress of *nothing!*"

Stunned by her outburst, Buford stepped away.

Caroline began to pace. "The only responsibility I have left to maintain my respectability in society is to entertain guests! And now you take that away from me!"

"I am sorry. It was not my intention." Buford pulled a face.

"You are unhappy."

"I am *not* unhappy. I would not trade places with anyone in the world. But all my life, I dreamt of being a great lady with my own home, entertaining my friends and acquaintances. I am a great lady, for I am married to you, and I have dear friends whom I love. But I am not mistress of any house."

"But…but our house in Wales—"

"Is the dower house," Caroline replied. "It belongs to Mother Buford. Do not mistake me. I truly love her and enjoy living with her. She asks for my opinions and assistance on household matters, and she has allowed our people to serve us. But do not deceive yourself into believing I forget for a moment it is *her* house. She will always have the last word on matters as long as she lives."

Caroline gestured at the room. "And here in London! Your brother is the most generous man I know. But this is *Rebecca* Buford's house, not *Caroline* Buford's.

"I accept this, John. I have made my peace with it. I know we are not in a position to have our own house. Perhaps someday, when you are stronger. I can wait."

During all this, Buford stood stock-still. He then dropped his head in despondency. "I have failed you."

Caroline took Buford's hand and kissed it, hoping her passionate defense of herself had not triggered her husband's despondency. "No, you have not. You have given me your love. You have given me Bea. I do not yet have a house, but as long as we are together, I have a *home*." She kissed his cheek. "I am content."

Buford's expression remained troubled. "I am sorry, Caro. You must know I love and respect you. I have been a blind fool."

Caroline did not argue the point, for he *had* been a fool. "I want you to be proud of me," she said.

"I *am*. I am proud of you." His voice was firm. "I shall never presume to speak for you again."

"Thank you, my dear." Caroline kissed him again. "Now, come

with me to the nursery. Bea has been wondering where we have been, I should not wonder."

She knew a mention of his daughter would bring the brightness back to his eyes. "Yes, let us go to my little princess." He then gave a roguish look. "Later, I must give my compliments to the queen of my heart."

Caroline smiled. "I am certain she would welcome them, my good sir."

# Chapter 4

L ady Fitzwilliam sat behind her Chippendale desk in her favorite small parlor, reviewing the household accounts. Unlike the rest of Rosings, this room had been remade to suit the taste of its current mistress. Gone were the dark, heavy drapes and the overcrowded, ostentatious décor. It was light and airy, the morning sun shining merrily through the windows. The only other furnishings in the room were three chairs, a fainting couch, a chest of drawers, and a dog bed under the desk for Romeo's use.

Anne adjusted her spectacles, biting her lip in concentration. She knew that, with the bad harvest, economy must be found in managing the estate. There would be no money this year to continue the redecoration of Rosings Manor. But forgoing their plans of making the great house more comfortable would not be sufficient. There were few outside expenses left to cut, for the Fitzwilliams had a duty to the poor of Hunsford. Anne had no choice but to retrench.

But where? Already she had forgone a shopping expedition to London. She planned no new gowns for the winter. The food budget might be trimmed—less beef, more chicken—but still it would not be enough. They might have to let a servant go.

Anne sighed. She would not trouble poor Richard over these matters—he had worries enough managing the estate. Mrs. Parks surely would have some recommendations.

The parlor door opened. "Lady Fitzwilliam, Lady Catherine de Bourgh ta see ya," a footman announced without knock or preamble.

Anne looked up, irritated. The new footman, Adam Shepardson, showed bad form, his uniform was a disgrace, and his wig sat askew on his head. He had been trained to do better, but Sergeant Gregory had reported difficulties with him.

"Show my mother in," Anne said coldly, "and fasten your jacket."

A slight sneer crossed the footman's face before he nodded and stepped aside. Lady Catherine swept in as though she still owned the place. "You may go," she ordered Shepardson.

"Mother, to what do I owe this visit?" asked Anne once the door closed. "As you can see, I am quite occupied."

"Too occupied to see your mother? Nonsense!" Lady Catherine's progress to one of the chairs was abruptly halted by a low growl. "*What* is that *animal* doing in here?" she cried.

Anne stepped between the Italian greyhound and the dowager. "Romeo, behave yourself, sir! Return to your bed." Romeo did as he was ordered, but the dog kept a gimlet eye on the intruder.

"Dogs in Rosings! What is this world coming to?"

Anne was well aware of her mother's aversion to her pet and thought it best to ignore it. "I am glad to see you well, but it is early for a visit, and I do have matters that require my attention."

"What matters are more important than your family? Do the servants now require your constant attention? It was not so in my day!"

Anne bit her tongue. Countless were the times she had witnessed her mother berate a servant of long standing and experience, demanding the most minute tasks be redone in accordance to her detailed direction. Anne knew nothing good would come of reminding her mother of her behavior, however.

"I must review the household accounts. Due to the unseasonable weather, we cannot trust that the estate profits will be what they were. We must economize."

"Nonsense! Richard is being cheated—depend upon it."

Anne gestured at the window. "Look for yourself. How shall we sell grain that does not grow? Where will the rents come from?"

Lady Catharine turned away from the window. "Pray do not address me in such a manner."

As usual, her mother refused to see what she did not want to see. "Thankfully, your fortune and settlement are invested in the funds. *Your* situation is not endangered, but Richard and I have greater demands upon us. The household, our people, Hunsford—"

"We owe Hunsford nothing!" the grand dame exclaimed. "Indeed, they owe us all gratitude and deference for allowing them to live on Rosings land and the honor of our patronage."

Anne was beginning to lose her composure. "Forgive me, but that sort of thinking is ridiculous! We do not own Hunsford. Our tenants pay rent and are responsible for the well-being of their workers and families. All are suffering due to this terrible harvest."

Her mother waved away her argument. "If they cannot do right by us, then let them find a new situation."

"Where? Misery covers the whole of England. There is unrest in the north—"

"Jacobian traitors, the lot of them!"

"Perhaps they are, or perhaps they are just hungry. In any case, *we* have a duty to *our* people, and we shall not fail them. If I must do without a new gown for a year, so be it."

"It is unconscionable for you to sacrifice for a horde of ingrates!"

Once again, Anne was struck by Lady Catherine's newfound antipathy for the tenants, with Hunsford, with...well, *everyone*. For most of her life, her mother crowed over the condescension she showed to all in the district. Lady Catherine knew everyone's business and did not hesitate to share her opinions and guidance. While rude and obnoxious, her advice was always excellent.

Now, the only words she had for the servants and locals were hostile. Anne knew not why; it was a mystery. All her inquiries were met with evasion and derision.

A knock on the door interrupted Anne's contemplation of yet another avenue of addressing her mother's bitterness. It was Mrs. Parks with a paper in her hand.

"Good morning, Lady Catherine. Pray forgive me, Lady Fitzwilliam, but here is the foodstuff inventory you requested."

"Thank you, Mrs. Parks." Both women ignored Lady Catherine's glare. "Mother, would you care for some refreshment?"

"Tea would not be unwelcome." The older lady turned to the housekeeper. "I expect lemon and sugar—"

"Nothing for me, Mrs. Parks," Anne broke in, smiling to soften the interruption. "Mrs. Parks knows well your tastes after sixteen years!"

The housekeeper's only response was a slight bow from her shoulders as she left the room, but Anne did not miss the warm look of thanks on the trusted servant's face. Mrs. Parks had been helpful to and supportive of the heiress over those sixteen years, never more than during the crisis last year that resulted in Anne's ascension and Lady Catherine's removal to the dower house. Gratitude was an insufficient word to describe Anne and Richard's feelings for the woman.

Lady Catherine was put out—not an uncommon occurrence over the last eighteen months—and was disinclined for conversation at present. She sat quietly, staring out the window. This suited Anne, and she returned to her work. By the time Mrs. Parks returned with Lady Catherine's tea, Anne had a question for the housekeeper.

"Cook is short on salt, Mrs. Parks?"

The housekeeper frowned. "Yes, milady."

"How is that so? The records show a considerable quantity of salt purchased earlier this year."

"I cannot say, ma'am. Cook has no answer, either. The shortage was only discovered during the inventory."

"We obviously have a thief in the house, Parks!" cried Lady Catherine.

"Mother, please. There may be a simple answer." Anne turned back to the housekeeper. "Is the salt kept under lock and key?"

"No, ma'am. It was not thought necessary."

Lady Catherine harrumphed. "Incompetence! Such a thing was inconceivable when I was mistress!"

Anne flinched at the insult.

"Begging your pardon, milady," Mrs. Parks responded respectfully, "but the salt has never been locked up—not in all my years here."

Lady Catherine was baffled. "Well...it should have been!"

"Mrs. Parks," said Anne evenly, thankful for the housekeeper's rejoinder, "instruct Cook that all the food and seasonings be locked up from now on, just in case."

"Yes, ma'am. I can report that Cook intends to do just that."

"Very good. You may return to your duties. Should I have any questions, we shall discuss them later."

The twinkle in Mrs. Parks's eye showed she understood her mistress very well. She took her leave of the ladies directly.

For the next few minutes, Lady Catherine was quiet. This allowed Anne to make some progress with her work. A knock on the door signaled the arrival of the older lady's tea. Soon, the only sounds were the scratch of Anne's pen and the clink of Lady Catherine's spoon.

"I wonder how Lady Llewellyn gets on."

Anne could not disregard her mother's non sequitur. "I suppose she is very happy in her situation."

"Of course, she is happy! She is a viscountess!"

Somehow, Anne resisted the impulse to roll her eyes. "No doubt, but I was referring to her husband rather than his estate."

"The Woodhouses are a very respectable family, but they should take more of an interest in society," Lady Catherine pronounced. "My sister's daughter should take her rightful place in the *ton*!"

Anne was hurt by this. She, after all, avoided town like the plague. Did she not live up to her mother's expectations? Was this another attack on *her*? "I do not think Georgiana is eager to involve herself in the workings of the first circles, Mother. She is very reserved and uncomfortable with London society—"

"It is the fault of that…that *woman* Darcy married!" Lady Catherine snarled. "Lady Llewellyn has been poorly directed. She should have been made to understand her destiny as a Darcy and a Fitzwilliam."

"Georgiana's decision has nothing to do with Lizzy—"

"*Elizabeth*, Anne! I despise pet names!"

"*Elizabeth*, then!" Anne ground out between her teeth. "You forget how Georgiana was before Elizabeth married Darcy. My cousin blossomed under her care and direction. She remains reserved because she is a *Darcy*—just like her brother! And Lord Llewellyn is just like her." Anne paused and pleaded, "They are happy together. Is that not enough? I know I have been a disappointment to you—"

"No, you are *not* a disappointment! Your delicate health in your youth prevented you from achieving your dreams."

*My health prevented me from achieving* your *dreams*, Anne thought.

"Now that you have recovered your strength," Lady Catherine continued, "you have fulfilled your destiny here at Rosings with Richard."

"Not completely," Anne could not help from pointing out. "I have yet to fulfill that most basic destiny as a wife." To her mortification, her eyes began to fill.

Lady Catherine's countenance was stricken. "Anne, you must not say so! You are well now. You *will* beget the heir to Rosings Park. I-I have every confidence in it."

It would have been easier for Anne to take comfort in her mother's declaration, had not Lady Catherine's voice wavered. But she chose to be satisfied with her mother's intention to relieve her fears.

"Then I have no worries, for if you say so, it must be done," Anne said with no trace of sarcasm.

"Of course." Lady Catherine held her chin up in triumph, but her lips trembled. She remained silent for the next few minutes as Anne endeavored to settle her feelings and return to her labors.

Eventually, the grand dame cleared her throat. "I own myself to be slightly weary. I shall return to the dower house to rest before dinner."

Anne rose, but Lady Catherine declined any assistance. "Very well, Mother. Richard and I look forward to seeing you."

Lady Catherine nodded but said no more until she reached the door, where she demanded Dawson attend her. As the door closed, Anne saw a footman dash towards the servants' quarters to fetch the lady's maid.

Alone at last, Anne broke down and cried.

ON THE FAR SIDE OF THE ROSINGS ESTATE, DEEP IN A STAND OF woods, stood an old blacksmith's shop. Eighteen years before, the abandoned, dilapidated shack had been transformed into a home for what remained of the Johnson family. Few people in the district knew where the place was and fewer visited.

The house was set off a bit from the trail through the woods. It was longer than wide, with a door in the left front and two windows to the center and right. There was another door in the center of the back, with a single window to the right. Behind the house was a privy, a coop, and a lean-to for the milk cow. Inside, a single room spanned the entirety of the house, save for a storage room close by the front door.

The house had seen neither hammer nor nail since the turn of the century. The roof was in poor condition, and the windows let in cold air. No maintenance had been performed by landlord or occupant. Only the great hearth, a relic of its blacksmithing days, made the shack habitable.

The few furnishings in the place were rough. A single table was close by the fire with a chair and three stools. Shelves built into the walls once stored iron, horseshoes, and nails but now held jars of flour, beans, and a few seasonings. Stored there, too, were several chipped plates and bowls, a few knives, spoons, and mugs. Spare clothes and blankets inhabited the lowest shelves. In the corner sat a single bed with a secured bedroll at its foot.

Mrs. Johnson bent over her work at the solitary table. Candles cost money, so she labored by the light of the cooking fire. She and her son Cork lived there rent-free by the charity of the Rosings family. She earned her bread and other necessities with needle and thread, and her simple-minded son brought in what coins he could by doing odd jobs in nearby Hunsford. And meat—Cork was good at acquiring meat—by means not always legal. This did not bother Mrs. Johnson overmuch.

From his birth, her son had been different. He was strong and sweet—and stupid. The villagers either shied away or mocked the lad. So many called him "cork-brained" that even she began to call him Cork. As the artless boy liked his new name, Cork he became.

Mrs. Johnson had just finished her work and placed the folded garment into a sack when the front door opened. "Cork," she called, not looking up, "have you brought food?"

"Yes, Mama, I got some fat squirrels, and—"

"The hell with that!" cried another voice. "Here's some real meat!" A haunch of venison landed on the table.

"Take a care! That's my work!" Mrs. Johnson glared at her son's companions. "An' where did you pinch that, Simon Shepardson?"

"Ask me no questions, Auntie, an' I'll tell ya no tales," he returned. His brother, Adam, was the last in. At least, he closed the door behind him.

The Shepardsons were the sons of Mrs. Johnson's late sister. She and her husband were taken by the influenza over a decade before, leaving fourteen-year-old Adam and twelve-year-old Simon adrift in the streets of Rochester and the docks at Chatham. Thievery kept them out of the salt works. Eventually, they made their way to Hunsford.

Adam, the clever one of the two, found work in the stables at a nearby estate. He now had a position at Rosings Park. Simon was a ne'er-do-well who got by with help from his brother, working the harvest, and petty crimes.

The Shepardson brothers did not live with the Johnsons. Adam had a room at Rosings and shared with his brother. But they often ate with their aunt to save money as the food at Rosings was only for servants, not their idle siblings.

Mrs. Johnson vacillated between greed and fear as she gazed upon the unexpected bounty before her. Venison would be a tasty change from their usual fare, but poaching deer was far more serious than taking the occasional squirrel. It could lead to prison or transportation. She wondered whether she should keep it or bury it in the woods.

It was Adam who made her decision. "He got th' haunch in th' woods off th' road to Tunbridge Wells. It weren't anywhere near here."

Mrs. Johnson was relieved. She doubted anyone would look for poachers so far away. But that brought up another question. "What were ya doin' way over there?"

"Oh, I were with Adam—" Simon's calm explanation was cut off by an angry Adam.

"I had business there, Aunt. Now, where's some food?"

"There's beans on th' stove now." She glanced at the venison. "Ain't got time ta cook *that* up, unless yer willin' to wait fer it."

Simon began to speak up, but Adam overrode him. "Beans'll be fine. We can have th' haunch tomorrow."

Mrs. Johnson frowned. "I'll have ta cook up th' whole thing—I ain't got enough salt to set it aside."

"Ya do now." Adam withdrew a small sack from his coat and placed it on the table.

Mrs. Johnson was more frightened of the sack than the venison. "So, ya pinching salt from Rosings now?" The salt before her was worth more than she earned in a year and, if discovered, would condemn her to Van Diemen's Land.

Adam's face grew hard. "Don't ya worry about where it come from, woman. Just get th' food. Cork, go hang th' meat in th' storeroom there."

Cork looked over at his mother. "Do as he says," she told him.

The giant obediently hefted the haunch over one shoulder and retrieved his catch of squirrels before carrying his burdens to a storeroom opposite the front door—another relic of the shack's blacksmithing days. In the meantime, Mrs. Johnson hurried to clean the table in preparation for the dinner of baked beans and day-old bread. The Shepardsons simply sat down, forcing her to work around them. There was no profit in scolding them. They would not listen, and it was unwise to anger Adam. He had a bad temper and a long memory, as Mrs. Johnson had cause to know.

Not that he ever struck her in front of Cork. The lad was a gentle soul who would never pick a fight or seek revenge, but he might defend his mother if someone hurt her before his eyes. Given his bulk and strength, Adam would not chance a beating at Cork's hands. He would wait until his enormous cousin was off to work or wandering in the woods before he "corrected" his aunt. He had done it before.

As for Mrs. Johnson, she expected nothing else. She had been beaten all her life—by her father, her husband, and now by her nephew. Her desire was not to give him any reason to do so.

It was the way of the world.

# Chapter 5

Richard sat back and studied the gentleman seated on the opposite side of his desk. This was the third applicant he had interviewed for the soon-to-be-vacant steward position, and Richard was tired of the whole business. He hoped that, with this candidate, he had found his man.

"So tell me, Mr. Evans, why do you wish to leave your current position?"

Philip Evans shifted in his chair and cleared his throat. "I have enjoyed my current situation, but my employer and I have reached an impasse over modernizing farming methods. I believe it is best for all that we part ways." He gestured to a document on Richard's desk. "You have his recommendation before you."

Richard had gotten the man's name from an acquaintance in town and was pleased that Evans was everything he had been told. "And what are your thoughts about modernizing?"

"I am in favor of it. The great minds of the age have studied the problem of the increasing population and the need for higher yields. I have read extensively on this matter and have seen the results. I am satisfied that the new techniques of crop rotation, enclosure, and other innovations are the way of the future."

"Here, here!" said Mr. Caruthers.

"Thank you, sir." Mr. Evans returned his attention to Richard. "My current master, good man that he is, is held captive by tradition. He does not wish to 'upset the cart,' as he put it, and distress his tenants, most of whom have tilled their leases for years and are loath to change with the times. They cannot see that they need to devise new and better ways of doing things, to produce more with less labor, even while their sons leave the farms for the factories."

Richard examined Mr. Evans. A man not quite thirty, rather short in stature and plain of dress, he sat straight in his chair and returned Richard's gaze steadfastly. He liked that. He could not abide a man who could not look him in the eye. He seemed eager to please, the recommendation from his former employer spoke of his propensity for hard work, and Mr. Caruthers's report had been excellent. Richard had but one last question for the gentleman.

"What is your preferred method for dealing with the tenants?"

Mr. Evans blinked and hesitated. It was clear he did not expect the question. He stared at Richard for a moment before speaking. "Of course, I would handle such matters as my employer wished."

"That is commendable, but I want to know how you would do things if you had your own way."

Mr. Evans paused to think, frowning. "*If* I had my own way," he said carefully, "matters generally would fall to the purview of the steward, particularly in the details of managing the tenants. The master would, of course, oversee the steward and control the outlay of funds. He would devise the overall strategy and, together with the steward, make plans. The steward would discharge the plans, leaving the master's attention free for other issues and investments. The steward could deal with the agents for the crops and wool, if that be the master's will."

Richard was pleased. Obviously, Mr. Evans would listen to his employer and endeavor to assure that his will was put into action. That was how things were done in the army. The commander devised the objective and overall strategy, and the subordinate figured how best to accomplish the mission. Successful regiments were staffed by men who could think on their feet and not have to scurry back to their leaders for every little decision. If a subordinate was well trained, a commander could order an officer to take a hill without having to tell him *how* to take that hill. This was the type of man Richard wanted.

"Mr. Evans, I believe you would suit very well. When are you free to start?"

"Thank you, sir. I can settle things with my current employer and be back in Kent within a fortnight."

"Excellent. We shall discuss my expectations further upon your return, but to give you an idea on how I see things, I can tell you I plan to turn the day-to-day operations of the farms over to you. All matters outside of Rosings House will fall under your purview, including the dower house. The exceptions are the stables and dog pens. Those are left to Sergeant-Major Gregory." He gestured at the burly man seated across the room. "Inside these walls, Lady Fitzwilliam and the housekeeper, Mrs. Parks, reign supreme."

Mr. Evans nodded at Sergeant Gregory. "Very good. I am sure the sergeant and I shall get along famously."

Richard suppressed a grin. "A word to the wise, sir. Lady Fitzwilliam's mother, Lady Catherine, is a woman of strong opinions. Dealings regarding the dower house require diplomacy."

"I understand. Sir Richard, what of the village?"

"That has yet to be decided. Lady Fitzwilliam has her duties there, and I meet regularly with a council representing the larger tenants and other gentleman of the district. You, of course, will be invited to attend."

"I would be honored."

"Very good. Now, let us discuss the terms of your employment."

RICHARD ESCORTED MR. CARUTHERS AND MR. EVANS OUT OF his study, feeling pleased with himself. Meanwhile, Sergeant Gregory poured his employer a glass of wine.

"Thank you," said Richard as he took the glass. "Pour one for yourself. I think the business went very well indeed."

"Having never been involved in such dealings before, I cannot venture an opinion."

"What think you of Mr. Evans?"

"He seems a capable man. Time will tell."

Fitzwilliam frowned. "You have doubts?"

Sergeant Gregory shook his head. "No, sir. I am just too set in my ways to praise a trooper before he proves worthy of his spurs."

"Hah! Lord knows what you thought of my horsemanship!"

The sergeant gave him a satirical look. "Why, it was of the best quality, Colonel."

Fitzwilliam threw back his head and laughed.

THREE WEEKS LATER, MR. CARUTHERS, MR. EVANS, AND Sergeant Gregory rode about the estate, Mr. Caruthers giving his successor the benefit of his years of knowledge of the area before he left Kent forever.

Many of the tenants were working the fields—finishing the sparse harvest and preparing for next spring's planting—so Mr. Evans was able to make their acquaintance. Sergeant Gregory noted that Mr. Evans greeted the tenants with cold civility, something that rubbed the former soldier the wrong way.

*Evans is supposed to be the steward of Rosings, not the master,* Gregory thought to himself. *It does no good for the man to take on such airs. He must work with these people and earn their allegiance.* Gregory always found that firm, fair, and friendly leadership worked to best advantage with his men.

The three took a rarely used trail back towards the main house and came upon a rough shack set off in the trees. The converted smithy was aged and in need of many small repairs. There was rubbish scattered about the overgrown garden. Mr. Evans inquired about it.

"That's the Johnson place. The Widow Johnson sometimes makes her living as a seamstress. She lives with her son." Mr. Caruthers made a gesture with his hand. "The boy's touched in the head, you see. Does odd jobs about the farm, mainly during the harvest."

Mr. Evans looked hard at the shack. "Sometime seamstress… son does odd jobs. Why does she live in a shack so far removed from the village? How can they afford the rent?"

Mr. Caruthers shifted in his saddle. "Funny thing, that. She was settled here before I became steward. My predecessor showed me the order drawn up by Sir Lewis, God rest his soul. She does not pay rent at all, and we are not responsible for anything but the most crucial of repairs. We never saw any reason to change things. It would be more trouble to run her off than the place is worth. So, we do not break our back keeping the place up, if you understand my meaning."

"Was there a reason Sir Lewis set the woman up?" Mr. Evans gave Mr. Caruthers a significant look.

Mr. Caruthers frowned. "If you mean what I think you do—no. That was not Sir Lewis's way, I have been told"

Mr. Evans rubbed his chin. "Is there anything else I need to know?"

"Things disappear from time to time," Mr. Caruthers continued. "Mrs. Johnson is from a family of thieves, so we suspect but cannot prove anything. Nothing out of the common way—a chicken every so often, coal, things like that. There was a pie last year."

"You cannot say that was her," said Gregory.

Mr. Caruthers shrugged. "I would not be surprised if it was."

At that moment, the door of the cottage opened, and a slovenly middle-aged woman peeked out. "Good day to ya, Mr. Caruthers." She spat on the ground.

"Johnson, come out here and make your curtsy," Mr. Caruthers demanded. "This here's the new steward, Mr. Evans. You will be dealing with him afore the month is out. Step quick now and none of your sass!"

The woman shuffled a few steps forward and paid the required honor by the barest of margins. She squinted up at the riders, her missing teeth visible.

"I see what you mean," said Mr. Evans to Mr. Caruthers. He turned to the woman. "Good afternoon, Mrs. Johnson. I am sure we shall get along famously."

Mrs. Johnson shrugged. "You'll get no trouble from me, sir."

"Is your son about?"

"Naw. Cork's out in the th' woods, throwin' rocks."

Mr. Evans looked at his companions.

"Cork—that is her son—likes to throw rocks," Gregory explained. "The boy is harmless."

"Big as an ox and about as strong," said Mr. Caruthers, "but gentle as a baby." He turned to the woman. "We take our leave of you, Johnson, but I am sure Mr. Evans will be back soon to see how things are."

"That I shall," Mr. Evans added.

The woman glared but said nothing as the men rode away.

# Chapter 6

The day was much like the others had been—cloudy and bitter cold. The Fitzwilliams had made themselves comfortable before the fire in the library, Romeo at Anne's feet, when the footman entered.

"Express for you, Sir Richard," he announced, the letter on a salver.

"Is the rider expecting a reply?" Richard inquired as he broke the seal.

"Yes, sir. He's waiting in the kitchen."

Richard paled as he read the letter. "Anne, we must leave for Matlock this instant! Father has taken ill!"

*Derbyshire*

THE CLOSER SHE DREW TO MATLOCK, THE MORE DISTRESSED Anne became. Her thoughts since the express arrived were occupied almost exclusively by concern for her husband and his relations' certain suffering. The anguish *they* were enduring amplified hers. The chilled coach and rough roads added to Anne's discomfort. The trip would have been unbearable but for Richard's consoling presence and Lady Catherine's surprising and merciful silence.

Anne gripped her husband's hand tightly, knowing he was

deeply distressed. Richard was sincerely attached to his father, yet the dear man exerted himself to calm Anne's worries. Anguish for her uncle was diminished by gratitude for her husband. Surely, no better man ever lived!

As for Lady Catherine's actions—or rather, *inactions*—they were a mystery suitable for particular consideration.

From almost as early in her life as she could understand, Anne knew Lady Catherine despised her brother. Throughout her childhood, Anne had been witness to her mother's rants over the ill treatment the grand dame had received from her own flesh and blood without knowing the reason for her kindly uncle's purported cruelty to his only surviving sibling.

In the last year, she finally was acquainted with the genesis of her mother's antagonism: her father, Sir Lewis, had made Lord Matlock and not Lady Catherine trustee of his will and manager of his estate, and that state of affairs had rankled the widow ever since. Lady Catherine had yet to forgive her brother for the impertinence of accepting this charge or for failing to attend her wishes in matters concerning Rosings.

When not tearful for Richard and Lady Matlock, Anne contemplated her mother's unusual behavior. It was surprising that Lady Catherine had insisted on joining them on the journey, and Anne had resigned herself to three days in a cold carriage, enduring her mother's constant vitriol without the comfort of Mrs. Jenkinson, her companion, who remained at Rosings. Instead, Lady Catherine spent the days gazing out the window, watching the passing fields and villages, and limiting herself to the infrequent remark about the unpleasantness of travel or the laziness of innkeepers.

Hope arose in Anne's breast. Might her mother see her way to reconciliation with the earl now that he was so dreadfully ill? Could it be that she desired to make her peace with her only brother before it was too late? It was an astonishing thought—so much so, that she had not yet shared her conjecture with Richard. It seemed that Lady Catherine's character was fixed and unlikely to alter, but things had changed in the last year. The old woman had accepted Richard as her son and had even graciously visited Pemberley. Anne prayed something good would come of this tragedy.

Thoughts such as these were Anne's only balm as she worried for her uncle and her husband.

The grand estate of Matlock Manor was far enough removed not to be bothered by the town of Matlock on the River Derwent and the spas with their increasing demand from those seeking cures without the society offered by the more fashionable Bath. Tall ridges of limestone ran throughout the area, giving Derbyshire its famous rugged reputation as the Peaks, but the estate was happily situated on good, rolling land. The manor itself provided excellent prospects of the park. The jagged cliffs were considered ill refined, and therefore were hidden from view by trees with middling success.

Richard had never found his birthplace a particularly welcoming house. For generations, the Fitzwilliams labored to bury their sheepherding Irish roots deep in the past by grandiose display and intensely proper English manners. Charles II had made Sir Cedric Fitzwilliam a peer, and Sir Cedric's son's reward for supporting William and Mary during the Glorious Revolution was a valuable earldom for the family. The Fitzwilliams were jealous of their power, purse, and prestige, and it was the task of every succeeding Earl of Matlock to further establish the family as a fixture in society.

Matlock Manor reflected this. Constructed of cold, gray stone blocks, the house was meant to impress. Comfort gave way to display. Cold elegance was desired and achieved. That a family lived there, that children might play within its halls, was not considered when improvements were undertaken.

Things were different at the beloved Fitzwilliam hunting lodge in Scotland. There, a man might sit in a soft chair before a cozy fire, his muddy boots on an ottoman, taking his ease after a hard day of shooting. Only Pemberley was as dear to an outdoorsman like Richard.

On arrival, the party from Rosings was escorted to the drawing room by the butler, and the travelers were greeted by Andrew, Viscount Fitzwilliam, the viscountess, and the Darcys. The embrace by the two brothers was as tight as Richard could remember. Elizabeth, of course, was as affectionate as ever, and Darcy tried valiantly to remain steadfast. The raw emotion displayed was a strong counterpoint to the austere formality of the room. Lady Eugenie, Viscountess Fitzwilliam, acted as hostess in the countess's absence, a fact remarked upon by Lady Catherine.

"She remains above stairs, madam, attending my father," said Andrew coldly.

Richard ignored his aunt. "What news, Brother?"

All were invited to sit before Andrew spoke again. "Nothing good since I wrote to you," said the viscount brusquely, as was his way when not in the fashionable salons of town. "The physician said the apoplexy has laid him low. His left side is paralyzed, and he is barely able to mumble. He gives little hope."

"Say not so!" cried Anne, her eyes watering yet again.

"Forgive me, but we must face things straight on. My father's time is short." He turned, and the pain in his eyes was palpable. "It is good you came as quickly as you did."

"But where are your sister and brother, the Montgomerys?" injected Lady Catherine. "It is most disgraceful they are not here. And the Llewellyns—Darcy, where is your sister?"

Darcy glared at his aunt. "Lord and Lady Llewellyn are expected from Ambervale Lodge by nightfall."

Richard noticed that Elizabeth had placed a hand on Darcy's arm, and that must have been the reason for her husband's relatively gentle reply.

"And as for my sister, Henrietta," the viscount spat out the words, "she and Lord Montgomery are wandering about the Continent, as you well know! It will be a fortnight before they can return, assuming they received my letter."

Lady Eugenie stood. "I am certain you all wish to refresh yourselves. I would be happy to show you to your rooms."

"It is good *someone* knows the courtesies," Lady Catherine said as she rose. "I expect I shall have my usual rooms."

It was not a question. And it did not go unnoticed that Lady Catherine had failed to show proper deference to Eugenie. Not only was the younger woman also the daughter of an earl, but she was the wife of a viscount and, consequently, above the widow of a baronet. However, Lady Eugenie, who could feign a smile with the best of them, reflected Richard.

"Of course."

"I thank you for my part," said Richard, "but I should like to see my father now."

"And I, my uncle." Anne wrapped her slender arm about Richard's broad one.

"Of course," said Andrew gravely. "I must see to Lady Catherine, but Darcy will take you."

The party moved up the grand staircase, their steps ringing unnaturally loud on the hard marble. Richard knew all the fires in the keep were set and attended, yet the house chilled his bones. Dread grew with every step despite Elizabeth's valiant attempts to engage Anne in conversation.

For not the first time, Richard blessed his cousin. Elizabeth's intelligent, generous nature was much like Darcy's, but her innate ability to put others at ease was magnificent. She knew Anne needed comfort and so accompanied them. For his part, Darcy's grim visage and stern silence made him useless at a time like this, despite his great goodness.

The door opened to a space as familiar to Richard as any could be. Rich, dark fabrics on proper English mahogany filled the space, dominated by a large bed. A fine desk was against one wall, and a pair of upholstered armchairs was before the fireplace. An exquisite carpet from a faraway land graced the floor.

Yet, it was not the same room that occupied Richard's childhood memories. It was dim and gloomy though the sun was still an hour from setting. The armchairs were turned the wrong way, towards the bed, the drapes were closed, and the air was filled with the distasteful scent common in sick rooms. Candles failed to chase away the shadows. His father's manservant moved quietly about the darkness. His mother sat in a wooden armchair close by the bed, dressed in drab colors, her prayer book on her lap.

Most horrible of all was the figure lying in the bed.

His father, the Right Honorable Hugh Fitzwilliam, fifth Earl of Matlock, had always been Richard's standard of what it meant not only to be a gentleman but a *man*. He had been strong in both body and mind. He was large in figure and large in life. He knew every acre, brick, brook, and tree of his beloved Matlock estate. He stood upon tradition, yet he exercised his mind and was not afraid of new ideas. A born and bred Tory, he was so confident in his beliefs and politics that he claimed friendships among his Whig opponents in the House of Lords, diverted by their good-natured arguments. He was English through and through—his favored meal: honest roast beef and potatoes—yet he cherished French wine. He was intelligent enough to marry an untitled gentlewoman who would stand up to him, rather than a simpering or ill-tempered aristocrat. He was fair and honest. Never had there been a whiff of scandal attached to his name.

To some, he was proud and gruff, hard and unforgiving—like the Derbyshire countryside that made him—with little conversation suitable for the drawing rooms of the *ton*. But with his family and true friends, he was gregarious and generous. As a father, he was loud and demanding. He jealously guarded his position as head of his family and allowed no one to challenge it. He expected his sons to live up to his example. And he loved his wife, children, and all his family with a love that was as fierce as it was complete.

Hugh Fitzwilliam was not one to lie in bed, his body so limp as to be enveloped by the covers. Richard recalled that his father dominated every space, be it a crowded ballroom, a dining table with family, or astride his favorite horse. But now he looked shrunken, old, and pale. Worse yet was the silence. The Lion of Matlock was *never* silent.

The oppressive stillness redoubled the sense of foreboding in Richard's breast. This was a room of death, and death was something he knew all too well. He feared his father would never stir from his bed again.

Alexandria, Countess Matlock, rose from her chair to embrace Richard and Anne. Her plump cheeks were pale, her eyes drawn and weary, and there was a slight tremble to her hands. Exhaustion and stress would surely be his mother's undoing, Richard feared.

"I am so happy you have come, Richard," she said, holding his head in her hands. "And you, too, Anne, my love. Thank you so much."

Anne reassured the countess. "We could not do anything but come—my mother, as well."

Lady Matlock froze. "Catherine is here?" Her lips tightened.

All knew of the mutual loathing between Alexandria and Catherine, but it was Elizabeth who moved forward first. "My dear aunt, should you not rest? Please come away. Richard and Anne will take your place for a while."

Lady Matlock looked at the figure in the bed. "But—"

Richard kissed his mother's cheek. "You will be nearby. Nothing will happen. Please rest, Mother, if but to reassure me. We shall be here until you return."

The countess bowed to her son's entreaty, turned back to the bed, and gently touched the earl's arm. In a voice both hopeful and fearful, she said, "Hugh? Look who is come. Richard is here and dear Anne too. My dear, Richard and Anne are here."

The earl stirred and opened his eyes. Richard immediately saw the damage done to his father, for the left eye was droopy; only the right eye seemed to have life in it. "R-Richard?" the Lion of Matlock managed to gasp.

"Yes, your son and new daughter have come home."

An inner light infused the earl's half-dead face. "R-Richard!" A trembling right arm reached out and was quickly grasped.

Richard struggled for something to say, but no words came, his emotions too overwhelming, except to utter, "Father." There was a world of love and respect and fear in the way Richard pronounced that single word. He held his father's good hand tightly, his eyes locked on the earl's, until Anne drew close.

"Uncle? It is I, Anne." Richard perceived his wife was holding back tears.

"Annie," the earl croaked. He released his son's hand to take both of Anne's, the right side of his mouth rising in a smile. "Good... see you."

Anne kissed his hand.

"You...happy, Annie? R-Richard treating you well?"

"Very well, Uncle."

Richard nodded to Lady Matlock, who after a kiss from Anne, allowed Elizabeth and Darcy to assist her to her rooms. Meanwhile, Anne took the chair vacated by her aunt while Richard moved another close to the earl's sickbed. Lord Matlock's manservant helped the earl to a more upright position before retiring to the dressing room. Anne reclaimed her uncle's hand.

"You...well? Both?"

"Yes, Father, both Anne and I are in good health," answered Richard.

Assured the trip from Kent was not too tasking, the earl managed some questions about Rosings. Richard suspected the earl only wanted to hear their voices, so he began a monologue on the joys and challenges of running an estate. Anne was content simply to hold her father-in-law's hand and laugh at Richard's occasional self-deprecating jokes. It was clear that the earl enjoyed the attention. He could also see that, while his father's body may have been rendered useless by his illness, his mind was whole. There was an air of frustration behind the earl's rapt attention. His father wanted to talk without slurring, desired to leap out of his sickbed and embrace his relations, but his muscles betrayed him. The Lion was trapped inside his fleshy prison, a condition painful for all.

Once Richard's conversation had wound down, Lord Matlock turned to his niece and daughter. "Annie, you look pretty. Very pretty. You…keeping this r-rascal," he gestured at Richard, "in line?"

Anne smiled, her spirits rallying. "I could not be happier, Uncle."

Richard grinned. "Rest assured she has the whip hand. My man, Sergeant Gregory, has been most diligent in instructing Anne on the finer points of managing me. I hardly have to make a single decision, as one or both have made them all for me."

Lord Matlock's head shuddered, either from an inability to laugh or an attempt to shake it in mock disapproval. He stared at his second son, his good eye glowing. "My boy. Sir R-Richard. So proud…of you. Have something to—"

Whatever he was going to say was interrupted by the bedroom door's opening and Lady Catherine's entrance. She walked in unassisted, peering at the earl with an unreadable expression. Richard and Anne rose immediately and not just from courtesy.

"Mother—" Anne began, but she was cut off by an imperious wave of Lady Catherine's hand.

"I have come to speak to my brother." She walked over to the foot of the bed, Richard and Anne watching apprehensively. "Well, Hugh, the reports are true, I suppose. Your illness has brought you low."

"Aunt Catherine," cried Richard as he moved to her side, "now is not the time or place—"

"Silence, Richard," she demanded. "I shall say my piece." It was clear she would brook no interruption.

Lord Matlock raised his hand. "Let her talk, R-Richard."

The grand dame looked down her nose at the patient. "I am sorry it has come to this. Surely, this is your reward for the injuries you have visited upon your only surviving sibling. Still, I take no pleasure in it. Always I have been celebrated for my feeling and Christian charity. You do not have my pity. You would reject it in any case, I am sure. But, for all the evil you have done me, I forgive you."

Lord Matlock's face twisted into as much of a sardonic expression as Richard assumed his father could now manage. "You are... kind, C-Cathy."

Lady Catherine seemed to accept the earl's words as thanks. "You are not in any pain, I trust?" The earl shook his head, and she nodded in return. "I shall leave you to your rest and the good company of my children." Without another word, she turned and left the room.

Lord Matlock glowered and mumbled something that to Richard's ear sounded like a mangled curse. The old, ill man then reached for Anne's hand. Once again, the ghastly half-grin appeared.

"You...only good thing...C-Cathy did." He squeezed Anne's hand tight. Anne sobbed and kissed her uncle. He seemed exhausted by his efforts, for he fell back and spoke no more. Within a few minutes, he was asleep.

Richard and Anne kept a silent vigil for the next few hours until Lord and Lady Llewellyn arrived at Matlock Manor.

OVER THE NEXT FEW DAYS, THE FAMILY TOOK TURNS CARING for Lord Matlock, the countess hardly leaving his side—all but Lady Catherine. She did not visit her brother again and remained in her rooms, except for meals.

The earl would have his moments of lucidity, and at those times, his visitors would try to entertain him with amusing family stories, many of them featuring some escapade of Richard's. Occasionally, the earl could manage a coughing laugh.

Mostly though, he lay peacefully, visibly content with his company. He seemed most happy with those he called "his girls"—his wife, Elizabeth Darcy, Anne Fitzwilliam, Georgiana Llewellyn, and even the impassive Lady Eugenie. His sons, Darcy, and Llewellyn stood like a guard of honor about the old man they loved and respected so much.

The physician declared that the earl's color had improved and was pleased to see that the damage from the apoplexy had not progressed. He thought the worst could be over, and the encouraged family began to make plans to have Lord Matlock moved downstairs during the warmest part of the day. Darcy wrote to town, inquiring about a Bath chair for his uncle's comfort.

Five days later, at three o'clock in the afternoon, all hope was dashed. Lord Hugh Fitzwilliam suffered a second and final apoplexy. The Lion of Matlock was no more.

# Chapter 7

The bright, cold sunshine of the bitter November morning seemed to mock the dark figures making their long, lonely, silent way back to the house, their most melancholy task done. Hugh Fitzwilliam now rested in the family crypt next to his third son, Geoffrey. Richard and Darcy walked together, as comfortable as two close friends could be after witnessing the old earl's internment. Lord Llewellyn was a step behind. Richard's eyes were on the back of his brother, now the Earl of Matlock. As usual, he outstripped the others—Andrew always walked as though he were late to some appointment. But instead of jauntily strolling, his shoulders were bent—the sign of a man bearing a great weight. Richard assumed it was caused by more than grief.

"It appears Andrew feels his new responsibilities greatly," Darcy remarked in a voice meant for Richard's ears alone.

Richard grunted his agreement. As a soldier, he recognized the look of fear in a man's eyes. He had seen it often enough before battle. There was no mistaking that terror warred with misery in Andrew's features during the service. Richard was sure his brother felt overwhelmed by his ascension to the seat of Matlock.

Indeed, so was Richard. The whole family knew Andrew would one day be the earl, but none were prepared for it. Men such as Hugh Fitzwilliam did not die; so great was his presence in the world, it could not do without him. But that ungraspable, inevitable day had come, and it was up to those left behind to carry on as best they could.

Richard glanced at Darcy. Surely, George Darcy's death had been a blow to Pemberley, but at least there had been Fitzwilliam—young, strong, clever, well-trained, and prepared. Even though Andrew had been overseeing the management of the home farm for several years, everyone in the family knew he was no Fitzwilliam Darcy—except perhaps Andrew's ambitious wife. With the country in a bad way due to meager harvests and depressed prices, this was no time for an untried captain to take the helm.

However, Destiny has her own calendar, and the trials of the Right Honorable Andrew Fitzwilliam, sixth Earl of Matlock, were upon him.

The gentlemen came through the front entrance of the great keep, handing their coats and hats to the footmen. The servants had been efficient, and black crepe adorned every window and looking glass. Matlock Manor had always been a cold house, but now it was gloomy and forbidding as well. A shiver ran down Richard's back.

Richard realized with a start that the house was silent too. The ladies were supposed to be in the drawing room awaiting callers, and with Lady Catherine in attendance, it should not have been quiet. It *could not* be quiet unless something was amiss. He turned to Darcy and Andrew and saw they noticed it too. With trepidation, the four gentlemen made their way to the drawing room.

Richard took in the scene. On one side of the fire sat Alexandra, the Dowager Countess of Matlock, Georgiana by her side. Opposite them was Lady Catherine, attended by Anne. Farthest from the fireplace were Elizabeth and Lady Eugenie. All sat quietly in black, a perfect portrait of the upper class in proper mourning.

A second look told the tale. Lady Alexandra's face was pale while Lady Catherine's was red. Both tried to hide their anger with little success. Georgiana's eyes were filled with unshed tears as she grasped her aunt's trembling hands. Meanwhile, Anne did little to hide her displeasure, and while she held hands with her mother, it appeared her goal was not to give comfort, but to restrain bad behavior. Elizabeth's cheeks were flushed, and her fine eyes were lit by indignation. Only Lady Eugenie appeared cool and collected, untouched by the extreme tension in the room.

Instantly, each man moved to his lady's side. Richard placed his hand on Anne's shoulder and felt the tautness there. His questioning eyes sought her furious ones, but before he or any of the men could speak more than a syllable, the butler announced visitors. Richard groaned. Explanations would have to wait.

FOR TWO EXCRUCIATING HOURS, RICHARD STOOD BY HIS WIFE as a steady stream of townsfolk paid their respects. Weather and distance kept the family's true friends and acquaintances in London. Some of the neighbors were sincere in their expression of sympathy, but most were simply pleased to have any excuse to be admitted to the splendor of Matlock Manor. Of the mourners, only Lady Catherine and Lady Eugenie seemed unfazed by the parade. Richard noted that Anne's mother was actually enjoying the attention. He knew not Eugenie's mind as she serenely observed the visitors. She was so closemouthed that Darcy was gregarious by comparison.

Richard had never taken to Eugenie. Only Andrew liked her, which was well, since the families involved had arranged the marriage. At times, they seemed to share a private joke at the expense of the rest of the Fitzwilliams. Richard knew she desired to be countess above all things, though Eugenie got along well enough with his father and mother. Richard assumed her good breeding served her well to hide her ambition. He also assumed that ambition was the lady's motivation to make a proper landowner out of Andrew.

However, there were signs that theirs was not a love match but a business partnership. Besides the complete lack of public displays of affection, there was the fact that there had yet to be any fruits from their union. Richard knew his mother and father had despaired of any grandchildren in that quarter. In comparison, his sister, Lady Henrietta Montgomery, had borne a son, even though she had been married two years less.

As for he and Anne, in spite of all their attempts— No, he would think of it no more.

Finally, the time for visitors was done. It was decided that all would retire to their rooms for a while before a late dinner was served.

"Anne, what occurred in the sitting room before the gentlemen returned?" Richard asked after they closed their door behind them.

Anne dreaded this conversation, for as much as she longed to release her vexation, she hated to upset her husband. "It was Mother."

"I assumed as much. What did she do this time?"

Richard's bitter comment stung Anne more than she had expected. Anne knew Lady Catherine's ways, but she was still her mother, and she loved her despite her faults. "She took it upon herself to offer her services to Eugenie for the redecoration of Matlock."

"*What?*" sputtered Richard. "With my mother present?"

Anne closed her eyes. "Yes. She assumed Aunt Alexandria would take immediate possession of the dower house and expected Eugenie would soon want to put her own stamp on the estate."

"Good God! I can imagine what that discussion was like! I am astonished we found all of you alive!"

"Actually, it ended quite quickly. Eugenie calmly stated that the dowager countess would remain in residence in the main house for as long as she liked, and that there would be no talk of redecoration until after the second mourning. Before Mother could respond to that, Elizabeth approved of Eugenie's plans and invited the Matlocks to Pemberley for Christmas."

Richard was nonplused. "While I cannot be surprised at Elizabeth's goodness, I own that I am pleased with Eugenie. I did not think her so thoughtful."

Anne said nothing. She suspected Eugenie acted more out of correctness than kindness. Anne also saw that Aunt Alexandria and Eugenie had already made their peace with the management of the household, and she expected the dowager would generously help ease her daughter's ascension.

"But Lady Catherine!" Richard continued. "Of what could she have been thinking?"

"I do not believe she was thinking at all."

"She has always hated my mother. But this is beyond everything—"

They were interrupted by a knock on the door. Richard opened it to admit an infuriated Andrew.

"Forgive my intrusion, but we must talk." He glanced at Anne. "Did you speak to Richard of what happened here while we were away?" Assured that she had, he turned to his brother. "Lady Catherine's actions are intolerable. To further distress our mother on this day, of all days! I will not stand for it."

Before Richard could say anything, Anne announced the decision she had contemplated for the last hour. "I understand, Andrew. We shall leave for Kent in the morning. Lady Catherine will have no further opportunity to insult your mother." She spoke not as the sweet former Anne de Bourgh, but as Lady Fitzwilliam, mistress of Rosings Park. Richard was visibly taken aback with Anne's pronouncement, but after a pause, he reaffirmed it.

"I am glad to hear it," said a relieved Andrew. "We would have you and Richard stay, but there is nothing for it. Your departure will not appear unseemly since the Darcys and Llewellyns are to leave as well. And I have finally received a letter from the Montgomerys. They are hurrying to reach the Channel ports and will arrive as soon as may be." He glanced at Richard. "I am sorry you will miss Henrietta, Brother. I think we shall all go to town early in the New Year, so perhaps we may meet then." Unsaid by the earl was that

Lady Catherine was not welcome.

Just as he was leaving, Andrew turned back. "There is something you should know. You would find out once the will was read, but I think this might lighten your spirits. Father and I discussed it some months ago. You are to have the hunting lodge in Scotland."

"I-I do not know what to say." Richard shook his brother's hand. "It is very good of you."

Anne was pleased for Richard, for she knew how much her husband loved traveling there with his male relations.

Andrew waved off any thanks. "Scotland is a nasty, cold country. Never liked it or the people. You have affection for the place for some reason, and I would just as soon rid myself of the responsibility." He shook his head. "This is a sad business, and the sooner all is settled, the better. Well, I expect I shall see you both in London in January. We shall say our goodbyes tomorrow." With that, the earl left the room.

Anne rose and moved to Richard's side, bestowing a kiss on his cheek. "I am happy for you. I know you are fond of the lodge."

She felt the tension ease from Richard's body. "It is like Father: old, hard, and comfortable. The times I had there! Oh, Annie, I miss him so!"

"Perhaps you can tell me about those times."

Richard smiled for the first time that day. "Later. Those are tales best told before a fire and mulled wine." He grew serious. "We must speak to your mother about our plans."

She agreed and steeled herself for the confrontation to come. The two made their way to Lady Catherine's room. Such were their feelings that they entered without leave, offering only a cursory knock to announce their intention.

Great was their shock. Lady Catherine was seated in a chair next to the window, quietly weeping into a handkerchief, a pair of miniatures in her other hand.

"Mother, what is the matter?" cried an alarmed Anne.

"They are all gone," she answered, her voice unsteady.

Anne knelt at her side while Richard asked, "Gone? Who?"

Lady Catherine turned to Anne, who beheld pain and fear on her mother's tear-streaked face. "Anne…and now Hugh. I am the last of my family." Her voice broke. "I am all alone!"

As Lady Catherine began to weep again, Anne noticed that the miniatures were of Anne Darcy and Hugh Fitzwilliam.

# Chapter 8

The return to Rosings Park was even quieter than the journey northward. The three passengers were lost in their private thoughts. Richard could make a good guess as to his wife's reflections. She had a particular affection for her Uncle Hugh, and she no doubt was consumed by grief. Lady Catherine de Bourgh's state of mind was a mystery, for she had spoken only a handful of words since her brother's funeral.

Richard contemplated a most fearful future. His father had been an influential figure in his life, but now that the great man was gone, his son began to grasp just how important he had been. Proud of his advancement and success in the army, Richard had forgotten that his father had helped him every step of the way. Richard's courage, zeal, and dash on the battlefield, in truth, could only get him so far without his father's guidance.

Lord Matlock's political instincts had been excellent and were far superior to those owned by either of his sons—or Darcy, for that matter. Matlock saw early on that the Wellesleys were a rising political family, despite their Irish roots, and quickly made himself their ally. His friendships with his customary opponents in the House of Lords gave him considerable influence for a mere earl from an insignificant seat. He never held high office, as he preferred the peaceful Derbyshire countryside to the turmoil of London. He advised Richard on who to trust and of whom to be wary, and it had made all the difference in his career.

Now Sir Richard Fitzwilliam, former colonel of Dragoons, was a gentleman farmer like his father before him. It behooved him to follow Lord Matlock's example, to succeed and nurture that which had been entrusted to his care. To honor his father's memory, he would, calling upon all that he had been taught. He vowed he would be a worthy son of Hugh Fitzwilliam.

UPON ARRIVAL AT HOME, THE PARTY FOUND THAT MRS. PARKS had seen to it that Rosings Park was properly adorned with all the trappings of mourning.

"Any problems, Gregory?" Richard asked his majordomo as he handed his heavy coat to a footman while Anne talked to the housekeeper.

"Mostly quiet, Colonel. Some of the horses escaped the stable a few nights ago. Spent some time in the dark gathering them all back in."

Richard frowned. "How the devil did that happen?"

Sergeant Gregory watched Lady Fitzwilliam and Mrs. Parks continue down the hall. "It seems some of the stall doors were unsecured," he answered in a low voice.

"That does not sound like an accident."

The sergeant nodded. "It wasn't. I'd stake my life on it. I've talked to the lads in the stable. They'll double-check the stalls before they retire for the night. It won't happen again."

"But if it is sabotage—"

"There'll be at least one man awake at all hours, sir. We'll catch him or scare him off."

Richard's gaze moved from Gregory to his wife, now standing by the stairs. "You have everything in hand, then. Do not bother Lady Fitzwilliam with this. She has enough on her mind."

"My condolences again, Colonel."

"Thank you, Gregory," Richard responded with a pat on the man's shoulder. He then hurried to escort Anne above stairs.

The next afternoon, the Fitzwilliams and Lady Catherine took their seats in the parlor and awaited the inevitable condolence calls. Joining them was Anne's longtime companion, Mrs. Jenkinson, who now made Rosings her home.

The first guests were, naturally, the Collinses. Indeed, Anne knew it was a miracle that Charlotte had prevented her overeager husband from calling at first light. Mrs. Collins was graciously received by all, but Lady Catherine's fleeting acknowledgement of Mr. Collins was a painful snub. Anne was mortified by her mother's humiliation of the loquacious vicar, knowing the grand dame had not forgiven the man for switching his alliance to the Fitzwilliams. That Lady Catherine had left Mr. Collins no choice in the matter meant little to her.

Anne did not wish to make a scene painful to all, so she and Richard spent considerable time speaking to the man—indeed, consoling *him*, rather than the other way around. His gratitude for their kindness, expressed at length as the Collinses took their leave, was embarrassing.

Lady Catherine, established in her customary grand chair, was out of sorts. She took no pleasure or comfort in the parade of visitors, mostly comprised of people from the surrounding country. She practically sneered at the attentions of Mr. and Mrs. Clarke.

Only the appearance of her longtime friend, Lady Metcalfe, raised Lady Catherine's spirits. She was surprised and delighted that the lady had traveled all the way from town to call. The pair retired to the couch next to Anne, speaking of the past. In the company of her old crony, Anne could see in her mother's face and voice a shadow of the lady she used to be—the virtual Queen of Hunsford, active and alive, who walked the streets of the village, accepting her due from the people and dispensing her wisdom to all and sundry. For not the first time, Anne wondered why her mother had changed so.

After Lady Metcalfe took her leave for London, Lady Catherine was more gracious to the sympathizers. Finally, the procession of mourners petered out, and Anne was about to have the door closed and call for tea when Wilkerson announced a final visitor.

"Mr. Kendrick, madam."

Anne gasped. Reginald Kendrick was the last person she expected to offer condolences to her family! But there stood her cousin, in a black coat and breaches, a little less than five-and-a-half feet tall and eighteen stone, if an ounce. The man waddled in and made his leg.

"Good afternoon, my *dear* aunt and cousins. Allow me to express my *deepest* condolences on the passing of my *esteemed* uncle." The sarcastic man was half in his cups.

Anne heard Richard's growl at Mr. Kendrick's mocking tone. Lady Catherine's face turned beet red, while Mrs. Jenkinson's paled. As it was, Anne could barely hold her tongue.

Reginald Kendrick, the only child of her father's sister, was her closest living relation on the de Bourgh side of the family. His connection to the Fitzwilliams was by marriage only. And given the contention that lay between the Kendricks and the Fitzwilliams, it was a connection neither claimed.

"Reginald Kendrick!" Lady Catherine exclaimed. "I am astonished by your audacity! How dare you come here!"

"Why should I not? It is *my* house, Lady Catherine." he snidely responded. "Oh! That is right—somehow Rosings Park did not descend to its rightful owner. I believe I have the late Lord Matlock to thank for that omission—that conniving thief."

Richard took one step towards the man but was held back by Anne's strong grip on his wrist. "Richard, no! He wants a scene. Do not give him the satisfaction."

"You…you scoundrel!" Lady Catherine waved her cane at him.

"I will not have you abuse the memory of my brother! Leave my house at once!"

"Bluster away, Aunt, but this is not your house. Is it, my dear Anne?"

Richard found his voice. "That is *Lady Fitzwilliam* to you, Kendrick! This is our house, and as its master, I order you to leave!"

"Pfft! I am not one of your soldiers. Keep your orders to yourself. I have a mind to visit with my dear family. Anne, will you not offer me a seat?"

Furious, Anne got to her feet. "What I am going to offer you, Mr. Kendrick, is an opportunity to leave the house under your own power."

Mr. Kendrick laughed. "Oh, ho! Are you going to set your husband on me? You should have married me. These Fitzwilliams are brutes." A nasty sneer grew. "But, perhaps you *like* brutes."

Richard cursed, but Anne would not relent her hold. "The Fitzwilliams are gentlemen—something you know nothing about," said Anne in a steely voice. "They know how to handle vermin. Do you not, dear husband?"

Richard took a breath. "Indeed, we do, my dear. Gregory, see to this person."

Standing at the door were Sergeant Gregory and two large footmen. "Aye, sir," Gregory said. To Mr. Kendrick he ordered, "You will come with us."

Mr. Kendrick turned towards the new threat, looked to say something, but instead nodded his head. "It seems I have a pressing appointment and must leave this *charming* family gathering." He bowed to the others. "Aunt Catherine, Anne, Fitzwilliam…" He looked at Mrs. Jenkinson. "Whoever the devil you are, farewell." With that, he allowed the footmen to grasp his arms and lead him out of the room.

"Gregory, I know it is tempting, but see him off the property in one piece, will you? Give him no reason to go to the magistrate."

"As you wish, Colonel," Sergeant Gregory said. "May I warn him off Rosings in my own style?"

"No bloodshed, mind."

The majordomo winked. "There'll be nary a scratch on him, sir. Ladies." He nodded and left.

"Of all the audacious, impudent, rude, degenerate...*monsters*," muttered Lady Catherine. "Taking the name of my brother in vain. The man should be horsewhipped! Horsewhipped, I say!"

Anne took her hand. "Mother, please, you must not distress yourself."

The old lady ignored her. "Was not all that fuss and bother years ago enough? Demanding the hand of my only daughter! As though I would allow it! He was told never to step on Rosings land again! And then—to claim Sir Lewis could not bequeath his holdings to Anne! His suit was laughed out of court! The man must be mad!"

"I am certain he is." Anne's eyes sent Mrs. Jenkinson a silent request for assistance.

"The Kendricks are a stain on the noble name of de Bourgh!" Lady Catherine gazed at her daughter, gripping her hand tightly. "You are in far better hands, Anne. Richard will care for you. Richard will care for all of us."

"Of course, I shall," Richard assured her.

Mrs. Jenkinson helped Lady Catherine out of her chair. "Madam, shall you not rest before dinner? Let us go up to the room set aside for you. It has all your favorite things you did not take to the dower house."

"Yes, yes...I should like that." Lady Catherine turned to her daughter, some of her usual firmness returning. "You should rest too, Anne. It is proper for a lady to rest in the afternoon."

"I remember, Mama."

The grand dame nodded and walked out of the room tolerably well. Meanwhile, Richard took a still-trembling Anne in his arms.

"Hush, sweetheart, all is well," he whispered in her ear.

"I am well, Richard. But of all days for that…*man* to appear, after all these years! Mother is right. He must be mad."

"That or intoxicated. How long ago was his suit claiming Rosings as his since he was the closest living male in the de Bourgh line?"

"Twelve years ago? Thirteen? He had just reached his majority. You are of an age with him, you know. But I had thought the suit referred to Mother, not me."

"Yes, we know how Lady Catherine hid the fact that Sir Lewis left Rosings to you."

"Let us not mention that again. What I never understood was why Cousin Reginald would claim something my uncle Cecil, his father, never did."

"Did you not know? Old Kendrick did make some ado about the will immediately after Sir Lewis's passing, but Father and Uncle Darcy set him straight. Father said it was the last time he ever saw or heard from the miserable miser."

"Again, something was kept from me! Richard, you must promise me never to do that."

"You know all my secrets, love."

"I had better."

# Chapter 9

Retired Colonel Christopher Brandon, a new member of Parliament, walked towards Number 28 St. James's Street. Brandon was in London early, for Parliament would not be in session until late January. He wanted his wife, Marianne, to enjoy the city with him before the work of government began.

The incumbent MP, Mr. White, unexpectedly died and, being the local magistrate, Brandon appointed himself for the remainder of his term. This saved him a considerable amount of money. The term was expected to be short, for all knew a general election would be called by 1818. Brandon would then have to decide whether the honor of sitting in the Commons was worth the thousands of pounds he would be expected to spend keeping the seat.

That was not his only concern. He was learning that politics was extremely complicated.

The Tory-controlled Parliament had recently passed the latest of the Corn Laws. The restrictions on cheap foreign grain importation was intended to protect farmers, the backbone of Britain's mainly agricultural economy. Yet things were not as clear as Brandon thought they should be. The minority Whigs argued that the country was becoming increasingly geared to manufacturing and that inexpensive food and raw materials were vital to wages and profits.

The increase in the price of grain put the businessmen in a quandary. High domestic grain prices meant food cost more. Workers needed to eat and required higher wages, but higher wages reduced profits, unless prices were raised. Higher prices for goods were extremely unpopular with the growing middle class. That could reduce sales.

It was a delicate balancing act. The aristocracy—who owned the land—and their farmhands were on one side, while merchants, factory owners, and their workers were on the other. Cheaper grain was better for the businessmen, but if farms all over the country failed and were abandoned, the nation would be at the mercy of foreigners for food. What would then happen to the farming towns across the British Isles and the people whose livelihoods depended on them? On top of that, the horrendous harvests of the current season dwindled the grain reserves. Prices were rising. Unrest was growing.

That Brandon himself was a landowner did not escape his conscience. He tried to be fair, but he had to look out for his people. What to do? Stand with his Tory friends or vote with the Whig opposition? He did not know.

Today Marianne was shopping with the wife of an old friend, so Brandon was preoccupied as he went on his way to his new club, Boodle's, to meet with his former comrade. As he approached the front door of the handsome stone and brick building, his friend was just descending from a hackney.

"Buford! Well met!"

Sir John Buford, accompanied by Corporal Frost, approached and took his hand. "Brandon, you old fox, I cannot say how good it is to meet again!"

Despite the cheerful greeting, the conversation over luncheon was strained.

Brandon had known John Buford for many years, since their

joint service in Italy. Buford was an excellent soldier, an extraordinary linguist, and a great friend. He was dashing, brave, intelligent, hardworking, and loyal. He was also a man of deeply held passions, usually hidden by a spirit of bonhomie.

Buford had his faults. He owned a fiery temper. In his youth, he enjoyed the company of women too much. His reputation as a rake had become notorious. To his credit, Buford had seen the error of his ways and reformed. His abilities were noticed by great men, and he was knighted for his actions, not his birth. His future was bright.

That was before Waterloo.

When Brandon helped Colonels Fitzwilliam and Denny carry the broken, battered, half-dead Buford from the field that terrible day, he did not expect his friend to live through the night. The surgeons performed what miracles they could, sewing up his face and leg, but they could not save his arm. Brandon wondered whether Buford would ever walk again after visiting him in hospital.

Brandon could not imagine what agonies Buford suffered in his recovery over the last eighteen months. He was astonished the man could walk and ride. His handsome face was not *too* badly scarred, after all; it almost lent an air of distinction to his profile. His limp was less pronounced every time they met. He seemed at peace with the amputation of his arm.

But all was not well. Buford had become exceedingly bitter and reclusive. A man once renowned for his dash and industry now could hardly be tempted to go to his club. He suffered bouts of despair. Friends had been neglected. Acquaintances had been shunned. Brandon was sure that his friend was in pain—and not just the physical kind.

Today, Sir John's countenance revealed no evidence of misery, but Brandon expected it was a façade. He wished to help Buford, but he knew not how.

After playing whist for a couple of hours, the gentlemen collected Corporal Frost, took their leave from the club, and made their way on foot towards Brandon's lodgings where they would have dinner. They had not gone far when they noted people noisily dashing about. They were not the usual sort seen near Hyde Park; they were tradesmen, laborers, and farmers. All wore panicked expressions.

"What the devil is going on?" demanded Buford.

Suddenly, a rough-looking individual appeared before them wearing a tri-color cockade pinned on his open coat. Dirty and unshaven, his eyes were wide, angry, and frightened. He nearly collided with the group.

"Take a care, you scallywag!" cried Corporal Frost.

The panicked man, instead of withdrawing, pulled a knife from his waist, screaming for the group to give way. In response, Buford brandished his walking stick like a saber.

"Buford," Brandon cried, "be careful!"

"Frost, your assistance," Buford commanded, never taking his eyes off their assailant.

Frost retrieved a pistol from inside his coat. The sight of the gun decided things for the man. He spun on his heels and ran down the street in the opposite direction for all he was worth. Moments later, soldiers appeared and chased after the assailant.

"Well, that was exciting," observed Buford.

Frost was not so sanguine. "We ought to hurry to the lodgings, Colonel, afore anything else happens." He kept the pistol in his hand.

"Quite right, Frost," said Brandon. "Let us leave this place."

"GOOD GOD, JOHN! WHAT WERE YOU THINKING?" CRIED CAROLINE, once she returned from her shopping expedition.

Buford wore a mixture of contrition and annoyance battling on his scarred face. "What was I to do? Let the beggar stick me?"

"Corporal Frost was there! It falls to him to see to such matters!"

Brandon tried to smooth things over. "And he did, Caroline, I assure you. We perhaps overstated the case." He turned to his wife. "We were in no danger at all."

Marianne believed none of it. "No danger! How can you say such a thing? The streets were filled with raging hooligans! The evening papers reported it! *Riots in Spa Fields! Attacks at the Tower!* People are unable to walk the streets of London in broad daylight without taking their lives in their hands! The government should do something!"

Brandon patted her hand. "Do not distress yourself. I am certain talk in the Commons will be about nothing else."

"Instead of the usual politics?" observed Buford sarcastically.

"They are all tied together, I think. The government will not be happy after the events of today. There will be strong measures taken. That is, after the usual debates."

"Politics—bah!" said Buford. "The more I see of it, the more disenchanted I become."

*You are disenchanted about a great many things other than politics,* thought Brandon as he studied his great friend.

Buford was not finished. "Take the borough of Beaumaris on the Isle of Anglesey. Mr. Lewis is a good man, I allow, but he lives in Radnorshire in the center of Wales. How can he know what happens on Anglesey, one hundred fifty miles away? Rotten boroughs[1] are a scourge on this country!"

"You have a point, my friend, but pocket boroughs serve a good purpose too," Brandon responded. "Not every young man of ability has the opportunity to enter Parliament. Consider Old Pitt.[2] Without a series of pocket boroughs, the country may never have benefited from his talents. Would you not say Lord Chatham was a great prime minister?"

"Aye, he was."

---

1  A pocket or rotten borough was a parliamentary borough or constituency in the United Kingdom that had a very small electorate and could be used by a patron to gain undue and unrepresentative influence within Parliament. They were abolished in the mid-1800s.

2  William Pitt, 1st Earl of Chatham, PC, 1708–1778, commonly referred to as William Pitt the Elder. He served as Prime Minster and Lord Privy Seal 1766–1768. His second son, who was the youngest PM in Britain's history (1783–1801, 1804–1806), is known as William Pitt the Younger.

"And Mr. Perceval.[3] A good friend of the army when you were in the Peninsula, he saw the nation as a whole rather than individual districts. He always said that if pocket boroughs were discarded, our whole electoral system was liable to collapse."

"There I must take issue with you, Brandon," responded Buford. "This country is far too strong to just collapse like the Frenchies."

"Peace, gentlemen!" cried Marianne. "Such talk will ruin our appetites for dinner."

"Very true," said Caroline. "Pray save your arguments for your port."

"You ladies are right, of course," said the colonel. "It shall be as you wish. But these are important matters."

Marianne was not moved. "Oh, how I despise politics! Sometimes, Christopher, I wish you had never joined Parliament!" She took a deep breath. "I am sure dinner is almost ready. Shall we retire to the dining room?"

Brandon was glad to see that Buford did not rebuff Caroline's assistance out of his chair. He knew that, despite appearances, he was leaning on her rather than the other way around. With relief, he offered his arm to Marianne. "Lead on, my love."

"By the way," Marianne said as the couples made their way into the dining room, "I received a letter from Lady Fitzwilliam. Anne and Sir Richard are to be in town after Christmas. Is that not a lovely thing? We should call on them after they are settled."

"They are in mourning, Marianne," Brandon pointed out.

"Mourning? What is that when there are good friends to be met? Caroline agrees with me. We shall console their feelings and lighten their hearts. We are determined!"

THAT NIGHT IN BUFORD HOUSE, CORPORAL DAVID FROST waited impatiently in the hallway after preparing Sir John for

---

3 Spencer Perceval, Prime Minster from 1809 to 1812, was the only premier of Great Britain ever to have been assassinated.

bed. He was of middling height and unremarkable features, save his moustache, a rarity in England. Frost grew his moustache to emulate his former adversaries and allies, to prove he was as good a soldier as any Frenchman or Prussian. Sir John hated his orderly's facial hair and had requested more than once that Frost shave the ridiculous thing off, but the corporal would not part with it. It was one of the few disagreements between them.

After the final peace, Frost retired from the army and joined Colonel Buford's service, helping his commander recover from his grievous wounds. The men were close, as only a selfless officer and loyal subordinate who had faced death together could be. Colonel Buford could not do without Frost, and the corporal would never voluntarily leave his colonel.

That loyalty had been tested, however, and more than once. During those times, Sir John lashed out at his caretakers, bringing Lady Buford to tears more times than either would ever choose to remember. Those were the only times Frost disliked his former commander.

But wife and batman stood by the colonel until Sir John's "Black Dog" would return to hibernation. Mortification and apologies would then flow and be accepted, but all would wait in dread for the reemergence of that malicious beast.

Thus, the cause of Frost's uneasiness: he had seen the telltale signs while undressing his charge, and he waited for confirmation from his mistress's maid.

The door finally opened, and Abigail stepped out into the hallway.

"Are they abed yet, Abby?"

"Aye, but the master's restless again." Her worry was apparent. "They'll get no sleep tonight, that's for certain."

Frost cursed softly. "Aye—I expected it after today. And he won't let me dose him, more's the pity. I suppose there's nothing for it."

"You know he can't abide that vile tonic."

"True, and I understand his reasons, but the mistress will get no rest." He reached out and touched Abigail's cheek. "You neither."

Abigail brushed his hand away. "Now, Davy, if you're thinking what I think you're thinking, you're daft," she hissed. "Not while we're in London! There's enough talk downstairs as it is. You'll just have to wait 'till we get back to Wales."

"You know, love, if you'd accept me—"

Anguished, the lady's maid took his hand. "Please, no more of that. My ladyship needs me, and himself needs you more. We'd be sent away, you know that."

Frost groaned. "*I* need you."

A sigh escaped Abigail's lips. "Soon, love, soon."

*He was weaving about the battlefield on his mount, the unholy din of cannon fire and musket shots deafening him. He waved his sword over his head, slashing down again and again against his enemies. Smoke obscured his vision. The smell of powder choked him. All about him were French uniforms. Where were the English? Where were his men?*

*Onward he rode, dodging, fighting, fear rising in his throat. He could not talk. He could not breathe. He could only scream. He struck and struck and struck, and yet the French kept coming. They were endless. He was exhausted. He could barely raise his blade.*

*Suddenly, his horse was cut down beneath him. Explosions raked the world.*

*He desperately scrambled to his feet, freeing his legs from his dead horse, barely managing to parry a French cuirassier's killing thrust. He slashed viciously at his opponent, his blow striking home, and the Frenchman fell in a heap at his feet. Instantly, a hundred more took his place, each larger and stronger. He tried to raise his arm but could not. The sword slipped from his blood-drenched fingers.*

*Terror gripped him. There was no escape—no escape—no escape!*

"John! John! Wake up!"

Buford awoke with a start, waving his ruined left arm, trying to shield his head. He was drenched in a cold sweat. He turned wildly towards the voice beside him.

"John, you are dreaming!" Caroline cried. "You are safe. You are safe in England with me."

Buford forced himself to calm down. He was not on some distant battlefield. He was in his bedroom at Buford House in London. He sagged against the mattress, breathing hard. He felt he had run for miles.

Caroline tentatively touched his shoulder. "Was it the nightmare again?"

"Yes," he gasped. "Did I call out? I am sorry—"

"Never mind that. Lie back and rest. Shall I call for Frost and the laudanum?"

"No! No more laudanum! I will not have it!" Buford tried to slow his breathing. "All will be well in a moment."

Slowly, carefully, Caroline slipped her arms about his trembling body. At once, he felt his tension fade away.

"Shall I hold you, Johnny?"

Buford swallowed thickly, tears forming in his eyes. He had no secrets from her—none at all—save one.

"Please," he sobbed. "Please hold me."

*Rosings Park*

THE DECEMBER AFTERNOON SUN WAS JUST DIPPING BELOW THE tops of the trees when Mr. Evans dismounted near the Johnson cottage. Smoke rose from the chimney, and movement within could be heard. He secured his horse, checked the pair of pistols tucked in his belt, and walked to the front door. His imperious knock was answered quickly.

Mrs. Johnson's face paled as she beheld the steward. "Mr. Evans. What can I do fer ya?"

Evans said nothing as he waved, demanding entrance. He made only a few steps inside before he stopped short, his hand unconsciously reaching for one of his guns. Cork loomed in the center of the room.

"G'day, Mr. Evans," said the giant.

Evans looked at the man's soot-covered hands. "Cork, have you been working?"

"I was with the smithy today, an' he paid me with coal." He gestured towards the half-filled scuttle.

Evans nodded. "Yes. Good for you. Pray excuse us. I need to speak with your mother."

"Go outside, boy," ordered Mrs. Johnson.

Cork nodded good-naturedly and left the house, retrieving his satchel on the way. Mr. Evans watched him go before turning his hard, dark eyes towards Mrs. Johnson.

The woman was nervous. "I'm…I'm fixin' supper. Kinda busy."

"Yes." Evans drawled the word out. "Venison, by the smell of it."

"Cork found it—dead—in th' woods."

Evans did not raise his voice. "Do not lie to me, woman. I am sure Cork found the animal dead—right after he killed it with his sling." At the woman's protests, he held up a restraining hand. "Do not bother denying it. That is poaching, Johnson. You both can be taken up for it."

"I don't know what ya mean." A look of fear, anger, and wariness filled the woman's face. "What do ya want? I ain't got nothin'."

"That is obvious." He sniffed and walked about the small room. "However, it is not right for you to live on Rosings land and not pay rent."

"Sir Lewis said we could live here fer free!"

"Sir Lewis is long dead," Evans pointed out. "You will pay me two shillings directly, once a month, beginning next month. No exceptions."

"Two shillings! Where do I get the money an' still eat?"

"That is not my concern."

"I won't get it off my back, if that's what you mean."

Evans looked as though he smelled something rotten. "If I thought you capable of that, I would have the constable run you out of the county."

"It'll be hard."

He glanced at the door meaningfully. "You have that oaf of a son. Send him to Rosings. We shall put him to work."

"An' you'll keep his wages."

"It will be laid against your rent."

Mrs. Johnson's fists shook by her side. "You're a right bastard an' no mistake."

"That language will not help you, woman. Remember what I said. I shall see you in four weeks to collect my money." With that, Mr. Evans left the shack.

# Chapter 10

Christmas came and went, and the people of Britain celebrated the start of the Year of Our Lord 1817 with activities either sacred, profane, or both, depending on their character. The country was uneasy, and the King's government was anxious to do something—*anything*—to restore stability.

It was a fool's errand. The world was changing though few saw it. Sustainable existence was no longer enough for the masses. *A Better Life* was the new byword. Industry was growing faster than the crops in the fields. Overseas trade was not a luxury but an integral part of the nation's economic system. Men and women left the farms for the cities and work. England's green and pleasant land was transforming into a forge that would build a new age of iron, coal, steam, and steel.

This was hot, hard, dirty, and dangerous work. Mechanical knowledge and science strove to create the solutions required for farms to produce ever more with fewer hands to work the fields and tend the herds. People struggled to carry on with the changes progress caused, yet families were torn asunder. Untitled men became captains of industry, rich beyond measure, and peers dabbled in trade. Competition between nations for raw materials and markets caused wars for colonies.

Workers labored to feed their children, but food was dear. The rising population outstripped the poor harvests. Many would die and many more would suffer over the decades to come before industry learned that compassion *increased* efficiency, not lessened it.

The Industrial Revolution had begun, and hardly anyone knew it. Britain and the world would never be the same.

*London*

SEVERAL DAYS LATER, THE BRANDON CARRIAGE PULLED UP before Matlock House on Grosvenor Square. A cold, cloudy day, London had been spared snow. It was chilly enough, however, for two couples to make their way quickly to the door adorned with the black wreath of mourning. The Brandons and the Bufords were expected, and within moments, they were in the vestibule of the house, and servants were helping the guests remove their coats.

Marianne looked about the place as the butler escorted them to the sitting room. This was only her second time in Matlock House; normally, she met with her friends either in her own house or at the Darcys. With the paintings covered and black bunting everywhere, the hallway seemed as cold and impersonal as the weather outside. Marianne Brandon reveled in warmth and light, so this bleakness, expected in a house in mourning, troubled her sensibilities.

The sitting room was just as dismal. The curtains were drawn, and black crepe draped the mantle, making the flame within its fireplace ominous rather than cheerful.

The people awaiting them were altered too. Sir Richard Fitzwilliam grasped Colonel Brandon's hand even as the butler announced them. His coat, vest, and trousers were all in black, rather than his habitually cheerful colors. His face was haggard. Anne was but a step behind, a pale, slim vision in ebony. No jewelry graced her, save the small cross at her throat. An instant later, Marianne was enveloped in her friend's embrace.

"Marianne," said Anne, "it is so good of you all to come." Anne and Richard then greeted the Bufords while the other occupants in the room made a more restrained welcome. The new Earl of Matlock appeared as he ever was—perfectly correct if slightly bored. Marianne had never warmed to Lady Eugenie, believing the woman esteemed a colonel's wife beneath her. Nothing in the countess's greeting showed any encouragement to further intimacy.

Everyone sought their seats, and the next few minutes were spent in expressions of condolence on the callers' part and acceptance of those assurances by the residents. After inquiring whether the weather had been any inconvenience to the visitors, the earl and countess rose.

"If you would excuse us," drawled Lord Matlock, "we have matters that require our attention. We leave you in the capable hands of our relations. You are very welcome to Matlock House." The countess spared the visitors a nod, and the two made their way out of the room.

Anne's apology was written on her face, but Marianne reassured her that none was necessary.

"Indeed," injected Caroline, "we can speak much freer now. I hope we find you both well."

Assured of the health of the parties, the conversation fell to questions about various relations. The Darcys were well, ensconced at Darcy House. The well-being of the Ferrars, Fitzwilliams, Dashwoods, Bingleys, Bennets, and the other families established, Richard asked about Colonel Denny and his bride.

"They have arrived in Calcutta," Brandon reported. "We finally received a letter from Denny a few weeks ago."

"I am curious how the new Mrs. Denny bears it," remarked Caroline. "I believe I am the only lady present that has been aboard ship, and while it was only to the Continent, I must say I liked it not."

"My late brother was in the navy," said Buford, "and I remember well his letters filled with complaints about bad weather, confined spaces, and weevil-infested food."

"At least the children were spared it," Marianne pointed out.

Lydia—foolish, childish Lydia—was a paradox. She was beautiful and jolly, and though she seldom knew her own mind, she always landed on her feet.

She abandoned her friends to run off with a rogue like George Wickham. It *should* have led to her ruin, but she ended up respectfully married, her reputation intact if not a little bruised. Her sisters had married well enough to help her when matters occasionally became uncomfortable. Her husband was rumored to have been dangerously unfaithful, but she apparently escaped any harm and had three healthy daughters.

Her despicable major fell at Waterloo, and within seven months, his widow married the excellent Colonel Denny. Her children did not risk their lives on a voyage halfway around the world. Instead, they were raised in society above their expectations by the Bingleys, the Darcys, and the Tuckers.

It did not escape Marianne's consideration that she had been much like Lydia Denny in her youth. Both had been spoiled by their mothers and allowed to follow the impulses of their feelings. Rational thought was a hindrance to their high spirits. It was all foolishness. Marianne's folly had led her to John Willoughby and near death. It was Colonel Christopher Brandon who saved, loved, married, and improved her. Maturity had given Mrs. Brandon respectability, a partner, and two lovely children. Might Colonel Denny do the same for Lydia? Her friends would not know for years.

The butler appeared and announced the arrival of the Darcys.

Darcy wore his customary dark and austere clothing, his black cravat standing out from his crisp white shirt. Mrs. Darcy was in deep grey, a great change from her usual attire. Their somberness was not reflected in their greetings for their friends, however.

"Here is a merry happenchance," said Marianne as she embraced Elizabeth. "I hope your ears are not burning, for we were just speaking of you. Nothing unkind, I assure you."

"Oh, Marianne, how I have missed you!" cried Elizabeth.

"Our attendance should be no surprise," said Darcy, "as our purpose in town is to wait upon visitors offering condolences." He shook Brandon's hand. "We are here most days."

"Otherwise, you would never see my cousin waiting on the *ton*," quipped Richard, "now that Georgiana is safely married."

Darcy spared a glare for his cousin before greeting Buford. "Are you well, Sir John?" Assured that he was, he bowed to the ladies. Elizabeth and Caroline exchanged kisses on the cheek, and soon all were assembled about the fireplace, engaging in small talk. Eventually, the men's discussions fell into politics and current affairs, while the ladies spoke of more heartfelt matters.

The hour passed quickly, and the time to depart was upon them. As the Brandons and Bufords were taking farewell of their friends, Anne made an offer.

"Richard and I have decided we would like to invite you all to join us at Rosings this summer, once the first mourning is done. Pray, say you will come." Marianne's stunned look was copied by her husband and the Bufords. Anne quickly added, "The Darcys will be with us, and we consider you to be as close as family. It will be a quiet time, but I believe you will find it enjoyable nonetheless."

While the Bufords assured Anne of their attendance, Marianne and Brandon shared a silent glance. It was Christopher who spoke at last. "You are very kind, Anne, but I fear we must decline. Parliament will surely sit until deep into July, given that it will not open until next week."

"And you plan to attend every session?" Richard asked. "Many do not."

"If I am to be an MP, I shall. I have a very good steward for Delaford, and my family will be with me."

Buford grinned. "You have some long nights ahead of you, Brandon. I do not envy you."

"It should not be too bad," Brandon claimed. "We shall be in session only three days a week, and then only after half past three in the afternoon."

"Except next week when Parliament opens," said Anne. "Are you looking forward to it?"

"Christopher?" Marianne laughed. "He loves nothing more than pomp and pageantry!"

"I have been too long a soldier not to," Brandon admitted. He and Marianne, along with the Bufords, then took their leave, promising to visit as often as they could.

JANUARY FLEW BY, AND THE MONTH WAS REACHING ITS END. Marianne was in the nursery, holding her young son, John Richard, while watching her daughter, Joy, play with the nanny. Christopher had left early that morning to attend the opening of Parliament, and she expected he would not return until well after dark. Therefore, it was a shock to hear familiar heavy steps rapidly ascending the stairs. A moment later, her husband burst into the room.

She took in his flushed and distressed expression in an instant. "What has happened?"

"Pandemonium has taken over Parliament!" he cried. "The Regent's carriage was assaulted outside of Westminster, and it is thought someone took a shot at him!"

"Are you saying someone tried to kill the Regent?"

"It appears that way," Brandon said as he sat next to Marianne, taking her and their son into his embrace. "The glass on his carriage was shattered."

"Heaven protect us!" cried the nanny. She scooped up Joy and handed her to her father.

Marianne wept into Brandon's shoulder. "What is happening to the world, Christopher?"

MEANWHILE, MATLOCK HOUSE WAS IN AN UPROAR. AMONG its inhabitants, the condemnation of the attack was universal. Their response to it was not.

Mrs. Darcy, who was visiting, confirmed her husband's intention to quit London. Sir Richard and Anne announced their return to Rosings. The earl and countess were determined to remain in town and showed little consideration for their relations' fears. A heated argument arose between Richard and Andrew.

Standing next to the parlor's fireplace, Andrew accused contemptuously, "I cannot believe that you, a soldier, wish to run away!"

On the far side of the room, only Anne's hand on Richard's arm prevented the knight from striding across the carpet and striking his brother. "Andrew," he growled at him, "I am thinking of Anne's wellbeing. There were riots in the streets last month, and now the Crown itself was attacked! I do not believe we can remain in London safely."

"Neither do I," Andrew shot back, "but that is why we have the army! They will set things to rights."

Richard bit his lip. Andrew regarded the army as the servant of the government, and it was, to a certain extent, but it also served as the protector of the British people. Facing their own citizens with steel and muskets was every soldier's worst nightmare, but that notion was beyond Andrew's grasp.

Richard tried another tack. "The army cannot be everywhere. You must agree that it is well Mother remains at Matlock."

"Of course. Mother does not need further distress."

"Then, should we not consider the feelings of our wives as well?" Andrew glanced at Lady Eugenie. "What say you, my dear?"

The countess, seated on a divan with Mrs. Darcy, simply shrugged. "I trust our footmen will do their duty and protect us. This Season is very important to you, Andrew. We are in mourning, but we must be seen about town as much as propriety allows to maintain the standing of the family. *That* is of the upmost importance." As usual, her tone was icy.

"There, you see?" said Andrew. "It cannot be seen that the

Matlocks are afraid. Our very position in society depends upon remaining in town."

At that moment, the sitting room door opened. "That is ridiculous, Andrew." Darcy walked fully into the room. Unlike his cousins' voices, his was level.

Before the clearly offended earl could answer, Elizabeth rose and joined her husband. "What did Mary and Thomas say?"

"You visited the Tuckers?" asked Anne.

"Yes," said Darcy before he turned to Elizabeth. "Thomas cannot come with us, but Mary and Rosanna will."

Andrew rolled his eyes. "So, you are scurrying back to Pemberley."

Darcy's face lost emotion, and Richard knew it was a sure sign of his cousin's displeasure.

"That is not possible," Darcy responded, "given the snow between here and Derbyshire. Instead, we shall visit my wife's family in Hertfordshire. Our stay there will be of undetermined length." He then narrowed his eyes a bit, warning Andrew to keep his opinions to himself.

The earl bit his lip and turned away. "Have it your way, then. You always do." He lifted his chin. "I shall, of course, prove the Matlocks are not cowards."

*And my cousin will prove the Darcys are not fools*, was Richard's silent rejoinder.

Darcy nodded dispassionately. "Then we shall leave you to it. You must excuse us, but we plan to leave at dawn tomorrow, and there is much to do." Elizabeth and he made a quick farewell before seeing themselves out.

"Damn that Darcy!" cried the earl once the Darcys left the house. "Not everyone has the freedom to do as he pleases! Can he not see I have no choice?" He stalked over to a side table and poured a measure of brandy. "Father would not have run, and neither shall I. It will not be said that the Earl of Matlock is frightened by a handful of ruffians!" He swallowed his drink in one gulp. "My consolation is that Darcy will have to bear the antics of Elizabeth's atrocious family! Mrs. Bennet certainly will be quite vocal in her delight at his condescension, I have no doubt, and I wish him the joy of it!"

Lady Eugenie giggled. Andrew gestured with his empty glass at his brother. "I suppose you need to see to your packing as well."

Richard glanced at Anne, who nodded. "We do, but we would not leave you in anger, Andrew." He walked to the earl and offered his hand. "You and Eugenie are welcome at Rosings Park should you require sanctuary."

The earl blinked, his bravado fading from his face. He shook his brother's hand heartily. "That is very good of you. We shall keep that in mind." He tried to grin. "I suppose it would be amusing to annoy Auntie Cathy for a time. She is in constant attendance upon you, is she not?"

Richard chose not to answer. "You will travel about with your largest footmen at all times, correct?"

He was happy to see his brother pale. It meant he took his warning seriously. Andrew nodded. "You will dine with us?"

Richard shook his head. "We plan to set off within the half hour. We shall sleep at Rosings tonight."

"Then, we shall not detain you," announced Lady Eugenie. "I shall have Cook prepare something for you to take on your journey."

Thanking the countess for her thoughtfulness, Richard and Anne went above stairs. True to Richard's word, the Fitzwilliams reached Rosings before nightfall.

# Chapter 11

The new Lord Matlock was proven correct in his prediction about Darcy's pleasure in visiting Hertfordshire. There was little to be had.

The positive influence of Elizabeth's marriage to Darcy on Mr. and Mrs. Bennet's behavior was disappointingly trifling and muted. Thomas Bennet's fears over providing for his children and widow after his passing had been wiped away by Jane and Elizabeth's advantageous marriages. So, he gave over completely to his indolent and insolent ways. As long as he had his steward, his book room, and his brandy, he saw no need to concern himself with the welfare or improvement of his estate or his wife. If he was less biting in his general remarks, it was too little for comment.

Fanny Bennet was accustomed to her husband's neglect. Mr. Bennet had not married her for her wit or understanding. His attraction was far baser. Over the first decade of their marriage, his interest in her waned in concert with the decline of her youthful beauty. In the absence of his affection, Mrs. Bennet busied herself with her children, her household, her sister, and her gossip. Her goal in life, besides safeguarding her security in old age, was to see her daughters well married, and she had succeeded beyond her wildest dreams.

True, these results added to her loneliness, for most of her girls left Hertfordshire, but that could not be helped. At least Mrs. Tucker spent a goodly portion of her time in Meryton and was happy to attend her mother when her responsibilities allowed.

Her wealthier sons had assured Mrs. Bennet they would see to her security in her sunset years, which gave her great comfort. Knowing there would always be a house for her settled her nerves considerably, a change that pleased her husband.

Another change in Mrs. Bennet was the ranking of her daughters in her esteem. Mrs. Denny remained her favorite, but Lydia was half a world away. Mrs. Tucker grew far more acceptable because Mary was nearby and visited, and the others did not. But it was now *Mrs. Darcy* who was chief in her mother's thoughts—her beautiful, talented, clever, and rich-beyond-measure Elizabeth was second in her heart. Mrs. Bingley and Mrs. Southerland were as *nothing.*

Therefore, a visit from the Darcys, no matter the reason, was a cause for great celebration. Of course, Mrs. Bennet was horrified over the events in London—*The Regent attacked! The Jacobins might invade Hertfordshire next! She was sure to be murdered in her bed!*—and she recalled the Darcys were in mourning. Therefore, they would be shown every courtesy in concordance with their grief. Surely, it was *necessary* for their four-and-twenty neighbors to pay their respects! Absolutely, it was *required* to purchase a new tablecloth and beeswax candles! Of course, the larder *had* to be filled with Mr. Darcy's favorite foods!

In addition to the above, the private chambers were not at all to Darcy's liking. None of the beds could accommodate two; therefore, the Darcys were forced to sleep apart.

The only reason Darcy did not run mad during the fortnight at Longbourn was the fact that the Bennets were affectionate grandparents. Mrs. Bennet lovingly doted on the children, showing only the slightest preference for young Bennet. Their presence drew their grandfather out of his book room for as much as a half an hour at a time. Longbourn House was once again filled with the laughter of children, and it was enough to bring a tear to Mrs. Bennet's eye.

Still, the Bennets were too kind, too obliging, and too much. It was understandable that Darcy, with his wife's encouragement, eagerly attended to the road condition reports.

February was but a week old when he learned the diminished snows in the north allowed safe travel to Derbyshire. Within a day, leaving Mrs. Tucker and young Rosanna safe in the bosom of their family, the Darcys were again on the road, happily anticipating the peace and quiet of Pemberley.

*February, a tavern in Kent*
*on the road to Maidstone*

THE SLOVENLY TAVERN GIRL MADE HER WAY THROUGH THE seedy, dimly lit room to the bar. The patrons were few and quiet tonight. The girl's parents had named her Hannah after the gracious mother of the prophet Samuel, but she was as far from gracious as could be. She was, however, perfectly suited for her chosen occupation.

Hannah slapped down her serving tray on the bar, her considerable bosom well displayed. "Two ales, Sam, fer the gents in th' back room."

The owner prepared the drinks. "An' where's the money, eh?"

Several coins appeared, and Sam swept up the money after placing the mugs on the tray. Hannah kept a shilling or two for herself, and she knew he was aware of it. It was a game they played. He would get it out of her in trade after closing time. Hannah flashed a quick smile, her missing teeth evident, before she carried the ales to her customers.

The back room was small, completely enclosed save for a single door. The only light came from a candle on the rough-hewn table surrounded by five mismatched chairs, two of which were occupied. Hannah gave the short, fat gentleman hardly a glance, even though he was the one who had paid her. Her attention was reserved for the younger man. His type was more to Hannah's liking—rail thin, hard, and dangerous looking. She made sure he got a good peek down her dress at her ample assets as she placed his mug before him, inspiring an agreeably dark and hungry look.

"That will be all, girl," said the fat man. They offered no names, and Hannah did not inquire. This was an establishment favored by those who wished to remain anonymous and paid in advance.

Hannah was only a few steps out of the room when she noticed one of her shoes had become undone. She knelt to refasten it and could not help but overhear a bit of the renewed conversation from the room.

"So, the colonel never rides alone?" It was the fat gentleman who spoke.

"Nay," answered his companion. "His man Gregory's always with his lordship."

"Hmm... Let us return to your idea. You have enough salt?"

"Enough ta do the job proper, don't worry."

"If you are caught, I shall not know you."

"You pay me enough, an' I won't be caught."

Hannah finished with her shoe and stood up. *Salt?* She shook her head, retrieved her tray, and returned to the bar, already forgetting what she overheard. It was a useful ability in her profession.

*March, Hunsford*

When the newly married Lady Catherine first arrived at Rosings Park, she was scandalized by what passed for an assembly hall in nearby Hunsford. After many years of complaining and badgering, Sir Lewis was convinced to replace the modest building for a structure more attuned to his wife's Fitzwilliam pride. Money was dear; therefore, it took far longer than anticipated for an assembly hall fit for Lady Catherine's attendance to be completed. In fact, Sir Lewis was in his tomb six months before the doors officially opened, Lady Catherine herself unveiling the plaque installed by the entrance, dedicating the hall in her husband's memory. It was the first and last time she stepped into the building she had long championed.

The place was slightly small for a village the size of Hunsford, but elegance, not comfort, was the point. Lady Catherine insisted upon the best of everything for the hall. The floors, woodwork, doors, and stairs were made of the finest British oak available. The windows featured beautifully glazed glass, and no less than four chandeliers hung from the high ceiling to light the space. Everything was polished to a fine gleam.

Of course, such a building required a great deal of maintenance. Unfortunately, Lady Catherine's benevolence ended upon the completion of construction. The care of the place was the village's problem, and there were always far more pressing uses for their funds. For the sake of its preservation, Hunsford Assembly Hall was hardly used.

*Hardly* did not mean *never*, however. On an evening in early March, the hall was thrown open so the tenants of Rosings Park could hear an address by Mr. Evans. Neither Sir Richard nor Lady Fitzwilliam was in attendance. Seated behind a long table set before the benches were Evans and the members of the tenant council. Once all were seated and the doors closed, the steward rose and spoke. He offered no salutation but began directly.

"Gentlemen, as you are undoubtedly aware, we have suffered a most unfortunate winter. The harvest was exceedingly poor, and many of your rents are in arrears." At the rising sound of protests, Evans raised a hand. "Sir Richard Fitzwilliam has graciously decided to forego collecting all that is due and will only require that the tenants partake in the maintenance of the estate's drainage and roads. For those who cannot pay, your labor shall be your contribution. Your *cheerful* participation is expected and appreciated. Now, we must talk of spring planting."

"Here now," called out a farmer from the rear of those assembled. "You expect us to break our backs rebuilding your roads?"

Evans glared at the outburst. "You are a tenant on Rosings property, are you not?"

"Aye, and have been these ten years, an' I've never—"

"You use those roads, do you not? Your family received food this winter—food from Rosings own larder, did it not?"

"Well," the man blustered, "we did—like everyone else. But there was nothing for it. There was no money."

Evans nearly sneered. "If you cannot pay your rent, then you must find other means of fulfilling your obligation to Rosings or find yourself another situation."

"By working like a slave?"

"Honest work is not slavery, sir. Do you find these conditions unacceptable?"

Mr. Clarke then spoke up. "Harris, sit down, you old fool! We all have to do our share. We're here to talk of *this* season, not *last* season." The other members of the tenant council mumbled their agreement. Still angry, Mr. Harris took his seat.

"Thank you, Mr. Clarke," Evans said. "Now usually planting begins in mid-March as soon as we are assured that we have seen the last of the frost. But this winter is such that it has been decided to postpone planting for a few weeks and allow the soil to warm up properly and thereby successfully accept our seeds. The first seeds shall be released at the end of April."

There was an explosion of complaints. "The end of April? I never heard of such a thing!"

"We'll only get two harvests in!"

"Two? We'll be lucky if we get *one*!"

"Give us them seeds now!"

Evans raised his hands. "Gentlemen! I understand your concerns, but you must listen. Setting back planting is regrettable but necessary. All scientific evidence shows that if the soil temperature is too low, the seeds will not—"

"Science! Bah! I've been farmin' this here land fer twenty years!"

"Let your men o' science till my land fer a change!"

"Order!" Evans cried. "Order, I say! Our plant seeds are too valuable to waste on antiquated ways! I shall not risk Rosings's future on such foolishness!"

A farmer in the front row stood. "Mr. Evans, can I speak?"

"You may, Mr. Wilkerson," Evans reluctantly allowed.

Mr. Wilkerson paused to gather his thoughts. "You're a very learned man, Mr. Evans, an' we're happy ta use th' new scientific methods. They work, to a fashion. But we've been workin' these fields for a lifetime or more, an' we've had bad winters before, you bet. There's ways o' doing things, we've learned. Like what ta do for a cold spring. We can plant th' seeds a wee bit deeper. That'll keep 'em warm till the frosts are passed."

Evans waved his hand impatiently. "All your experience aside, I must tell you the decision has been made. The plant seeds will be distributed the last week of April. Are there any other questions?"

Mr. Wilkerson blinked before sadly shaking his head as he took his seat. The others sat in silence.

"Fine." Evans turned to the council. "We shall now discuss the schedule for the road repairs. Mr. Clarke, you are in charge of that, I recall."

ON A CHILLY MORNING, RICHARD SAT BEFORE THE FIREPLACE in his study and opened his latest letter from Colonel Brandon.

*My dear Richard,*

*Marianne and I send our warmest greetings to you and Anne. We are all well here, Dickie is growing larger every day, and Joy delights in the office of older sister...*

Richard sighed. He knew things were now quiet in London and

that his old friend was more than capable of protecting himself and his family should matters turn perilous, but it was a relief to have his belief verified. He skipped ahead to the real news in the letter.

*Parliament has responded to the unrest in the country as I predicted. Habeas corpus is now suspended, and a new Seditious Meetings Act was passed, the latter more restrictive than the one established over twenty years ago. Yesterday, it was made high treason to assassinate, speak of killing, or even to imagine doing away with the Prince Regent. The papers are referring to them as the Grenville and Pitt Bills and the Gagging Acts.*

*Parliament was frightened out of its wits over the Spa Fields riot in December and the attempt upon the Regent in January. Now this Blanket march in Manchester has them terrified. This is no longer about Luddites losing their custom to the factories in the north. There is loose talk of a Jacobin revolution in the air. No one now speaks of reform, only maintaining the law and social order.*

*Our friends are as divided as the country. Buford is disgusted over what he calls the "cowardice of the government" while Tucker supports Liverpool. There is no room for compromise as long as the Crown believes the country is in danger. Parliament will stay in session deep into the summer, I fear.*

Richard was unsurprised by Brandon's report. The papers were full of the debates raging in the House. What was disheartening was his old comrade's depressing insights.

*Richard, this is not what I imagined when I took over poor Mr. White's seat. Politics is a hard, messy, and altogether unpleasant business. Late each night, I return dispirited to my rented London house, which distresses my poor Marianne terribly. Oh, how I wish I could be taking my ease in my favorite chair at Delaford, a fire in the grate and my family beside me, contending only with the usual petty disagreements between my tenants! At this time, I doubt I shall stand for office at the next election. I know this will be a bitter blow to Tucker and our friends in government, but to my own conscience I must be true.*

*I close this lengthy monograph assuring you and dear Anne of all the love Marianne and I can spare from the children. Alas, we shall not be able to satisfy our dearest desire to accept your kind invitation to Kent in June. I shall write to Buford. Pray give our regards to the Darcys.*

*Your obt. servant,*
*Brandon*

Richard refolded the letter in low spirits. That the Brandons would not be visiting this summer was the least of the bad news. When his friend took his seat in Parliament, Richard had high hopes that Brandon's calm demeanor and excellent understanding would prove to be an asset to the country. Judging by this letter, it seemed that the give and take of governing was not to Brandon's liking. He preferred the quiet of his estate. It was more than likely that Brandon would return to Dorsetshire, and his voice would be lost to the country.

First Buford had rejected politics and now Brandon. Who, Richard wondered, would challenge the fools and charlatans in Parliament?

*April*

CORK JOHNSON ENTERED HIS MOTHER'S RUN-DOWN COTTAGE at the end of another disappointing day to find her at the kitchen table weeping, head bent in her arms.

"Maw! Maw!" Dropping his bag of rocks on the floor, he quickly lumbered to her side. "What's wrong?"

Mrs. Johnson wiped her face with a soiled hand cloth. "Did the smithy pay you, Cork?"

"No. He had no work fer me today."

"Oh no, oh no." She wept anew.

A nearly panicked Cork was at a loss to know what to do, but he rubbed her shoulder, as she did to him sometimes, and begged her to tell him what troubled her.

"It's...it's the end of the month, an' I've had no sewin' nor mendin', an' that bastard Evans'll be here in the mornin' looking fer his money. What'll I do?"

"I'm sorry, Maw. I've been tryin' ta find work, but there ain't none. Rosings don't need me—too cold ta work, they say. An' the smithy didn't need me this week. I'm tryin', Maw."

"He'll throw us out fer sure." She sobbed into the hand cloth.

Just then, the Shepardson brothers strolled in. "What's for dinner?" demanded Simon. Looking at his aunt, he asked, "What's th' matter with you?"

"We ain't got the rent money, an' Mr. Evans is comin' tomorrow," Cork explained.

"Yeah," observed Adam. "He's a right bastard, that one."

Simon laughed. "Someone ought ta stick 'im in the ribs, huh?"

Adam frowned. "I told ya—none o' that kinda talk." He turned to his aunt. "How much does he want?"

"Two shillings," she managed.

Adam cursed under his breath and dug in his waistband. From there he extracted a money purse. A moment later, two coins were dropped on the table.

"This ought ta settle 'im," Adam said. "Now get us some dinner, Auntie."

Both Cork and Mrs. Johnson stared at the money. "Where'd ya get that?" Mrs. Johnson demanded.

"Don't worry about it."

The woman was terrified. "You ain't stealin' from Rosings, are ya? They'll hang ya—an' us too!"

"No, I ain't stole nothin'."

"Then where'd ya get it?"

Simon chuckled. "Adam's got him a friend, don't ya, Adam?"

His brother turned on him. "I *told* ya to shut up 'bout that!" Adam continued, "I said not ta worry 'bout it, Auntie. I ain't got this from Rosings. Don't you worry 'bout Rosings either. They'll get theirs, you bet. Now do as I said, woman, and get us some dinner!"

Both flinched away from Adam Shepardson's anger. Mrs. Johnson hurried to the cooking pot while Cork moved to retrieve his bag of throwing stones.

"Hey, Cork," Adam said, "they'll be work fer ya at Rosings in a for'night. You too, Simon."

"Aw, hell, Adam," Simon complained. "Do I have to?"

"Yes, ya have to," Adam growled. "We gotta make things look good 'til—" Adam caught himself. "You just do as I say, right?"

"All right." Simon reached for the bottle of wine and poured a couple of glasses. Meanwhile, Cork hung his bag by the front door, the curious look on his face going unseen by the others.

# Chapter 12

The Darcys' carriages arrived at Rosings just after midday. The Fitzwilliams, Lady Catherine, and Mrs. Jenkinson awaited them on the steps of the great house as a footman moved to open the lead carriage's door.

Darcy was the first to emerge. He then helped Elizabeth out with Frances in her arms. Bennet and Chloe Wickham followed with the nanny. Though mourning was not required, all still wore dark colors. To Richard's surprise, Elizabeth handed her daughter to Darcy before grasping their son's hand. They then walked to the bottom of the stairs, Mrs. Nivens following behind with Miss Wickham.

Richard and Anne came down to greet them, the ladies embracing while the men shook hands. "Good to see you, Darce!" cried Richard. "How did you find the roads?"

"Tolerable," Darcy dryly returned.

"Tolerable to you, sir," Elizabeth exclaimed, "but I assure you I felt every mile!"

"Miss Franny, what a big girl you are!" said Richard as he gave her head a caress.

Anne rose from kissing Bennet. "Oh, let me see her!" she cried. The Fitzwilliams exchanged places, and Richard bent down to shake Bennet's hand while Anne cooed over Frances.

Elizabeth kissed Richard's cheek. "I pray we find you well."

"Well enough, Cousin. Your rooms await you."

Lady Catherine cleared her throat and drew their attention to the top of the steps.

Richard winked. "We are summoned."

The grand dame awaited their attendance like a princess of the realm. The Darcys approached and offered their bows and curtsies.

"Lady Catherine," said Darcy, "I see we find you well."

"I am in excellent health, as always, Darcy," she proclaimed.

He nodded. "You, of course, remember Mrs. Darcy and my son, Master Bennet."

Lady Catherine eyed the boy neutrally as his mother urged him to bow.

"And this young lady," Darcy continued," is my daughter, Anne Frances, much grown."

"A pretty child, to be sure, Darcy, but why are you holding her? That is quite irregular!" She turned and glared at the nanny. "Is your servant incapable of doing so?"

"I hold my daughter because I wish to. Besides, Mrs. Nivens is occupied. Let me present my ward, Miss Chloe Wickham."

The child curtsied, which drew a sneer from Lady Catherine. Ignoring the girl, she turned her attention to Elizabeth. "Mrs. Darcy, if you have not lost the power of speech, you will tell me how you do."

Richard felt Anne stiffen. For her part, Elizabeth only smiled.

"I am very well, your ladyship, and very happy to enjoy the grandeur of Rosings after so long an absence."

Lady Catherine huffed. "Of course you miss Rosings! Have I not said that distance only increases one's affection for it?" She turned to Darcy. "You have neglected your duty to me and to your wife by staying away so long! I expect you will reform your behavior."

Richard did not know whether Darcy was biting his tongue; as for himself, he hoped he did not draw blood. The only evidence of his cousin's irritation was his hesitation before bowing his head.

"I shall keep that in mind," he said evenly.

"Excellent! Well, there is no call for us to stand about like common folk in this weather. You shall all come inside," Lady Catherine commanded before turning to walk through the doors.

"*Mother!*" Anne's voice was a hiss. Lady Catherine halted, and the others did not move.

With a grim look, Anne marched to the doors. "I thank you all for coming to *my house*." Anne's voice pitched higher in obvious aggravation. "Pray, come in," she indicated with a sweep of her arm. She then pointedly walked in before her mother. As the others followed, Richard observed Darcy and Elizabeth sharing a knowing look.

Once their coats had been handed over to the servants, Lady Catherine once again attempted to take charge. "You must all be quite tired. Your rooms should be ready for you now."

"Mother!" murmured Anne again. "If you will, I require your opinion on a private matter." To the others, she weakly requested, "Pray excuse us."

Richard had no doubt that everyone assembled knew Anne was going to take Lady Catherine to task for usurping her responsibilities as hostess. He doubted the old bat would oblige her daughter today any more than she had before. He then felt a tug at his pants leg and looked down to see Chloe Wickham smiling up at him.

"You said that Aunt Lizzy is your cousin. Am I your cousin too?"

Richard had not seen Darcy's ward since Georgiana's September wedding at Pemberley, and he had spent little time in her presence there. The passage of time had only enhanced what he had noticed then. The girl owned her father's eyes. Those damned laughing George Wickham eyes. Mocking eyes. *Hated eyes.*

Richard shuddered. "No, child, you are not," he replied coldly.

The smile slipped from Chloe's face.

"Chloe!" cried Mrs. Nivens. "Come here, dear. It is time to go see your room."

The little girl ran to her nanny's side, Richard's gaze following her. He then realized that Elizabeth had observed the encounter. She pierced him with a hurt, accusing expression. It was but a moment, and then she followed the rest of their party up the staircase to their rooms.

"I COULD *SCREAM*!" CRIED ANNE.

Richard crossed the length of their sitting room with a glass of wine. "Here, sweetheart. You must not let your mother upset you. We know how she is."

Anne accepted the glass. "*I* am mistress of Rosings. *I* am. Why will she not stop interfering?"

"Take a sip. It will do you good."

His wife turned her glare on him. "I shall thank you not to imitate my mother, sir! I shall drink my wine when I choose!" She then drained half the glass.

Richard ignored her outburst. "Lady Catherine has been an interfering woman her entire life. Why should she change now?"

"Do you not see the insult done to me? She diminishes me not only with every shopkeeper in the village but in my own home! Why are you defending her?"

"Take care waving your arms," said Richard dryly, "lest you spill your wine."

"Stop being so calm! Show some appreciation for my feelings!"

Richard knelt down and gently took her glass. "There is nothing I appreciate more than your feelings, Annie. That is why I *am* calm. There is no profit in battling Aunt Catherine, so I shall not go to war with her and upset the house. She is rude and overbearing and has been so her entire life. You know this better than anyone, for you have borne the brunt of it. She will not change, no matter how much we rail against her."

He placed the glass on a table and began to caress his wife's hand. "She loves you dearly as her daughter, but that fact also brings a discord between you. You are her darling little girl and *always will be*. She cannot accept that you are grown, that you are a wife and the mistress of Rosings, and you do not require her guidance." He chuckled. "She is not far different than was my dear father in that regard."

"Hardly." Anne's tone was considerably calmer. "Lord Matlock respected you and took pride in your accomplishments. He only wanted the best for you."

Richard shook his head. "And he gave his advice whether it was sought or not. There is something in the Fitzwilliam blood that makes one overbearing." He sat beside Anne on the sofa and drew her onto his lap. She tucked her head into the crook between his shoulder and neck.

"You are not like that." Her voice was muffled as she spoke into his neck cloth.

"True, and neither is Henrietta—or even Andrew, for all his arrogance. It must be my mother's tempering influence. Now, Darcy can be an insufferable arse at times. Hah—he is more a Fitzwilliam than we are!" He held her close and kissed her hair. "Annie, you should not permit your mother to upset you. You are the mistress of this house and every servant knows that. If she becomes unbearable, pray allow me to deal with her. Her games do not work on me. Make use of me, sweetheart."

Anne returned the kiss but on his cheek. "My noble knight in shining armor, ready and willing to slay my dragons! What should I do without you? I adore you."

"As I adore you. Now, sweet girl, give me a proper kiss."

"You are upset," Darcy observed once they were ensconced in Elizabeth's rooms.

"Of course, I am upset!" Elizabeth cried from a small settee near the fireplace. "Your cousin hurt Chloe's feelings!" Elizabeth felt her body shake in anger. "I expected Lady Catherine's dismissal of

Chloe. Indeed, I was relieved she did not do worse. But for Chloe to be rejected by Richard—kind, amusing, loyal Richard? It felt like a blow. At this moment, I want to repack the trunks, load the carriages, and return to Pemberley."

"I saw Richard's look," Darcy said in that steady, flat voice he used to indicate his disapproval, "and I share your displeasure."

"How could he treat a child so?" Elizabeth turned her attention to Darcy and saw that, while he was unhappy, he was not discomposed. Little could unsettle her unflappable husband, but not to be affected by this was very telling. "You expected this?"

"I am not surprised is more accurate. He avoided her at Pemberley." Darcy looked out the window as was his wont when he wished to settle his thoughts. "We have discussed my unforgiving temper. How once my good opinion is lost, it is lost forever."

"Yes," she replied, "and you believe this disposition is a result of your Fitzwilliam heritage." She frowned. "You believe Richard owns unreasonable resentment?"

Darcy glanced at her. "Unreasonable resentment is the true Fitzwilliam curse."

"I find nothing unreasonable about *your* resentments, my dear."

A small smile graced his otherwise stony features. "You are very kind, my love, but I must own my shortcomings."

"You do yourself an injustice. You are the best of men. There are many who can learn from you." In a lower voice, she added, "Including some in Kent."

He nodded. "You speak of my aunt, which proves my point." He turned to the window again. "All the Fitzwilliams bear this curse to one extent or another, including myself and my mother. She was nothing compared to my aunt or uncle, of course, but I was not blind to Mother's occasional antipathy to individuals who at worse deserved merely lack of notice. Father was the forgiving one in the family. In this, Georgiana takes after him, thank goodness."

*Forgiveness is not always a blessing*, thought Elizabeth, *when it is bestowed on the undeserving like George Wickham. I am sad to recall that Charles and Jane overlook the behavior of others they should not out of misplaced mercy.*

"Richard never liked or trusted George Wickham," her husband continued. "After the Ramsgate ignominy, his hatred of Wickham was complete. It took me hours to talk Richard out of challenging him, and only his concern that the resulting scandal would damage Georgiana forever stayed his hand."

"So, his hatred for the father has been transferred to the daughter. Fitzwilliam, that is outrageously unfair!"

"I shall not argue that you are wrong, but I know that to angrily confront Richard over his unreasonableness will do more harm than good." He offered a small smile. "Fitzwilliams are known to be stubborn in their opinions as well."

Elizabeth blushed and looked down. "As are Bennets, I must admit."

Darcy leaned over and kissed her cheek. "Do not distress yourself, my love. You did offer me a second chance, after all."

"No—I was wrong and changed my mind." She smiled at him "Dispute that if you dare!"

He joined her on the small settee. "Indeed, I dare not! I know well my wife's temper."

"Fitzwilliam!" She moved into his arms. "I am not so terrible, am I?"

His lips moved to her forehead. "Bingley is wrong. *You* are the true angel."

She sighed. "Then there is nothing to be done?"

"Only to have patience, my dear. I shall speak to him and insist that he be civil. Richard is not unreasonable. In time, he may see that Chloe, for all her resemblance to her father, is nothing like him."

"Or, he may not."

Darcy nodded.

DINNER THAT NIGHT WAS FAR LESS TAXING THAN DARCY anticipated. Surprisingly, this was due to the attendance of Mr. and Mrs. Collins. Elizabeth, overjoyed with the prospect of renewing acquaintance with the lady who had once been her particular friend, largely spent her time in close and happy conversation with Mrs. Collins, Anne, and Mrs. Jenkinson. She had little discourse with Sir Richard; therefore, her coolness to his cousin was undetected.

The burden of entertaining Lady Catherine, therefore, fell to Darcy, and in this he was joined by Richard and Mr. Collins. That task would have been easier without the tiresome, simpering observations of the Hunsford rector, but it was a burden with which Darcy was well acquainted, and he carried out his duty with perfect composure.

Lady Catherine and the Collinses did not leave until it was nearly nightfall. The ladies excused themselves and retired above stairs. Darcy was not of a mind to play billiards, so he and his cousin had port in the library. Richard took his ease in a chair while Darcy, glass in hand, perused the bookshelves.

"I see you managed to procure a copy of *Waverley*. I am impressed," said Darcy.

"It was a gift from Father—one of the last I received before his illness. He was not one for novels, but he loved the book. I suppose I should read it." Richard gestured at the chair beside him. "I am tired of straining my neck to look up at you. You are far too tall. Come and sit—and tell me why your wife is annoyed with me."

Richard's comment caught Darcy off guard while he was in the act of sitting. He paused, and then slowly made himself comfortable. Apparently, Elizabeth's feelings were detectable after all. Darcy needed a sip to settle his thoughts.

"Well?"

Darcy set down his glass and glared at his cousin. "She took offense at your dismissal of Chloe."

Richard stared at him as though he thought Darcy had lost his mind. "You cannot be serious."

"I am."

Richard sat forward, his face working. "You expect me to welcome Wickham's brat into my home?"

"Richard. You are speaking of my niece and ward. I shall thank you to keep a civil tongue in your head."

Richard flushed in anger but nodded. "I mean no offense to you or Lizzy, but I cannot set eyes on that child and not see Wickham's lying face."

Darcy beat down his first impulse—to pack his family and leave Rosings at first light—and attempted to speak rationally. "You are a reasonable man, Fitz. Surely, you know Chloe is innocent of Wickham's sins."

"I know that!" Richard snorted. "It is just that…" He waved his hands, seemingly unable to say more.

A horrible thought occurred to Darcy. "Pray tell me you do not subscribe to Aunt Catherine's appalling notion about bad blood."

Richard shook his head. "Of course not." He dropped his elbows to his knees and held his face in his hands. Darcy could see his cousin was struggling, but he offered no solace. The man deserved no such relief.

"It is her eyes," Richard mumbled.

Darcy did not respond. He simply waited for the rest. It was not long in coming.

"She has Wickham's eyes, Darce. I *hate* those eyes." He looked up at his cousin. "I look at your ward, and I see all the pain that man caused our family.

"I saw it when we were young. I saw he was nothing but a jealous, devious bully and scoundrel. He used everyone and cared for no one. You were blind to it at first. You were so young, so lonely. You wanted a friend badly. I did what I could to protect you, but I was either at Matlock, or school, or the army. You had no one but

Wickham. When your blinders finally fell, my uncle would not listen to you. He would do nothing!"

Darcy took a deep breath. "You know how charming, how persuasive Wickham could be, even in his youth. Father felt sorry for him, given the woman who was his mother. He thought I could be a good influence on his godson.

"Later, after Mother's death, Father lost his way. She was his joy, and joy left him when she was gone. Wickham was agreeable, he was amusing, and I...I was serious and reserved. I was the heir. I was the responsible one. I was the one he depended on to care for Georgiana and Pemberley. He told me this in his last days—"

"Bah!" Richard cut him off. "Uncle George refused to accept what Wickham was! Sending him to school, paying off his debts. He should have cast him off! He should have been more concerned for you!" He clenched a fist in his other hand. "You cannot know how much I hated Wickham. I wanted to kill him, you know. After Ramsgate, I could have cut him down in the street at the slightest provocation."

"I am happy you did not," Darcy said, reaching out and tapping his cousin on the knee. "I have grown used to your annoying presence, as has Georgiana."

Richard returned his gaze to him.

"I have made my peace with my childhood. I have forgiven Father. No man, no matter how good, is perfect. I certainly am not. I have learned that hate and resentment are a poison to one's soul.

"Wickham is dead, Fitz. But even he did something good. He left the world three lovely little girls. The Bingleys have Phoebe, and the Tuckers Rosanna. Elizabeth and I are honored we have been given the charge to raise Chloe, and we shall do so to the best of our ability."

"Yes, you are very generous—"

Darcy cut him off. "This is not *generosity*, not in the least. You may as well call us selfish at once, because in our hearts, Chloe is *ours*—Elizabeth's and mine. We shall raise her as our daughter. And once she is old enough to make the choice, we shall adopt her if that is her wish."

Richard was shocked. "You...you would adopt Wickham's—"

"We stand ready to adopt *my ward*—my *sister* Lydia's child," Darcy stated firmly. "A sweet and loving little girl, virtually abandoned by her mother. We care not who fathered her. *I* shall be her father now." He paused. "And we require our relations and acquaintances to respect our decision and accept my family. My *entire* family." He offered a smile and softened his tone. "She would like another cousin."

"I...I do not know if I can do that." He bit his lip. "I am well rebuked for my treatment of—of your ward. I shall do better. I shall offer her every courtesy. But pray do not ask more of me."

"You have much to think on."

"I do." He looked up bleakly. "I owe you and Lizzy an apology."

Darcy shrugged. "For myself, I require nothing. Elizabeth is generous, as I have reason to know."

"And...the child?"

"Treat her well and we shall have no complaints."

Richard nodded and changed the subject. "Care for another port?"

Darcy eyed his nearly empty glass. "I believe this was your father's favorite vintage."

"Yes, the last of the case from his cellar." At Darcy's astonishment, he laughed ruefully. "Port is made to be drunk, Darce. Besides, I think Father would approve. Nothing was more important to him than family."

"True." After Richard refilled their glasses, Darcy raised his, looking up at the ceiling. "To Hugh Fitzwilliam and George Darcy—the two men who taught me what it means to be a father."

Richard smiled, staring straight at his cousin. "To fathers."

# Chapter 13

At sunrise the next morning, Darcy tore himself away from his sleeping wife. Usually when visiting friends, the Darcys took the opportunity to lounge a bit in bed. Of course, the Darcys' definition of lounging was unique. They never kept town hours, even at the London house. The typical routine was to wake soon after daybreak and walk together in the gardens before an early breakfast. When visiting anyone other than family, they would forgo the morning walk and spend the early hours in the privacy of their rooms. Today, however, Darcy had a mission: inspecting Rosings Park on horseback.

He quietly made his way from Elizabeth's room to his own, where his valet was waiting as planned. Soon, Darcy was in the stables, surprising the men mucking out the stalls. A horse was saddled, and Darcy rode out onto the plantation.

He had not gone far before he pulled his mount to a dead stop. He could not believe his eyes.

After a moment, he called out to the gardener, "You there! What has happened to the vegetable garden?"

A young man, hoe in hand, turned from his labors in a huge patch of nearly lifeless ground. "We don't know, sir! Mr. Evans, he has us workin' the ground with manure, but it don't help!"

Darcy nodded. "Thank you. Carry on, then," he said. As he

made his way deeper onto the plantation, Darcy could not help looking back at the wasteland.

As he traveled through the home farm, Darcy was relieved that the general condition of the crops was not the disaster found in the gardens. Still, things should have been better, even with the abnormal weather. Soon, he entered the fields rented by the tenants.

Darcy required answers and directed his mount to a certain farm. Sure enough, he found a middle-aged man hard at work with his laborers.

"Mr. Wilkerson! Good morning to you, sir!"

The man looked up. "Why, bless my soul! Mr. Darcy!" Mr. Wilkerson walked to the edge of the tilled field, removed his hat, and bowed from his shoulders. "How are you farin', sir?"

Darcy nodded in greeting from his horse. "I am well, thank you. And you and your family?"

"Why, thankee sir, we're all well. By God, it's been an age, I declare! What—four years since you've been here?"

In years past, when Darcy had been tasked with assisting Lady Catherine in managing Rosings Park, he learned much of the estate's true condition by riding the fields with Mr. Caruthers and speaking to men like Mr. Wilkerson. The cantankerous farmer was unafraid to speak his mind, something Darcy liked and appreciated. He hoped Richard did the same.

"Indeed." Darcy looked over the field. "Your sons, I assume. They are much grown."

"Yes, sir, that's them, exceptin' my second boy." Mr. Wilkerson's voice dropped. "He went and left me. Lookin' to make his fortune in the mills." He spat on the ground. "It broke his maw's heart, it did."

Darcy had no answer for that. "I see your fields are in no better shape than those at Pemberley." He thought it odd. The winter should have been milder here.

"Sorry to hear 'bout Pemberley, sir. This cursed weather!

Mr. Evans set plantin' behind by six weeks! We'll be fortunate to get in one harvest this season."

"I see one field left fallow."

Mr. Wilkerson squinted as he looked out. "Yes, sir. Old Caruthers had us take up that four-field rotation. I figure it works. Look over there." He pointed to the south. "That field was let fallow last year, an' it was the first we planted. It's the best crop we'll get this season. We'd have gotten two harvests outta there, at least, if we'd planted in the early spring like always."

"It looks as though Mr. Smith has finally taken up the new scientific ways, as well," Darcy observed, standing up in his saddle to look over to the next farm. "I never thought he would do so."

Mr. Wilkerson spat again. "That ain't Smith's farm no more, Mr. Darcy. Pensioned off, he was. Mr. Clarke's got it now."

Darcy was surprised. "I do not know Mr. Clarke."

"Young man—barely outta leading strings, if ya ask me. Still, he's a hard worker." He paused. "People call him Fitzwilliam's Favorite, ya know."

A frown grew on Darcy's forehead. "Are you insinuating Sir Richard gives him preferential treatment?"

Mr. Wilkerson shook his head. "I ain't sayin' the colonel is, and I ain't sayin' he ain't. But that's the word 'round Hunsford. Puttin' a young man like Clarke on the tenants' council is bound to have some with their nose outta joint. His wife is friendly with Lady Fitzwilliam too." Mr. Wilkerson paused. "The Clarkes are good people, sir, but that don't stop the jealous types, you understand. I get along with him just fine."

"How is Mr. Evans working out?"

Mr. Wilkerson's open face became guarded. "Mr. Evans knows his farmin'."

Darcy heard what Mr. Wilkerson did not say. "That is good to hear, but there is more to being a good steward than expertise in agriculture."

"I wouldn't say that—beggin' your pardon, Mr. Darcy."

"I do not take your meaning."

The farmer looked about, as though afraid of being overheard. "Mr. Evans, his advice is good, but it seems to me like he speaks from rote—like from a book. It don't seem to matter if conditions aren't what they should be—just do as he says or else. Now, old Caruthers wasn't so set in his ways. He'd listen to a man and talk things over. He didn't get the tenants upset."

Darcy was disturbed by what he heard, but it would not do to state his feelings. His expression grew impassive. "Mr. Caruthers was a good man. I am sorry to hear about Mr. Evans. Have you spoken to Sir Richard?"

"Sir Richard? Nah, we don't see the colonel exceptin' on Sunday at church."

Darcy could not hide his shock. "Sir Richard does not ride the fields?"

Mr. Wilkerson was suddenly uncomfortable. "Mr. Darcy, I don't like sayin' anything against the colonel. I'll never forget what he did for us back in '15 afore he went off an' beat Bonaparte—the rent holiday when things were bad. He's a good man. Always got a kind word to the wife. But he don't pay the attention to the fields like you used to. He left that to Mr. Caruthers an' now to Mr. Evans. We see Sergeant Gregory sometimes, but that's all from Rosings."

Darcy fought to regain his composure, a difficult task as he was deeply troubled. From his youth, almost since he could ride a horse, his father taught him the *Darcy way* of running an estate. It required personal interaction with the servants, hands, tenants, clergy, and merchants whose livelihood depended upon the patronage of the family. A competent steward was certainly essential, as were the housekeeper, butler, secretary, and stable master. It did not excuse the master or mistress from their particular duties, not the least of which was the supervision of those individuals.

How could the master manage the steward if he did not see what the steward saw, heard what the steward heard? It was impossible. Master and steward had to have complete trust and confidence in one another, like his father and Old Wickham had or himself and Mr. Thompson. Darcy had been taught that the success or failure of the estate rested ultimately with the master and mistress and no one else. He was convinced it was the only way to properly manage an estate. He feared his cousin was failing the people of Rosings.

He was about to ask Mr. Wilkerson more about Mr. Evans, but the questions died on his lips. The tenant farmer looked beyond Darcy, his eyes wide and lips drawn. His expression seemed a mixture of anger and fear. Darcy turned and saw a short man in a brown coat riding towards them, his horse at a trot. By his dress, Darcy assumed this was Mr. Evans. He did not display a friendly countenance.

"Good morning, sir!" The short man's voice was not friendly either. "You find yourself on Rosings land. If you are lost, I would be happy to direct you to your destination. Otherwise, I must ask you your business here." By now, he was about ten feet away.

With skill developed from years in the saddle, Darcy smoothly repositioned his horse and stood next to Mr. Wilkerson, facing the presumed steward of Rosings. He raised his chin and looked down his patrician nose.

"My business, sir, is speaking to this honest fellow. Our conversation is done, and I shall be on my way." He turned to the farmer. "Good day, Mr. Wilkerson. My best to your wife and family."

"Thankee, sir, an' God bless ya."

The other rider narrowed his eyes. He apparently did not take well to being dismissed. "Allow me to escort you to the road," he managed through clenched teeth.

Darcy's riding clothes were of the best quality, afforded only by a wealthy gentleman. His interrogator surely realized it but chose to make no remark on it. He was either a fool or a bully, Darcy decided. "That will not be necessary," he responded carelessly, "as my business is elsewhere."

"And where is that business?"

"Wherever I wish." Darcy knew his insolence enraged the man; in fact, that had been his purpose. He had not liked what he had heard about Mr. Evans, and his animosity had not lessened now that he was in his company. Pushing a rude and unpleasant man to his limit was a quick way to establish his true character. If this gentleman was indeed Mr. Evans, Darcy wanted to know just what sort of man he was.

The red-faced gentleman fidgeted in his saddle, his hands twisting the reins in irritation. "We do not look kindly on trespassers."

"As I well know."

"I can have you escorted away."

A corner of Darcy's mouth quirked up. "I doubt it."

Finally, the short man's temper broke. "Devil take it! I am the steward of Rosings Park! Who are you to speak to me in such a manner?" He brandished a short whip.

Darcy had not asked for an introduction, wondering how long it would be before the interloper remembered his manners. His rude outburst could hardly be considered a request, but it would do. Darcy had achieved his goal and successfully goaded him to reveal his temperament, and he now knew Mr. Evans was a very unpleasant sort of man.

Without removing his eyes from him, he asked the farmer, "Mr. Wilkerson, would you do the honors?"

Mr. Wilkerson's voice trembled a bit—from fear or amusement, Darcy did not know. "Mr. Darcy, this is Mr. Evans, steward of Rosings Park. Mr. Evans, this here's Mr. Darcy of Pemberley, nephew of Lady Catherine."

"I am a guest of my cousins, the Fitzwilliams," Darcy coolly informed him.

Mr. Evans paled, his eyes wide, and the whip fell to his side. "M-Mr. Darcy, I beg your pardon...I did not know."

Darcy chose to be magnanimous. "Of course not, Mr. Evans. We arrived less than a day ago. I am sorry we had not the opportunity to meet before. As for my business, it is my custom when I visit Rosings to tour the plantation, see to the state of the farms, and speak to the tenants. Such was my practice when, for five years, I oversaw Rosings." Darcy felt no need to further diminish Mr. Evans. He had made his point.

"I…I hope you are pleased by what you saw, sir." The change in Mr. Evans's manner was almost humorous.

"The fields are in decent condition," Darcy allowed. He left unsaid that they should have been better. "Mr. Wilkerson's, particularly, are in fine shape." He turned and congratulated the farmer, who thanked him in return.

"But, Mr. Evans, the vegetable gardens are in a shocking state. Whatever can be the matter?"

Mr. Evans by now had recovered his composure. "Apparently, sir, the gardens have suffered grievously from the cruel winter just past. I have the gardeners working more manure into the soil. Unfortunately, this has delayed planting. We must now look towards a harvest in the fall."

Darcy's brow creased. Was the winter *that* harsh in Kent? Richard's letters did not indicate that. "It is extraordinary that a winter, severe as it was, could cause such damage. Have you considered the possibility of other causes?"

"Such things I leave to the gardener," Mr. Evans replied carelessly. "I trust he knows his business. May I join you on your ride, sir?"

"Another time, perhaps. I must return to the house for breakfast." He took his leave of both men and set his horse towards the stables. Still, he could not stop himself from glancing at the Mr. Wilkerson garden as he passed. It was lush and green.

Darcy rode on, contemplating the mystery. *What is wrong with the Rosings gardens? And why is Mr. Evans so unconcerned over it?*

It was a disappointed Elizabeth who stepped into the breakfast parlor to find only Sir Richard within. She was slightly out of sorts. She had awakened by herself and not in her favored attitude, lying in her husband's arms. Elizabeth expected Darcy had ridden out to view the farms—the man was so predictable—and she hoped he would be back in time to break his fast with her. Sir Richard was a poor substitute for Fitzwilliam Darcy. She returned her cousin's greeting very civilly if not completely cheerfully.

Her companion rose when she entered. "Elizabeth, pray accept my apology for my behavior yesterday. I own I was a blackguard."

Elizabeth was expecting this. Darcy had told her of his conversation with Richard before they slept. With cool graciousness, she accepted Richard's apology and his promise to treat Chloe better and sat down for a breakfast of dry toast and tea.

"I say, Lizzy," Richard managed after he washed down a mouthful of kippers with coffee, "is there nothing else on the sideboard to tempt you? Shall I have Cook prepare something else?" The stench of oily fish was quite pronounced.

Elizabeth hid her queasiness well. "Do not trouble yourself. I am perfectly happy with tea for now. I am awaiting Darcy in any case." She did not reveal that Richard's choice of food was revolting to *someone else* who had yet to make his or her presence known to anyone other than herself and her husband. "Is Anne well?"

"Yes. She is with her lover now." He took another bite of his breakfast.

Elizabeth choked on her tea. "I beg your pardon?"

Richard grinned. "Morpheus. You know how my wife hates to tear herself away from her bed in the morning."

Elizabeth shook her head and smiled. "You wicked, teasing man!"

"I have my moments." Indeed he did, for the jest broke the tension in the room. Richard drained the remains of his cup. "You must pardon me. I have business with Gregory this morning."

"Fear not, Cousin. Elizabeth is in better company now." Darcy, still in his riding clothes, strode into the room as though he owned it, as was his way.

"I am happy you decided to favor us with your attendance," Richard countered good-humoredly. "Your wife quite despaired of seeing you."

"Pay no attention to him, my dear," said Elizabeth as she turned up her cheek for Darcy's kiss. "He is only jealous that Anne prefers her paramour to him in the morning."

"Ah, yes—her bed," Darcy responded. At Elizabeth's surprised look, he continued. "Anne is well-known in the family for keeping town hours in the morning and country hours at night."

Richard stood, patting his lips with a serviette. "Before, it was due to illness," he said seriously. "Now, the habit is ingrained, I suppose. I expect she will be down soon." With that, he took his leave.

Darcy sat next to Elizabeth and kissed her hand. "I am sorry to have left you so early, my love, but I could not bear to disturb your rest." Worry was present in his dark eyes. "You are well, I trust?"

"We are *both* well, Fitzwilliam." She caressed his strong, dear face. "I only require that you do not have kippers this morning, or I shall not answer for the consequences!"

A bark disturbed their tête-à-tête, and Darcy turned toward the source. "What is *that*?"

Elizabeth laughed. "*That*, my dear, is Anne's other lover! Come here, Romeo!"

The dog eagerly approached Elizabeth, his tail wagging constantly. He jumped up, his front paws on the chair seat, begging for attention. She complied, petting his soft, short fur.

"I had no idea there was a dog in the house. Is it a puppy?"

"No, it is an Italian greyhound. They are always this small." She smiled. "They are not like those great beasts at Pemberley!"

Darcy was slightly offended. "Lysander and Penelope are not beasts. They are a fit size for greyhounds." He pointed at Romeo. "Unlike this creature."

"He is a dear, sweet little thing," his wife insisted as Romeo tried to lick her face.

"Perhaps," Darcy said as he rose from his chair, "but that does not make him a proper dog."

"Why do you have an aversion to small dogs? I recall you do not care for Kitty's Pug."

"Small dogs are useless," he declared and changed the subject. "Have you stomach for anything other than toast? May I tempt you with a chop?"

Every day, Elizabeth fell more in love with her Fitzwilliam. What other husband would not only fill her breakfast plate, but recall her changeable food aversions while with child? There was no better man in the kingdom. "Thank you. A bit of cake and honey—a very *little* honey—would set me up famously."

A suitable plate was soon before her. Her husband dined on rolls and cold meat, along with coffee. Elizabeth wrinkled her nose, for she could not abide coffee in the morning. How Fitzwilliam could drink the vile, bitter brew so early in the day, she knew not.

"How was your ride this morning?"

"Troubling." Darcy glanced at her. "In general, the fields are disappointing. The weather, while not ideal, is better than last summer, but the farms have not recovered to the extent one would expect. The vegetable garden, in particular, was shocking."

"Could it be that the winter here was worse than you thought?"

Darcy shook his head. "It would be surprising indeed if that were the case. Longbourn is to the north of London; surely, it was colder *there*. But it is in better condition than Rosings, and your father reports the other farms in the district are satisfied with the improvement over last season."

Elizabeth knew her husband well. "You have an idea as to the cause."

He gave her a knowing glance. "Perhaps. It requires further study."

"Fitzwilliam, have a care. This is Richard's realm, not yours. I do not think he would take kindly to any interference."

Darcy waved off her warning. "Of course, of course. I would not dream of interfering. But managing an estate has been my profession these ten years. What sort of cousin would I be if I did not offer my assistance?"

Elizabeth's eyes narrowed at her husband's condescension. He sounded vaguely like Lady Catherine. "We are speaking of Richard, not Charles."

Darcy placed a hand on hers. "Trust me to know the difference. Richard and I have a strong, brotherly affection for each other. We have always been open and honest in our opinions and counsel. There is nothing we would not do for each other. This matter will be no different."

Elizabeth bit back a sigh. There was little hope of changing her husband's mind now that it was set. She could only hope he was right.

It was an hour before midday when Anne regretfully left her apartments to break her fast. She had forgotten her guests were early risers and were probably awaiting her in the breakfast parlor, if they had not finished their meal already.

As she busily berated herself for her thoughtlessness, a noise not heard for decades in the halls of Rosings nearly escaped Anne's notice. It was the sound of giggling, and it was coming from the nursery. Anne was drawn to peek in and see what had amused the children. She was unprepared for what she beheld.

Elizabeth was sitting in a chair, holding her daughter Frances with one arm while her free hand covered her mouth, smothering light laughter. Chloe and Bennet were happily crawling over a figure lying on the floor. Incredibly, it was Darcy in his shirtsleeves, flat on his back, allowing the children to abuse his person while he, in turn, tickled his tormenters.

Anne could not help herself. "Darcy, what in the world are you doing?"

Her outburst captured the attention of everyone in the room, including the nurse who stood near the far wall, calmly taking in the unimaginable sight.

Darcy looked up at Anne. "The children are playing King of the Hill, and I am the hill," he stated as though it were patently obvious.

"Uncle is tickling us!" cried Chloe.

"The hills of Pemberley are very ticklish," Darcy pointed out.

Anne was completely nonplussed. In her wildest dreams, she never thought she would behold such a sight: Darcy, her staid, serious, slightly boring cousin, playing with his children in such an undignified manner! And not embarrassed about it in the least. He was on the floor, for goodness sake! What had come over him?

A hopeful Chloe interrupted Anne's thoughts. "Have you come to play too?" Meanwhile, Bennet resumed his attempt to climb atop his father.

Anne turned to Elizabeth, to see a twinkle in that lady's eye. "The children might like to see what the hills of Rosings are like," she impishly suggested. "The Longbourn hills are occupied at the moment."

"Ah…I see," Anne managed. "I thank you, no. Another time, perhaps. We are to call on Charlotte this afternoon."

Elizabeth nodded. "I remember. I shall attend you later." Chloe meanwhile turned her attentions to Darcy again.

Anne quietly left the nursery, vowing never to tell her mother of this. The Darcys and she would never hear the end of it otherwise!

Telling Richard, however, was another matter entirely.

IT WAS EARLY AFTERNOON BEFORE ELIZABETH WAS HANDED down from Anne's smart little phaeton by Mr. Collins. Vociferous were his numerous compliments to his generous patroness and noble cousin. A full five minutes was insufficient for the loquacious vicar to express his indescribable delight at the honor bestowed on his humble abode by two such exalted personages. It fell to the lady of the house to remind her husband that their visitors would find it far more comfortable inside the cottage than without. Mr. Collins's numerous heartfelt apologies for his unforgivable bad manners were cut short by his wife's reminder of his intention to collect his ordered treatise on beekeeping from the village book seller. That led to an extended leave taking.

With the ladies finally seated in the parlor and Mr. Collins off to the depths of Hunsford, Elizabeth was allowed to express her joy at being in Charlotte's agreeable company after a long absence. It had been over three years since they had laid eyes on each other, and while the post had made a tidy profit in the meantime, given the numerous letters exchanged between Hunsford and Pemberley or London, written words were a poor substitute for deep, personal conversation between dear friends.

Charlotte was the woman she remembered—sensible, kind, patient, and observant. The most apparent change was a fullness in face and figure, something expected of a lady three times a mother. But there was one other alteration, something only hinted of in her letters. Charlotte was more than contented in her marriage. She was *happy*.

It was not only from joy found in motherhood or from pleasure found in her office of parson's wife, although these delights were considerable. From her letters—and Anne's too—Elizabeth knew much of this change was due to an alteration in Mr. Collins.

In the spring of 1815, after years of verbal abuse of himself and his family from Lady Catherine, the Reverend William Collins found his courage and threw his complete support behind Anne de Bourgh's ascension to mistress of Rosings Park. This was no little thing. Collins had risked his position and his family's security. Had the bloodless coup failed, it was certain that a resentful Lady Catherine would labor to find—or manufacture—misconduct on the cleric's part that would cost him his living. Failing that, she undoubtedly would make his life a living hell.

But the man surprised all with his steadfastness—even himself. His reward for his bravery was his new patrons' gratitude, the community's respect, and his wife's growing affection.

Charlotte wrote of the happy surprise—that her husband had become a man she could respect and even—at times—admire. Now in her company, Elizabeth could see matters were even more pronounced than reported. Her friend was well satisfied with her situation, and it was within the realm of possibility that she might grow fond of her husband.

It was not to say that Mr. Collins had changed *completely*. He had not. His tendencies toward pomposity, obsequiousness, impulsiveness, and self-righteousness were unabated. His learning and understanding were suspect. He owned a pathetic need for acceptance by his superiors. He was at once single-minded and easily distracted.

However, he was loyal. He owned few vices, save a tendency towards gluttony; he had gained at least three stone in the last five years. He was delighted with his daughters, Catherine, Anne, and Elizabeth, and he adored his wife.

He could be moved to better behavior if encouraged by that lady. His dress and table manners were improved. His bodily hygiene could no longer be faulted. He ceased all resentments against the Bennets—including Elizabeth—over the events in 1811, and he accepted the fact he could be overbearing in conversation and struggled (unsuccessfully) to curtail that most offensive facet of his character.

Charlotte once said happiness in marriage was a matter of chance. To Elizabeth's mind, it seemed her friend had won a qualified prize in the end.

As the visit continued, it became apparent to Elizabeth that Charlotte had won another prize, one not as satisfying to the mistress of Pemberley. Mrs. Collins's particular friend was no longer Mrs. Darcy but Lady Fitzwilliam.

It should have been no surprise. Elizabeth's relationship with Charlotte had taken a blow when her friend agreed to marry Mr. Collins. Elizabeth's subsequent union with Mr. Darcy added physical distance to the emotional one caused by Charlotte's choice. Still, Elizabeth held Charlotte close to her heart and thought those feelings were returned.

It was an unreasonable expectation, Elizabeth now recognized, as was the jealousy she felt by her friend's defection. Occasional letters could not replace daily face-to-face interaction, especially with a person as kind and generous as Anne Fitzwilliam.

After a short struggle, Elizabeth resolved to be sanguine. After all, had not Kitty and Georgiana become her particular friends? Was it a betrayal to Jane that these two ladies were now chief in her thoughts, outside of Darcy and the children? She should rejoice that Charlotte had gained such an agreeable friend. She vowed to be happy for her.

And anything Elizabeth set her mind to do usually met with success.

# Chapter 14

S everal days later, a rut in the road shook a carriage in a particularly violent manner. "Are you well, dear?" asked Lady Buford.

Buford did not respond, his attention fixed upon the horse and rider escorting the carriage. Corporal Frost worked the stallion effortlessly, as a cavalryman should. Hannibal was Sir John's favorite horse, and he observed his movements with barely concealed envy.

"My dear, are you well?" asked his wife again.

"Perfectly, Caroline," he responded brusquely, his eyes never straying from the horse. *As well as one can be in this blasted, overcrowded carriage*, he thought to himself.

It was well most of his companions did not know his unkind and ungracious thoughts. There were five people in the carriage, but only four took up seats. The nurse, Mrs. Foley, held his infant daughter Beatrice in her ample arms. She sat opposite him, next to Lady Buford's maid Abigail. Normally, Abigail would travel in the luggage carriage, but that conveyance was unavailable for this trip. A wagon was pressed into service, and Corporal Frost rode alongside.

Buford sat next to the window, his good right arm bracing his body from the worst of the shaking. His injured left leg was extended as far as it could be in the crowded compartment, the extra cushion his wife insisted upon failing to fully alleviate the stiffness he felt while traveling. Caroline shared his seat.

The carriage swayed violently again, sending a sharp shot of pain through Buford's leg. Oh, how he wished this journey were over!

"Sir John," said Mrs. Foley, "I am concerned that all this rocking will disturb the wee babe. My arms—they are not strong enough to protect her. Might I trouble you to—"

"What?" Buford cried, his attention fixed upon his daughter. "What would you have me do?"

She glanced down at her charge. "Miss Beatrice…"

He understood her in an instant. "Here, hand her to me." A moment later, Buford cradled his daughter in his strong right arm. "I need a blanket."

"Here, John," offered Caroline. "Use mine."

He accepted his wife's offering without a word. Together, they wrapped the blanket to serve as padding between the child and the side of the carriage. During the whole of the maneuver, Beatrice only cooed with pleasure. She adored being held by her father.

Buford gazed into the child's bright blue eyes—eyes that mirrored his own—with a tight smile. As always, the warmth of a doting father's love grew in his breast. *This is my child. This is my darling girl. Nothing will harm her. Nothing!* His foul mood faded.

Preoccupied as he was with Beatrice, Buford ignored the jerking and swaying as they continued through the Kent countryside. He never saw the wink the nurse offered Lady Buford.

The Rosings party, including Lady Catherine, stood outside to greet the Bufords. The unremarkable brown carriage, lacking a coat of arms, came to a squeaky stop before the steps while the open luggage wagon continued towards the servants' entrance in the back of the manor.

The driver's assistant, in the unassuming livery of the Buford family, climbed down from the box, let down the step, and opened the door. The carriage shook somewhat, caused by movement inside. Then Sir John appeared, almost leaping out of it as though fleeing something unpleasant. However, with a smile, he instantly took the coachman's place to hand down the others.

Elizabeth was unsurprised at Sir John's black coat and trousers. Like her husband, Buford favored dark hues. What was surprising was Lady Buford's drab dress. Caroline's usual choice was strong or bright colors—green, red, orange, white—but today she wore dove gray. One would think she was in mourning.

Her own dress—steel gray with black trim—was much like Lady Buford's, except for that lady's lack of black gloves and ribbons. It slowly dawned on Elizabeth that Caroline had chosen her colors deliberately, to honor the grief felt by her hosts. Such a depth of feeling was not expected from a woman like Caroline Bingley!

*But, then again*, Elizabeth recalled, *she is Caroline Bingley no longer.*

To Elizabeth's surprise, Sir John handed down a large woman holding a child and then assisted Caroline's personal maid. Commonly, such a service was left to a servant, but the Bufords were very odd about such things. Lady Catherine's snort of disapproval indicated that she, too, had noticed the peculiar behavior.

The Bufords greeted their hosts—Sir John in proper English manner with handshakes and bows while Caroline adopted the French style of kisses on both cheeks favored by her husband's mother. Having visited the Buford's house in London on many occasions, Elizabeth was accustomed to the unorthodox sight.

Lady Catherine was not. Her obvious look of disapproval was a clear sign of that. Fortunately, the Bufords' greeting to her followed the proper protocol.

"Lady Catherine," said Sir John after he and his wife gave their bow and curtsey, "allow me to introduce my daughter, Beatrice Albertine."

It had been several months since Elizabeth had last seen her. Now at eighteen months, the cute baby was becoming a beautiful toddler, inheriting her mother's pale-rose complexion and raven locks, paired with her father's blue eyes. From the safety of the nurse's arms, Beatrice stared with uncertainty at the older woman.

"Harrumph, a pretty enough child, I suppose," the grand dame said in judgment. "What sort of name is Beatrice Albertine? There is nothing suitably English about it."

Elizabeth was mortified on Caroline's behalf. Darcy was grim, and the Fitzwilliams were embarrassed.

However, Sir John spoke diplomatically. "Very true, milady. Albertine is for my mother, who is originally from France. As for Beatrice—Latin for *blessed voyager*—well, if it is good enough for our friend Lady Beatrice, it is good enough for our little girl."

"Lady Beatrice? You mean to say this child is named for Lady Beatrice Wellesley, cousin of the Duke of Wellington? That you *know* her? Preposterous!" Lady Catherine pompously insisted.

Sir John turned to his wife. "I suppose it is too late to request that her ladyship rescind her permission, my dear?"

"Indeed so," Caroline managed through clenched teeth. "Her name is recorded in the baptismal register. Besides, it would never do to so offend Lady Beatrice or the duke."

Buford gave Lady Catherine an apologetic shrug. "It seems there is nothing for it, milady."

Lady Catherine was not finished. "How could someone like *you* know Lord Wellington or his cousin?"

"Mother, that is quite enough!" cried Anne. "Sir John served on the duke's staff for a time, and Lady Buford befriended her ladyship in Vienna. Lady Buford was kind enough to share her letter from Lady Beatrice, expressing her delight at the Bufords's consideration of using her name, and it was dated prior to the birth. You owe the Bufords an apology."

"Well, it seems I was uninformed of all the facts! No offense was intended, Lady Buford." She shook her head and huffed. "One can never tell about these jumped-up Irishmen like the Wellesleys."

There could be no reply to that. Indeed, it could be said the

Fitzwilliams were once jumped-up Irishmen, so the Bufords turned their attentions to the Darcys. As they exchanged kisses, Elizabeth whispered to Caroline her regrets for Lady Catherine's behavior. Caroline nodded but was clearly still outraged.

Anne announced her intention of escorting Lady Buford, Miss Buford, and their servants above stairs to the rooms set aside for them to refresh themselves and rest before dinner. Elizabeth chose to accompany them. The first destination was the nursery. Upon entering, they were affectionately assailed by Chloe Wickham.

"Aunt Lizzy! Aunt Lizzy! Did you bring— Oh!" The child came to a dead stop only steps before them. "Is *that* the baby?" She pointed at the child in Mrs. Foley's arms. "You said a baby was coming."

Elizabeth excused her ward's exuberance. She *was* Lydia's daughter, after all. "Yes, my dear, but I must introduce her mother first."

Chloe stood in nervous excitement as Elizabeth presented her to Lady Buford. "And this," she continued, "is Miss Bea Buford." It had been decided that the children could easily manage *Bea*, rather than attempt *Beatrice*.

A frown creased Chloe's face. "She is too big for a baby."

"Yes, but she is a year younger than Bennet."

Chloe tried to make sense of this. "She is bigger than Franny. Is she older than Franny?" At her aunt's nod, she proclaimed, "Bea is a funny name." She giggled. "Bea! Like a bumble bee!"

Anne hid a laugh as Caroline joined the conversation. "Her real name is Beatrice."

"Like Franny? Her real name is Fran...Fran—Oh, it is too hard!" Chloe smiled. "There are too many big names!"

Mrs. Nivens then brought Bennet over to his mother. With well-practiced efficiency, Elizabeth knelt to pick up her ward in one arm before receiving her son in the other. "There! Now you both may see Miss Bea better."

Two-and-a-half-year-old Bennet was not as interested in the new arrival as his four-year-old cousin. He focused on hugging his mother. While the children were thus occupied, the nannies were introduced, and Mrs. Nivens volunteered to show Mrs. Foley the nursery rooms. She also reported that Miss Frances had been put down for a nap. The ladies spent a little more time with the children before taking their leave, promising to look in again before dinner.

As they followed Anne to the Bufords' rooms, Caroline turned to Elizabeth. "Miss Chloe is a strikingly beautiful child, Eliza. While I can see the resemblance to Phoebe and Rosanna, they are nothing to her." She paused. "You may have trouble with Chloe."

Elizabeth's first response was to be offended—that is, until she perceived the small smile on Caroline's lips. "Ah, you know her parents were both quite handsome. I fear my husband may be more protective of Chloe than even Franny in the years to come!"

Caroline laughed. "I remember well Darcy's protectiveness of Georgiana! Woe to the gentlemen who attempt to dally with his girls. Miss Chloe is in safe hands."

DINNER WAS A CASUAL AFFAIR, EVEN WITH LADY CATHERINE and the Collinses in attendance. Sir Richard sat at the head of the table. To his right were Lady Catherine, then Sir John, Mrs. Collins, and Mr. Darcy. Anne was at the other end, with Lady Buford to her right, then Mr. Collins, Mrs. Jenkinson, and Mrs. Darcy. Caroline was relieved that her husband's black mood had lifted, particularly as he was seated next to Lady Catherine.

The soup course passed without incident, but things changed after the bowls had been removed. Two nice fowls had been roasted to a turn, and the flesh had been sliced in the kitchen. Lady Catherine served herself from the platter, and the maid unthinkingly held it out to Buford.

He stared at it, and realization exploded throughout the room. *How can Sir John cut his fowl?*

Caroline turned red and then white in an instant. The current custom with the Bufords was that plates were assembled in the kitchen, all meat and other items pre-cut into bite-sized pieces. The plates then were set before the diners. No one cut anything at table. Indeed, knifes were not even set out. Caroline had not cut her own meal for nearly a year so as not to diminish her husband. She had meant to speak to Anne about it, but in her excitement to share Beatrice with her friend, she had forgotten.

Caroline was frozen in indecision. She was dismayed, embarrassed, and angry. She wanted to dash to John's side and be useful to him, but nothing came to mind that would not intensely humiliate her husband.

The maid and the majority of the table were struck by the same hesitancy—except for Lady Catherine. She turned to the young maid. "Stupid girl! Can you not see that Sir John is a cripple?"

The statement echoed about the room. Caroline bit back a gasp.

Buford's eyes flicked to the grand dame and then back to the hovering platter. With a rather forced grin, he took the leg from the platter with his hand, placed it on his plate, and indicated that Mrs. Darcy was next, as though it was an everyday occurrence. By then the maid was stuttering her apologies, but Buford would have none of it. He waved her away, declared the leg the choicest part of the bird, and asked if he could bother her for an additional serviette.

"We cannot dirty Lady Fitzwilliam's table, now can we?" Buford said cheerfully. He then took the leg in his hand, took a bite, and nodded in Lady Catherine's direction.

"Well, I never!" cried Lady Catherine.

"My lady, you ought to try it. That is how we ate in Spain, eh, Fitz?"

Caroline almost cheered.

~~~

RICHARD SAT BACK, SIPPING HIS PORT AFTER THE LADIES retired to the parlor. The men remained at the dinner table, enjoying their particular after-meal libation. All took port rather than brandy, but only Darcy and Richard chose to partake of the Fitzwilliam cigar offerings. Buford had never developed a taste for tobacco. As for Mr. Collins, his first and only attempt to smoke a year ago had resulted in a coughing fit that shook the paintings on the wall.

Mr. Collins had commandeered Darcy's attention. Richard felt a bit guilty for his cousin's discomfort and for his lack of desire to relieve him of talking with the fawning fool. *I deal with Collins every day, Darcy. Tonight, it is your turn.*

Richard turned to his old comrade in arms. "So, how are you faring, Buford?"

"I have no complaints."

Buford's flippant comment caused Richard to frown. "You traveled from your brother's estate in Wales, I believe."

"Yes. The roads were in a sorry shape, but other than that..." Buford waved his hand. "The family is well, even Mother. Which reminds me—how is your mother's health?"

So deftly had Buford changed the subject that Richard had no choice but to follow. A discussion of their various absent families ensued, bringing the attention of both Darcy and Collins. Family matters invariably brought up the current political situation. When that subject was fully discussed, it was time to rejoin the ladies.

CAROLINE WAS IN HER NIGHTDRESS AND ROBE, SITTING AT HER looking glass as Abigail braided her hair, when she heard Sir John knock on the bedroom door as he came in. They had been given separate rooms as propriety demanded, but as there were no adjoining rooms in the guest wing, Sir John's chamber was across the hall. His reflection showed him in a robe, standing by the bed, gazing at her back in an affectionate manner.

"John, I am sorry for what happened at dinner."

"No harm done, Caro." Buford was nonchalant.

Caroline was relieved that Sir John's mood remained good. It seemed he had other matters in mind. "I meant to talk to Anne but was distracted by Bea. Forgive me."

"Hah! I can certainly see how my daughter is distracting. Reminds me of another beautiful Buford lady."

Abigail blushed, and Caroline, perturbed for her sake, regretted Buford's habit of flirting with his wife before the servants.

"All done, milady," said the maid. Caroline dismissed her with a smile and turned to her husband.

"You embarrassed her, you know," she said once Abigail had left the room.

"I think she is amused, rather."

"I know *you* are amused," Caroline said as she stepped into his embrace. "I was proud of you tonight."

"For what? 'Tis not the maid's fault." Buford's strong hand caressed her back through her robe.

"I meant Lady Catherine's remark. Horrid woman!"

"What? I *am* a cripple."

"Do not say that!" Caroline demanded with passion.

"Why not? It is true." He began to kiss her neck. "It does not follow that I am completely helpless," he murmured against her soft skin.

Caroline arched into him. This was another of Sir John's habits—making love to her their first night during a visit. She supposed he was proving himself. Not to her—*she* had no doubts. For her part, she was tired. But if it made him happy…

"Show me, Johnny," she purred in his ear. "Show me how accomplished you are."

*He was galloping through the mist across a featureless landscape, his lady sharing his horse. She sat behind him, astride, her soft arms wrapped desperately about his waist. They were fleeing the nameless, faceless terror chasing them. They rode as fast as they dared. With the ground level and the horse surefooted, they had a chance of escape.*

*He would be enjoying this ride, given the feel of her curves against his back and the tightness of her grip on his person, were it not for the seriousness of their situation. Concern triumphed over lust. He would see his love safe, even at the cost of his own life.*

*The mist had turned the world to gray. It was difficult to see more than a few yards ahead. The pair traveled mostly by instinct. Forward was safety. Behind them was death.*

*He had just consoled her, telling her once again all would be well, when the air cleared. Before them were scores of figures in black, each upon an ebony horse. The horror surrounded them. There would be no easy escape. He had to fight his way through their enemies.*

*His right hand let loose the reins, intending them for his left while he drew his sword. But there was no left hand. His arm was missing. Desperately, he gripped the horse's flanks with his thighs, pain shooting through his damaged hip. The pair fought to maintain their balance as they wheeled about, their enemies drawing closer. He pulled his blade.*

*Caroline's screams filled his ears as the figures fell upon them.*

"John! John! Wake up! 'Tis the dream again!" cried Caroline.

Buford awakened. He was lying in bed, drenched in sweat, and his wife was shaking him.

"You are well. You are safe," she softly said, stroking his shoulder.

"I-I...Forgive me," Buford managed, fighting to stop shaking, anger replacing his fear. "I woke you."

"It is no matter."

"Yes, it is!" Buford bit out the words. "You were asleep, and I awoke you! Again! You should not have to tolerate this!"

"John..."

"No!" Buford rubbed his hand across his face. "I should sleep elsewhere."

There was a long pause. "You wish to leave?"

"Yes! No! I—" Buford stared at the bed's canopy. "You need

your rest, and I—I am a…distraction."

"Is that what you think you are? A distraction?"

*At the very least*, he thought. *A burden, a curse.* "I do not wish to be a bother."

There was another pause before Caroline responded. "I would choose for you to remain, if I am not a *bother* to you, of course."

"It is not you who are the bother. I am."

Caroline moved to lightly embrace him. "Perhaps, but I knew that when I married you. You *bothered* me until I accepted you." She kissed his shoulder. "You were very persistent."

The last of Buford's mortification and frustration melted away. He reached over and gently stroked her cheek with his fingers. "I do not deserve you."

She kissed his palm. "Perhaps. Or perhaps we deserve each other. In any case, I am yours. Go to sleep, my love."

# Chapter 15

Richard was at the breakfast table early the next morning in his riding clothes, eating a bit of the fowl from the night before, when Buford limped in. "Good morning. I left a leg for you."

"Some people would take offense at that, you know." Buford poured a cup of coffee.

"I have said worse." Richard then noticed that Buford looked terrible—his eyes red and his complexion pale. "I say, old man, do you wish to put off our ride this morning?"

"I am well, I assure you," he said, making a point of dropping the leg onto a plate. "Let me gnaw on this a bit, and we shall be off. Does Darcy join us?"

"No, he has already eaten and left."

Thirty minutes later, the two gentlemen made their way to the stables, accompanied by Sergeant Gregory and Corporal Frost. Quicksilver and Hannibal were saddled and ready, as well as a mount for Gregory. Frost helped his master to the mounting block, and soon Sir John was safely astride his horse.

"Let Lady Buford know we have gone," Buford instructed his man. "We should be back before midday."

"Aye, sir. Good ride, gentlemen." Frost waved as the three men set out.

It was a fine, June day, if a bit cool. The sun was high in the sky, and the grass was green. Richard led the way, slowing Quicksilver's pace in deference to Sir John. His friend did not like it.

"Deuce take it, Fitz! I am not in leading strings! Ride on!"

Buford spurred Hannibal into a gallop, forcing the others to give chase. The three dashed along the hills and dales of Kent, enjoying the exercise and comradeship. They slowed as they neared the village.

"I must leave you, sir," said Gregory. "I have business with Mr. Evans and Mr. Clarke." The majordomo rode towards Hunsford, and the two former cavalrymen loped off in the opposite direction.

The pace easier, conversation could be had. "I say, the crops here are as bad as they are in Wales."

"Blasted weather! Mr. Evans tells me the planting was at least a month late. If the weather would just warm!" He turned to Buford. "You take an eager interest in my harvest. Since when did you pay the least attention to farming?"

"I had nothing else to do, living with my brother."

Richard frowned at that. The pair came to a creek, and Fitzwilliam suggested they rest the horses. He quickly dismounted and rushed to his friend before he tried to climb down from the saddle.

"Leave off! I can do this," Buford growled at him.

"Stop being a mule and allow me to help you."

"Go to the devil, Fitzwilliam!"

Richard grinned. "No doubt I shall. Caroline will make certain of it should any injury befall you, so be a good fellow and take my hand."

Buford glowered and reluctantly did as he was bidden. The horses were secured to a low branch, permitting them to graze, and the gentlemen made their way to a fallen log. Buford sat down, but Richard did not. Instead, he tossed his friend a small flask.

"Brandy," Richard answered Buford's unasked question. "Drink up and tell me how you are faring. And none of that folderol from last night. We are brothers in arms, blast it, and you will tell me true!" He crossed his arms.

Buford managed to open the flask with one hand and took a sip. "I have been better. Is that what you want me to say?"

"Are you in pain? Is there nothing you can take for your relief?"

Buford stretched his leg. "No, nothing. The hip is not so bad most days—just stiff. Other times…sitting in a coach for hours is hard work."

"And the arm?" Richard leaned against a tree.

Buford glanced down at the half empty sleeve. "I am coming to terms with it, I think. Oh, it does not hurt in the least. Strangest thing though. Sometimes it itches. Not the stump—my forearm. The missing forearm." He looked up at Richard. "How can I feel something that is not there?"

Richard shook his head. "I never heard of such a thing. What does the doctor say?"

"Macmillan says it is usual in cases like mine but gives no other answers. It is deuced distracting, I can tell you."

The two old comrades were silent for a time, enjoying the morning air.

"Do you have nightmares, Fitz?" Buford asked quietly.

"Sometimes. Not as much as when I first came home. You had one last night, I take it?"

"I look that awful? No, do not answer me. Yes, I did, a bad one. Too often I get no rest."

"Surely, Mr. Macmillan can concoct a draught of—"

"By the infernal, no!" Buford cried. "Do you remember General Norwich, who lost his leg in Spain? The man is now a complete drunkard. I may be useless, but I shall not lose myself in drink or draughts!"

"Yes, I saw poor old Norwich in a sad shape last year at Boodle's. But what is this about being useless? You are not useless, Buford— far from it!"

"That is easy for you to say. I cannot fence, or shoot, or fish. All sport is beyond me."

"That is not true." At Buford's furious look, Richard quickly added, "I do not mock you. You know me better than that. You can ride, for example."

"Yes, the cavalry taught us to ride one-handed," Buford held up his right arm, "but with the wrong hand! I am still not used to using the reins with my right."

"You have no need for a sword in England, Buford."

"I might, with your impertinence!"

Richard laughed. "You would have to catch me first, and you have never been able to do that."

"Just wait, you popinjay! I shall have you singing another tune soon!"

"I look forward to it. And what is this about fencing? You still can hold a foil."

Buford sighed. "The balance is all wrong. Besides, with this hip, I cannot push off in attack."

"Then I might actually have a chance against you."

For the first time, Buford grinned. "That I doubt!"

"We shall practice together and strengthen that leg. And Darcy gave me a pair of rifled pistols. What say to a spot of target shooting, eh?"

"I suppose." He took another pull of the brandy.

"Buford, forgive me, but all this sitting about does you no good. You are like me. You must have an occupation. What happened to your plans to stand for Parliament?"

"I may still do that…someday."

"What are you waiting for? If there is no open seat in Wales, you can find some pocket borough that will suit! My family controls a few in the north."

"I dislike the idea of rotten boroughs, Fitz. Besides, where would I get the thousands of pounds I would need to get elected?"

"As you will. What about the Foreign Office or Whitehall? Surely Castlereagh or York can use a man with your gift for languages."

Buford was incredulous. "Go back into the army or work as a clerk?"

"That is not my meaning! You know there are many gentlemen, even peers, who serve the King in Whitehall. Write to Wellington. You worked with him before. He likes you and few have his connections. He will help you if you but ask."

"It may mean travel outside the country."

"What of it? Caroline adores travel. She glows when she speaks of Vienna. She is not attached to an estate, and to tell the truth, I do not think she would care to be." At Buford's incredulous look, he added, "I know a fashionable country house is expected of a gentleman, and Caroline is a wonderful hostess, but an estate is more than that. Think of your brother's responsibilities. He thrives because he is like Darcy. There is nothing that needs to be done that he does not do himself. He and Mrs. Buford are hardly in town. I do not think that is the life Caroline desires."

"True," Buford allowed.

Richard saw that Buford was carefully considering the idea. "If you need another opinion, talk to Darcy or write to Brandon."

Buford looked at his friend. "I shall think on this, Fitz, I promise you. Thank you." He tossed the flask back to Richard. "But I believe the ladies should be at breakfast by now. Shall we ride back and join them?"

ANNE CAME DOWN FROM HER ROOM, NOT SURPRISED TO FIND Elizabeth and Mrs. Jenkinson already at the table. She partook of a light breakfast and tea, enjoying inconsequential conversation with her friends until Lady Buford joined them.

Anne saw in an instant that Caroline was out of sorts. "My dear Caroline, are you well?"

Twin spots of color bloomed on Caroline's pale cheeks. "Perfectly well, I assure you." She sat at table rather than helping herself to the sideboard. To a maid, she requested dry toast, tea, and orange marmalade.

This was most unlike her friend! Anne's innate *de Bourgh* personality burst forth. "Caroline, such a breakfast! I insist you tell me what ails you!"

"I beg your pardon. I simply adore your marmalade. You must tell me where you get it."

Anne could not abide evasion. "That is not what I mean!" Her sharp words caught Mrs. Jenkinson's attention, and she gave a disapproving look to her former charge.

Anne regained her composure. "Caroline, excuse me, I do not intend to offend. It is unlike you to eat so little, and it raised my concern for your health. I do not mean to pry. Pray ignore my outburst."

"It is forgot, Anne. Sir John had a restless night, is all. My sleep was interrupted."

Anne's eyes grew wide. She could hear her husband from his bedroom? Anne had heard nothing, but the guest quarters were on the other side of the house.

Caroline's face turned red. "Oh, I should not have said that!"

Anne realized what Caroline's words had revealed. *Sir John had been in Caroline's bed all night!* Anne was mortified for her friend. She then noticed that, while Mrs. Jenkinson was as embarrassed as she was, Elizabeth was not.

Caroline attempted to recover her dignity. "I love the Bufords dearly," she said dryly, "but close contact with my family does have its hazards. On occasion, I forget that the informality at Buford Manor is the exception in polite society, not the rule. I hope I do not shock you."

"Of course not," Anne prevaricated. "But if your rooms are unsatisfactory—"

Now Caroline laughed. "It would make no difference, I am afraid." Her eyes darted to Elizabeth. "That your friends should suffer this state of affairs cannot be a surprise to you. I know you have spent much time at Pemberley." She hid a grin as she sipped her tea.

Anne colored. All of the family knew of the Darcys infamous practice of sharing a bedroom. Pemberley was one of the grand houses in Derbyshire, and the mistress's apartments were the envy of many, yet it was used only as a dressing room. The younger generation leniently ignored it, her late uncle put it down as an eccentricity Darcy had obviously inherited from his father, and Lady Catherine was scandalized, certain that this behavior was evidence of the pollution Mrs. Darcy infected on Pemberley's shades.

Apparently, the Bufords shared the Darcys' custom in sleeping arrangements! Anne's face grew hot.

Elizabeth spoke calmly. "I see nothing wrong with such a practice." Her eyes twinkled.

It was left to Mrs. Jenkinson to salvage the conversation. "Nor should you, Mrs. Darcy. Such business is the concern of those involved and no one else. Would you pass the tea?"

Anne was eternally grateful that the gentlemen chose that moment to join them from their morning ride. Conversation moved to safer subjects.

ONCE THE LADIES WERE FINISHED, THE GENTLEMEN EXCUSED themselves to attend to letters of business. Lady Buford and Mrs. Darcy announced they were for the nursery, while Mrs. Jenkinson intended to go to the village. Anne decided to join her friends, and within a few minutes, she watched with amusement as the once haughty Miss Bingley knelt on the carpeted floor of the room, joyfully playing with her infant daughter while Elizabeth bounced her youngest on her lap. Bennet Darcy stood by his mother, quietly clutching her skirt while Chloe Wickham watched Caroline with interest.

"Come, Bea," said Caroline, "say 'Mama.'"

Beatrice looked up at her mother, smiled prettily, and said, "Papa."

"No, no!" laughed Caroline. "Mama."

The child giggled, her ebony curls bouncing about her pink face. "Papa, Papa, Papa!"

"Is the baby too little to say 'Mama'?" asked Chloe.

Caroline smiled ruefully at her friends as she gathered Beatrice into her arms. "Perhaps. She only has eyes for her father, I am afraid. He is her favorite, and the feeling is quite mutual. I can get nothing out of her, save 'Papa.'"

"Papa, Papa, Papa!" Beatrice exclaimed, as she buried her face in Caroline's chest.

"I can say 'Papa,'" Chloe proudly proclaimed.

"Of course, you can, dear," said Elizabeth to her ward before reassuring Caroline. "I should not worry. She seems happy where she is. Such a grasp she has on your dress!"

Caroline kissed the top of her daughter's head. "She is a dear, sweet child."

"She has the look of Sir John about her, particularly the eyes," claimed Anne.

"And your hair," added Elizabeth.

Anne laughed. "If she grows up half as handsome as her mother, you will have suitors all about!"

"Heaven forbid!" cried Caroline. "Sir John cannot bear to think of it. He has already loaded his pistols!"

"You have done well with her," observed Elizabeth.

Caroline slowly stroked the wiggling girl's black tresses. "I own myself astounded, Eliza. Years ago, I was mocked that I would feel this way. It was at my engagement ball on New Year's Eve in the year fourteen—do you recall? I was teased that I would be the most attentive of mothers, that I would allow no one to touch my children but myself. Mrs. Norris said it to be cruel, but how right she was!" Caroline hugged the baby to her breast. "I adore her—I, who never thought of children before in my life! Is that not strange?"

Elizabeth reached down to caress Bennet's hair. "Not so strange."

Tears pricked Anne's eyes, and she tried not to sniffle. Her friends' words brought back what she had lost last year. She forced herself to smile. *I must not be despondent. Our time will come.*

Caroline seemed to sense her mood, for in the next instant, she offered Beatrice to Anne. For the next half an hour, the three ladies took turns holding and playing with the children. Chloe fairly glorified in the attention. Bennet, ever his father's son, tolerated the troublesome fussing with a scowl. Frances's impressions were a mystery. Finally, Beatrice yawned, which was the signal for the nurses to reclaim their charges.

The ladies left quietly and parted in the hall. Elizabeth desired to practice her music, and Anne accepted Caroline's request to take a turn in the gardens.

ANNE HAD A SERVANT BRING ROMEO TO HER FOR THE OUTING, and the ladies were amused for a time watching the little dog dash about the gardens at an astonishing pace, chasing insects and sunbeams. It was not long before the beast tired itself out, and when Anne and Caroline sat on a bench, Romeo dutifully made himself comfortable at his mistress's feet.

"I own I have never seen a dog run so fast," admitted Caroline. "He seems a sweet little thing."

"Yes," said Anne fondly, "he is my darling boy. Have you an interest in Italian greyhounds?"

Caroline looked scandalized. "Oh, no thank you, Anne. Your house is yours, and you shall do as you please, but I have no interest in a house dog. Sir John enjoys his hunting dogs well enough, but happily, they live out-of-doors at Buford Manor. What they do I neither know nor care as long as my house is safe from them. I could not stand the hair."

As Anne adored her pet, she could not but be a little nettled at Caroline's statement. Her expression must have revealed her feelings, for in the next moment, Caroline was all apologies.

"Not that I have any complaints about Rosings! No, indeed! I must compliment your servants. Why, one would not know there even was a dog in the house."

Anne coolly assured her that she would pass along her praise.

Caroline held a hand to her forehead. "Pray, forgive me, dearest. I have yet to overcome my tendency to speak too freely. I meant no insult, truly."

Anne, mollified, took her friend's hand. "It is all forgot."

Caroline looked at Anne in her dove grey and white. "How are you bearing up, Anne?"

"It is well you have come. The last six months have been weighing on us. My uncle Hugh was so…so much larger than life. He was exceedingly kind to Richard and me. It is hard to accept that he is gone." She sighed and pulled her wrap tightly around her, thankful for the sunlight. "With the troubles in Derbyshire and Ireland—you know my Fitzwilliam cousins have property there—and this most unusual weather, I own we need diversion."

"It is the same in Wales. We hope things are better this summer than last. I am worried for Charles and Jane, and the Darcys too."

"Elizabeth said things are calm at Pemberley. What is the news from Mayfield?"

"There is as much unrest in Nottinghamshire as Derbyshire. I love my brother dearly, but"—she sighed—"Charles is not Darcy. Pemberley is the only place I know where the servants are as loyal as our people at Buford Manor."

Anne glanced at Caroline. "I have heard of no disturbances here." Anne also knew that despite all attempts to build loyalty, most of Rosings's servants were not steadfast in their fidelity. Memories of Lady Catherine's misrule were too ingrained. Only the housekeeper, the butler, and Sergeant Gregory were unquestionably trusted.

"Oh, no!" Caroline assured her. "Kent is peaceful and quiet. Almost too quiet for my taste. I must admit I enjoy the noise and diversions of London." She played absently with the ribbon from her bonnet. "Anne, there is another reason I was out of looks this morning. It seems I am with child again."

Anne cried out joyfully and hugged her friend. "I am so happy for you!" She tried to ignore the flare of jealousy that coursed through her. "Does Sir John hope for a boy this time?"

"He said no, but I do not believe him," Caroline said firmly. "Gentlemen want boys." Her face became hopeful. "Do you have any news for us?"

Pained, Anne turned away. "No."

Caroline groaned. "Forgive me! I was thoughtless again. You must not mind me. Your time will come. I am sure of it!"

Anne forced herself to hide her disappointments and fears. "I am sure you are right."

ELIZABETH HAD BEEN AT THE INSTRUMENT ONLY A SHORT TIME when she was distracted by a gentleman's entrance.

"Pray, do not let me disturb you," Darcy said.

She gifted him with a bright, private laugh. "It has been many years since your presence disturbed me, my love. Did you enjoy your ride?"

Darcy frowned as he unconsciously glanced at himself. He had changed out of his riding clothes. "It was...informative."

Elizabeth shook her head. Darcy again rode the grounds of Rosings to inspect them. She needed to rid herself of her slight irritation at his scrutiny. She rose, extending her hand. "Come—I long to enjoy a good walk with you."

A handsome half smile graced his face. "I am at your disposal, as always, my dearest."

SOMETIME LATER, THE DARCYS WERE DEEP IN THE GROVES OF Rosings Park. The two conversed about topics important only to themselves while walking comfortably, nearly hip to hip as happily married people often do. Elizabeth, both arms wrapped about Darcy's, was laughing over her husband's droll commentary about

Mr. Collins's latest foible when she was brought to a halt so suddenly that she nearly lost her footing.

"Fitzwilliam! What on earth?"

Darcy stared straight ahead, his expression a mixture of distaste and mortification. "Forgive me, my dear," he managed after a moment. "Let us turn back to the house."

"But why?" Elizabeth looked about. "The weather is not uncomfortable, and I wish more time with you. Are you well?"

"Perfectly. There is a path over here."

"If you wish." Elizabeth could not understand Darcy's actions. There was nothing amiss with their present location. It was a well-worn path along a fence. There was a gate nearby.

"Come, Elizabeth." Darcy practically tugged her along.

"What is wrong? You act as though you wish to flee this place."

"You cannot want to be *here*!"

Elizabeth was taken aback at the pain in her husband's eyes. Such a statement could only cause her to glance about her again. There was something familiar about that gate.

"*Oh…!*"

"There, you see?" Darcy moaned. "I should have minded my steps better."

Elizabeth was frozen in place. This was the spot she received his letter—*the* letter—the missive that had so changed her life.

The entire incident flashed before her mind. *Her disjointed early morning stroll, her thoughts, both angry and regretful. His surprising appearance. The thick letter extending over the gate in his long fingers. His haughty request at war with his weary, pained, defeated expression. His stiff, measured escape. His written words—his terrible, awful, horrifying, wonderful, charitable words.*

"This was the place," Elizabeth whispered, her eyes wide. "How could I forget?"

"I am so sorry, my dear. I have ruined our walk. Come away from here."

"You have ruined nothing, Fitzwilliam," she returned, refusing to be moved, still staring at the gate. "I can only wonder at my negligence. This spot should be burnt into my memory."

"You wish to remember my dreadful behavior?"

"No!" Elizabeth turned to him, taking both his hands in hers. "Do you not see, my love? This is the place of our beginning!" At his frown, she continued. "Before that day—before your letter—I was a proud, blind fool. You opened my eyes, and I saw myself for the first time. I realized how in love with myself I had been—how stupidly I had acted."

"I was worse!"

Elizabeth smiled, her fingers stroking his firm, chiseled jaw. It calmed him, as she knew it would. "Our motives were different. You acted out of self-preservation and love of your family and friends. I had no idea how hunted you had been by the women of the *ton*. Who could imagine the pain and disappointment Georgiana suffered at the hands of Wickham or her fear of exposure? With Charles, you acted as a friend, for you could not see emotions Jane refuse to display."

"I should have," Darcy broke in. "I should have known her by my own example."

She laughed. "I shall allow that! But your reserve was not the only reason I misunderstood and misjudged you."

"My thoughtless comment at the assembly was inexcusable." He grimaced in disgust.

"It was rude, my dear, and a bad start but not inexcusable. You showed your interest in me only a few days later at the Lucas's party and again at Netherfield. If I had been in my right mind, I would have forgiven you and fallen in love at once. I certainly never should have paid Mr. Wickham any notice at all! But there was nothing noble in my actions. I intended to hurt and belittle you for the petty crime of bruising my vanity. I was an angry little girl."

She turned her attention to the gate. "At this place, I became a new creature. At this painful, wonderful place, my heart was opened, for I then saw it was incomplete." Her dark, sparkling eyes were on Darcy again. "It was at Pemberley that I finally admitted what my heart was missing: you, my dearest love. *You.*"

There was only one way Darcy could respond to her declaration. He swept his wife into his arms and kissed her senseless. In turn, she wrapped her arms about his neck and returned his passion fully. They only stopped for the need to breathe.

Darcy tilted his head so their foreheads touched. "I must disagree, Elizabeth. You did nothing wrong. I deserved your refusal, your censure. I was a fool. You are the saving of me. You have made me a better man."

"Impossible."

He shook his head slowly. "I shall no longer argue with you for the greater share of the blame. Instead, I vow to labor that you never have cause to regret marrying me."

She grinned. "Impossible."

Darcy chuckled. "It is you who are impossible! However can I convince you?"

Her voice was a caress. "Kiss me again."

Sometime later, as they stood in a close embrace, Elizabeth said, "I have a request to make, my dear. I need to change your mind about this blessed spot. We shall have a picnic here one day—just the two of us."

Darcy was unconvinced. "How will that change our memories?"

Elizabeth gave her husband her most playful look. "We shall think of something."

# Chapter 16

The next morning, Anne remained above stairs due to her monthly indisposition. Her guests despaired of her company yet found the courage to continue with their plans. Darcy rode out again early, his destination known only to him.

The day being fine, the other gentleman decided on pistol shooting for their sport and left for the far side of the estate where, it was hoped, their planned destruction of hapless straw bales would alarm no one.

Elizabeth never failed to take advantage of pleasant weather to enjoy a good ramble, but when Lady Buford indicated an interest in joining her, Elizabeth's plans for a longer walk were deterred, and she had to be satisfied with a stroll about Rosings's gardens.

Elizabeth tied the black ribbons of her bonnet as Caroline descended the stairs. She felt a short jolt of envy, for Caroline's pale-yellow gown was just the color that suited Elizabeth's fancy. As it was, propriety demanded she remain in half mourning, and she consoled herself that her lavender dress was attractive, even with black trim. With a minimum of conversation, the ladies left the house.

Elizabeth's walks were more than a simple morning constitutional. She used her time out of doors to clear her thoughts and settle her feelings. Sometimes she simply strolled about, allowing the sunshine and fresh air to soothe and refresh her. Other times, she used the peace and quiet to ponder questions and decide matters. Today was to be the latter, the reason being the presence of her companion.

As they moved silently along the rose bushes, Elizabeth glanced at Lady Buford. There was little outward change from the Miss Bingley she knew. Caroline remained a strikingly handsome lady with black hair and green eyes. Taller than she, Lady Buford moved with a practiced grace that could only come from endless repetition at a lady's seminary. Caroline's sense of fashion had always been very fine, though perhaps it was a little less showy now that she was married.

It was Caroline's character that confounded Elizabeth. Upon meeting her, Elizabeth had settled that Miss Bingley had been a rude and grasping snob. Intent on setting aside her roots in trade, she had flattered her betters and dismissed those she considered beneath her, using titles and income as her guide. She had been malicious and ridiculous in her pursuit of Mr. Darcy. Worse, she had been one of the instigators in separating her brother, Charles, from Elizabeth's sister Jane. Caroline Bingley had been Elizabeth Bennet's enemy.

However, two years after she had made that judgment, Elizabeth began to note a change in Miss Bingley. She had sincerely apologized to Elizabeth and to Jane, now Mrs. Bingley. She became a useful member of the Bingley household. She withdrew from the company of the cruelest members of the *ton*. And most astonishing of all, Caroline had befriended Mary Bennet of all people.

*Mary!* The thought caused Elizabeth to blush with guilt. It was no secret that, growing up, Elizabeth had felt closest to Jane. Kitty and Lydia had been inseparable until Lydia's elopement with Mr. Wickham. Poor Mary had been left to her own devices.

After her marriage to Mr. Darcy, Elizabeth took Kitty into

her home, her intention to improve both her and her new sister, Georgiana. The plan worked to perfection: Kitty became sensible and Georgiana livelier. Both would marry well and, to Elizabeth's joy, settle in Derbyshire.

Mary was left in Jane's care. At the time, the Bingleys resided at Netherfield, and Mary expressed a desire to remain in Meryton. But soon, Jane fell with child, and there was no time for her sister. Instead, Mary had been left with only the company of Miss Bingley.

Even now, Elizabeth could not understand the ladies' friendship. How was it that a strait-laced, simple girl and a disappointed sycophant could suffer to be in the same room, much less form a close and endearing attachment? To her regret, Elizabeth knew Mary had grown more devoted to Caroline than to her.

Elizabeth's great fault was the same as her husband's: she hated being wrong. But wrong she had been about both Mary and Caroline. Elizabeth had ignored and, to her shame, occasionally belittled Mary Bennet. Once her sister became Mary Tucker, married to an intelligent, remarkable, and affectionate young man, she turned into a rather impressive lady. Elizabeth was proud of her and ashamed of her previous sentiments.

As for her opinion of Caroline Bingley, despite Elizabeth's precept of remembering the past only as it gives you pleasure, she could never forget the terrible year of 1815. The peace for which they had so long prayed was shattered by Napoleon's escape from Elba. Many of their friends were called to fight him: Richard, Colonel Brandon, Sir John—even George Wickham, Lydia's husband. And when the battle was done, the horror continued. Wickham was dead, and Sir John was grievously wounded. It was feared Buford would die.

It was then that Caroline rose to the occasion. Without a word of complaint, she nursed her husband, saving his life and remaining limbs—all while carrying their unborn child! Elizabeth had witnessed this. She had been impressed and surprised—and humbly grateful *she* had not been put to such a test.

Lady Buford was a woman to respect. Why, then, was she not her true friend? Why did they remain only pleasant acquaintances? Whose choice was that?

"I must say the roses are quite beautiful," observed Caroline, breaking the silence.

The offhand comment interrupted Elizabeth's increasingly troubled thoughts. "Yes, they are."

"Anne is fortunate in her gardener."

Elizabeth could not suppress a giggle. "She is fortunate in her *parson*, rather."

Caroline came to a dead stop. "I beg your pardon?"

"The Rosings gardener follows Mr. Collins's suggestions," Elizabeth responded, her eyes sparkling, "whose talents in the garden are unquestioned. The few books in the parsonage library are of a horticultural bent. It is his passion, unlike sermon making."

Caroline nodded while Elizabeth reviewed her last statement with regret. Why could she not praise Mr. Collins's accomplishments without demeaning his shortcomings? Why could she not be kinder to him?

"He is your cousin, I believe."

Elizabeth could not help but be suspicious of Caroline's meaning. "He is." They continued their walk.

"And heir to your father's estate as I recall." Caroline glanced at her. "Are you resentful it will not remain in your immediate family?"

"No, I am not. I have had all my life to prepare for that eventuality as I have no brothers. Charlotte will make an excellent mistress of Longbourn. For obvious reasons, I pray it is not too soon."

"Certainly." Caroline frowned. "I admit I would not be so generous were I in your place."

Elizabeth smiled to herself. That remark reflected more of the Caroline she knew! "Would you have married the heir, then? Becoming mistress of Longbourn is a delightful accomplishment."

Caroline stopped abruptly again, her eyes wide and lips tight.

She was obviously holding back an insulting comment, which caused Elizabeth to laugh delightfully. "You do not have to answer! Instead, let us be thankful for the gift my cousin has given Rosings by marrying Charlotte!"

Caroline smirked. "You are very wicked, Eliza!"

"An attribute we share?" she returned good-naturedly.

Caroline's smile disappeared, and Elizabeth's happy mood evaporated at her companion's sudden discomfort. Elizabeth's apology was on her lips when Caroline spoke again.

"I try no longer to be so." The lady was uneasy.

"Forgive me. I tease far too—"

"No," Caroline interrupted, "you do not. There is a world of difference between playful teasing and hurtful comments. I should know."

Elizabeth took her hand. "As I have told you before, it is all forgot."

Caroline offered a small smile. "And as *I* have told you before, I am not as generous as you. I must remember ere I fall back into bad behavior."

"Is there bad behavior in your treatment of Mary? You are her friend, and that alone makes you mine." As she said it, Elizabeth realized it was true. Caroline Buford was her friend, and it was astonishing!

"Mary…" Caroline bit her lip. "She is a true sister to me. I cannot say how it came to be, but there it is." She looked at Elizabeth, apprehension in her eyes. "You do not resent it, I hope?"

"No! How could I when she is so happy?" That Elizabeth felt guilty over it she did not say. "All she talks of is her Thomas and you."

"And Rosanna," Caroline pointed out.

Elizabeth laughed. "Yes, and Rosanna!"

"She is fortunate to have her. There is no Rosanna for poor Anne," Caroline said with surprising insight.

Elizabeth squeezed her hand. "They have not been married two years. All in God's time." Elizabeth hoped more than believed this.

"I thank the Lord for Beatrice."

"And I am thankful for my children." Elizabeth grinned. "But surely you are thankful for more than just your daughter?" She gave a pointed look at Caroline's waist.

Her companion was stunned. "How did you know?"

"My aunt could always spot the signs, and so can I."

"I shall not ask your secret, Eliza. I would be mortified to know."

Elizabeth laughed again. This had proven to be a delightful walk! Why on earth would she wish to be alone? "Caroline, if we are to be friends, I should like to be Lizzy to you."

"*Lizzy?*" Caroline looked as if she bit into something distasteful. "Indeed, I could never call you by a child's name like Lizzy. You are *Eliza*," she said firmly.

Elizabeth pursed her lips. "Of my friends, only you and Charlotte call me Eliza."

"Then, that proves she is a wise woman."

"Shall I call you Caro, then?"

"Pray do not!" Caroline cried. "Only one person is allowed to call me that." She smiled. "He is jealous of the privilege."

They both giggled at that.


Darcy walked towards the Rosings home farm vegetable gardens in the bright, late morning sun with a very unusual companion.

"Forgive me, sir, but are you certain you can determine why the gardens are failing?"

Mr. Collins bowed. "Mr. Darcy, I thank you for your generous condescension. While it is my solemn duty to care for the spiritual needs of my flock, what passion I can spare from my dearest Charlotte and sweet children I spend in my garden. It is my most perfect joy to study the words of Our Lord, but I do take some little time to devour any book or pamphlet I can procure on horticulture. It is not proper, I know, to boast of one's abilities, but I believe I can humbly say that my gardens are some of the finest in the district."

Somehow, Darcy refrained from rolling his eyes at the man's pompous chattering. He never would have called on Mr. Collins's help, except that no one at Rosings could explain why the vegetable gardens were failing. Money intended for repairs to the estate and support for the needy had to be used instead to purchase food for the manor's table.

Richard left the enquiry to Mr. Evans, but Darcy was unimpressed with that man's efforts. Evans owned some talent, he allowed, but the steward spent much of his time disparaging the tenants' work and flattering Lady Catherine's vanity. It appeared he had taken Mr. Collins's place in humoring the grand dame's sizeable conceit. Evans simply ordered the gardeners to redouble their efforts, and he was disinclined to investigate the cause of the crops dying.

In Darcy's mind, this was foolish and irresponsible. True to his exacting nature, the master of Pemberley took it upon himself to learn why Rosings had suffered such a calamity. It had been his obligation in the five years following his father's death to assist Lady Catherine and oversee Rosings's steward. Though he had lost that duty in the wake of his marriage to Elizabeth, it was hard to break the habit.

All of Darcy's inquiries had come to naught. Baffled, he reluctantly agreed to Mrs. Collins's suggestion that her husband might prove useful. Thus, he now found himself walking beside the heavy-set cleric, followed by a livery-clad footman holding a folded blanket.

"And you can tell us what is wrong with the gardens?" Darcy repeated.

"I can promise nothing, my dear sir, but I shall use all my knowledge and faculties in the service of my generous patroness."

Darcy was struck by a certain word. "Faculties, Mr. Collins?"

The vicar nodded, his attention focused on the gardens. It was in shambles. Few plants had grown, and of those, most were brown and wilted. The rest of the patch was a mixture of dead plants and bare soil.

"A disgrace, sir," Mr. Collins said, an uncommon frown marking his countenance. "An absolute disgrace."

Darcy abstained from pointing out that the rector was stating the obvious. "Extra manure has been introduced with little success. The gardener is at a loss what to do next."

"I am not surprised," Mr. Collins mumbled. He then caught himself and continued in a louder voice, engaging in voracious commendation of the Rosings staff for their loyalty and diligence. Darcy was sorry to hear it. He liked and respected succinctly blunt honesty and had no use for flowery, long-winded false praise.

"I am certain the field hands will welcome your approbation, Mr. Collins. To the matter before us—have you anything to offer that might reverse this state of affairs?"

"It cannot be the weather," Mr. Collins stated with some authority. "It is unnaturally cool, to be sure, but it is not impossible to grow vegetables, as proven by the bounty in my own humble garden. If you will permit me…"

He turned to the footman and retrieved the blanket he insisted the man carry. Mr. Collins then placed the cloth on the ground, knelt on it, and handed his squat, wide-brimmed hat to the servant. To Darcy's utter astonishment, the man bent over until his nose was an inch above the soil. He then began to sniff the ground, much like fox hounds during the hunt.

If Darcy thought this behavior bizarre, what happened next caused him to doubt the cleric's sanity. He had pinched a bit of soil and placed it in his mouth!

Mr. Collins returned to a kneeling position, a look of satisfaction on his face. "It is as I feared. Mr. Darcy, these gardens must be abandoned. The soil has been salted."

It took a moment for Mr. Collins's words to be understood. "Salted? Are you certain?"

"Oh yes, there is no doubt about it. Would you care for a taste?" The fool was serious! "I thank you, no."

Mr. Collins surveyed the expanse before him, his hands on his knees. "It is no wonder the Rosings gardener was defeated. A cursory examination would be unprofitable in determining the cause. There is no smell or visible evidence, you see, save the dead plants. Only a small amount of salt is required to produce these results; therefore, the gardeners would not see it, particularly after a rain. I suspected such a thing, and the lack of odor made me confident in my speculation. However, tasting the soil was the only method to prove my hypothesis."

The large, heavy man struggled to rise, and Darcy grasped his upper arm to help him to his feet. "Thank you, my dear sir! That my cousin's noble husband, a man of stature and importance in the world, should show such consideration to my undeserving self is condescension indeed! Pray, use my handkerchief to clean your hand!"

"Thank you, no, Mr. Collins," said an embarrassed Darcy as he stepped back and withdrew a square from his pocket. "I always use my own."

"Of course, of course!" Mr. Collins replaced his hat on his head while he contemplated the gardens. "Yes, this plot must be abandoned. The salt has ruined the soil, and no amount of manure can save it. New gardens must be prepared at no little distance from here, lest the salt leech into the good soil."

The cleric turned to Darcy in a fury. "Whoever did this should be severely punished. This cannot be an accident, Mr. Darcy. This was deliberate! This was malicious! To destroy, perhaps forever, a part of the Lord's world…this lovely garden—" He shut his lips into a tight, white line as he struggled with his anger. "Who could have committed such a wicked deed?"

"I have no idea." Darcy thought Mr. Collins's behavior interesting and revealing. The cleric showed more true, honest emotion over a small plot of land than he ever displayed for his family, his position, or his congregation.

*Mr. Collins is ill-placed in his profession,* Darcy concluded. *He should have been a farmer. Perhaps Longbourn shall one day have a master worthy of it. For all of Mr. Bennet's admirable qualities, Mr. Collins may prove to be a better steward of the land than Elizabeth's inattentive father.*

"We must advise Sir Richard at once!" Mr. Collins declared. Before Darcy could respond, the tall, heavy man had spun about and run into the footman, knocking the servant to the ground. "Clumsy fool! You should take better care where you stand!" the vicar cried as he quickly continued on his way.

Without a word, Darcy assisted the hapless footman to his feet, thinking that the next master of Longbourn may not be worthy of the estate, after all.

# Chapter 17

"Salted? You say the vegetable gardens have been salted?"

An incredulous Richard sat at his desk in the study, Sergeant Gregory standing at his side while Mr. Evans sat in an armchair across from the desk. All looked at Darcy and Mr. Collins, who stood before them.

Darcy gestured to Mr. Collins. "I suspected something extraordinary had happened to the gardens, and Mr. Collins was kind enough to share his expertise."

Mr. Evans gave a snort of dismissal.

Darcy frowned but continued. "He was able to prove to my satisfaction that the soil had been contaminated with salt, poisoning the space and making any attempt to improve the earth pointless."

"Sir," said Mr. Evans with the barest veneer of civility, "are you saying that in order to prove this supposition, you sought not the advice of the head gardener but the...proficiency of the local minister?" He sat back, a slight sneer on his lips. "I must wonder at it."

Darcy turned his cold eyes on the steward, but any response died on his lips as Mr. Collins spoke up.

"Indeed, it is a wonder! I am exceedingly honored that such an august personage as Mr. Darcy should seek my advice and guidance." The cleric managed to talk and bow at the same time. "While I have been trained from infancy to serve the spiritual needs of my parish, I humbly admit an intense pleasure in gardening. Due to the closeness of our families—a condition for which I give thanks every day—my cousin by marriage, if I may be so bold as to claim the relation, is aware of my interest and sought my opinion. This I was privileged to do, not only to please my cousin's husband, but to perform a service for Rosings Park and the combined Fitzwilliam and de Bourgh families, the source of my family's delightful situation!"

Richard had held his gaze on the papers on his desk during Mr. Collins's oration, trying to keep his anger in check. "And it is your opinion that the garden has been salted?"

"If you would forgive me, my dear sir, it is not an opinion but a decided fact."

"What drivel!" cried Evans.

At this, Mr. Collins puffed up with indignation. "A decided fact, I say! There can be no doubt about it." He raised his proud chin. "If you wish, Mr. Evans, I would be happy to prove it to your satisfaction."

"And how would you do that?"

"It is exceedingly simple, sir. One need only taste the soil."

"You *eat* the dirt?" Mr. Evans huffed and turned to his employer. "Why are we listening to this?"

Richard was wondering the same when Sergeant Gregory said slowly, "I have heard of this practice. You are certain the soil is salty, Mr. Collins?" Assured that it was, the majordomo leaned over to Richard. "If he's right, Colonel, the garden's done for. We'll have to make a new one."

"Exactly!" cried Mr. Collins.

"The proper application of additional manure would cure all ills," proclaimed Mr. Evans. "I shall redouble the men's efforts."

Mr. Collins sniffed. "That would be an utter waste of time! The soil is ruined beyond remedy, save that from the Almighty."

"Are you questioning my competence?" cried the steward.

Before Richard could demand a stop to the argument, his cousin took command again. "That is enough, gentlemen," ordered Darcy. "Given that it is late in the season, I believe the question before us is how quickly a new garden may be prepared."

Richard had had enough—of Evans, Collins, and Darcy. "Yes, you are correct, Cousin," he barked as he took to his feet. This was *his* command, dammit, and *he* would deal with this matter! "Mr. Evans, it is my decision that we err on the side of caution. The gardener shall begin to establish a new vegetable garden today, at a spot of his choosing. See to it."

The steward was clearly disappointed that his advice had been rejected. "Sir Richard, I am certain it is not necessary. A few more days would set things to rights."

"Mr. Evans," Richard said slowly, "if—I say, *if*—the present gardens are salted, will your efforts repair it?" Anyone who had served under Colonel Fitzwilliam in the army would have blanched at his dangerous tone of voice. It portended a severe dressing down.

"Well, no, nothing can," Mr. Evans admitted. "But I am not convinced that they are."

"We shall take no chances," Richard continued in the same voice. "Your first concern is to prepare a new garden. Once that is done, you may continue efforts to remedy the fault in the existing place."

Mr. Evans was disgruntled but bowed to his master's will. "It will be done. I shall need additional help, probably the grooms—"

"The stables are *my* domain," said Gregory, "and I cannot spare anyone."

"I shall need more men!" Mr. Evans insisted.

Richard slammed his hand flat on the desk, the sharp sound stopping the argument cold. "And you shall have them! Gregory, put off what work you can and release those grooms to Mr. Evans's direction. Evans, the new garden is your highest priority. Are my orders clear?"

The two men, red-faced and angry, glanced at each other with mutual loathing before nodding to their employer.

"Then, see to it." In a more conciliatory tone, he said, "Mr. Collins, thank you for your advice. Good day."

While Mr. Evans and Gregory left the study quickly, Mr. Collins's exit was long-winded and prolonged. It was several minutes before he finally left. In the meantime, Richard's anger toward his cousin had hardly abated.

From childhood, Darcy was more of a brother to Richard than Andrew. Because of it, he knew his cousin's ways as well as he knew his own. Darcy was perhaps the most exceptional man he had ever met. He was remarkably intelligent, unquestionably honest, extremely hard-working, utterly loyal, and incredibly generous. He was open-minded and sought new knowledge constantly.

Unfortunately, he was also stiff, stubborn, proud, curt, and persistent. Darcy knew well the extent of his intellectual powers and failed to consistently restrain his few shortcomings. To his benefit, he was reserved with the world at large, or he would be more unpopular with society than he was currently. Among family and close friends, however, he occasionally set aside his aloofness and shared his views and opinions brusquely, purporting his statements as established facts. Darcy was often right in his advice, and he meant to be a service to his friends, but it made little difference to them. At those times, his behavior made him as insufferable as Lady Catherine.

This was one of those times.

"I can provide you with a revised list of candidates in a few days, Richard."

Darcy's abrupt statement broke Richard from his musings. He then realized his cousin had not departed the study with the others; instead, he was looking out the window at the fields beyond. "What was that?" he asked sharply.

"A list of replacements for Mr. Evans. I shall request that my secretary in town forward the names I had previously collected for you."

All of Richard's offended feelings over Darcy's high-handed behavior merged with his deep-seated fears over his own inadequacies in managing Rosings, causing the former colonel of Hussars to lash out at his cousin.

"You will do no such thing!" Richard leapt to his feet. "How dare you!"

Darcy stood silent, pale faced, and clearly shocked at the outburst.

The lack of reaction only fueled Richard's ire. "You come striding in here like Moses descending the mountain top with your acolyte at your heels, presuming to tell me how to run my estate! The great and all-knowing Fitzwilliam Darcy, practically ordering me to dismiss my steward and replace him with one of your choosing!

"Do not deceive yourself that I am unaware of your recent actions! Since your arrival, you have been riding the plantation and talking to my tenants as though you were the master of Rosings! Never in my life have I seen more arrogance and conceit! Allow me to remind you, sir, that this is not Pemberley and that the care of Rosings is entrusted to me, not you!"

Darcy's face lost all expression. "My intention was to be of service to you."

"I am sure it was—taking poor, stupid Richard in hand, teaching him his duty. I am not a child, Darcy! Your help is neither needed nor desired!"

After a long pause, Darcy spoke in a quiet, level voice. "I am certain you wish me gone. Elizabeth, the children, and I can be off to London as soon as may be."

Richard dropped his chin to his breast. "No. Anne would feel it dearly if you left. This matter is between the two of us. I would not wish to hurt your wife or mine."

"My presence will not disturb you?"

Richard bit the inside of his cheek. Darcy could not hide the hurt in his voice. "We are gentlemen. I trust it is not beyond our ability to act as such in company. For Anne's sake, I bid you remain."

Darcy's reply was cold. "As you wish. I shall keep our contact to a minimum."

Richard, fuming, heard him move towards the door. "You always have to have the last word, do you not, Darcy?"

A dark part of Richard's soul rejoiced at Darcy's hesitation before exiting the room. A moment after the door closed, Richard walked over to a table loaded with bottles, poured himself a measure of brandy, and gulped it down.

*Damn the man!*

The tension at Rosings remained thick throughout the remains of the day. Fortunately for the peace of the house, Lady Catherine had decided to take dinner at the dower house. It was unpleasant enough, as Darcy and Richard refused even to look at one another, and the tradition of an after-meal cigar and port was set aside. The ladies, and Buford too, knew nothing of the quarrel between the cousins, and they shared questioning looks during Caroline's performance at the pianoforte.

Eventually, the three couples retired to their apartments to change, rest, and attend to whatever matters required their attention before the party would share supper. Upon finding Elizabeth in the nursery, Caroline cautiously inquired whether she had an explanation of the matter between Darcy and Richard.

"I have no idea," Elizabeth admitted as she held Franny in one arm and hugged Bennet close to her side with the other. "Richard did seem out of sorts. Has Sir John said anything?"

For her part, Caroline held Beatrice while Chloe attempted to tie a ribbon in the child's hair. "He knows no more than I." To herself, she thought, *Sir Richard is not the only one out of sorts, but perhaps Eliza is immune to Darcy's closed and forbidding façade.*

"Mama, Mama, Mama," Bennet wiggled free of Elizabeth's grasp, attempting to crawl into her lap.

"No, no, my love," she gently scolded him. "We must be careful of your sister."

Bennet turned his large, dark eyes to the babe, his lip in an adorable pout. Then, to Caroline's astonishment, his face went blank, he straightened and clearly said, "Yes, Mama."

*Heavens! He looks the very image of his father!*

Elizabeth frowned at Bennet's actions. "Chloe," she said, "pray take Bennet to play with his blocks."

"I want to give Bea a bow," was Chloe's response. "Bea bow!" she giggled at the nonsensical joke.

Caroline smiled at the child. "It is a very pretty bow too, but Bea is too little to stay still. You should play with your cousin."

Chloe accepted this logic and took Bennet by the hand. Within moments, they were engrossed in building a great castle.

"Bennet is very much like Darcy," offered Caroline carefully.

"Yes, and I wish sometimes he were not. I fear he is too serious for his age. He should laugh more." Elizabeth smiled at her cooing daughter. "Like this one."

"I am no expert on children, Eliza, but Bennet will be what he is meant to be. There are worse examples for a boy than Darcy." She smirked. "Why, he might grow up responsible and marry an impertinent girl!"

Elizabeth laughed. "And what of Bea?"

"She shall marry royalty," she proclaimed with mock severity. "Royalty—or her papa will run those young men off!"

# Chapter 18

Midmorning the next day, Sir John Buford hefted a fencing foil in his hand, feeling for the balance. It had been over a year since he had held such a thing, and he wondered whether any attempt to wield it was not certain to meet with failure.

One of the first changes Richard made to Rosings was to construct a fencing studio. Situated on the ground floor in the back of the mansion, it had previously been Mrs. Jenkinson's room. She and her pianoforte had been relocated to a better room above stairs, and the space now served as Richard's retreat.

In the middle of the room was a fencing pad. At one end, a fencing dummy was positioned with targets marked across its chest. Buford, in shirt and breeches, eyed his "opponent" while flexing his knees. As he expected, there was stiffness in his left hip. Would that leg be strong enough for him to move properly? This was what Buford was attempting to learn.

As he prepared to attack, foil extended forward, he immediately realized the missing half of his left arm threw his balance off. He shifted to move over his right leg, and in a sliding motion, made his first thrust.

He missed the target badly.

Slowly moving in reverse, Buford shook the foil about to fine-tune the balance and then struck again. This time, he missed the center by a few inches. He repeated the exercise but only hit his target half the time. All the while, pain grew in his hip. Buford gritted his teeth and tried a more complicated move. His back leg gave out, and with an oath, he fell to the mat.

"Bloody hell!" he cried as he tried to regain his footing. Suddenly, there was a hand extended in front of his face.

"If you would allow me," said Darcy.

"I would be obliged," Buford grunted as he extended his hand. "Where the devil did you come from? I did not hear you come in." Buford was soon on his feet.

"I am not surprised. You were very intent upon your practice. Are you well?"

"Well or not, I must work out this leg." For the first time, Buford realized Darcy was also dressed to fence. "It is useless. You may have the mat."

"If you wish," said Darcy carefully, his gaze taking in Buford's appearance. "I do not wish to disturb you. You should continue."

"What would be the purpose? I cannot fence on my arse."

"Is it balance? You are favoring your left leg."

"Aye. This blasted wound. The leg is as weak as a baby's."

"Then we must strengthen it. Here is your foil. Take your position." Darcy gestured at the target. "Come now. Right foot forward."

Slowly, Buford assumed the attack position, all the time questioning Darcy with his eyes. Darcy studied his posture and then suggested minor adjustments. Working together, Buford went through the classic moves of fencing—lunge, parry, and riposte. From time to time, they would halt and adjust Buford's stance. The pain in his hip was constant but manageable.

"There," Darcy declared, "you are moving much better."

"Aye, but I have no power behind my thrusts."

"That will come in time. Do you fear for your leg?"

The door of the room opened. "Well, well. Just the man I was looking for," a languid voice intoned.

Buford and Darcy watched as Richard Fitzwilliam approached, a weapon in his hand.

ANNE GREETED CAROLINE IN THE HALLWAY LEADING TO THE stairs, and together they descended to the first floor and towards the breakfast room. The subject of the quarrel between Richard and Darcy was to be avoided, so the two friends settled upon discussing the weather. They agreed that summer had at last arrived by the time they were close enough for the footman to open the breakfast room door. They beheld Elizabeth having a rather stilted conversation with Mrs. Jenkinson.

"Good morning," said Anne. "Have the gentlemen already broken their fast?"

Elizabeth frowned. "I cannot say. Darcy always rises at daybreak, but he has not yet returned from his constitutional. I have not seen Richard or Sir John."

"John arose early as well. It was unusual, but I thought nothing of it." Caroline glanced nervously at Anne.

For her part, Anne shuddered. "Richard...Richard never rises early." She clenched her dress as terrified thoughts seized her imagination. Richard was so angry with Darcy yesterday! Was he angry enough to challenge his cousin? Bile rose in her throat. "P-pardon me."

On shaky legs, she walked over to the footman by the door. "Do you know where Sir Richard may be found?"

The man shook his head. "I'm sorry, ma'am, I've not seen him. I've just come on duty. Shall I look for him?"

One of the downstairs maids walked by. "Beggin' my lady's pardon, but I just saw the master going below stairs, carrying a sword."

More than one lady cried out. Anne grasped the maid's arm. "Where was he going? Was he headed outside?"

"I-I don't know, my lady. He was going to the back of the house when I saw him. He might have gone outside." The maid whimpered. "Ma'am, my arm—it hurts!"

Anne jerked her hand back, releasing the maid, as Caroline mumbled, "Oh, good God, they are fighting."

"We do not know that," responded Elizabeth in an uncertain voice.

Caroline's conjecture was precisely what Anne feared. She ordered the maid to show her exactly where she saw Sir Richard. Caroline and Elizabeth followed to the ground floor and towards the back of the house. The sound of steel upon steel could be heard down one hallway.

Giving up all pretense of propriety, the three ladies dashed down to a closed door. Anne threw it open without hesitation.

"*Stop it this instant!*" she screamed.

The sight before the ladies was not what they expected.

Richard, disheveled and sweat drenched, was indeed on the fencing mat in a fighting position, but holding a foil, not a sword. Darcy was not opposite him. Instead, it was Sir John in a similar state as Richard. Darcy stood nearby, his weapon tucked beneath one arm, observing the pair. All had turned their heads towards the doorway, wearing expressions of bewildered astonishment.

"What is going on here?" cried Anne.

"John!" injected Caroline. "Why are you fighting Richard?"

"I am exercising my leg," Buford explained as though it was obvious.

"Is something amiss?" asked Darcy. "You object to our sport?"

Elizabeth looked between the gentlemen. "Fitzwilliam, you are not fighting Richard?"

"I intend to exercise with Richard in a moment," he replied, "once Buford is comfortable with our instruction."

"We are simply practicing," Richard pointed out, spreading his arms wide. "Buford wishes to rehabilitate his leg and hip, and Darcy and I are aiding him."

"Then," queried Anne, "you are *not* dueling?"

"No!" claimed all three gentlemen in unison.

Mortified and yet amused, the three red-faced ladies glanced at each other. "Forgive us our intrusion," Anne said for the group. Blithely, she waved a hand. "Carry on."

The other ladies reluctantly agreed, for the gentlemen appeared rather dashing with their damp shirts clinging to their torsos. However, they reserved their giggling admiration until the door was firmly closed behind them.

"Richard and I made our peace over breakfast," Darcy explained to Elizabeth later in her chambers, once he had bathed and dressed. "I agreed I acted like a fool, and he agreed to look into the behavior of his steward. There was never any danger of our dueling, my dear."

"I am glad to hear it. Pray do not give me cause to think so ever again!" She softened her next words by sliding close to him on the sofa they shared, taking his hand, and gracing his cheek with a loving kiss. "Fitzwilliam, you are as good a man as ever lived, but you really must give over this notion that you are obliged to be of use to everyone."

"Am I to look the other way when my friends are in danger of mistaken or foolish behavior when, with but a word, I may be of service?" Darcy's mien was a mixture of sternness and confusion.

"*Yes*, my love!" Elizabeth answered earnestly. She was not distressed by his forbidding expression. She now knew his ways as well as her own. "Not everyone is like our brother Bingley. They see your interference, well intentioned though it may be, as a slight if not an insult. Richard has risen to high office on his own merit in his previous profession. He will not tolerate unasked for guidance."

"The army is not estate management."

Elizabeth was gentle, for scolding would not serve. "That is so, and you have surely forgotten more about estates and farming and investments than many other gentlemen will ever learn." She stroked Darcy's arm. "But you must recall that Richard is your elder and has his own considerable pride." She kissed him again. "And stubbornness."

"You are trying to sway me," Darcy pointed out without anger.

Elizabeth playfully batted her eyes. "Am I succeeding?"

Darcy's groan turned into a laugh. "Yes, you minx, as you well know!" He took her hand. "I am sorry, my dear. I am well rebuked. In future, I shall recall that I must keep my opinions to myself unless requested."

Elizabeth leaned her head against her husband's shoulder. "If Richard becomes concerned or frustrated, he will seek your advice. You know this."

"Yes, I do. But I own it is hard to watch him make mistakes."

"Is he, Fitzwilliam?" She had simply thought her husband was displaying superior knowledge in estate manners. She had not considered that Rosings was in danger. "Is Richard making mistakes?"

Darcy nodded. "I fear he is. He is falling into the trap of taking little interest in the farm, leaving its care entirely in the hands of the steward. It is the custom of most gentlemen, and all would be well if the steward is industrious, honest, and fair-minded.

"Mr. Evans seems to know farming, but he is too fixed in his thinking. The prosperous farmer is as flexible, as changeable, as the weather that makes a prosperous or poor harvest. Not so Mr. Evans. If his pamphlet says to do a certain thing, it must be done, no matter the current conditions.

"On the home farm, his supervision is lax. He issues orders imprecisely and faults the men when their methods fail due to confusion over his intentions.

"He does not inspire the confidence of the tenants. They are wary of him. Some are even frightened. Evans rejects persuasion in favor of command. It is well he sees the superiority of the scientific methods. But it is ill-done to ram it down the throats of tenants with twenty years' experience or more.

"All this would become apparent to Richard if he paid it any mind. But he does not ride the plantation or visit the tenants. Instead, he has established a council filled with men who either owe their allegiance to Richard or are favorites of Mr. Evans. They will not pass along the complaints of the other tenants, particularly if Evans is in attendance. Except for the stable, which is Sergeant Gregory's domain, Richard knows nothing of what is happening."

Elizabeth's gaze was fixed upon the window and the fields beyond. "This is grave, indeed. It is not the way you manage Pemberley."

"I follow my father's teachings though it is not the only way. Matlock Estate, for example, cannot be administered in that manner unless Andrew neglects his seat in the Lords. Matlock is prosperous because of the quality of its steward."

Elizabeth thought about that. "The same could be said for Longbourn or Mayfield. Neither my father nor brother have your talent for management."

Darcy affectionately squeezed her hand. "Precisely. Which is why considerable time has been taken in finding the right men to serve as stewards to your father and Charles."

"*Your* time, you mean, my dear," Elizabeth maintained, and Darcy did not dispute her. "So, the issue here is Mr. Evans."

"That is my thinking."

"Well, there is nothing to be done," declared Elizabeth, closing the discussion. "Richard and Anne are not fools. They will find their own way. Now, give over gloominess, Husband! This fine weather needs to be enjoyed!"

Darcy grinned. "And what do you suggest, Wife?" He leaned in, clearly desiring a kiss.

Elizabeth laughed. "I am sorry to disappoint you, but Anne has other entertainments in mind!"

THE SUMMER'S DAY WAS SUNNY AND WARM FOR ONCE, AND Anne would not waste the opportunity to have a picnic, which sent the house into a flurry of activity. Sooner than one would expect, the Rosings party gathered in an idyllic spot about a hundred yards from the main house. It was near the wood that blocked the western sun. A large rug was laid upon the grass, and for the comfort of the party, cushions were available.

The kitchen outdid itself given the short time available to produce a feast. Baskets of cold meats, cheeses, breads, cakes, and fruits of the season made the trek from the house along with wine, ale, and milk. Yes, milk—for the Collins family was invited to bring their children, which delighted Chloe Wickham.

The ladies sat upon the cushions, enjoying the food and conversation and watching the children run and play with Romeo. Elizabeth held Franny, Caroline held Bea, and Charlotte held her youngest. Bennet was doing his best to keep up with Chloe and the Collins girls, and Mrs. Nivens kept a sharp eye on him. Anne's half mourning of grey and cream was in sharp contrast to Elizabeth's dress of yellow and the pale green worn by Caroline.

The only woman not sitting upon the rug was Lady Catherine. She insisted upon a chair, and her favored seat was retrieved from the parlor. Like the Queen of Rosings she still considered herself to be, dressed in black, she gazed upon the proceedings from her throne with a benevolent eye, her maid Dawson attending her.

The shade offered shelter from the warm sun. The air was fresh and clean. All found the food delicious, the company excellent, and the children well-behaved. As far as the ladies were concerned, they were in paradise.

Except for the sharp report of pistol fire.

The gentlemen declared they could not have an outing without their sport, and mindful of Buford's limited abilities, a pistol-shooting tournament was arranged. A hay bale adorned with a paper bull's-eye served as a target, and two sets of rifled dueling pistols, courtesy of Richard and Darcy, were the weapons. All the gentlemen participated, including a reluctant Mr. Collins. Ten rounds were the agreed upon contest. Corporal Frost loaded the guns while Sergeant Gregory served as judge.

The gentlemen doffed their coats and hats for their competition. After several rounds, Sir John had taken a slight lead over Darcy. Sir Richard acquitted himself well, but it was rare for the nervous Mr. Collins even to strike the hay bale. He never endangered the bull's-eye.

Initially, the ladies were alarmed over such a dangerous competition when children were present. It became immediately apparent, however, that the youngsters held no interest in such frighteningly loud things as pistols. Instead, they took great joy in screaming at the top of their lungs each time the gentlemen fired—at least until, to their mothers' relief, that entertainment grew tiresome.

Finally, the last retort echoed through the trees. The gentlemen shook hands and slapped each other upon the back. They returned to their ladies, coats and hats in hand, while the servants removed all evidence of their violent sport.

"Behold the champion!" cried Richard, holding up Buford's arm, causing him to lose hold of his garments. "Oh, I beg your pardon."

"'Tis no matter, Fitz. Frost will see to my coat." He flashed a grin at his batman, who shook his head in mock outrage. "I could use an ale."

The gentlemen took their seats by their ladies as servants filled their glasses. All were in high spirits, save Mr. Collins.

"I am afraid shooting is not my forte, my good sirs," he said dejectedly. "It is my sincere desire that my poor showing did not diminish your satisfaction with your outing."

"Nonsense, Collins!" cried Richard. "You have never handled a pistol before. You did as well as could be expected, I dare say. Would you not agree, Darcy?"

Privately, Darcy thought a blind man could have done as well, but he generously said, "Richard is correct. As my aunt says, perfection is only achieved through constant practice." Darcy could never be described as a toadeater, but the gentle encouragement of his wife had softened his manners to the extent that he could speak so to Mr. Collins without gagging. His reward was pleased smiles from Elizabeth, Mr. Collins, and Lady Catherine. He pretended not to notice Richard's raised eyebrows.

Caroline sidled up to her husband as closely as propriety allowed. "So, the honors are yours, my dear?"

"Barely," Buford allowed. "I feared for my victory after Darcy's last shot."

"It is why I hate hunting with my cousin," claimed Richard good-naturedly. "He always outshoots me."

"Then, never hunt with Mr. Charles Musgrove," returned Darcy after he sipped his wine. "The man is uncanny." He turned to Buford. "Have you hunted much with pistols?"

"Not often, no. My choice has always been rifles or fowling pieces. Pistols were for the battlefield."

Darcy raised his glass to him. "Then you are a natural shot. My congratulations."

Buford was interested. "You hunt with pistols?"

"Sometimes. The woods at Pemberley can be thick with brush. Pistols are better for small game in such spots."

"Hmm," Buford mused. "I have never thought of pistols for hunting."

Richard gestured with his tankard. "I am sure Darcy can set you up with an excellent brace of rifled pistols, eh, Cuz?"

"Enough of such talk!" cried Anne. "Guns, indeed! It is time for the ladies to perform. Elizabeth, will you lead off?"

"Spoken by the lady who cannot sing," Elizabeth teasingly whispered to her husband.

"Then, shall you sing for me?" he returned in like voice.

"Traitor!" she laughed.

The impromptu *a cappella* concert then began with a solo by Elizabeth, followed by first Caroline and then Charlotte. The ladies, at the encouragement of their onlookers, finished the recital with a trio of voices of middling quality, improved with intermittent giggling by the performers. The enthusiastic applause they received was due more to the level of affection held by the audience for the singers than the quality of the performance. Even Lady Catherine seemed to enjoy herself, though her praise was tempered by a reminder that the ladies should practice more.

It was then the grand dame announced her intention to retire to the dower house. This was a signal for the nannies to collect their charges for their afternoon naps. The Collinses, too, took their leave with their children, their departure delayed by Mr. Collins's prolonged thanks for his patrons' kind condescension in issuing an invitation to their outing, sport, and concert.

Thus, it was that the six friends were left on their own. In the more relaxed atmosphere, each couple assembled themselves in their preferred state. Darcy sat against a tree with Elizabeth lying her head in her husband's lap. The Bufords copied it, with the alteration of Caroline using no backrest as she sat with Sir John's head in her lap. Richard simply stretched out, head propped on one hand, while Anne sat on a cushion near him. The servants, knowing their presence was neither required nor desired, moved closer to the manor, out of earshot. Conversation flowed easily, the ladies mainly talking to each other while the gentlemen took their ease, occasionally injecting their observations and opinions.

In this pleasant manner, the afternoon passed with the strengthening of friendship among the participants. When it was time for the party to return to the house, dark clouds from the west signaled the fair weather was changing.

By nightfall, the rain fell heavily and continued intermittently throughout the next two days. On the third day, the sky had lightened. At breakfast, an express from Pemberley arrived.

# Chapter 19

The news from the north was grim.

"My steward writes of an uprising," Darcy reported, his face taunt and pale. "Armed men are roaming throughout Derbyshire and Northamptonshire. There are reports of looting and murder."

There were gasps all around the dining table. "Charles and Jane!" cried Caroline. Buford, feeling the tension in the air, took her hand.

Darcy studied the letter. "Thompson writes only of Pemberley. Our people are troubled and frightened, but no harm has befallen them yet." He glanced at his wife and Caroline. "He has no news of Mayfield."

"And Matlock?" asked Richard. He was seemingly calm, but Buford saw his clenched fists.

Darcy shook his head. "If Pemberley was spared, perhaps Matlock was as well—and the Llewellyns too." He folded the express. "This news is two days old. I must leave at once."

Richard stood. "I shall go with you."

"No!" cried Anne.

There was a note of anger in Richard's reply. "My mother and brother may be in danger."

"What can you do?" demanded a distraught Anne. "Your responsibility is to Rosings!"

Richard started to reply and then stopped. Buford watched his old friend struggle to find the right words. "I have a duty to my family."

"Your family is here, Richard." Darcy's words were calm and quiet.

"So is yours!"

"True, which is why I am relying on you to protect them in my absence."

Buford spoke up before Richard could respond. "Forgive me for inserting myself into a family discussion, Fitz, but Darcy is right. Pemberley is his estate. He must see to it and his people. That is *his* duty. Matlock is your brother's."

"And you would not rush to Wales if your family were in danger, Buford?" Richard spat out the question.

"I have no estate. You do." He hoped to stop this discussion before Richard turned this disagreement into a shouting match.

Richard leaned on his fists over the dining table, his shoulders tense, his head down, mouth working, obviously struggling with his emotions. Anne, by his side, looked upon him with concern and fear. Still and quiet, Elizabeth had taken one of her husband's hands in hers, tears pooling in her eyes. Darcy stood tall, his gaze fixed upon his cousin.

The tension in the room finally broke. "I trust you will go to Matlock once you set Pemberley to rights." Richard's voice was tight with anger.

Darcy nodded. "My intention is to send messengers to Lord Matlock, Lord Llewellyn, and Bingley once I reach Pemberley." To Elizabeth, he said, "I shall call upon Franklin and Kitty in Kympton personally."

Elizabeth's reply was to lay her head on Darcy's shoulder, her eyes glistening with unshed tears.

"Elizabeth! What troubles you, dearest?" He held her tenderly, not caring that they were surrounded by their friends.

"It is nothing, my dear—just something in my eye. I must see to your packing." With a tearful smile, she left them.

After a moment, Darcy cleared his throat. "I must have my carriage readied."

"Speak to Sergeant Gregory," Anne suggested.

Darcy nodded and made his way out of the room. The others stood about in various states of concern, mortification, sadness, and in Richard's case, displeasure. He turned to Anne.

"Pray excuse me. I must send a letter to my brother. I shall be in my study." Richard's voice was cold, and with the barest of acknowledgement, he left them.

Anne was visibly shaken. "I…I must see that Darcy has provisions for his journey."

"Shall I help you, Anne?" offered Caroline.

"If you wish," Anne responded absently. Caroline gave Buford a hard look before taking Anne's arm and went to find the housekeeper.

Buford well understood his wife's silent message. Gritting his teeth, he made for Richard's study.

RICHARD, WHO HAD JUST SEATED HIMSELF AT HIS DESK, JUMPED when Buford entered the study without knocking.

"Just what the devil are you about, Fitzwilliam?" He slammed the door for emphasis.

"This is none of your concern." He glared as his best friend strode over to the desk and leaned over it.

"By blazes, it is! You are acting like a bloody fool, and I am prepared to knock some sense into that thick head of yours!"

Richard rose. "Buford, I shall not stand for any interference."

"Open your eyes and shut your mouth, Fitz! Can you not see what is going on? Darcy is going into what well could be a battle area, Elizabeth is terrified, and you are being an arse, nursing your hurt feelings!" Buford's scar stood out in white relief against his angry, red face. "Darcy has entrusted his wife and children into your care while he risks his life to do his duty!"

Richard met rage with rage. "His is not the only family in danger! What of Matlock? My mother, my brother—"

"They are not your main concern any longer!" Buford slammed his fist on the desk. "*Rosings is!*"

"Rosings is not in danger."

"How can you be certain? For all you know, this could be the prelude to a civil war!"

"What are you saying?" gasped Richard, taken aback.

"Do you not remember what happened in London over the winter? Do you not read what Brandon writes? It is all over the papers. There is unrest throughout the kingdom." Buford calmed down. "This might be an isolated event, like the frame-breaking by the Luddites a few years ago, or it might not. Your duty is *here*, protecting Rosings, protecting Anne. You knew that when you married. *This* is the duty you signed on for, Sir Richard!"

Richard could no longer bear the glare from the man who was like a brother to him. He looked anywhere but at Buford. "You should not speak to me so."

"I shall speak to you in any manner I choose if it is for your own good." He grinned. "You have done the same for me."

Buford's audacious smile did away with much of Richard's antagonism. "Nothing has changed since Spain, has it?"

"No."

Richard pinched the bridge of his nose. "I suppose you are correct."

"Your ability to recall that is one of your best qualities, Brother. Now, be a good host and pour me a glass of wine."

Richard grunted but moved to a side table lined with bottles. "Would you care for something stronger instead?"

"Too early in the morning. I need my wits about me—as do you."

Richard gave him a glance before pouring two glasses of Burgundy. "Here, it is from Darcy's uncle in trade. An excellent vintage."

"Thank you." Buford gestured at the desk. "Write your letter. Darcy will be leaving soon. And prepare an apology to Anne." He raised his eyebrows.

Richard sat, dropped his head in his hands, and groaned.

ELIZABETH WAS NEARLY COMPOSED WHEN SHE INFORMED Darcy's valet of his master's immediate return to Pemberley. She also told him the reason why his charge needed to leave, for the Darcys kept few secrets from their personal servants and thereby insured their total loyalty. Bartholomew appeared shocked by the news, a rare sight for one whose expression was typically so fixed, but he went about his task with his usual efficiency.

Her mission completed, Elizabeth searched for her husband. She found him in the first place she looked—the nursery. Darcy was seated silently on the sofa with Franny in his arms, Bennet and Chloe snuggled in close beside him. The nurses and Miss Buford were not in attendance.

Hesitating a moment, reluctant to disturb the touching scene, Elizabeth quietly asked from the doorway, "May I join you?"

Darcy's dark, serious eyes searched hers. "Please."

Chloe stubbornly remained on her uncle's right, clinging to his arm, so Elizabeth picked up her wiggling son and sat on Darcy's left. Bennet immediately wrapped his fat little arms about his mother's neck and laid his head upon her breast, one eye focused on his father.

Of course, it was Chloe who spoke up. "Uncle Darcy is to go away!" she cried. "Make him stay, Aunt Lizzy!"

Though that was the great wish of her heart, Elizabeth slowly shook her head. "Your uncle must go on important business to Pemberley. Of course, we shall miss him, but we must not complain and make him unhappy. Let us instead give him our love and best wishes and hope he can return to us very soon."

Chloe began to cry. "No! I want him to stay!" She buried her face in his arm.

*So do I*, thought Elizabeth.

Darcy freed one hand from supporting Franny and stroked Chloe's hair. "No tears, now. You are the eldest, and your aunt will depend upon you to help with the little ones. You do not want your aunt to be sad, do you?"

Chloe shook her head.

"There's a good girl." Darcy bent down and kissed the top of the child's head. He turned to Elizabeth. "I must prepare for the journey."

It took all of Elizabeth's strength not to weep. She touched the hand supporting their child. "Your man Witherspoon is packing even now. Have you spoken to Sergeant Gregory?" When Darcy acknowledged he had, she asked, "Are you taking the carriage to Pemberley?"

"I am. The holiday for our coachmen and footmen is over. Fear not, my dear. They are all former soldiers, well-armed and well-trained in the military arts. I shall be as safe as the Prince Regent."

"The Regent was attacked six months ago."

"And escaped unharmed," Darcy reminded her.

Elizabeth frowned. Her husband could be so flippant sometimes! But she knew he was trying to calm her fears, and she loved him for it. "I hate the idea of your going," she whispered in his ear.

"You know why I have to."

"Yes." She kissed that ear. "But I still *hate* it. Pray, linger with us as long as you are able."

Darcy nodded and turned to the woman he adored. "I hate going too."

"ANNE?" RICHARD CALLED FROM THE DOOR OF HIS WIFE'S STUDY.

Anne was expressionless as she turned from the window and looked at her husband, Romeo at her feet. She had spent the last hour reflecting on her hurt and surprise at his response to Darcy's express. Knowing he felt his duty was more to Matlock and the

Fitzwilliams than to Rosings and her, was a knife to her heart.

"Yes, Richard? Is your packing completed?" She desired to be strong and struggled not to weep.

"I am not going."

Anne's jaw dropped open. "But…you said downstairs—"

"Pray, let us sit so I may explain." Richard gestured to a pair of armchairs. "First, I must credit Buford for pointing out how stupidly I spoke. I am in his debt. I should have made it clear that my alarm over Matlock was because it was in danger, and I do not think Andrew is up to the task of protecting it." He looked intently at Anne. "I love my mother and brother, but my first concern is and always will be you. Pray forgive my beastly temper downstairs."

"Of course. You were very worried, I am sure." Anne took his hand. "But, is this wise if you truly believe Andrew is incapable of safeguarding Matlock?"

"Andrew has not my experience in the army and has spent a goodly portion of his life in pursuit of the usual pleasures of young heirs. It was not until he married Eugenie—an arranged marriage, as you recall—that he showed any interest in the management of the estate. I do not know what he would do in a crisis."

"He is a Fitzwilliam," Anne reminded him. "Would he not act as Uncle Hugh and protect his land and people?"

Richard grimaced. "One would think so. Father was certainly fearless. But I have seen war, Annie, and what it does to men. Some of the largest, toughest recruits became paralyzed with fear in the face of battle, while far less promising men charged into hell like heroes. None can say how a man will act when brought to the test."

Anne squeezed his hand. "Then, why do you not go?" She hoped her voice did not give away her disquiet.

Richard sighed. "I fear for him and Matlock, but Buford is right. My duty is here in Kent with you. Should Andrew or Darcy have need of me, I trust they will send word." He kissed her hair. "Until then, I shall remain with my sweet rose of Rosings."

Anne wept, but in relief.

By midday, the London papers had arrived, filled with stories of the uprising in the north. For all the alarming reports contained within, there was little new information, something that offered scant relief to the people at Rosings.

The party gathered on the front steps to see Darcy off, Elizabeth holding their daughter and son, their niece clutching her skirt. The day was far too bright and pleasant for such a melancholy gathering.

Darcy took his leave of the Bufords, then the Fitzwilliams, before he turned to his little family. A tearful Chloe kissed her uncle's cheek, promising to be a good girl. Bennet was not certain what was happening, but when his father requested a hug, he dutifully complied. Darcy bent and kissed Franny's forehead, and then focused his attention on Elizabeth. The others looked away, giving the couple a bit of privacy, but it was unnecessary. Too well schooled in propriety, they simply gazed into each other's eyes before Darcy graced his wife's hand with his lips. The only breach of decorum was that he held it a bit longer than proper. A moment later he was in the carriage, and it pulled away from the house.

The party slowly made its way inside, save for the Darcy family. They remained until the carriage disappeared down the lane.

# Chapter 20

Elizabeth filled the next few days with diversion: music, needlework, walks, letters, books, and especially attending to her children. Yet, never far from her mind was the distance between Derbyshire and Kent. She knew she had to fill her mind with *something* now that Darcy was off to Pemberley and danger, or she would run mad.

*Three days—it was three days by coach to Pemberley. Several days for Fitzwilliam to survey the situation in the area, including Kympton. Two days to Matlock and back. Then, if all was well, at least a se'nnight at Mayfield. Three weeks before I hear from him? More? Oh, what is happening?*

Her friends did what they could, but as their thoughts were not entirely different from Elizabeth's, their efforts failed to console. Elizabeth's walks offered no peace, for the silence gave her too much time alone to ponder and worry. Her nights were agony. Even the children were occasionally a trial, particularly the one yet to be born. They reminded Elizabeth how much the family depended upon Fitzwilliam—his labors, his wisdom, his attention, his love. Only in the Rosings library was she able to totally escape from her worries for a time.

Bennet, being so young, hardly knew what had happened. Chloe was a different matter. A precocious four-year-old child abandoned by her mother, she had witnessed too much in her young life not to be aware of Darcy's absence. She adored her uncle and cried for him repeatedly. It was Chloe who needed Elizabeth most.

Finally, five days after Darcy's departure, Elizabeth shook off her gloom and gathered her courage. Pining and worrying for her husband would serve no good purpose, and the children needed her to be strong. She would not fail them.

The day was gloomy, the sun unable to break through the clouds, but the air was tolerable. Elizabeth decided on an outing with her niece and walked to visit the pond with the intention of feeding whatever waterfowl that happened to be there.

Alas, the two found themselves alone. This was not to Chloe's liking, so Elizabeth suggested they sit upon a bench and wait for winged visitors. The spot was most agreeably situated with a view of the great house across the pond. For a while, Chloe was content to sit and wait, her little feet swinging high off the ground.

After a few minutes, the child broke the silence. "When will Uncle Darcy come back?"

Elizabeth took her hand. "I do not know. His business took him to Pemberley, and that is a great distance away."

Chloe screwed her lips into a pout. "I do not like business. It takes Uncle away. I want him to come back!" She looked and sounded so much like Lydia, Elizabeth had to bite back a laugh.

"He will return as soon as he can." She squeezed Chloe's hand for emphasis.

"I want to play King of the Hill." She turned to her aunt. "But there is no Uncle Darcy to play with us."

"I shall play with you."

Chloe huffed. "You are too little. Uncle Darcy is big!" She thought for a moment. "Would Sir John play with us?"

"I do not know, dear. He suffers still from his wounds."

"Oh. Maybe Sir Richard would want to play?"

Elizabeth could not help but frown. "I doubt it."

"I remember. He does not like me." Chloe stared at her shoes.

Elizabeth's insides roiled. While Richard did apologize for his rude greeting of Chloe and had not mistreated her since, he did not go out of his way to engage the child. His attitude was benign neglect. Did he not see how hurt Chloe was by his unfriendly behavior?

There was nothing Elizabeth could do to improve Richard's manners. Chloe's feelings were her priority. "My love, Sir Richard is a busy man. He oversees the running of Rosings Park. It is a big place, is it not?"

Chloe looked up. "Yes."

"He does not play with Bennet or Franny or Bea, does he?"

"No."

Elizabeth ran her fingers through Chloe's wavy brown hair, so reminiscent of her mother's. "Perhaps we may visit the parsonage tomorrow. I am sure the Collins girls will be happy to play with you."

"Catherine is my age?" Chloe referred to the Collinses's eldest.

"Yes, she is."

Chloe smiled. "That will be fun."

"There!" Elizabeth exclaimed as she got to her feet. "Now, let us see if we can find any ducks, shall we?"

Chloe happily took her aunt's hand and began the quest.

THAT NIGHT, AS ANNE SAT AT HER DRESSING TABLE WHILE THE maid prepared her for bed, her thoughts returned to her great dilemma. Above all things she desired to give Richard a child, but to date she had failed. Meanwhile, her friends had succeeded not once but multiple times.

They had consoled her but offered contrasting advice based upon their varied experience, character, and situation.

She knew Charlotte had married Mr. Collins for security. His income and situation were more than adequate for the plain daughter of a shopkeeper turned landowner. Mr. Collins's other qualities were few. He had been cruelly beaten into submission by a miserly father, becoming vain yet servile, and of weak understanding. No one could call him handsome or romantic. However, his heart was good. Though he meant well, his actions, at times, could be in conflict with his intentions. Because he wished to be both of use and admired, he was easily led. Charlotte, more thoughtful and wiser than Mr. Collins, was able to guide him gently and kindly to better thinking and actions. At the same time, she slyly encouraged his affection and dependence on her. Never expecting to find love in marriage, she was not dismayed in her lack of passion for him and was content in her children, her household, and the peculiar form of affection she held for her husband. Charlotte, a mother of three girls, simply said to trust in the Lord.

Caroline also came from trade, but she was as different from Charlotte as the sun from the moon. The recipient of a proper ladies' education in London, she was beautiful, graceful, and accomplished. She had also been grasping, willful, and spiteful in her youth. Thanks to a providence not often offered to the mean and jealous, Caroline came to recognize her faults and labored to reform herself. Supported by a husband that by all accounts was her equal in previously reprehensible behavior, she was a new creature, loving and loyal. Caroline owned rough edges still—it would be impossible, Anne judged, to exorcise them all—but her ambition and will was now directed to nursing and promoting her injured beloved Sir John.

Caroline adored her husband and seemed to think her custom of sharing a bed with him was the source of her success in conception. Caroline had fallen with child almost immediately, Anne recalled. In fact, it was well that Beatrice was born ten months after the wedding or tongues would have wagged! And now she was with child again.

"*I heartily recommend our habits to promote true understanding and affection—and conception,*" she had declared with a laugh during a recent conversation.

Elizabeth was now carrying her third child. She scoffed at Caroline's reasoning and the example she offered made perfect sense.

*"Oh, hang Caroline!"* Elizabeth had cried without rancor. *"What does she know? She fell with child practically from the off! Anne, you are aware Darcy and I share the same sleeping arrangements as the Bufords, but Bennet was not born until fifteen months after the wedding. My parents have never shared a bedroom, but my mother was safely delivered of five healthy girls in seven years. Certainly, the Collinses do not share a room."*

Anne knew she was not barren. She had suffered a miscarriage. While she feared another failure, her desire for motherhood was stronger than her apprehension. She would try anything.

Anne donned her robe, dismissed her maid, and made her way into the small parlor that separated her rooms from Richard's. As expected, he was in his usual chair reading a book, waiting for her. A small fire warmed the room, exactly to Anne's taste. She affixed her most fetching smile and proceeded to settle herself not in her chair but on her husband's lap. She anticipated he would be surprised, and he did not disappoint.

"This is a pleasant thing indeed! To what do I owe the honor?" he exclaimed as she took his book and placed it on a side table.

"Do I need a reason, Husband?" She nibbled at his ear, something experience had taught her drove Richard to distraction.

"No, indeed." He kissed her neck hungrily while his hands sought her slight curves. "You are so beautiful, Annie."

"You may come to me tonight."

"Hmm," he murmured while continuing his attentions, "I think I shall."

He occupied himself in this manner for some time, which confused Anne. In her present position, she knew of his desire—indeed, she could not help but know of it—yet he seemed disinclined to take advantage of her willingness. Perhaps he was teasing her, building her desire. Well, that was unnecessary. She was ready *now* and wanted the preliminaries ended! She pulled away slightly and forced herself to look directly into his eyes.

"Richard, pray take me to bed." There, she had said it!

An infuriating, teasing grin hung on his adorable face. "Sweeter words have never been spoken." Yet on his lap she remained.

Caught between confusion and mortification, she cried, "If you mean to do nothing about it, then I shall return to my room!"

"Not by yourself, my love." Richard rose from the chair, effortlessly lifting her in his arms.

Anne wrapped her arms about his neck. "You are a terrible, teasing man! I should lock you out of my room!"

"But you will not, will you, my sweet?" he whispered in her ear.

LATER, THE LOVERS LAY INTERTWINED, ANNE SLOWLY STROKing Richard's bare chest. She lost herself in the contentment she always felt after lovemaking. For so long she had loved him, for so long she had felt she would never have him. That he was beside her, a caring, faithful husband and companion, was truly a dream come true.

She raised his hand and compared it to her own. "So big a hand," she said.

"Not too big, I trust," he returned suggestively.

"Richard!" she affectionately scolded him. To her embarrassment, Richard enjoyed talking of intimate details, something Anne could never bring herself to do.

His chuckle rumbled deep in his chest as he turned to place a kiss on her forehead. "So prim and proper, and in such a place! No, do not argue. I know the truth about you!"

"I do not deny I love being with you."

"And I adore being with you." He kissed her lips. "And I especially adore looking at you at close quarters!" His eyes moved down as his hand opened the top of her gown, exposing her small breasts.

"Richard, please," Their lovemaking had been intense, and her breasts were a bit sore from his amorous attentions.

"I cannot help it. You are the loveliest woman in the world."

She rolled her eyes. "You are sweet, but that is not true."

"It is," he insisted. His arm wrapped about her and caressed her back.

For the life of her, Anne could not understand why Richard insisted on paying her such compliments. There was no standard of beauty in which she excelled. She was short and slim to the point of being bony. She had no bosom to speak of, was unremarkable of face, mousy of hair, and not particularly graceful. She needed spectacles to read. She had no talents and even less conversation than her cousin Darcy. She had been ill most of her life. Yet, her husband spoke of her as though she were a goddess.

She wondered whether Richard labored to convince himself that he did not make a mistake marrying her. After all, what had she brought to their union besides Rosings and her dowry? She could not elevate him in society. In fact, she knew that many in town assumed Sir Richard had taken pity on his plain, timid cousin.

Anne struggled to drive such thoughts from her mind. Richard loved her. His affection was constant. She should not—must not—doubt him.

Richard's caresses were very relaxing. She wiggled closer to him.

"You like that, do you, my pet?" Richard pulled her tight and groaned. "Ah, Annie! What you do to me!"

"Is something wrong?"

"Nothing, except you drive me to distraction. If I was not so tired…I suppose I should return to my chambers."

Anne smiled, knowing her decision would please him. "I am very happy where you are, sir."

"What? Do you mean I should stay here all night?"

"Richard, I should be beyond pleased if you would stay with me." She kissed his cheek, already covered in stubble.

"I would like nothing better."

Unfortunately, no good deed goes unpunished.

"Richard, wake up!"

"Uh—what? What is it, Anne?"

"You are snoring. Stop it."

"Oh, sorry. I shall just turn over, shall I?"

A few minutes later, there was a shove.

"Richard, you are doing it again."

"Mmm…" It did not serve.

"Richard…please!"

Awake, Richard grumbled. "Forgive me, but I cannot help it." He rose and yanked on his robe. "I suppose I should take myself to my bed."

Tears gathered in Anne's eyes. "Richard, I am sorry."

"Do not be." He leaned down and kissed her tenderly. "The fault is mine." He gently caressed her cheek. "There was a reason few wished to share my tent in Spain. Ask Buford about it sometime."

"I love you, Richard."

"And I love you, Annie. I am distressed that I keep you from your rest. Sleep, my dear, and I shall be happy."

Richard kissed her again and slipped out the door. With a sad sigh, Anne gathered a blanket around her and went to sleep.

*A tavern in Kent*
*on the road to Maidstone*

"I must tell you," said the gentleman across the table from Adam Shepardson, "I am disappointed with your efforts to date. I expected more for my money."

Adam set down his tankard of ale with a thump. "I've done what I can. I took care o' that garden, didn't I?"

"And what else? Damaging a few fence railings? Opening a stall or two? I wanted sabotage, not pranks!"

"Then I need more money."

"Why?"

Adam rubbed his grimy face with his dirt-stained hand. "I can bribe a few fellers—get 'em drunk—that'll help—"

"Bah!"

"Look," Adam demanded, his angry, nervous face glimmering in the candlelight, "I'm takin' all the risks. His lordship an' that damn Gregory is looking fer troublemakers. They know these ain't accidents. You owe me."

"I owe you nothing." The gentleman sneered. "If you want more funds, accomplish something."

"Like what?"

"That is for you to determine." The gentleman rose from the rough table. "But make it telling this time. I want to *hurt* them."

Adam frowned. "Why's that so important to ya?"

"I told you before—that is my concern and my concern only. Do not ask again, or our association is over." He gave Adam a hard look. "And do not think to blackmail me. Those who try are dealt with—permanently."

"Then why don't *ya* deal with his lordship?" Adam was not intimidated in the least.

"I have my reasons. Contact me only when you have something of worth to discuss." He tossed a few coins on the table. "Pay for the ale out of that. You will get no more money until they are made to suffer!"

With that, the gentleman left the back room of the tavern.

*Rosings*

HOURS LATER, AS THE MORNING SUN FORCED ITS WAY THROUGH small gaps in the window curtains, a half-asleep Anne felt her bed move. Had Romeo escaped from the kitchen again? She turned to find two eyes studying her closely.

"Richard?" She blinked. "What are you doing?"

"Looking at you," he said as he pulled the counterpane over himself.

Anne grew more awake. "No. Why are you here in my room? Is something wrong?"

"I simply thought you might like my company." He grinned. "I snore very little in the morning, you see."

"Oh." She blushed. "Pray forgive me about last night."

"Say nothing of it. It was my doing, after all. Here, does this make amends for my beastly behavior?" He took Anne into his arms.

Anne laughed. "Beastly, indeed." She snuggled deeper into his embrace.

Richard kissed her forehead. "Go back to sleep, my Annie. I shall keep you warm."

A few minutes later, she gave him a light shove. "Richard?"

"Yes, love?"

"I am not sleepy anymore."

# Chapter 21

Anne sat at the desk in her study, the letters and account books before her forgotten. She was caught up in pleasant contemplation of the previous night and that morning. She was brought back to her surroundings by the sound of Mrs. Parks's voice.

"I beg your pardon, milady, but there is a problem with tonight's dinner."

Anne sighed and waved the housekeeper to a chair. "What is the difficulty?"

As her mistress reviewed the menu, Mrs. Parks reported, "There is to be a roast beef, but the joint is barely large enough to feed the table with Lady Catherine in company. There will certainly not be enough for the staff."

Anne glanced up. "Our people need to eat. Why is there not enough for soup or pie?" Her face darkened. "Am I to assume that Cook's order was changed *again*?"

"Yes, milady."

"I thought we made it clear to the butcher that he should take orders from Rosings only."

Mrs. Parks refused to meet Anne's glare. "Beggin' milady's pardon, but Lady Catherine can be very...persuasive."

"*Threatening*, you mean."

"Aye, madam."

"Very well." Anne got to her feet. "Pray excuse me, Mrs. Parks, but I have a sudden appointment at the dower house. In the meantime, is there any other meat in the larder?"

"We have bacon, milady."

Both knew it was too late to acquire more meat for dinner from the butcher. "Beef and bacon pie will have to do for the staff. Pray give them my apologies."

"Thank you kindly, but that will hardly be necessary. Cook makes a very good pie."

Anne offered a slight smile. "Then that might have to be on the dinner menu some night. In the meantime, be so good as to call for my phaeton while I dress for my visit."

WHILE SHE EASILY COULD HAVE WALKED, ANNE KNEW APPEARances were important. It simply would not do for her to stomp all the way from the manor to the dower house. The servants would gossip, and the tale would be all over Hunsford by nightfall. No, by using her phaeton, Anne could promote the fiction that this was an ordinary call on Lady Catherine.

The dower house possessed no stable, but footmen came down from the front door to help Anne out and see to the horse. One of the servants escorted her into the house and took her driving coat and hat. Waving away any more assistance, Anne made her way up to the first-floor parlor and her mother. She burst into the room unannounced. She wanted no witnesses.

"Mother!"

Lady Catherine, seated in her favored chair near the fireplace on the far wall, jumped at the sound of her voice. In her surprise, she dropped a letter onto a small table by her side. "Anne, what is the meaning of this?"

Anne stalked across the room. "It is past time we had an important conversation. *Long* past time."

Lady Catherine turned away. "Not now. I am not in a humor for guests."

"You will listen, Mother!" Anne would not be put off. "You will be silent and listen for once!"

"How dare you speak to me—"

"SILENCE!" Some dark part of Anne's soul cheered as Lady Catherine drew back in alarm. "Did you not agree that *I* am mistress of Rosings Park as Father desired? Have you not been allowed to manage the house provided for you as you wished? Have I not seen to your every comfort without touching a penny of your fortune? Have I interfered with your servants? Can you answer yes to any of this?"

"Anne, I do not understand—"

"Answer my question, Mother!"

"No," the old lady admitted, shaking her head. "You have seen to your duty to me as you should."

"No, I have done *more* than duty requires of me. I could have let you fend for yourself, relying on the interest from your dowry, either here or in town. You know this! You also know I can *withdraw* my support, and I will if you continue your interference in my household!"

"I have done nothing of the sort!" She seemed totally nonplussed.

"You do, Mother! You do it constantly! Just this week you changed my order from the butcher again!"

"What—oh, that!" Lady Catherine recovered a bit from her shock. "Your cook ordered too much meat. I corrected the order. It would not do to waste it."

"There would have been nothing for the servants. You know they have what is left over."

"There would have been more than enough," her mother shot back. "You are only six at dinner."

"Seven to nine, if you and the Collinses come. And there are the Darcy and Buford servants. What of them?"

Lady Catherine seemed genuinely confused for a moment. "I forgot."

Those two words had an enormous effect on Anne. "You *forgot?*" Such an admission was stunning. Lady Catherine de Bourgh forgot *nothing.* Most of Anne's righteous anger drained away.

The grand dame waved her hand in dismissal. "A temporary lapse of memory. It is of no moment. I was only looking after your best interests, Anne. There is no cause for you to berate and threaten me." Still, her mother refused to look at her—a sure sign she was mortified.

Anne slowly sat down in the chair across from her mother. "Mama, are you well?" For the first time, she noted that Lady Catherine was pale, her eyes bloodshot.

"Well enough, though I am here all by myself." Her lip trembled, as did her hand.

Anne glanced at the side table. Next to the open letter was a crumpled, wet handkerchief. "Have you received bad news?"

At first, her mother shook her head, but then she nodded. "I-I received a letter…Lady Metcalfe…her daughter writes that she has consumption—" Lady Catherine broke down in tears.

"Oh, no!" Anne was horrified. Lady Metcalfe was her mother's dearest friend. She grasped her hand. "Mama, I am so sorry."

A moment later, Anne was on her feet, cradling her weeping mother in her arms. "All my friends are gone," Lady Catherine wailed. "I am all alone!"

"No, Mama, you are not." Anne stroked her back. "We are here—Richard and I. We shall always take care of you."

Lady Catherine pulled away a bit so she could raise her face to her daughter's. "Yes! Richard is here! Richard will protect us!" Her tear-filled eyes were red and wide. "Oh, Anne, please do not leave me alone!" She was almost frantic.

"Never, Mama. You must not worry."

Lady Catherine hugged her daughter. "I am sorry. I-I only mean to help you. You are so young…you do not know things. People are so dishonest. They will cheat you. They will take advantage of you."

"I know more than you think. You have taught me well," Anne prevaricated. "I shall be careful, and I always have you and Richard to help me."

"It is good that Richard is here. I had thought only Darcy would do, but Richard is strong. He will protect us."

*Protection?* thought Anne. *What does Mama believe we need protection from? The villagers?* Anne considered it unwise to ask. Her mother was already upset. It was probably something that existed only in her imagination, in any case.

Anne released her hold and knelt down to face Lady Catherine. "I think you should rest. I shall call for Dawson." To Anne's continued unease, her mother meekly agreed.

*Forgetting things? Submissiveness? Apologizing? This was not Lady Catherine at all! She must be truly distressed.*

Dawson had heard some of the earlier argument and came downstairs, for Anne found her just outside the parlor door. The two of them assisted Lady Catherine to her feet. The long-time servant slowly helped her mistress up the stairs to her bedroom, Anne watching in confused concern.

*1797, Rosings Park*

"MR. KENDRICK, MILADY," ANNOUNCED THE BUTLER.

Lady Catherine de Bourgh pursed her lips at the intrusion by the husband of Sir Lewis's sister but followed propriety and rose at his entrance. At five and thirty, the former Lady Catherine Fitzwilliam had lost little of the brilliance of her earlier years. Then, she had been a tall, curvaceous society beauty. Now, she was the handsome mistress of Rosings Park. Her gown was the latest style with a full skirt featuring a high empire waist to emphasize her breasts. Her hair was piled high, left in its natural color of soft brown, powdered hair being no longer fashionable. She dismissed the custom of a wife's cap, for she was exceedingly proud of her tresses.

Cecil Kendrick was a man of average height, but his riding clothes were stressed to their limits by his stocky build. Except for his wig, the man could have been mistaken for a merchant or solicitor. He certainly did not possess the pleasing elegance of Sir Lewis de Bourgh.

Her visitor made his leg. "Good afternoon, Lady Catherine."

"I am afraid my husband is unavailable. He is occupied with the steward."

Mr. Kendrick smiled. "I came to visit with my family, milady."

Trapped, Lady Catherine could either dismiss the man or invite him in. She chose to be gracious and offered the gentleman a seat and refreshments. The first he accepted, closing the door, taking a chair next to the couch she occupied, and making himself comfortable. The second he refused. Mr. Kendrick offered no conversation but examined Lady Catherine closely.

The mistress of Rosings Park refused to be intimidated. "What news of Glendale Farm, sir? I trust Mrs. Kendrick is well?" She declined to use a more familiar address with him, even though he was married to Sir Lewis's only sibling.

"Unfortunately, no. Her health remains poor." His melancholy voice was contradicted by his relaxed features. Lady Catherine was certain he owned little concern over the fate of his wife. "My son, Reginald, however, is in excellent health. And how does my niece fare, may I ask?"

"Anne remains above stairs. Other than a slight cold, she is well."

"Ah." Mr. Kendrick sat back and crossed his legs, gazing about the parlor. The white walls were covered with gold leaf and landscape paintings. Clawfoot furniture and an oriental carpet graced the parquet floor. The room was Lady Catherine's pride and joy. She had spent much time and many pounds to bring it to the pinnacle of French Baroque elegance.

Mr. Kendrick sat forward. "It has occurred to me that our children are of an age. It is as though they were formed for each other."

Eyes wide in disbelief and revulsion, Lady Catherine recoiled. "Mr. Kendrick, surely you are not proposing a union between our houses!"

"Why not? We are what remains of the noble de Bourgh line. Would it not be wise to keep the estate in the family?"

"The de Bourghs are not the only noble lineage in *my* family," Lady Catherine said icily. "The Fitzwilliams, for example—"

"The Fitzwilliams!" Mr. Kendrick cried. "A bunch of jumped-up farmers! The de Bourghs came over with the Conquest."

"And lost most of their lands and titles," she retorted. "*My* family earned much favor and many honors from our sovereigns. My father is an *earl*. My sister's family, the Darcys, is of Norman stock, and they have *increased* their holdings. The only title left for the de Bourghs is a hereditary baronetcy, which is *my* husband's province."

"Reginald can take the de Bourgh name."

Lady Catherine waved her hand. "The de Bourgh baronetcy is of the usual kind: it can descend only through *heirs male of the body of the grantee*. It cannot be assumed either by the son of a daughter or husband of a daughter."

Mr. Kendrick grew thoughtful. "Then, unless you produce an heir, the title dies with your husband, and the lands forfeit to the Crown."

Lady Catherine shrugged. "So be it. There is no land left of the original grant due to the extravagance of your *noble* de Bourgh family," she scoffed. "Rosings Park is another matter. Sir Lewis purchased it himself. It is apart from the baronetcy."

"Still, it would be pleasant to keep the title, would it not? All you need is a son, but I doubt you will get one from Lewis."

The man's boorishness knew no bounds. "Sir! You speak of matters that are outside of polite conversation! You will desist at once!"

"Come, Catherine, you know as well as I that pompous scarecrow is no man for you. I doubt he is able to arise to the occasion these days." His eyes raked over her form, a hungry smile on his fat lips. "You are lovely and need a gentleman who can take advantage of it."

Deeply offended and a little frightened, she rose from her chair. "Mr. Kendrick, you will leave this instant!"

"Now, you do not mean that," he said with a hearty laugh as he got to his feet. "How long has it been since a man touched you, my girl?"

Lady Catherine, realizing her danger, turned to flee, but Mr. Kendrick was too quick for her. She found herself pinned against the mantelpiece, Mr. Kendrick trying to kiss her. "Help! Help me!"

"Stop fighting, Catherine! It will be so much nicer if you cooperate. Besides, I locked the door."

"Then, it is well that there is a servants' entrance," came a languid, almost bored voice.

The two looked over to see Sir Lewis de Bourgh, still in his riding costume, ebony walking stick in hand, just inside the hidden servants' door, wearing an amused expression.

"Lewis, thank Heavens!" cried his wife.

"You are interrupting private business, Brother." Mr. Kendrick released Lady Catherine and stepped away. She took the opportunity to flee to her husband's side.

"Lewis, he is lying!" Her voice was high and disjointed. "It is not what you think!"

"Nonsense, my dear," Sir Lewis responded in the same half-amused voice. "It is *exactly* what I think. Pray excuse me." With that, the baronet disengaged himself from his wife's grasp and walked over to his sister's husband.

"Every time I take your measure, Cecil, you manage to surprise me. As little as I respect you, even in my darkest dreams, I did not think you would stoop to rape and incest." Sir Lewis shook his head. "My poor sister. I warned Marie off you, you know, but she would have you, no matter what." He sniffed. "You should be exterminated."

"What are you about, you popinjay?" Mr. Kendrick crossed his arms over his broad chest. "Are you to call me out?"

"I would not dirty my hands on you." Sir Lewis's response was a bark of a laugh. "Leave *now*, Cecil, and do not return."

Mr. Kendrick raised an eyebrow. "And if I refuse?"

Just then, there was the noise of a key in a lock, and the parlor door opened to reveal the steward and two burly footmen. Sir Lewis indicated them with his chin. "There is more than one key in this house. These gentlemen will escort you off Rosings property. Goodbye, Cecil."

Mr. Kendrick turned to Lady Catherine. "Until we meet again, my lady." He affected a slight bow, and therefore did not see Sir Lewis rear back with his walking stick. With a vicious blow to the back of Kendrick's head, he laid his wife's attacker nearly insensible on the floor.

The servants dashed forward to the prone figure while Sir Lewis leaned over him on the self-same walking stick. The hard, ebony-painted walnut cane was unblemished. "Still with us, Cecil? Excellent! Then there will be no misunderstanding. Leave Rosings and never return." The baronet faced his steward. "Perkins, see this man off the grounds, and let the word be spread throughout the estate and Hunsford that Cecil Kendrick is not to step foot on Rosings. Should he be found here after today, he is to be shot on sight. Are my instructions clear?"

"Aye, sir." Perkins turned his attention to Mr. Kendrick. "You heard the master. Get up, and mark what he says. Take him out, lads."

"Very good, Perkins. Oh—" Sir Lewis turned to the butler. "Apparently, Mr. Kendrick has bloodied the carpet. Pray have a maid clean it up."

By now, Mr. Kendrick had found his voice. "I-I will have you taken up for this, de Bourgh!"

Sir Lewis, unconcerned, gazed at his angry brother. With blood running down his neck, Mr. Kendrick was held up by his arms by the footmen. "Ah, Cecil, you still have not thought things through. *I* am the magistrate for this district. It is well known I have standing orders to shoot trespassers. As of now, you are a trespasser." Sir Lewis shrugged. "I could have you killed now for attacking Catherine, and that would be an end to it. Could I not, Perkins?"

"Aye, milord."

"Fortunately for you, I am a Christian man, and for my sister's sake I give you your life—*this* time." To the footmen, he ordered, "Take him away." Once a protesting Mr. Kendrick was frog-marched out of the room, Sir Lewis shut the door.

Lady Catherine, frightened and shocked by the sudden violence, slowly approached her husband.

Sir Lewis swung around. "Did I not decree that you should not entertain gentlemen without my presence?"

Lady Catherine stopped short, her hand to her throat. "I am mistress of the house, Lewis! It is my duty—"

"It was my will that you not entertain gentlemen outside of my presence. You will do as I say." His voice was like a whip.

"You…you cannot mean…you think I would—" She was horrified. "Lewis, I would *never* dishonor myself in such a manner!"

Sir Lewis smirked. "Of course not—not intentionally. You hardly *dishonor yourself* privately with your husband."

Lady Catherine flushed with shame.

"However, my dear," he continued, "you are far too handsome and far too trusting in your suspect judgment to be left to your own devices. This incident proves my point. You never should have received Cecil alone." He shook his head. "It shall not happen again. I shall so inform the butler and housekeeper."

By now, Lady Catherine had recovered a bit of her Fitzwilliam temper. "So, you do not believe I am capable of managing your house? Must you diminish me?"

"I do not diminish you, Catherine. In essentials, you are much as you were the day we married."

"Hateful, hateful man!"

Regret washed over Sir Lewis's face. "No, Catherine, you can never accuse me of hating you. No matter how you treat me, I shall protect you as I promised your father and brother."

The aggrieved matron seized upon that word. "Protection—yes! We must speak of that! That terrible man suggested we pledge Anne to his horrid son! We must make sure that never happens!"

"Of course not," Sir Lewis assured her. "Kendrick's son will never receive my permission."

"But we must prepare for any eventuality!" Lady Catherine put a hand to her head. "If we pledged Anne to someone else—someone noble—inside the family." Eyes aglow, she looked at her husband. "Anne and George's Fitzwilliam! He would be ideal!"

Sir Lewis was incredulous. "Arrange a match between your sister's son and our daughter? What mad idea is this? We are not of the peerage. We have no title to defend."

"Fitzwilliam would be perfect!" she continued, not heeding his assertion. "We would unite our great estates! We would improve the standings of three noble families. Anne would be protected by the Darcy name as well as ours!"

He dismissed her idea with a wave of his snuff-stained hand. "Anne is my heir. She need look to no one for protection unless it is her choice. I shall give her the ability to marry for affection."

"Affection? Only fools marry for affection!" she cried thoughtlessly.

"The greater fool marries without it, as I have cause to know," he responded sadly.

Insulted, Lady Catherine shot back. "I must wonder why you married me!"

The baronet sighed. "I often wonder about that myself. As the pretty daughter of an earl with a sizable dowry, one would think you would have a brain in your head and a heart in your breast. Either one would be welcome. Pray, inform me when you acquire one or the other." He bowed. "I am off to visit my daughter. Until dinner, madam." With that, he opened the door and left her.

Aghast, Lady Catherine could only stare at the opened door before she broke down in tears.

# Chapter 22

Two days later, Richard, dressed in his riding clothes, stood talking to Mr. Evans near the stable. Buford, who had accompanied him, leaned against a nearby fence.

"The gardener has begun planting in the new garden, sir," Mr. Evans reported.

Richard frowned at the plot. Only two men—the head gardener and a farmhand—were attending to the task. "Do we not have more men to work the soil? Where is the undergardener?"

"They are all seeing to the recovery of the old garden." Mr. Evans's tone was slightly dismissive.

"I was of the impression that salted soil was utterly ruined."

"Assuming it *is* salted, sir." Mr. Evans sniffed. "It is my opinion we can bring the old plot back to life."

Richard raised an eyebrow. "Then you think something else was the cause?"

Mr. Evans shrugged. "There could be any number of reasons. Sir Richard, you are a busy man. Leave everything to me."

"Have you tasted the soil, Mr. Evans?" called out Buford.

Mr. Evans's eyes flamed in anger. "Of course not! What does a parson know? Ridiculous notion!" The steward then caught himself. "That is no reflection on you, Sir John."

"Of course not," the knight returned. "But let us satisfy an old soldier's curiosity, shall we? Would you care to join me, Fitzwilliam?" At that, he righted himself and strolled to the ruined garden, Richard and Evans following in his wake. Buford walked well into the upturned soil and then faced his companions, gesturing at the dirt. "Would you care for the honors, Fitz?" Meanwhile, the workers toiling in the garden stopped to watch.

With a huff, Richard bent over and took a pinch of the black dirt. Buford did the same, Mr. Evans joining in after a brief hesitation. One by one, the gentlemen put the soil in their mouths.

Richard grimaced and spit it out. "Bah! It tastes like dirt!"

"True," responded Buford with a smirk, "but I do detect a hint of salt. What say you, Mr. Evans?"

The steward, who had also spit out his sample, reluctantly said, "There might be...it is hard to tell."

Richard took another pinch. This time, he concentrated. "Yes, I do taste salt. But it is very faint." He again spit out the revolting stuff. "How much does it take to ruin the soil?"

He called for the undergardener to join them. "Well?" Richard inquired of the steward. "How much does it take?"

"I...I am not certain." Mr. Evans was clearly embarrassed.

Richard asked the undergardener the same question. In his opinion, only a bit of salt would destroy a garden.

"Then we are wasting time here," Richard declared decisively. He spoke to the undergardener. "Take all the men from this place and have them assist planting the new gardens. We shall concern ourselves with this plot later. You may go."

The undergardener hastened to follow his master's orders, leaving a fuming Sir Richard with Mr. Evans. "The new gardens are a priority, Mr. Evans. Do you agree?" It was not a question.

"Of course, sir." Mr. Evans's face was red—from anger or mortification, Richard could not tell. "We shall finish the planting as soon as may be."

"Good." Richard marched out of the garden without dismissing

Evans, so great was his annoyance. Buford caught up with him near the stables.

"Are you still willing to ride out, Fitz?"

Richard swallowed his bad temper. "Of course." Just as he was about to call for the horses, he noticed a bit of cloth peeking out from behind a barrel next to the stable wall. The cloth was blue and white—and moving.

Richard leaned over to his left to better see what it was. "Miss Chloe?"

The child squeaked and squeezed back farther behind the barrel.

"Come out from there, child," Richard commanded. The little girl only whimpered.

The two gentlemen moved to the barrel. "What are you doing there?" asked Buford kindly. "Playing at hide-and-seek?"

Chloe answered in a nervous voice. "No."

Richard squatted on his heels. "Come out, Miss Chloe. There is nothing to fear."

"Yes, there is," the girl cried. "Mrs. Nivens will make me go inside, and I want to see the horsies!"

Richard grinned. He well remembered feeling the same when he was a lad. "Come out, and I shall show you the horses." He held out his hands.

Slowly, the frightened little girl moved towards Richard. She held a small wooden horse in one hand. Chloe stopped just out of arm's reach. "You promise?"

Richard gave her a stern look. "Miss Chloe, I always keep my promises."

"Oh, I do not know about that," chuckled Buford. "There was that time in Spain… What was the name of that village?"

"Enough, Buford." He gave his old friend a glare. "What happened in Spain stays there. Or, shall I bring up that incident In Lisbon?"

Buford smiled and held up his hand. "Have it your way, Fitz."

Returning his attention to Chloe, Richard gestured. The girl closed the distance, and Richard gathered her in his arms and stood up. "Good girl. So, you wish to see my horses, do you?"

Chloe looked at him with uncertain eyes and nodded her head.

Richard turned to the stable master, who had just come out of the barn. "Edwards, pray have the pony brought to me."

Mr. Edwards touched his forelock with a closed hand. "At once, Colonel."

Chloe closely looked at Richard. "You are a colonel?"

"I was." He turned so that she could see Buford. "Sir John was also a colonel." Buford acknowledged it with a wave.

"Oh." Chloe seemed to think. "My papa was a soldier like you. He is in Heaven now. Did you know my papa?"

Richard had tried to think of this little girl as simply the Darcys' ward, but Chloe had just reminded him she was the offspring of one of the few men he had ever hated. He cleared his throat. "Yes, we both did." He seriously doubted Wickham was anywhere near Heaven.

"I have a new papa now, and he is a colonel too," Chloe said sadly. "But he and Mamma went far away."

"I know. That is a soldier's lot."

"Uncle Darcy and Aunt Lizzy are nice, but I miss my momma."

"Of course, you do. I am sure she misses you too." Richard knew nothing of the sort, but he desired to cheer the girl. "Ah, look! Here is the pony."

He turned again so Chloe could see the animal being brought out by a lumbering stable hand and Mr. Edwards. The full-grown pony, used for hauling carts about the estate, was a little over ten hands tall. It owned a dark brown coat with bits of gold at its nose and hindquarters. Its mane was dark and long. An intelligent creature, it turned its attention to Chloe.

"He is pretty!" Chloe judged.

Richard whispered in Chloe's ear. "Actually, he is a she. This is Annabelle." Richard's attention was caught by the large stable hand. "Cork, is it not?"

Cork Johnson nodded. "Good day to ya, Colonel." The young man stood patiently by the pony, smiling. His usual malodorous aroma was enhanced by the smells of the stable, as his trousers were covered in manure.

Richard turned to Mr. Edwards. "Cork works in the stables?"

"Only when we're short of hands," said the stable master. "But he works hard, he does."

"Ah. Keep up the good work, Cork." The compliment earned a big grin from the simple-minded giant.

Richard's attention returned to the child. "Do you wish to touch Annabelle, Miss Chloe?"

Eyes wide with excitement, Chloe could only nod. Slowly, she reached out and stroked the pony's shoulder and withers. Chloe sighed contentedly as her fingers skimmed over the shiny, soft coat. They moved to the pony's head, and Chloe giggled when Annabelle gave a happy snort when she petted her nose.

"I think you made a friend," Richard observed.

Chloe's smile could light up the sky. "She is soft."

"Fitz," said Buford, "I think someone here is looking for our fair guest." He gestured toward the house. Mrs. Nivens was hurrying across the lawn towards the stable.

"Oh, no!" Chloe buried her face in Richard's shoulder, who was surprised to find how pleasant it felt.

"Chloe Wickham! There you are!" Mrs. Nivens cried. "Sir Richard, I apologize! I hope Miss Chloe has not caused you much trouble."

"Not at all," he assured the nanny. "We were enjoying Annabelle's company, were we not, Miss Chloe?" The child's response was to burrow deeper into Richard's shoulder.

"She has a habit of sneaking out of the nursery," Mrs. Nivens explained as she held out her hands for the child. "Now, Miss Chloe, you know you should not be outside without me or your aunt."

"Shall I be punished?" Chloe whimpered, pouting.

"Hmm." The nanny seemed to think it over. "If you do not make a fuss, you shall still have a biscuit this afternoon. Come along, now," she ordered with a smile.

Once Chloe was exchanged, she looked back at the pony. "Bye-bye, Annabelle."

Richard felt something warm inside him. The child was delightful, full of spunk and good humor. It was wrong of him to place the crimes of her father upon such an innocent. She could not choose her parents. Something started to shift in his mind. This sweet little girl was *Miss Chloe*, not *Miss Wickham*.

Impulsively, he offered, "When your aunt and uncle decide you are big enough, would you like to ride Annabelle?"

Chloe's eyes grew wide. "Yes! Yes!"

Richard laughed. "Then, be a good girl, and mind Mrs. Nivens." He leaned close. "An afternoon biscuit is serious business, is it not?"

She nodded and hugged the nanny as they returned to the manor, Richard quietly watching their progress. At the same time, Cork led Annabelle back to her stall while Mr. Edwards saw to saddling horses for Richard and Buford.

Buford broke the silence. "Miss Wickham is a lovely child."

"Yes," Richard returned thoughtfully. "You would not think it possible with such parents."

"You cannot blame a child for Wickham's crimes. I, for one, pity her—being she was abandoned by her mother."

"Was she?" Richard glanced at Buford. "There is no doubt she and her sisters will have a better life with their aunts in England than with Mrs. Wickham—Mrs. Denny now—in far-away India. Perhaps it was not so much abandonment as a great gift for their futures."

Buford grunted. "Caroline does not think well of Mrs. Denny. Most likely, the decision was her husband's. He may have talked her into it."

"Perhaps, perhaps. We may never know." Richard changed the subject. "Well, where do you wish to ride today?" The sound of hoofbeats from the road caused the two to look toward the front drive. "Hold! That is an express rider!"

Buford took a few steps forward. "News from Darcy, do you think?"

"It must be!" Richard hurried to the entrance of the stable. "Edwards, unsaddle the horses! I must return to the house this instant!"

Without waiting for a reply, the two retired colonels ran to Rosings manor.

THE LADIES OF ROSINGS SAT IN THE BLUE PARLOR, ENGAGED IN needlework. The others were making better progress than Elizabeth. Sewing was never a favored activity, and her personal concerns robbed her of even the tiny bit of attention she usually gave to it. All work came to a stop as Buford and Richard stormed into the room.

"Here is an express just come for Lizzy." Richard waved the message.

Conversation ceased as Elizabeth rose to receive the letter. A glance at the express calmed her. The writing was in Darcy's strong, tight hand. Surely, he was safe if he could write her!

Elizabeth quickly skimmed the letter. What she read brought a bright smile to her face. "If you will permit me, I shall read it aloud."

*Dearest Elizabeth,*

*Let me at once settle any fears you may have. I have arrived safely at Pemberley and in good time. While the alarming incidents that caused me to hurry to our home left great unease and fear among our people, let me assure you that no wickedness has befallen Pemberley, Lambton, or Kympton. I have heard the same from our brothers Bingley, Southerland, and Llewellyn, as well as from Matlock. Everyone is well.*

"Thank heavens Darcy is safe!" cried Anne.

"Charles and Jane too?" inquired Caroline.

Elizabeth nodded and returned to the letter. Her voice grew solemn as she continued.

*Mr. Thompson's alarm at the late events was justified by the number of people involved, the goals of the criminals, and the blood that was spilled. Their proposal was no less than the overthrow of the government by armed insurrection. Their objective was evil indeed, and their intent to commit rebellion is proven by at least one murder.*

"Damn them!" cried Buford, earning him a reprimand from his wife.

*The perpetrators' ability to accomplish their revolution, however, is far more doubtful. From what I have learned, the traitors intended to march from Derbyshire to Northampton on the night of the ninth, gathering men and weapons, building an army of the dissatisfied and angry, and eventually moving against London. Somehow, the government learned of their plans.*

*The march started near the village of Pentrich, between Derby and Matlock. The crowd went from house to farm, demanding food, weapons, and men. The crowd grew—how much I cannot say. Reports have it between a hundred to over three hundred. Drink was plentiful. However, most of the good people of the district wanted nothing to do with them. They hid, refusing to answer the ruffians' demands. In Pentrich, the Widow Hepworth's poor servant was murdered by the chief traitor.*

*The drunken louts continued through the night in the heavy rain to Nottingham, their number diminishing with every step due to the wet weather and disappointment over lack of support. The remaining marchers were met by the Hussars at Giltbrook, where they were routed. About forty are in the gaols. The leaders, however, have so far eluded capture.*

*While these sad events are not in the neighborhood of either Pemberley or Mayfield, dangerous individuals are still at large, and it is wise to exercise every precaution. I go this day to meet with Bingley and thence to Matlock the following day or the day after. Andrew and I hope to call on his Grace the Lord Lieutenant at Chatsworth before week's end.*

Elizabeth abruptly stopped and blushed. "The rest of the letter is…about mundane matters at home." She folded it. "I shall peruse it later."

While most of the assembled seemed satisfied with her statement, to Elizabeth's mortification, Caroline grinned. "*Mundane*, Eliza?"

*Teasing is far better than being teased*, thought a red-faced Elizabeth. "Perhaps *private* is a more accurate term, Caroline." That earned a short laugh from all attending.

"So, Darcy and our friends are safe," remarked Buford. "Good! Hopefully, the rest of the rabble will be rounded up soon. Damned traitors!"

"But, why?" was Anne's inquiry. "What did these people hope to accomplish? Overthrow the government? Preposterous!"

"I beg your pardon, Anne, but it is not preposterous at all." Buford took a seat next to Caroline. "Remember Spain, Fitz?"

Richard nodded. "Aye. The *guerrillas* rose up to take their country back from the French. Just farmers, shopkeepers, and the like, but they fought like *banditti*, from the houses and behind the trees. They struck anywhere, anytime. They kept the Frogs off-balance and destroyed their supplies. I do not think we would have freed Spain without them."

Anne clutched Richard's sleeve. "Do you believe that can happen here?"

"My dear Anne, would you have believed those mad Americans could have beaten us twice?" Buford said mildly.

"*Once*," argued Richard, "and that was with French help."

"And what would you call the late war? All of Admiral Cochrane's plans came to naught, especially at New Orleans."

Richard crossed his arms. "We did not lose that war!"

Elizabeth decided such talk was enough. "Darcy writes that all is now calm in the north, and the Duke of Devonshire will personally investigate what happened and why. His Grace is a good man, well respected, and not beholden to the current government."

"Aye, that is so," Richard agreed. "Parliament will listen to him."

"I have much less faith in Parliament than you." Buford earned a glare from Elizabeth for that, but he continued. "But Lizzy is right. Devonshire's word carries much weight."

"I, for one, care little about that. Charles and Jane are safe!" cried Caroline.

"And everyone at Matlock," added Anne. "Does my cousin say when he returns, Lizzy?"

Elizabeth rescanned the letter. Her joy was tempered by what she read. "He says he shall be occupied with Andrew and His Grace for several days. He will write again when he has more news." Elizabeth bit her lip in distress.

The others consoled her, Caroline adding, "Fear not, Eliza. Darcy is very clever. No harm can come to him while in the Duke's company, surely."

Such kind words did little to soothe Elizabeth's heart, and she soon excused herself from company. In the privacy of her chambers, she allowed herself to weep.

A few hours later, Richard received a letter from Brandon in London.

*The trial of the Spenceans has come and gone. Apparently, the government had a spy in the crowd, and the jury was convinced that he instigated the Spa Fields riot. The men were acquitted. I have no opinion of the verdict as I was not present at the trial. It is well, I think, that the government is keeping close watch on these people, but it looks very bad if our agents are encouraging insurrection for appearances' sake.*

*The government remains shaken, especially now over the late events in the north. Revolution is in the air, they say. I fear the feeling in Parliament is that strong action is necessary.*

Richard frowned. He had honorably served his King and his government all his life. To learn there were those in the ministry who would stoop to using spies was unsettling. If there was an infiltrator at Spa Fields, was there one, too, at Pentrich? And if so, did the spy simply observe the leaders of the march, or was he an instigator himself?

Government spies stirring up rioting! Troops used against the people! What the devil was happening to the country he loved?

MRS. JOHNSON WAS PREPARING THE NIGHTLY MEAL WHEN THE front door slammed open, and Adam and Simon Shepardson walked in.

Adam was in a foul mood. "Food, woman, an' be quick about it!"

It was a Tuesday, and the Shepardson brothers usually visited on Sundays and Wednesdays. Mrs. Johnson could not restrain her irritation. "You'll have to wait. I have little enough for Cork and me as it is."

Her remark had been a mistake. Adam took two strides and delivered an open-handed blow powerful enough to take her to the dirty floor. "I'll have nothin' out o' you, woman! We want food now!"

Mrs. Johnson cursed herself for not holding her tongue. It was not the first time she received a blow from one or the other of the Shepardsons. She wiped away a trickle of blood from the corner of her mouth. As she did so, her eyes fell upon a new and dangerous addition to Adam's belongings—a flintlock pistol.

Mrs. Johnson became truly frightened. Beatings were one thing—shootings were something else entirely. She kept her eyes lowered as she returned to her feet. It would not do to further enrage an armed Adam Shepardson.

The brothers were at the table, sharing a bottle of wine, when Mrs. Johnson noted that Simon was similarly armed. She was not foolish enough to inquire about the guns. Surely, they were stolen, and questions raised would lead to another beating.

"Th' food—" She paused to spit out blood. "Th' food will be ready soon." She knew there would be little for Cork or herself that night—again. The brothers did not respond, occupied as they were with drinking.

Simon finished his glass. "So, what's this idea o' yours ta make us rich?"

"Pour me another glass there," ordered Adam. "I've been doin' some thinkin'. We've gone about this thing all wrong. What we need ta do is—" He glanced at Mrs. Johnson and frowned. "Later, Simon."

The brothers were shoving the stew into their mouths when Cork returned home. He only smiled when his mother placed a gravy-covered slice of stale bread before him. Mrs. Johnson had the same, and the two ate in silence as the Shepardsons drank themselves into a stupor.

Mrs. Johnson was uneasy over the brothers' illegal activities. They were planning something different than petty larceny—something dangerous. She did not know what, but she feared that she was already caught up in it, and that terrified her.

The notion of informing anyone about her concerns never entered her mind. Whatever those two were planning, Mrs. Johnson's sole thoughts pondered whether she and Cork would live through it.

# Chapter 23

The trouble in Hunsford was caused, like many before and since, by the deadly mixture of a woman desired by two men and copious amounts of ale.

The girl was named Jenny, a comely serving wench known to be rather free with her favors. Her father owned the local pub and source of the ale, The Crowing Cock.

The rivals were a laborer and a farmer. The former was Joshua Tanner—handsome, foolish, gregarious, popular, and poor. The latter, Mr. Barnard, was everything young Joshua was not—fat, conniving, irritable, disliked, and middle-aged. He also owned his own cottage, which compensated for some of his shortcomings. Besides a lust for Jenny, the only thing the two men had in common was their excessive fondness for The Crowing Cock's excellent ale.

It was well known in Hunsford that the two men loathed each other. More than one angry argument between them had been witnessed. Some said afterwards that the tragedy could have been adverted had Jenny made her choice known, but the imprudent girl seemed to relish playing her two suitors against one another. And the tension in the village caused by the terrible growing season did not help matters.

Inevitably, one evening, it came to blows between Joshua Tanner and Mr. Barnard at The Crowing Cock. No one was certain who threw the first punch or pulled the first knife, but by the time the fight was over, both men suffered slashes and stab wounds. Mr. Barnard got the worst of it, lying dead in a pool of blood with a blade in his chest.

Young Joshua was taken in hand by the constable's men, and his wounds were attended to in the local gaol. There was no question as to his guilt. The men hated each other, a dozen witnessed the fight, and Barnard was dead. Normally, the only question would be the laborer's fate: face the noose or suffer transportation overseas.

But things were not normal that June. Hunger, frustration, and fear had changed Hunsford. What should have been a straightforward case of two drunken loudmouths fighting over a lightskirt was turned into a conflict between the classes.

A MAN COULD NOT BE CONDEMNED BY LOCAL OFFICIALS, FOR that was a pleasure reserved for the lords of the Crown's Courts in London. The procedure was for the local magistrate to review the evidence and, if sufficient, request that the man be sent to face justice in the capital.

The office of magistrate was typically entrusted to the major landowner in the district. There was a difficulty in Hunsford, for the largest estate nearby was Rosings Park, and in years past, was believed to be owned by Lady Catherine de Bourgh. Being a woman, she was forbidden the honor, so the village turned to another—at least nominally.

Mr. Lionel Hibbert owned a small estate a mile from Rosings. The gentleman had served as magistrate for many years after the untimely death of Sir Lewis de Bourgh. Mr. Hibbert was old and kindly, and very submissive to his betters. He might have held this high office in name, but everyone in the village knew the final decision belonged to Lady Catherine, and Mr. Hibbert always deferred to her judgment.

Now, he looked to Sir Richard Fitzwilliam for guidance, knowing soon he would gratefully turn over his office to him.

As colonel of a regiment of his majesty's cavalry, sitting in judgment of a man's life was not unknown to Richard. Meting out punishment had been one of his more unpleasant duties. He had served on several boards of court-martial and, more often than he liked, had to vote to hang thieves and murderers.

This, however, was a new experience for him. He had limited authority in the regiment, and he had never presided over a court-martial. With the magistrate relying on his judgment, Richard's was the deciding voice. By his word, the man could be sent to the courts, and it was rare indeed if the prisoner was not convicted.

Richard and Mr. Hibbert heard the case in the assembly hall. At their side were Mr. Evans, Mr. Clarke, and the constable. Witnesses told what they had seen, the apothecary testified as to the cause of death, and the character of the two men involved was discussed. Three other men observed the proceedings: Mr. Collins, Sergeant Gregory, and Sir John Buford.

Richard rubbed his brow, feeling Mr. Hibbert's eye upon him, the weight of responsibility heavy on his conscience. The verdict was a foregone conclusion, for there could be no doubt that Joshua Tanner had caused the death of Mr. Barnard.

In his short time at Rosings, Richard had become acquainted with the two men. The bullying Mr. Barnard had been a thorn in his side due to the man's stubbornness over adapting modern methods of farming and the unpleasant way he expressed his disagreement with new ideas. Young Joshua was a jolly, stupid boy with a hot temper who lacked a firm hand to guide him. Both men undoubtedly had been in their cups.

Privately, Richard knew Hunsford was a better place without Mr. Barnard, and he wished Young Joshua could simply be impressed into the Royal Navy. *They* would drill some discipline into the man, but that could not be. The war was over, a man was dead, and Richard had no choice.

Mr. Hibbert tapped his fingertips on the desk. "Have you anything to add, Sir Richard?" By his tone, Richard knew Hibbert was asking for his decision.

He sat up straight. "I have heard enough. I believe there is sufficient evidence for you to proceed."

"Very well," said Hibbert. "The charge is manslaughter, and the prisoner shall be held in gaol until such time as he can be transferred to the proper authorities in London." He raised his gavel.

Buford cleared his throat.

Richard glared at his old friend. Was he challenging his decision? He whispered to Hibbert, "We need to discuss this privately."

Hibbert nodded. To the room, he proclaimed, "This court of inquiry shall go into closed deliberation. All others please leave the room."

"Except Sir John and Sergeant Gregory," Richard added.

The witnesses left without comment, but Mr. Collins rose. "My dear gentlemen, surely you mean for me to remain as well! I flatter myself that as God's humble representative in Hunsford and one of Sir Richard's closest counselors, I should be at his side to offer what consolation you may request! Of course, I am not worthy to hold such a lofty office, and I am forever grateful that you have entrusted me—"

Richard cut him off. "As unique as your advice usually is, I think the needs of Mr. Barnard's family are paramount, Mr. Collins. Your kind words of consolation are what is required in the present circumstances."

"But Mr. Barnard has no family in the village, except for a cousin—"

"Indeed, sir! And is not a cousin a family member? After all, consider your connections."

The reminder that he was related by marriage to the august Darcy family clearly assuaged the vicar's massive sense of self-importance. "You are right, you are very right—as always, my dear, dear Sir

Richard! Cousins are as important a relation as any, I always say. Of course, Mr. Barnard's cousin has need of my office. I shall provide the looked-for succor, never fear!" The man nearly ran out of the building.

Sergeant Gregory grinned as he approached the bench with Buford. "You're gettin' very good at handling him, Colonel, if you don't mind me sayin' so."

"That man is addlepated," retorted Mr. Evans.

The remaining men frowned at the steward's insulting comment. "He is a very loyal man, sir," returned Richard sharply, "and I do not undervalue loyalty. It has served me well more than once on the battlefield," he turned to his old brother-in-arms, "eh, Buford?"

"Very true, as well as rude honesty between comrades."

Richard colored. "You believe the verdict wrong?"

"About that young fool in gaol? No. I am only concerned about the consequences. Things are not what they should be out there." Buford gestured at the lone, high window.

"I would listen to him, Colonel," said Sergeant Gregory. "There's a lot of grumbling in town. Young Joshua's very popular."

"Don't like that," said the constable.

Mr. Evans snorted. "Why should that be a concern of ours? May I remind you that a farmer has been killed—by a drunken laborer no less? We must maintain order."

Gregory scowled. "Order is important, but so's justice. Barnard was a right bastard."

"So, he deserved to die?" Mr. Evans shot back. "You shock me, Sergeant."

"You know I don't mean that."

Richard had to reestablish control. "Gentlemen, quarrelling will not serve. Mr. Clarke, what is your opinion?"

Clearly, Mr. Clarke wanted to be somewhere else. "Sir Richard, I don't think we have any choice. Unpopular as he was, Mr. Barnard was a tenant farmer. The rest of us look to you for protection. There must be law and order in Hunsford.

"Look here, I told Young Joshua time and again that his wild ways would be the death of him. I'm just sorry that it has come true. I'm sure he didn't mean to kill Mr. Barnard, and maybe we can say so to the court."

Gregory threw up his hands. "That won't do any good!"

"Gregory, be silent!" Richard ordered. "Continue, Mr. Clarke."

Clarke could not look Richard in the eye. "Sir, the tenants depend on you. You've my trust, you know that—I owe everything to you. But like you said, loyalty's important. It goes both ways. You expect that we be loyal to you, and you should—"

"But the tenants expect that their loyalty be returned," Richard gently finished. "I understand."

"It does not matter that this boy is popular, Sir Richard," Mr. Evans stated coldly. "The law is clear."

"Would you say the same if things were the other way around? If it were Barnard in gaol and Tanner dead?" Gregory sneered.

During the preceding argument, Buford had remained silent. He now rose to his feet, ending all talk. "This discussion is pointless. May I speak bluntly, Fitz?"

"Why not? Everyone else has." Richard felt a headache coming on.

Buford looked pointedly at the others. "This is not about whether that boy is guilty or not. My opinion is that he is, but that is not the problem before you. The question is whether you can ship him to London without causing a riot."

Mr. Evans scoffed. "A riot? Oh, come now, Sir John!"

Buford ignored the steward. "We have seen this before, Fitz. Remember that little village in Spain when supplies were running low? The locals were infuriated that the quartermaster was requisitioning so much from the town stores. We almost had to turn our guns on the very people we were trying to liberate."

"If that supply train had been delayed another few days, we would've had to defend ourselves," added Gregory.

"It was very nearly an uprising," Buford continued, "and things would have gone very badly indeed had not the general talked to the village elders, telling them we were as hungry as they.

"The point is that it is not important *what* we are doing. What is important is what it *appears* we are doing. We have to talk to the townspeople."

Richard looked Buford in the eye. "You mean *I* have to talk to them."

"Is that not what you signed up for?"

Richard sighed. "Spoken like a second son who does not manage an estate."

His best friend shrugged.

"I think that would be wise, Sir Richard," Mr. Hibbert hesitantly offered. Mr. Clarke nodded his agreement.

"Very well." Richard turned to his steward. "Mr. Evans, arrange a town meeting for tomorrow night, if you please. Mr. Hibbert, I believe the decision stands. Send Tanner to London as soon as may be."

CORPORAL FROST WAS TAKING HIS EASE BEFORE ATTENDING his duties, drinking a tankard of wine in a small sitting room reserved for the servants and wondering what Abigail was doing at that moment, when Sergeant Gregory appeared.

"Any more o' that left, Frost, or are you drinking my master out of house and home?"

Frost reached over to a sideboard for another tankard while Gregory sat opposite him. "How'd it go in town? You look right put out." He poured a drink and handed it over.

Gregory took a large gulp. "Education's mightily overrated, if you ask me. All that sitting 'round, listening to fat dons in their funny hats, drives common sense out of a fellow! They can't see what's right before 'em."

"I take it things didn't go well."

Gregory leaned over the table. "This town's ready to explode, but their lordships can't see it"—he jerked a thumb up over his shoulder—"except maybe your Sir John." He explained what had been decided.

Frost frowned. "Tomorrow? Blast, Gregory, they ought to be talkin' to 'em tonight out there in the taverns! You don't wait to put out a fire."

"You're right there an' no mistake. Everybody'll know by noontime tomorrow that Young Joshua was shipped out during the night. What happens then, eh? Nothin' good."

Frost cursed. "Can't you talk Sir Richard out of it?"

"No. The colonel's listening to that fool Evans."

Just then the door opened. "Corporal Frost, Sir John is preparing to retire," said Mrs. Parks.

"Thank you, madam. I'll bid you good night, Gregory. Get some sleep. Things will look better in the morning." Corporal Frost left with Mrs. Parks, and Sergeant Gregory was left to his dark thoughts.

"I hope you're right, Frost. I hope to God you're right."

# Chapter 24

The next afternoon, Sir Richard was working on the accounts in his study when Anne walked in without ceremony. "I want to go with you."

Richard's head jerked up in surprise. "Where? Do you mean to the meeting tonight?" He set down his pen, a slightly patronizing expression on his face. "My dear, you cannot go with me."

"And why not, may I ask? I am the patroness of Hunsford."

"But Anne—ladies at such a meeting? It simply is not done, as you are well aware."

"Hang propriety! They are my people. I should be there."

"Anne, you are being unreasonable."

"Unreasonable? Rosings Park belongs to me!"

Richard flinched as though he had been struck. He slowly got to his feet. "It was my understanding that Rosings was *ours*. I hope I have given you good service, madam." His lips were taunt and white.

Anne knew how deeply she had hurt her husband. In her anger, she had forgotten he was insecure and sensitive about his position at Rosings. "Oh, Richard, let us not quarrel. Of course it is ours. You have done a remarkable job managing the estate, but I believe I should attend this meeting with you."

She was relieved to see Richard relax. "I understand your feelings, my dear, and in a manner of speaking, you are correct. You are indeed the patroness of Hunsford. But you are also my wife, and it is your husband who requires you to remain here, safe and sound."

"You speak as though there is danger!"

Richard waved his hands. "No, no. I phrased it poorly. Anne, there will be farmhands, laborers, and such at this assembly. They are rough people, and there will be rough language—certainly, nothing fit for a lady's ears. I seek only to protect you. It will be a short assembly in any case. I shall inform them of the things you and I decided to do in case the harvest goes bad again. The villagers will be appeased, and I shall be home before you miss me." He took her hands. "I promise I shall speak to them in our name."

Anne was only slightly appeased. "But if I am not needed, why should you go? Would not Mr. Evans do as well?"

Richard shook his head. "I do not think so. The army has taught me that men want to hear from their commanding officers. To leave too much to subordinates hurts morale. A good officer always leads from the front. By this, he wins their hearts and loyalty. I believe the same applies to landowners." His mood darkened. "Besides, I believe I have made a mistake taking on Mr. Evans."

Anne frowned. "What has he done?"

"It is not so much a matter of what he has done as how he does things. He is proficient in all his duties except ensuring loyalty. He is all pride and insolence to those beneath him, including the tenants."

"I know your man Gregory does not like him."

"The feeling is mutual, and Gregory is not one to hide his abhorrence. It has led to many quarrels. I shall have to have a word with them both once this matter is behind us." He sighed. "But that is a matter for another day."

Anne glanced at the clock. "I have a light dinner planned, and it should be ready. Shall we retire to the dining room?"

Richard, smiling roguishly, took Anne into his arms. "Not until I have my dessert first, my sweet."

Anne lost herself in the kiss, putting aside her fears for a time.

"ANNE IS WORRIED, AND SO AM I." CAROLINE SAID AS CORPORAL Frost helped Sir John dress for dinner. "Is this speech truly necessary?"

Buford winced as Frost tightened his cravat. "It is, my dear. Fitz cannot leave the townspeople uninformed. To do so would only increase suspicion and unrest." He turned to his wife. "We Bufords have always been open with our people, and it has served us well."

Caroline shook her head. "But this is Rosings Park, not Buford Manor."

"The people of Kent are no different than our good Welsh folk."

His wife was not so sure. The former Caroline Bingley had learned much since her marriage, and many of her lessons deposed closely held beliefs. Instilled at a young age was her superiority to servants and the working class. Life at Buford Manor had shown her a different way, a different life. At her husband's ancestral home, respect between the classes was the rule, not the exception. It was not hard to build trust, she had been told. All that was necessary was to talk to those under their protection and patronage. Talk *to*, not talk *at*.

It was simple, difficult, and revolutionary—and to her incredulity, it had worked.

Caroline constantly struggled to disregard habits and opinions implanted by her parents and schoolmates. That she did spoke volumes of her determination to please her husband. She did not like the idea of Sir Richard facing an angry mob and hated that John was determined to stand at his comrade's side, but she knew her husband would not be swayed. His character would allow nothing else. Acceptance of the ways of a brave and honorable officer—or former officer—came at a price that was sometimes high.

While she disagreed with her husband's estimation of the people of Hunsford, she could not have him leave with cross words between them. Experience had shown her humor was the best way to soothe him. Therefore, Caroline took his hand.

"Are you saying the people of Kent are equal to the Welsh?

Goodness, sir, shall you never again wear the leek on St. David's Day?"

The cocky smile she loved grew on Buford's ruined, adored face. "You know me better than that. Ah, you are a game lass, my vain Yorkshire beauty! I shall be back soon." He added in a serious tone, "Stay close to Anne. She needs you."

Caroline would have kissed him, had the corporal not been there. "Frost, I shall depend upon *you* to stay close to Sir John!"

"I shall be his shadow, my lady. And here is our insurance." He slipped a brace of pistols into his belt.

As the sun set, the men of the district filled Hunsford Common. The village green was in the middle of the town, bordered on the west side by the church. Along the north side was the main road, and it was there most of the shops were located, as well as the inn. On the south side were the houses of the more prosperous personages, as well as the assembly hall. A public house, the stable, and the smithy took up a portion of the east side, which gave way to woods. Trees lined the edges of the common on all sides, and the overhanging branches reflected the torches that lit the area, adding to the uncertain air.

A flatbed wagon sat at the end of the common nearest the church. It was obviously a stage. Four chairs were upon it, and steps up from the ground had been constructed. There, the tenant farmers, constable, and other leaders of the community huddled, eying the growing throng in the center of the space. The green was filled with disgruntled farmhands and other laborers, many walking over from the town's taverns. They milled about, mumbling amongst themselves and casting dark looks at their betters. There were a few women in their midst even though it was not their place. The shopkeepers stood apprehensively along one side close to their establishments, some holding clubs, for they knew that if things got out of hand, their shops would feel the brunt of any riot.

The party from Rosings rode up to the makeshift stage. That

seemed to be a signal. Mr. Evans, Mr. Collins, and the constable ascended onto the wagon bed.

"Gentlemen, gentlemen," cried Mr. Collins, "your attention, good men of Hunsford! And…and ladies too, I see! Peace, my friends, peace! We have gathered here at the request of the honored consort of our beloved patroness! Our Savior requires obedience. Please quiet yourselves and bow your heads as I give the invocation."

After suffering through a long and thoroughly muddled prayer, the crowd finally murmured their amens, and Mr. Evans strode forth. "People of Hunsford, as you are aware, a terrible crime has occurred. Mr. Barnard, a valued and honored member of the community—"

"Valued and honored, my arse," grumbled one of the farmhands.

"Mr. Barnard has been viciously cut down in the prime of his life," Evans continued. "What makes this most tragic is that this foul deed was perpetrated by one of our own. The criminal has been apprehended and handed over to the proper authorities."

The crowd started to jeer.

Mr. Evans grew more strident. "No man is above the law, no matter who he is! Justice will be served, I promise you!"

"*Whose* justice?" cried a voice from the throng.

"Rich man's justice?" yelled another.

"Enough of that!" Mr. Evans demanded. "English justice is fair and swift! But you are summoned here not to debate one man's guilt or innocence! We have condescended to speak to you, to inform you about what has occurred, and what steps will be taken to prevent happenings such as this from occurring again!"

Buford leaned over towards Richard, saying in a low voice, "What is that fool doing?"

"Evans is makin' things worse, Colonel," added Sergeant Gregory.

Richard nodded. "I had best see to this." He dismounted and climbed the stairs. "A moment, Mr. Evans," he called out cheerfully.

His steward was obviously put out at being interrupted. "Sir

Richard, there is no need for you to waste your time talking to this—"

Richard cut him off. "I shall take things from here, my good man." His calm words belied his growing temper.

"Sir, I must protest!"

Richard moved close to Mr. Evans, his expression now thunderous. "You are relieved, sir." His sharp whisper lashed Mr. Evans like a slap. "You shall *never* question me again." Richard's lips hardly moved, his voice low and slow, but each word hammered into the steward.

Mr. Evans blanched. "Of course, Sir Richard." He reluctantly bowed and stepped back.

The knight's blazing eyes left his steward's distraught face only when he nodded. Richard schooled his features, and by the time he turned to the crowd, he was his usual affable self.

"Good people of Hunsford, I thank you for coming tonight! This meeting has been called to discuss several matters facing all our families. One has already been raised"—he gestured at Mr. Evans— "a sad business that strikes at the very heart of Hunsford. This is a tragedy, there can be no doubt, and it is natural that feelings are high." The crowd growled in agreement. "But, my friends, we are Englishmen! We are all equal before the law! We must put our trust in the law!"

A few jeers arose and Richard cut them off. "We are—we must! I fought for that. You know me, my friends. Most of my life I wore the King's uniform. I fought our enemies up and down the length of Europe. I have seen with my own eyes how foreign folk suffer under the yoke of tyranny. What they would not give to trade places with you in Jolly Ole England!"

The crowd's response was mixed. Heckles vied with cries of "Here, here!"

Richard spoke gently now. "I know you are angry. I am angry too. Such a calamity never should have happened, not to us."

"That's easy for you to say, northerner!"

Richard did not change his tone. "True, I was not born here. I came from the untamed wilds of Derbyshire. I have *chosen* to live here."

A few men in the crowd murmured. "I have! I do not have to live at Rosings to profit from it. Many in London choose to reside in the city, leaving their estates in the hands of stewards and overseers." Richard noted the grumbling at the mention of a steward. "But Lady Fitzwilliam would not have that, and neither would I. Rosings Park is our home, my home, here in the lush, rolling hills of Kent. Happy are the people who reside in the garden of England! Lady Fitzwilliam and I know our responsibility to Hunsford.

"The last year has been hard, I know, and I would be honest with you. We fear this year will be difficult too." He turned to Mr. Collins. "We, of course, send our prayers to the Almighty to save us from hunger and hardship." He turned back to the crowd, "But while we pray for the best, we must steel ourselves for the worst. This is the reason I wished to speak with you tonight."

"What do *you* know of hardship?" someone in the back of the crowd called out.

To the surprise of those gathered, Richard laughed. "You have never served the King, I take it!" He pointed at a man near the front. "You there—Henry Baker! You were with us at Corunna! Tell them how we pitched our tents in the freezing rain. Tell them how we held off charge after charge of the Frogs with our backs to the ocean!"

Mr. Baker, a shopkeeper, said nothing, but nodded his head in agreement.

"And you, Thomas Donaldson! You have a son in the navy, do you not? Bosun's mate, if I recall."

"Aye, sir," answered the proud tenant farmer.

"Would you say living on hardtack and bad water was easy?"

"Hell, no! Um, beggin' your pardon, sir." Mr. Donaldson's

response drew laughter from the crowd, and Richard joined in.

He gestured at Buford, Gregory, and Frost. "Would you gentlemen call Waterloo a ride in the park?" His long glance at Buford's missing arm was noted by all.

The master of Rosings lowered his voice. "Hardship comes in many forms, my good people." He then stood tall, hands on his hips. "Which is why Lady Fitzwilliam and I shall see to it that no one goes hungry this winter!"

The people cheered. By good humor and honest words, Richard had skillfully taken most of the crowd into his hands. The support for Joshua Tanner was a symptom of the fear and dissatisfaction infecting Hunsford. By addressing the people's real anxiety, he had turned the crowd away from the violence that was simmering below the surface.

Richard's brief discourse on his and Lady Fitzwilliam's plans was interrupted by a farmhand asking dolefully, "But what about Joshua?"

Most of the crowd, their attention now turned to their own concerns, tried to shout the man down, but Richard would have none of it.

"Aye, what about Joshua Tanner?" he sadly observed. "I shall not lie to you. This is a most serious matter. And like us all, he must reap what he has sown. I think it does us well to pray for him, and Mr. Barnard too. No good can come of this. It is a tragedy and no mistake.

"Let us all return to our homes and embrace our families. Life is short, and we must keep our loved ones close. Mr. Collins, a benediction, if you will?"

As the rector stepped up, Richard whispered, "A *short* one would be best, do you not think?"

RICHARD DESCENDED FROM THE WAGON WITH MR. COLLINS and walked over to where Buford held his horse's reins, Mr. Evans trailing behind him. Mr. Collins, as was his wont, prattled insistently over his patron's performance before the crowd, declaring it the finest speech ever delivered in Hunsford. Richard allowed the foolish man's blathering to wash over him, his mind fixed on the problem of Mr. Evans.

As loath as he was to admit it, Richard saw that Darcy and Gregory had been right. It had been a mistake to hire Mr. Evans. The man's knowledge in the new scientific ways were more than offset by his arrogant and offensive manner with the tenants and villagers. The man almost caused a riot!

The question was what to do with him. Was his steward hopeless of remedy? Could he be led to better behavior by training and example, or should he dismiss Mr. Evans only months before the harvest? There were no good answers to those questions.

"Bravo, Fitz!" said Buford as he handed over the reins. "You calmed that mob right down."

"Aye, Colonel." Sergeant Gregory leaned over his saddle. "Why, they were eating out of your hand there at the end." He glared at Mr. Evans. "Of course, if the crowd hadn't been incited in the first place—"

"Enough, Gregory." Richard noticed Mr. Evans's red face, and he did not need an argument between the two men on the village green. He turned his attention to Mr. Clarke as he approached the group.

"Well done, Sir Richard!" the farmer cried. "A few of the tenants are taking their ease in The Crowing Cock, and we'd be happy to drink in your honor."

"Thankee, Mr. Clarke." An idea came to Richard. "Would you object if I bought a round?"

"Why, you honor us, sir!" cried the surprised man. "But you need not trouble yourself."

Richard tossed his reins to a stable hand. "Nonsense! In fact, I would like to join you, if you would not mind."

Mr. Clarke was not the only man stunned. "Sir Richard, you are not seriously—" Mr. Evans was silenced by his employer's dark look.

"Evans, I do not need a nursemaid." Richard glanced at a smirking Sergeant Gregory. "No advice from you?"

The majordomo shook his head. "One can take Colonel Fitzwilliam out of the army, but one cannot take the army out of Red Fitz."

Richard laughed. He had been known to down a pint or two with his men. "And do not forget it, Troop Sergeant-Major! Do not wait up for me. I shall see you in the morning. Come, Mr. Clarke, before the ale runs out."

The remainder of the Rosings party rode back to the estate in the dark. About halfway there, an uneasy Corporal Frost gave Sergeant Gregory a significant look. The two surreptitiously slowed their mounts, allowing Sir John and Mr. Evans to ride ahead.

Gregory lowered his voice. "What is it?"

Frost turned in the saddle, glancing back at Hunsford. "You think it's all right to leave Sir Richard alone?"

"Of course." The sergeant frowned. "You disagree?"

"I...well, the crowd was unruly before. Are you sure everything's quieted down now?"

"It is for now. The mob's thinking more about their bellies getting filled than that stupid bugger sittin' in the gaol. By this time tomorrow, after he's shipped off to London, they'll have a hard time remembering his name. I should have known the colonel would see to things."

"Yes, he did all right..." Frost knew that Gregory's assurances made sense, but the corporal could not escape a feeling of unease. He had a sense of increased awareness when matters were not as they first appeared. It had kept him—and Sir John—alive in Spain.

"What has you so troubled?" asked his companion.

Frost knew he was not infallible. He had been wrong before and laughed off the false alarms. Still, the hairs on the back of his head had not been like this since Vitoria.

"I don't like riding in the dark, that's all."

"Hah, the colonel ain't the only man to need an ale! Ride on, Frost!"

# Chapter 25

Sir Richard Fitzwilliam stirred, slowly coming to the realization that something was wrong. He was dazed and in pain, his head hurting, his mouth as well. It was pitch black though his eyes were open. Something was covering them. He tried to rub his face, but he could not move his hands—they were secured behind him! *What the devil?*

He kicked his feet, only to discover that, like his hands, they were tied together! His mind worked urgently while he instinctively struggled. His inability to see was caused by a blindfold. The fullness in his mouth was a gag. He was bound hand and foot. He was a prisoner!

He was seated on some sort of mat. His jerky attempts to free himself had rolled him onto a hard, rough surface. His nose worked—the space smelled awful. He tried to yell, but all he could manage were muffled grunts and squeals.

They must have been loud enough, for he heard a door open and close, footsteps drawing near. He turned towards the sound, rage replacing panic.

"Awake now, are ya?"

The uncultured male voice was slightly muffled. Richard tried to speak, but the gag served its purpose, his inaudible curses amusing his visitor, if his chuckles were any indication.

"Ya might as well save yerself th' trouble, yer highness. Yer never gettin' out of them knots."

Richard struggled to sit up, only to be slammed painfully back down on the wood floor. "Did I tell ya to sit up?" the man growled. "I'm in charge now! Be still if ya knows what's good fer ya!"

Richard lay quietly, realizing there was no profit in resisting.

"Not so high an' mighty now, are ya?" His captor sounded pleased—and familiar, even muffled. Where had he heard that voice before?

"This is the way it is, yer highness. Yer ta be our guest fer a time. I expect yer family'll be wantin' ya back, so's we have a little bargainin' ta do. If'n everybody's reasonable, you'll be back in yer big house in no time. If not…well…" He punctuated his statement with a kick in Richard's ribs. He gasped in pain.

"Don't cause no trouble, or yer'll get worse than that, ya can be sure. An' keep quiet, or yer'll be shut up fer good. Ya understand, rich man? Nod, damn ya!"

Richard did so.

"Good. Yer'll be fed twice a day. Don't try nothin', or we'll kill ya." He heard the man stand up. "Good day, yer highness." Footsteps moved away, and the opening and closing of a door signaled that his captor had gone.

Left alone, Richard struggled to free himself. That proved unsuccessful, so he settled for twisting around until he could sit up. It took him some time to locate the mat again. Thin and stinking, it was better than the unyielding wood floor. Fortune was with him, and he was able to wedge himself into a corner.

Richard called on his military training, concentrating on his situation. He was being held captive for ransom. Therefore, he was in no immediate danger, but it was cold comfort. He was a member of the aristocracy—son of an earl and knight of the realm—and that made this kidnapping a hanging offense. His captors would grow desperate, he was certain.

He shook off his fear by concentrating on his enemies, for he was certain there had to be more than one man involved. The question was how many. If he did free himself, could he defeat them? If only he knew the number!

His head pounded, and his side ached, but Richard forced himself to relax. His only chance of escape was to make his captors think he was paralyzed with fear and wait for them to make a mistake. His time would come, he told himself.

With the genesis of a plan, he permitted himself to think of Anne. By God, how long had he been here? What must she be thinking? Try as he might, Richard could not but be distressed by what Anne must be suffering.

This fueled his anger. *By all that is holy, these men will pay for this!*

Anne had not slept well and was eager to dress, go down for breakfast, and speak to her husband. To her surprise, Richard was not at the breakfast table.

"Has anyone yet broken their fast?" she asked a maid.

"No, madam," the girl reported. "Sir Richard has not come down yet, and neither have Sir John or Lady Buford. Mrs. Darcy is out walking in the gardens."

It was unusual for Richard not to rise before her, but Anne told herself not to fret over it. Surely, he had not returned until late. Disappointed, she sat down to her first cup of tea for the day. It was not long before she was joined by Sir John.

"Are you not eating?" he inquired after greeting her.

"In a moment. I am waiting for Richard."

Buford laughed. "So, you share breakfast together. I cannot be so gallant, for Caroline loves her bed in the morning more than breaking her fast, and I would grow hungry awaiting her!"

Buford filled a plate, and the two fell into an easy conversation. They were soon joined by Elizabeth who had returned from her morning walk. It was the appearance of Caroline that reminded Anne of her missing husband. She rose and went to look for Mrs. Parks.

"Pray send a footman above stairs to inquire when Sir Richard will join us," she asked the housekeeper.

Mrs. Parks seemed perplexed. "Milady, did you not know? Sir Richard did not return last night."

Anne was stunned. "What? Why was I not informed?"

"I was just told myself. It was known he was making merry at The Crowing Cock until late. It is thought he slept at the inn."

"What is this?" Buford approached them from the breakfast parlor. "I could not but overhear. Fitzwilliam did not return last night?"

"No, he did not." Mrs. Park's voice grew concerned.

"That is not at all like him," Buford declared. He turned to Anne. "In Spain, he always returned to his quarters, no matter how much he drank. I should know. I often shared a tent with him. He said it was a point of honor."

"Oh, good heavens," cried Anne. "What could have happened to him?"

"I am certain there is a good explanation," Buford said lightly, in an attempt to calm her. "If you will excuse me, I shall make inquiries in Hunsford."

"Take Gregory with you!"

"I shall." Buford took Anne's hand. "Do not worry. I shall have him home in a trice."

TWO HOURS LATER, IT WAS APPARENT TO BUFORD THAT HE would not be able to keep his promise. Both Richard and his horse had disappeared. Details were very unclear.

"I left the tavern before Sir Richard," reported Mr. Clarke. "He did not appear to me to be foxed. Indeed, he drank very little."

The publican corroborated Mr. Clarke's statement. "He was th' last to leave an' said good night most gentleman-like. It were a fine thing for him to come in."

Questions posed to those at the stable were no help.

"I'm sorry, sir," said a stable hand. "I had to answer a call o' nature, an' when I got back, Sir Richard's horse was gone, saddle an' all. Nothin' strange about that. I've seen th' colonel saddle his horse afore instead o' waitin'."

Richard was not at the inn.

"This makes no sense!" Sergeant Gregory said in a huff. "Where the devil is he?"

"Perhaps," Mr. Evans allowed, "he is at a private house. Gentlemen are known to have…friends."

Gregory turned on Mr. Evans. "Here now! Just what are you implying?"

"Come, sir, we are all adults." The steward smiled. "Sir Richard is a charming man."

Buford quickly stepped between the two before a growling Gregory could do harm to the sanctimonious steward. "Mr. Evans, by voicing that statement, it is clear you do not know your employer at all. He has been my friend for almost half my life, and I can report with absolute certainty that he has never engaged in the behavior you insinuate."

"I can vouch for that as well!" cried Gregory.

Mr. Evans nodded. "Forgive me, sir. I am sure you both are correct."

Buford was certain Mr. Evans's apology was not sincere, but he had other matters with which to contend—namely finding Sir Richard Fitzwilliam. "Gregory, form a search party," he ordered. Fortunately, the Rosings majordomo accepted his command.

"Sir John, is that really necessary?" asked Mr. Evans.

"I would not request one for my amusement, sir," Buford snapped at the steward. To his satisfaction, the overbearing man blanched. "And, Gregory, notify the magistrate." He faced Mr. Evans. "Just in case."

"THERE YA GO, SIR RICHARD." THE MAN GAVE RICHARD'S BONDS a sharp yank.

"He ain't getting' outta that!" giggled his partner.

Richard kept his still-aching head down, forcing himself not to show any reaction. When the kidnappers returned with food, they decided they had better things to do than hand feed their captive. Richard's hands were now tied before him, rather than behind his back. A length of rope had been tied between his hands and feet. He could touch his mouth, but only when he sat.

Because he could also reach his eyes, the kidnappers had removed his blindfold. Thanks to a lone candle brought in by the villains, Richard could survey his prison. It was a small, windowless room with shelves on one side, probably used for storage. It was empty except for himself, a thin mat on the floor, and a bucket.

He could not escape while his bonds were changed, for one of the villains held a blade to his throat while his confederate worked. They both hid their identities by covering their heads with sacks, holes cut for their eyes.

It did not matter. Richard now had a good idea who his enemies were.

The head kidnapper—Richard had so named him for he seemed to be in charge—set down a plate with a bit of bread next to his hand. "Yer breakfast, yer lordship," he mocked.

Richard said nothing as he ate, thankful the man was unable to be silent. *Morning, eh? Another mistake, you bastard.*

The man gestured to the bucket. "I think even a gent like yerself can figure what that's for. Mark it well. It'll be damn unpleasant should ya overturn it in th' dark."

"I shall keep that in mind," said Richard as neutrally as he could, his blood still boiling over his mistreatment.

"Ya better!" cried the other man. "I ain't cleanin' it up!"

The leader took the plate and candle. "Remember what I told ya. Make not a sound, or you'll get the gag again. Understand?"

"I do."

The kidnapper gestured at his comrade and the two left the room, the sound of the turning lock echoing in the darkness. Richard chewed on the half stale bread and thought.

He had recognized the leader's voice. Adam Shepardson, former footman and current stable hand at Rosings, had the annoying habit of occasionally referring to Sir Richard as "yer lordship." The stupid fool had neglected to guard his tongue. He also had a layabout brother in Hunsford. It was obvious they were his captors.

Shepardson had made more than one mistake. In the darkness, Richard had no idea what day it was. Now he was fairly certain it was the morning after the meeting in the village. And by tying his hands in front, he could reach the ropes that secured his feet. Richard had all the time in the world to loosen those bonds and free his legs. When the opportunity presented itself, he would rush the door when it was opened.

He had to be patient and careful though. Surely, the scoundrels would take great care when they came again. Richard would have to wait until they grew overconfident.

Richard leaned against the wall and planned his escape.

IN THE LATE AFTERNOON, ANNE MET WITH SERGEANT GREGORY and Mr. Evans in Rosings's small parlor. Sir John, Caroline, and Elizabeth were also in attendance. It was a taxing event. While Anne valiantly attempted to project the calm comportment of a gently bred lady, inside she struggled not to give over to fear. Thank goodness Elizabeth was holding her hand! "Allow me to understand you rightly, Sergeant Gregory. Sir Richard's horse was found on the road to Tunbridge Wells?"

"That's right, milady."

"But my husband was not with his horse?"

"We have examined the immediate area thoroughly, Lady Fitzwilliam," Mr. Evans assured her. "There was no sign of him. Of course, we shall continue to search."

Anne shook her head. "But why was Sir Richard riding to Tunbridge Wells?"

"Perhaps he had an appointment."

"In the middle of the night, Mr. Evans?" To her horror, Mr. Evans smirked.

The majordomo ignored the man. "My lady, we do not know why. Perhaps the master was more in his cups than we were led to believe and simply lost his way in the dark."

Anne turned to Elizabeth for comfort and noticed her attention was elsewhere.

Elizabeth raised an eyebrow. "I believe Sir John has another opinion, do you not?" She was not teasing but coldly serious.

Buford only tightened his lips.

"John?" Caroline inquired.

The former colonel spoke slowly, as though the words were wrenched out of him. "We should consider the possibility that Fitzwilliam was...prevented from returning home last night."

"Prevented!" cried Anne. "What do you mean?"

"I know Fitz. If he was on his horse, he was returning to Rosings. He intended nothing else." He glared at Mr. Evans. "Gregory suggests he lost his bearings. That is unlikely but possible. But if he fell from his horse or was thrown, we would have found him on the road or near it. We did not." Buford paused. "Therefore, we cannot dismiss the possibility that some unknown person is involved in this matter."

"Someone has hurt Richard?" Anne screamed.

"Anne, no!" Buford assured her. "I think he has been hidden away somewhere."

"Kidnapped?" clarified Elizabeth.

"Yes, Mrs. Darcy."

"Ridiculous!" cried Mr. Evans. "Who would do such an absurd thing?"

Anne, while terrified for Richard, grew more and more angry with Mr. Evans's rude behavior.

Buford showed great patience. "Taking into account Sir Richard's sterling character, we cannot yet dismiss this possibility out of hand. He is not off somewhere else. He has either been injured and made insensible or has been abducted."

"You have a point, Sir John," allowed Gregory. "As outrageous as it sounds, it is not impossible."

"Anne," said Buford gently, "we shall continue to search, not just for Fitzwilliam, but for clues that indicate he has been taken prisoner. We shall not give up."

IT WAS TIME FOR DINNER, AND RICHARD SQUATTED QUIETLY in the corner, his elbows braced against the walls. He had removed the loosened ropes about his ankles. His eyes were fixed on the door, waiting for a crack of light, waiting for his moment. He was a coiled snake, prepared not to strike but to flee.

Richard had been utterly compliant, and it had served. His captors grew confident and careless. Only one kidnapper bothered to attend him now. They thought they had broken his spirit. Richard was ready to prove them wrong.

He had been in this attitude for half an hour. His legs ached, but he forced his mind away from the discomfort, away from the murmurings from without. He focused instead on his homecoming with Anne. He would not leave her bed for a week!

Then, he heard the jingling of keys and the scrape of metal on metal. Richard released all his hoarded rage. *Strike hard! Strike fast! No quarter!*

The door started to open. Richard pushed against the walls. In three steps, he was across the room. The opening was just wide enough for him to slip through and slam his fists and shoulder against one of his tormentors. The man, knocked off his feet, cried out in pain, there was the crash of something on the floor, but

Richard paid it no mind. The door to the house was before him. Nothing could stop him!

He allowed himself to fall against the wall near the door. His still-bound hands struggled with the latch. *Open, damn you!*

Ignoring the screams and shouts from behind, he worked the latch and swung the door open. *Freedom!*

Richard's head exploded with pain, and everything went black.

# Chapter 26

"You shouldn't had tried that, Colonel," the masked man whispered as he gently dabbed Fitzwilliam's bleeding face. "They hurt you bad."

An agonized Fitzwilliam, lying on the thin mat, was forced to agree. After hours of planning and preparation for his escape, he found himself back in his prison with a split head as his reward. He was sluggish and dizzy, and the light from the man's candle danced before his eyes. It was all confusing. He had thought there were only two kidnappers. Where had this man come from? Where had he heard his strange voice before? If he was one of the criminals, why was he being kind to him? The more he tried to concentrate, the greater the ache in his head became.

Though still dazed, Fitzwilliam realized his captors had changed his confinement. His legs remained free, however, a rope now ran from his bound hands to a hook in the ceiling. It was impossible for him to loosen the knots. He was trapped.

The man finished his ministrations and rose, leaving a bit of bread and a cup of water within Fitzwilliam's reach.

"Wait," he croaked as he raised himself on one elbow. The man stopped. He was tall and broad, his face covered with a sack like the others. The candle failed to illuminate his eyes behind the holes in the cloth. "Thank you," he managed.

The candle shook in his hand. "Don't you do that again, Colonel," he whispered. "They'll do more to you next time than hit you with a staff."

Fitzwilliam's confused brain remembered that voice. "*Cork? Cork Johnson?*"

The giant moved at a speed that belied his size. He slapped one large hand against Fitzwilliam's mouth, an action that caused agonizing pain to reverberate through his skull. His scream was effectively muffled by Cork's fat fingers.

"I'm sorry, Colonel," Cork urgently whispered. "I'm really sorry, but you gotta be quiet. Cork can't let Sim—can't let *them* know you knows me. It'll be very bad. Very bad."

At that moment Fitzwilliam could not imagine things becoming any worse than at present. "Can you help me?" he said between Cork's fingers.

"Can't, Colonel." The bag moved side to side. He drew his hand away.

"Why are you doing this? Why are you with them?"

"D-don't you say that, Colonel." Cork sounded as though he were about to cry. "My maw—they said they'd hurt my maw." He looked over his shoulder. "Cork has to go now."

A moment later, he was gone, and the room fell back into darkness. The clink of the door lock signaled the end of the encounter.

Fitzwilliam lay on his back, staring up into the blackness. He had failed to escape, and there was little chance he would get a second opportunity. All he could do now was wait and hope the kidnappers would release him when the ransom was paid.

*If* the ransom was paid. *How much are they demanding? Could Anne raise the funds?*

*Darcy! He would help. He would pay. Andrew would help.*

*Damn!* Tears leaked down his unshaven cheeks. Useless Richard Fitzwilliam would cost his family a fortune, and there was nothing he could do about it.

A new thought occurred to him. *Would the scoundrels release him? What guarantee did he have? Would it not be better for them to kill him?*

Alone in a small, dank room, Richard feared he might never see Anne again.

THROUGHOUT THE NEXT DAY, MEN SCOURED THE AREA, LOOK-ing for Sir Richard. They focused on the Tunbridge Wells road and did not bother to search the tenant cottages of Rosings or the houses in Hunsford.

It was likely he was injured somewhere in the woods or fields. All the inhabitants in the district who could be spared from their duties volunteered to help. In effect, Hunsford was deserted.

Mr. Evans and Sergeant Gregory led the quest. Evans insisted on the main area of search. At first, he was as eager to find his patron as the colonel's friends, but as the hours passed and the search proved fruitless, the steward's enthusiasm dimmed.

"Do you not find it odd where Sir Richard's horse was found?" he mentioned to Sir John over a quick lunch of thin soup and bread.

Buford did not immediately respond. "What is your meaning, sir?"

Mr. Evans looked about and lowered his voice. "Why would Sir Richard ride in the opposite direction from Rosings?"

"I can think of several reasons. Most likely he was overcome by drink and lost his way."

"Certainly, certainly. That must be our first notion, but I find it curious that the horse was found a mile from Hunsford along a deserted stretch of road. Would you not say it was the perfect spot for a private meeting?"

Mr. Evans had captured Buford's attention. "A meeting in the middle of the night? For what purpose?"

"Come, come, Sir John," said Mr. Evans with a knowing smirk. "You are a man of the world. Surely, you can think of a reason a man may wish for a rendezvous in the small hours of the morning, far away from inquiring eyes."

Buford knew Fitzwilliam like a brother. He knew Fitz was absolutely devoted to his Anne. Evans's suggestion, which was totally against Fitzwilliam's character, was absolutely insulting.

But all this, along with his anger with the man's insolence, Buford kept to himself. Carefully, he said, "We have no evidence that Sir Richard met with anyone, save perhaps highwaymen."

"Highwaymen?" cried Mr. Evans. "In Hunsford? Ridiculous! I assure you I have swept the district clean of gypsies and such scum. There are no highwaymen here, my good sir."

"Criminals travel."

Mr. Evans deflated a bit. "That is so."

"I have eaten enough." Buford pushed his bowl away and stood from the table. "Come, Mr. Evans—daylight is burning."

ANNE WAS GOING MAD.

For hours she had attended her guests in the blue parlor. Elizabeth, Caroline, and Mrs. Jenkinson were joined by Lady Catherine and Charlotte Collins. They meant well. All were concerned about Richard and wanted to be a comfort to her.

*If only they would stop talking!*

Actually, the fault fell to Mrs. Jenkinson, Charlotte, and most especially Lady Catherine. Elizabeth and Caroline thankfully said little, and when they did speak, it was to blunt the most upsetting talk from the others' conversation. But their valiant efforts were for naught, for no one could override her mother when she was in high dudgeon.

Lady Catherine was certain—*absolutely certain*—that the villagers in Hunsford had done *something* to Richard. What that *something* was, she did not articulate. Instead, she went on and on about inbred wickedness and disloyal ingrates. Charlotte attempted to temper Lady Catherine's assertions, politely giving examples of the townspeople's support and faithfulness. Mrs. Jenkinson took it upon herself to act as mediator, agreeing first with her ladyship and them with the rector's wife. The three would not give over the discussion, ignoring the numerous attempts to change the subject by Elizabeth and the murmured caustic remarks from Caroline.

Richard had been missing now for two days. Anne's agony increased every moment, and the ladies closest to her were too busy debating to offer comfort. She would scream if it would do any good.

Suddenly, Elizabeth stood. "Pray, pardon me, ladies, but it is time for me to look in on the children." She threw a significant look at Caroline.

"Ah, yes." Caroline rose to her feet. "I shall go with you, Eliza. I am sure Beatrice has been looking for me." Both curtsied to the assembled and escaped the room.

*Traitors*, thought Anne.

Lady Catherine sniffed. "In my day, young children were brought to their parents, not the other way around. It does no good to spoil them!"

Mrs. Jenkinson nodded. "You are very right, milady, but—"

"Eliza is a most attentive mother," Charlotte broke in. "I am certain that she would not ruin them."

"Of course not!" Lady Catherine cried. "She is the mother of the Darcy heir! Darcy will see that his son is raised to meet his duty. Why, look at Lady Llewellyn. Darcy did well by her."

"I am sure of it," replied Mrs. Jenkinson. "Oh, I hope all remains well up north and Mr. Darcy returns safely!"

Lady Catherine banged her walking stick. "The Regent should raise the army and see that these ruffians and revolutionaries are dealt with most severely, but he is too busy drinking and whoring in Carlton House!"

Anne tried desperately to block the others' conversation when the butler approached. "Lady Fitzwilliam, a small matter has arisen that requires your attendance," he quietly informed her.

Lady Catherine's age had not diminished her hearing. "What is that? What is the matter? Speak up, man!"

The butler was unperturbed. "A household matter, milady."

"Mother, such things fall to me," Anne almost growled. To the others present, she stated, "Pray, do not disturb yourselves. I shall have additional refreshments brought in." With that, Anne and the butler moved into the hallway.

The butler gestured to the staircase. "If you would accompany me, madam."

Anne was puzzled as they ascended. What household matter had arisen in the bedrooms? Her confusion was complete when they proceeded to the nursery. The butler opened the door.

"Lady Fitzwilliam as you requested, Mrs. Darcy."

Upon entering, Anne was astonished to find both Elizabeth and Caroline on the floor playing with the children. Elizabeth thanked the butler and turned to Anne.

"Would you care to join us for a time? I believe the distraction will prove advantageous."

It was a relieved Anne who gracefully took her place next to Caroline and took Chloe into her arms.

IN HIS HALF SLEEP, VOICES FLOWED THROUGH RICHARD'S consciousness. Slowly, he awakened. While he knew not what time it was, the pitch darkness had enhanced his other senses. He could hear one of his captors through the back wall arguing with another man outside the house. Was it Adam?

"I'm telling ya, th' plan's perfect."

"Kidnapping him for ransom? Are you mad?"

The other man spoke in a low, cultured voice. Richard frowned. Had he heard that voice before?

"Mad, am I? I'll show ya mad!"

"Keep your voice down, fool!"

"Who's ta hear? There ain't nobody about, 'cept my brother."

"And the other two? The idiot and his mother?"

"Don't ya worry 'bout them," Adam sneered. "They'll get th' same as his lordship."

"You should have killed him."

"What, an' give up all that lovely money?"

"You will never get it. Here, I shall pay one hundred pounds if you do it tonight."

Richard's blood ran cold.

"A hundred pounds ta do 'im in? I don't think so. A thousand pounds or we'll do this my way this time."

"A hundred or I shall leave you to your own devices. I want nothing to do with this kidnapping scheme."

"Too late, gov'nor. You're in this up ta your fine, fat neck. But don't ya worry. Ya wanted 'im ruined. This'll do th' trick proper."

"How will his death get me Rosings?"

Richard finally recognized that other voice. *Kendrick!*

"Simple. We'll demand £5,000 from Lady Fitzwilliam for 'is return, with a thousand first as good faith money. They'll pay, figurin' they'll catch us when we deliver th' colonel for th' rest. But we'll fool 'em! We get th' first payment and slit th' colonel's throat, sail for America, an' ya get ta console th' widow."

"It will never work. They are searching for him everywhere."

"Everywhere but here. That fool Evans thinks the th' colonel went to Tunbridge Wells. Th' rest think he's lying hurt in th' woods. By th' time they think to check all th' cottages, we'll be gone. That's where you come in."

"By using one of my wagons," Kendrick groused. "I do not like it."

"Too bad, Kendrick. Get that wagon here tomorrow night. There are a lot o' back ways outta here. We'll be deep in London by mornin', where they'll never find us. You do that an' you'll get Rosings."

"Hmm. And the others?"

"We'll bury 'em deep. People'll think they just ran off."

There was a pause, which allowed Richard to consider the bloody plans of his captors. He had to fight the terror that threatened to overwhelm him. He had faced death before and lived. He would do so again.

"I…I do not know whether I can acquire a wagon by tomorrow," said Kendrick. "It will take time to find one untraceable to me."

"Tomorrow, Kendrick. We need it tomorrow."

"Why not kill him now?"

"Because they might ask for proof he's still alive. Look, gov'nor, we've done everything yer way up to now. Saltin' th' garden, openin' th' stall doors, an' th' rest. Now we'll do this *my* way. Ya don't like it? Too bad. Remember, if they catch us, ya'll hang too."

"Do not threaten me."

There was a loud thump as the wall behind Richard shook. Kendrick squealed a painful oath.

"I'll do like I please. *I'm* in charge, now. Ya get that wagon here tomorrow, or ya'll be sorry."

"All right, all right. Let me go." Kendrick was having trouble speaking. Adam must have been holding him by the throat. "You will get your wagon."

"You best keep yer word, Kendrick, or I'll be comin' fer ya. Understand?"

The voices faded as the two moved away from the rear of the cottage. Richard now knew that his friends had only a day to find him. After that, he would have to save himself, and he had no idea how to do it.

# Chapter 27

The exhausted searchers gathered in the late afternoon at The Crowing Cock, drowning their failure to find Sir Richard with mediocre ale. The Rosings footmen and Hunsford villagers talked amongst themselves in low tones. Sir John, tired, dirty, and discouraged, sat at a corner table, rubbing his forehead in exasperation. With him were Sergeant Gregory, Corporal Frost, Mr. Evans, Mr. Clarke, Mr. Collins, and Mr. Hibbert, who were arguing over what to do next.

It was a dispute Buford had been forced to deal with for the last two days. Gregory wanted to redouble their efforts along the Tunbridge Wells road. Frost suggested expanding the search, allowing Buford's suggestion of a kidnapping might be the case. Mr. Hibbert dismissed the idea of anyone from Hunsford abducting Sir Richard. Mr. Clarke wanted guidance, and Mr. Evans was sure Fitzwilliam was not missing at all but off on a romantic adventure—an idea with which Gregory and Mr. Collins violently disagreed.

Buford was too weary to enter into the quarrel. His belly was empty, his hip ached, and his heart was heavy. His best friend was missing—perhaps grievously hurt—and so far, he had been unable to do anything about it. His mind was filled with pity for Lady Fitzwilliam, for the agonies her worries must be causing.

Buford dipped a bit of stale bread into the watery excuse for soup before him. At least the ale tasted…well, somewhat like ale. Just then, the publican approached and addressed those gathered.

"Beggin' yer pardon, masters, but young Cork Johnson be wantin' to talk to ye." He jerked a filthy thumb over his shoulder. "He's by the kitchen door. I tried ta run him off, but he swore he knows where the colonel's at an' won't leave."

"*What?*" Suddenly, Buford was no longer exhausted. "Bring him to me at once!"

"Sir John, really, That boy is an idiot!" cried Mr. Evans.

He leveled his fiercest glare at the steward. "I shall thank you to keep your thoughts to yourself. Simpleton or not, if that boy knows something, I wish to hear it." Buford looked about the table. "That goes for all of you. I trust I am understood." He sat back and took a breath. He had not used his *command* voice in almost two years, and damn, it felt good!

The innkeeper escorted a large young man to the table. Cork Johnson's clothes were only little better than dirty rags, and his odorous essence preceded him. For once, Buford wished he owned a dandy's perfumed handkerchief.

"Sir John," said the publican, "this here's Cork Johnson." He turned to his companion. "Now, none of your foolishness, Cork! Sir John's an important man."

Buford eyed Johnson. He was clearly anxious; his massive hands cruelly twisted the floppy hat he held. "You have something to tell me, young man?" asked Buford in a neutral voice.

Cork gave the innkeeper a nervous glance.

Buford turned to the publican. "Thank you. That is all for now."

The owner of The Crowing Cock grunted, gave Cork a scowl, and bowed before he returned to the bar. Cork stood, shuffling his feet.

"Sit down, Cork, and tell me what you know."

Cork took the lone empty chair, apprehensively eying Mr. Evans. "I-I…You're lookin' fer the colonel, Cork heard," he managed.

As calmly as he could, Buford said, "Yes, we are. I am told you claim to know something about that."

Cork stared down at the table. "Y-yes, sir."

"Speak, you damn fool!" Mr. Evans shouted. Cork flinched.

"He is conversing with *me*, Evans!" Buford spat out. He turned back to the frightened young giant. "What is it you know?"

Cork swallowed. "My maw—she had nothin' to do with it, Cork swears! They made us do it!"

Buford leaned in, his patience close to the breaking point. "*Who* made you do *what*?"

"Th-they'll kill my maw. They said they'd kill my maw."

"No one will hurt your mother. That is my promise." Sir John placed his hand on Cork's. "Tell me. Where is Sir Richard?"

Cork looked into Buford's eyes. "They've got him at my maw's house."


THE NEXT HALF AN HOUR WAS FILLED WITH CONTENTION AND confusion at first, until Sir John took firm command. All were astonished by Cork's news—that the Shepardson brothers dared to hold a knight of the realm for ransom. The claim that Sir Richard was being held captive in a cottage on Rosings's land, not two miles from the main house, was stunning to most and unbelievable to one.

"This is outlandish! Sir John, surely you see that this is the mad raving of a lunatic!" Mr. Evans dismissed Cork's tale in its entirety. "You cannot march on a broken-down shack based on the word of a simpleton!"

"And I say Cork Johnson is an honest young man," cried Gregory. "But I must wonder at you, Evans! It sounds to me as though you do not wish Sir Richard to be found. Were you part of this conspiracy?"

"How dare you!" screamed Mr. Evans as he scrambled to his feet.

"That is more than enough from both of you!" Buford shouted. "We shall have no more wild accusations or willful disobedience. By Lady Fitzwilliam's leave, *I* am in command, and you both will obey my orders!"

The two men glared at each other in absolute loathing but fell silent. The rest sat with various degrees of concern or anxiety on their faces.

Cork was clearly terrified. "Mr. Evans, he don't like Cork," he mumbled to Buford.

"Never you mind, lad. You are with me, and I believe you," Buford put a hand on his shoulder. Throughout his army career, Buford had to look into many a man's eye and in an instant, judge him cowardly or courageous, trustworthy or unreliable. His life and the survival of those under his command depended upon his judgment. It had seldom failed him, and Buford trusted it did not fail him now. "Let us review. You were sent out to get supplies?"

Cork nodded. "Aye, Sir John—beans an' flour, my maw says."

Buford turned to his batman. "Take Cork and purchase everything he requires."

"Sir?" Frost was confused.

"I shall explain my plan when you return. Cork, go with Corporal Frost. Off with you." To Sergeant Gregory he said, "Go to Rosings and return as quickly as possible with every able-bodied footman, groom, and farmhand."

Gregory frowned. "But won't that alert the Shepardsons?"

"Cork, did you not say Adam and Simon were at the cottage?"

The boy assured him that they were.

"Excellent. Gregory, you have the keys to Sir Richard's gun case. Bring all the arms with you—powder too. Do not forget Sir Richard's rifled pistols—I require them. Ask any man unfamiliar with guns to bring staffs and the like."

Sergeant Gregory raised his eyebrows. "It sounds like we're going to war, sir."

"We are," Buford grimly returned. "Mr. Clarke, gather any man in the village with military experience and bring them here."

The farmer nodded. "Armed, sir?"

"Yes. Mr. Hibbert, I suggest you send for the constable and await him here. He will have to take any prisoners we may have in hand."

Mr. Collins was nervous. "I-I would be honored to accompany you, Sir John, but as a man of peace I have no weapon or—"

Buford patted the man on the shoulder. "Your loyalty to the Fitzwilliam family is unquestioned, sir, but I believe your talents are better served summoning the apothecary in your chaise and assisting Mr. Hibbert relaying messages between the various groups and Rosings Park."

"You may depend upon me, Sir John!" Mr. Collins cried. "I shall be as swift as Mercury!"

"Good man!" The retired colonel of Hussars then turned to the Rosings steward. "Mr. Evans, as you believe we are on a wild goose chase, I think it best you continue your search for Sir Richard along the Tunbridge Wells road."

"Rosings Park is my responsibility, Sir John. I should go with you."

"At this time, my authority supersedes yours, sir." Buford drew close to Mr. Evans. "I shall only bring men who will obey my commands without question," he stated sotto voce. "I do not trust you to do that. In fact, I do not trust you *at all.*" Mr. Evans's outraged face grew red, but Buford did not give him the opportunity to respond. "Take your handful of followers and get out of my sight. Pray one of us finds Sir Richard, for he is the only one who can save your situation. If he is not recovered alive, I shall see you dismissed without a character. Search well, Evans."

To the assembled he said loudly, "You all have your instructions. Go quickly. We set off after dark."

THE MOOD AT ROSINGS PARK WAS AN INTENSE MIXTURE OF fear and uncertainty. Sergeant Gregory would not say more to Lady Fitzwilliam than that they had expanded the search and expected good results. This news was accompanied by Gregory removing a small arsenal of guns from Richard's study. When Anne demanded he explain himself, the majordomo only would say that he did so at Sir John's direction, and the weapons were needed "just in case."

"Just in case?" Anne repeated. "Why would you need them unless…" She paled. "My God, Richard *is* being held prisoner somewhere!"

"My lady, you must not distress yourself."

Her voice rose. "Sergeant Gregory, I *insist* you tell me what is happening!"

"Everything is well in hand, Lady Fitzwilliam," Gregory replied. He tried not to sound patronizing. "We have many men searching for the colonel. These," he waved at the men bearing the arms out the door, "are just a precaution. Pray, excuse me, but I must be away."

Anne would have none of it. Shaking in agitation, she protested anew, but she was interrupted by Caroline taking her shoulders.

"You are distraught, my dear," she said in a soothing voice. "Come away and allow Sergeant Gregory to return to the others." She led Anne back to the couch, giving the majordomo a baleful glare over her shoulder.

Mrs. Darcy would have her share of the conversation. "Sergeant Gregory, I would detain you a moment to remind you of the concern we all feel for Sir Richard's safety." Elizabeth raised one eyebrow. "I trust you will keep us *fully* advised as to your progress?" She smiled without mirth. "Be on your way with our best wishes for your *swift* success."

# Chapter 28

An hour later, Sir John and his impromptu rescue force began the journey to the Johnson house. Fortunately, the full moon made finding the way easy, for Buford had rejected bringing lanterns. Should Sir Richard be held at the remote cottage, the element of surprise was essential for a successful assault, and torches would give the game away.

Buford's company included ten men from Rosings, Mr. Wilkerson and his eldest son, as well as another farmer and field hand recruited by Mr. Clarke. All but Cork were armed with guns, staffs, swords, or heavy tools. They brought with them two horses but no wagon, out of concern over the noise such a conveyance would make.

Buford was more convinced than ever that they would find Fitzwilliam at the cottage. Cork was weak of mind, but he owned a good memory and provided many details of the place. He reported that Fitzwilliam was kept in a windowless storeroom, its door facing the front entrance. There was a back door opposite a huge fireplace, the single window facing the rear broken and boarded up. There were no side windows. Two front windows faced the road.

Cork said that the Shepardson brothers were armed with pistols and long knives, and Simon Shepardson also had a favorite club. He insisted his mother had nothing to do with the abduction. Indeed, she was as much a prisoner of the Shepardsons as Sir Richard.

A rough plan grew in Buford's mind. Once the group neared the cottage, Corporal Frost, along with Mr. Clarke, Mr. Wilkerson, and the Hunsford contingent, would sneak through the wood to the rear of the house and guard the back door. Once they were in position, Buford, Gregory, and the Rosings men would force their way through the one at the front.

Over Gregory's protests, Buford gave the most important task to Cork. He would distract the Shepardson brothers, making sure they could not harm Fitzwilliam before the rescuers gained entrance. To do this, Cork needed to go into the house as though returning from his errand. Frost added a bottle of wine to Cork's sack to aid in the distraction. Apparently, Simon Shepardson relished the bottle.

It was a simple plan: not completely thought out and fraught with risk. Buford had no idea of the opposition he would face. Was Fitzwilliam really there? Had the kidnappers moved him to a new location? Could they break down the door before the villains harmed Fitzwilliam? Were there only two enemies? Cork reported that Adam Shepardson met with a mystery man only yesterday. Had this man returned?

Buford forced his doubts aside. He required a calm mind and a clear purpose. War had taught him that complicated plans often failed upon contact with the enemy. It was claimed that the famous Admiral Nelson once said: *Never mind maneuvers; go straight at them*. It was good tactics for the army too. *Up and at them, boys!* The brute way was sometimes the only way.

About a quarter mile from their objective, Buford called for a halt. Using whispers and hand signals, he sent Frost and his men off the lane into the wood. The rest of the force slowly made their way closer to the cottage, keeping low and out of the moonlight. They advanced to about thirty yards before they halted again. Sergeant Gregory signaled for the men to crouch down. Buford crept forward to a large oak and peered around it.

The converted smithy was a low, wide, rough building. About

twenty yards from the trail and surrounded on three sides by the forest, the land before the cottage was devoid of trees, save the single oak that stood on the right near the lane that served as Buford's makeshift command post. The building's front door was on the left, and a chimney showed the fireplace was along the center of the front wall. Broken, open windows flanked the chimney. Candlelight flickered through them.

Buford ground his teeth in apprehension. While the moon was not high enough to light the space and reveal their position, those open windows could prove a grave problem. They were excellent spots from which to shoot, particularly with the brick of the fireplace offering protection from returning fire. As much as he wanted to free his friend, he had far too few men to waste on a bloody assault. Buford's small force had to be quick and fall upon the enemy before they could mount a defense. Speed was of the essence.

Buford turned to Cork and whispered, "It is time. A stout heart is needed now. Do you remember what to do?"

A frightened baby's face on a giant's head nodded, staring at the house. "A-aye, Sir John. Cork guards the colonel, an' you'll save my maw."

Buford nodded. "Good man. Take courage. Look for us in about a quarter of an hour."

Cork took a deep breath, shifted the sack on his shoulder, and moved towards the front door. Meanwhile, Buford drew Sergeant Gregory near to finalize the assault plan while keeping close attention on the house.

"ABOUT TIME YA GOT BACK, CORK!" SIMON SHEPARDSON CRIED from the table. "We're starvin'!"

"What took ya so long, eh?" Adam Shepardson demanded as the young man carefully closed the door.

Simon sniggered. "Maybe he's got hisself a girl in the village. She as ugly as you?"

Cork said nothing as he crossed the floor and presented the sack of supplies to his mother. She took his offering without a word. That changed when she looked in the sack.

"What's this, then?" Mrs. Johnson pulled out a bottle of wine.

"Uh...th' blacksmith, he owed Cork some money," Cork mumbled, his eyes downcast. "Thought you would like it."

Simon quickly snatched the bottle from Mrs. Johnson. "Too right, there! Cook up some food, woman!"

"You talk to anybody in Hunsford?" Adam asked.

"No. Lot of people there, lookin' for the colonel. Cork don't say nothin'."

Mrs. Johnson held out a package. "Bacon, too?"

"Must have been a lot o' money," Adam said thoughtfully. "Got any left?"

Cork dug a couple of coins from his pocket and tossed them on the table. "Spent most of it."

"Too bad." Adam shouted at Simon, "Save some o' that wine fer me, ya great bull calf!"

Cork picked up a bit of bread and shuffled over to the storeroom.

"Hey, what are ya doing?" demanded Simon.

Cork refused to turn. "Gonna feed th' colonel." He unlocked the door and went in.

"Ya fool, ya forgot th' mask!" Sure enough, the bag mask remained hanging on the nail next to the door. Simon got up to follow, but Adam grabbed his arm, halting his progress.

"It don't matter. It's not like his lordship's gonna be able ta say anything."

Simon laughed.

Mrs. Johnson shuddered. She did not dwell on what the Shepardsons had planned for the colonel, but Adam's chilling statement brought back dread of what *her* fate might be. She and her son were witnesses, after all. She swallowed her fears and focused on preparing the food. It was then she noticed that her knife was missing.

Aching and hungry, Richard leaned against the corner of the lightless room, half awake, his unshaven cheek against a wall. The sudden brightness from the open door startled him, and he raised his hands to shield his eyes. A moment later, Cork was kneeling beside him.

"Stay still, Colonel," the giant whispered. There was a tug on his wrists, and suddenly large hands grasped his shoulders.

Fear laced through Fitzwilliam's empty belly. "Wait—no! What are you doing?"

"Keep quiet, Colonel!" Cork whispered. There was a clink of metal against wood and then Richard's world spun about him. He thought he might cast his accounts. Then he realized that Cork had hoisted him over his shoulder. He must have cut his bonds!

The young man did not hesitate a moment. He stood and moved quickly out of the room, his living burden bouncing in the air. Shouts and screams filled Fitzwilliam's ears. There was an instant of dizziness when Cork stopped, twisted, and moved again. Lights faded as his nose breathed in fresh air. Fitzwilliam forced his eyes open as he bounced about, only to behold a bright flash and thundering roar—a jolt of agony—and then darkness again.

Buford, kneeling, was in deep conversation with Sergeant Gregory when one of the footmen grasped his bad shoulder. "Sir John, look!"

Wincing, Buford turned to the cottage and to his astonishment beheld Cork running out the door with something over his shoulder. *My God! Cork is running out of the house carrying Fitzwilliam!*

Buford was on his feet, pulling one of the pistols from his belt. "Gregory! Come on!"

No sooner had the words left his lips than the quiet of the night was shattered by a pistol shot. Cork fell upon his burden.

A horrified Buford dashed forward, shouting, "CHARGE!" He moved as quickly as his bad hip allowed, a pistol in his hand, his men flowing past him. The backlit figure that filled the doorway looked up, holding a handgun. Buford halted, smoothly raised the pistol to eye level, and pulled the trigger in a single motion. There was a blinding flash and sharp explosion, followed by the acrid smell of burnt gunpowder. By the time the smoke cleared, the man was out of sight. Before Buford could exchange his spent gun for its twin, Gregory and the others reached the still-open door.

Buford fell to his knees beside the two bodies. Fitzwilliam and Cork were now his concern. He ignored the shots and screams from the house. He had to see to Cork's injuries and Fitzwilliam's too. Cork was still alive, if his soft, pitiful groans were any indication, but his left shoulder was covered in blood.

Two of the footmen assigned to follow Sir John appeared at his side. "Help me turn Cork," Buford ordered. Gently, they moved the moaning giant to reveal the silent, unmoving body of Sir Richard, lying on his side. Buford bit back a gasp and placed his hand on Fitzwilliam's neck. His relief at finding his friend's pulse was indescribable.

"Cork has been shot. See to his wound!" he ordered one of the footmen. He shouted to the other, "Sir Richard is insensible. I believe he injured his head when Cork fell. Bring the horses here at once!" The other footman dashed away while Buford rolled Fitzwilliam onto his back. "Fitz, Fitz! Damn you, talk to me!" Buford snarled, his eyes filling with unshed tears. "You do not have my leave to die, you blasted, useless, pain in the arse! You saved my pitiful hide in Belgium, and I shall damn well save yours!"

"Sir?"

Buford looked up to see that Corporal Frost had arrived. "Cork was shot carrying Sir Richard out of the house. Sir Richard lives, but he must have struck his head when Cork fell. I have not been able to speak to him." Buford wiped his eyes with the sleeve of his missing arm. "What has happened within?"

"I don't know, Sir John. We came around front when the fighting stopped. I believe it's all over now. How is Cork faring?"

"I think it's his shoulder, sir," said the footman attending Cork, "but I ain't the apothecary. They're bringing the horses up now."

A panting Sergeant Gregory joined them. "All secure inside, sir, and Mrs. Johnson's safe."

Buford repeated what he had told Frost and asked about the Shepardsons.

Gregory's face grew feral. "Those two will never kidnap anyone again." It was then Buford noticed the blood on Gregory's shirt and coat.

Buford coldly gestured at the stain with his chin. "Which one?"

"Adam," responded Gregory curtly. "You did Simon, sir. Excellent shot, if I may say so."

The bloody banter ended with the approach of the horses and Mrs. Johnson. She stood pale and still over her son, a Rosings stable hand holding her up by one arm.

"Will...will he live?" she asked unevenly.

Buford rose. "That is up to God." He was too tired to worry over blasphemy. He pointed at the groom. "Take a horse and get to the village. We need a cart for Cork."

"Sir," said Mr. Wilkerson, "my farm's closer. My boy will fetch th' wagon."

"Very well. Have him take the horse." To the others, Buford said, "Help me up on the other horse, and then hand up Sir Richard. We have to get him to Rosings."

"Aye, Sir John," said Gregory, "But you'll not carry him. I will."

"The devil you say!" growled Buford.

"Sir," said Frost softly, "Gregory is right." He looked pointedly at Buford's left sleeve. "You're in charge *here*, in any case."

Though furious and embarrassed, Buford had to give way, and soon Gregory and Fitzwilliam were galloping toward the manor. Sir John took out his angry feelings on his men.

"All right! This has been a bloody cock-up! You—keep some

pressure on Cork's wound. We must stop the bleeding. The rest of you—search the house! We must learn whether there was anyone else involved in this!"

NOT FAR AWAY, ALONG THE TRAIL FROM THE OTHER DIRECTION, a two-horse cart moved slowly through the dark. Two men sat in the seat, one short and stout. Upon hearing sounds of gunfire, the driver abruptly stopped the horses. The men sat for several minutes.

The driver turned to the other man. "Should we continue on, sir?"

The fat man said nothing for a moment. "Turn around. Something has gone amiss. Turn around and head back. Quietly, or you will answer for it."

The driver nodded. He knew well his master's ways. "Yes, sir, Mr. Kendrick."

# Chapter 29

In the main parlor of Rosings, the ladies sat quietly near the roaring fireplace, working on embroidery in the stifling dread. It was something to do while waiting for the men to find the missing Sir Richard.

Lady Anne Fitzwilliam sat staring out the window, trying to calm her unsettled feelings, her needlework efforts untouched in her lap. Fear was ever-present, but so were impatience, anxiety, despair, and even anger. She could not eat. She could not rest. Her thoughts were solely fixed upon her dear husband.

*Where was Richard? Was he injured? Why have they not found him?*

Surely, if he had met with misfortune during his ride back to Rosings, he would have been quickly found. There were no places an insensible man could lie undetected. Anne fought valiantly not to think of any worse fate for him.

Sergeant Gregory's actions suggested Richard was being held somewhere against his will. *Why else would they want guns? Who would take Richard and why? For money? Horrible men!*

But what if he had not been taken away? His horse was found abandoned on the Tunbridge Wells road. *Could he have met someone there? Could he have left on his own?* Anne would not believe it. The idea was ridiculous!

*Was it not?*

Anne knew she was not the wife Richard deserved. Her moods were cross and agitated and changeable rather than happy, steady, and teasing. Richard was a passionate man, and she had failed at that most basic obligation of marriage—producing a child.

Richard claimed time and again he was happy with her. But how could he be? She was thin, pale, and awkward in company. She had no conversation or accomplishments. Her mouth was too wide, and her eyes were too weak. No figure, no grace. All she had was Rosings Park.

Was *that* the reason he married her?

Anne put her hands to her temples. *Stop it*, she commanded herself. *Richard is honorable and true. He says he loves me. I must trust him. I must!*

She turned away from her unhappy musings, for what felt liked the hundredth time, and picked up her embroidery. She was making handkerchiefs for Richard, their initials intertwined with roses. She noticed the *A* for *Anne* was crooked.

As she began to remove those stitches, her glance fell upon her companions. Caroline was the perfect example of a society lady as she bent over her work, sitting at the front edge of her chair, back straight, feet well hidden under her skirts. She worked steadily, with purpose. Given the seriousness of the day, she had made few comments. She appeared calm and collected, almost emotionless.

Elizabeth's deportment was something else entirely. Her posture was not as precise as she made herself comfortable on the couch. She worked in spurts, tongue between her lips, constantly checking her progress. More than once, she sighed as she pulled out several stitches.

Anne grew resentful of her friends. There they were, just as she had observed them in happier times, contented and untroubled. Both enjoyed the total devotion of their spouses, and both rejoiced in the delight of their children. They knew where their husbands were. And they were both with child. How dare they be happy when she was miserable!

"Anne, are you well, my dear?"

Anne's vile thoughts were broken by Mrs. Jenkinson's worried inquiry. Anne had dismissed her companion from her thoughts, for she had been at Rosings so long, she was as much a part of the place as the chimneypieces Mr. Collins admired. Anne blinked and saw the others' anxious gazes upon her. There was no judgment or superiority, only true and abiding concern.

"Pray, pay no mind. I am well." Anne's hand shook as she took her wine glass from the side table and took a sip.

"Is there nothing I can get for your relief?" asked Mrs. Jenkinson.

"I believe there is only one thing that will comfort Anne," said Caroline, not unkindly, "and it is not found in the house."

"They will find him, Anne," declared Elizabeth.

"Of course, they will, Eliza," proclaimed Caroline with no little pride. "My John will not fail."

Ashamed, fighting back tears, Anne could not trust herself to speak. Her anxiety had made her angry, her anger had made her jealous, and her jealousy had made her foolish. How could she think her friends were unaffected? They had been her constant companions since Richard's disappearance. Nothing was done for Anne's ease that they did not see to themselves. And these ladies were struggling with their own fears and uncertainties.

Darcy was still in the north, and no one knew whether those counties were not still in open revolt. As for Sir John, he was leading the search for Richard, and if he were indeed held captive, it would be Sir John to lead an armed rescue. Anne was not the only wife who worried for her husband's safety. They were among her dearest friends, and she had begun to resent their good fortune. How despicable of her.

Anne had removed yet another stitch when there was a clamor without. All the ladies turned towards the commotion, and Anne had just risen to her feet when the door crashed open.

"Lady Fitzwilliam!" cried a disheveled and blood-splattered Sergeant Gregory. "Pray come quickly. We found him!"

"Oh, thank God!" cried Anne.

"The colonel is injured!" The man then shouted over his shoulder to the men who followed him in, "No, do not put him down! To the master's chambers!"

An unnatural quiet followed, and all time seemed to stop.

The silence was shattered by Anne's scream. "RICHARD!"

THE NEXT HOUR SPED BY IN MASS CONFUSION FOR CAROLINE. Amid shouts and stamping of feet, servants rushed about every which way. And above it all was Anne, screaming and sobbing. Caroline fought to remain focused on the task before her: to bring order to Rosings.

Upon discovering the extent of Sir Richard's injuries, she and Elizabeth quickly divided their attentions. Elizabeth would stay with Sir Richard and Anne, while Caroline dealt with Mrs. Parks and the staff.

Mrs. Jenkinson claimed her place was at her former charge's side and refused to leave her, while Mrs. Collins was in a panic over the safety of her husband and children. Never had Caroline been so happy to see Mr. Collins as when he arrived with the apothecary in tow. No sooner had that gentleman entered Sir Richard's rooms than Mr. and Mrs. Collins rushed home to the parsonage.

It was only at that moment that Caroline sought out Sergeant Gregory. "My husband—where is my husband?" she demanded. "Where is Sir John?"

"Back at the cottage. I must return to—"

"Why has Sir John not returned with you? Where was Sir Richard found? How did he become injured?"

Clearly, Gregory wanted to be gone, but Caroline's cold stare and unflinching stance stopped him short. Caroline was sure the majordomo bit back a low growl, but in the end, he took the time to tell her what he had seen. Her blood ran cold. It *was* a kidnapping, and John led the rescue!

"My husband, he is well?"

"Aye, milady. Nary a scratch on him."

Caroline's relief was apparent. "And the malefactors?"

Now Gregory did growl. "The men who did *that*," he jerked his head towards the stairs, "are all dead. But there might be others. That's why Sir John remains with the men."

Knowing there was likely more criminals about did nothing to settle Caroline's fractured nerves—neither did the dried blood on Sergeant Gregory's clothing. Yet, with quiet composure, she managed, "I shall not detain you another moment, sir. Go—do what you must. I shall see to matters here. But, pray, see to my husband."

"Calm your fears, milady. Frost is with him." He glanced upstairs. "But the colonel—"

"—is in good hands," she assured him.

Sergeant Gregory nodded and dashed out the front door, leaving a terrified Caroline in his wake.

ANNE WAS STILL SHAKING AS SHE GATHERED IN THE PARLOR with Caroline and Elizabeth to hear the apothecary's pronouncement.

"I have done all I can," Mr. Lloyd said. "Sir Richard has suffered a serious blow to the head. The bleeding seems worse than it is," he said to Anne. "Head wounds are notoriously bloody. Unconsciousness is not uncommon in these cases and may indeed be a blessing. But I cannot yet tell if the skull has suffered a fracture until the swelling has gone down. I recommend bleeding him to release pressure and expel evil humors."

"You will not bleed him," Caroline stated firmly.

The apothecary was offended. "Lady Buford, I am a man of science—"

"By God, sir, you will not bleed him!" Caroline repeated with passion. She had nursed Sir John during his convalescence and had learned much by watching and listening to the London physicians who attended him, including the respected Mr. Macmillan. She had come to the opinion that bloodletting did more harm than good.

Elizabeth calmly stepped in. "Sir Richard needs his strength, and you would weaken him?"

"Ladies, you speak of things you cannot know." Mr. Lloyd's manner was conciliatory and condescending. "Lady Fitzwilliam, I most strongly recommend that we call for the surgeon."

"Anne, do not allow it!" Caroline insisted.

"Lady Buford, please," said Mrs. Jenkinson. "We must listen to the apothecary."

"Sir, pray forgive Lady Buford's tone," said Elizabeth. "She has gained great experience with matters of this sort, overseeing her husband's recovery."

The apothecary harrumphed. "That is all well and good, but I have been in practice these twenty years!"

Elizabeth turned to Anne. "Let me send an express to Mr. Macmillan in London. He can be here tomorrow. He will know what to do."

Anne was barely mistress of her emotions. Eyes bloodshot, face tear-stained, hands shaking, she grasped Mrs. Jenkinson's hands with a grip that left all fingers white. "Sir, could this procedure be put aside for a day or so?"

"Mr. Macmillan's reputation precedes him, and I, of course, shall bow to *his* diagnosis. Very well, my lady. Should you wish it, I shall delay calling for the surgeon, but Mr. Macmillan must come in good time."

Elizabeth sought to placate the man. "Thank you, Mr. Lloyd. If you will permit me, I shall write an express this moment—with your compliments."

The man's mood lightened at the flattery. "I would be most honored, madam." Turning to Anne, he continued. "Sir Richard's room should be kept warm and quiet. A wet compress applied to the head will help with the swelling. Do not attempt to feed him, but give him water, should he be able to swallow it. We should not force anything at this time.

"Now, I understand there is another who needs my services?"

"Yes," said Elizabeth. "Cork Johnson was shot during the rescue."

"Then if you will permit me, Lady Fitzwilliam, I shall attend to him. I assure you that I shall return tonight if called." He turned to Caroline. "And tomorrow I shall *consult* with Mr. Macmillan."

Anne rose wearily and held out her hand. "I thank you for all you have done, sir. Pray excuse me, but I must return to my husband. Should you wish any food or refreshment, Mrs. Parks will see to it." With Mrs. Jenkinson's assistance, Anne left for the stairs.

The apothecary raised an eyebrow. "Lady Fitzwilliam needs rest. I suggest laudanum—if that meets with *your* approval, madam?" He directed the last words to Caroline.

She graced him with a small nod. "I fully agree with *that* recommendation, sir."

Elizabeth gestured to the door. "Mrs. Parks will see you out, Mr. Lloyd. Forgive me, but I have an express to compose."

An hour later, Caroline stood just inside the front door, a wrap against the cold firmly around her shoulders, watching as the express rider began his journey. She felt a presence at her side.

"Is Anne resting yet, Eliza?" she asked, her attention remaining on the galloping horse fading into the darkness.

"Mrs. Jenkinson will give her a draught soon." Elizabeth placed a hand on Caroline's arm. "And I have sent expresses to Matlock House in London and to Pemberley."

"Yes, that would be advisable," Caroline said absently.

"Caroline, I—"

"Pray, Eliza." She cut her off, covering her eyes wearily. "I cannot bear your scolding just now, no matter how much I must deserve it. I know I overstepped my place, but—"

"You misunderstand me. Should you have not said anything to Mr. Lloyd, *I* would have. I am only concerned for you. You must rest as well."

Caroline wearily shook her head. "I cannot, not while John is still away."

Mrs. Parks entered the foyer. "Forgive my intrusion, milady, but we shall see to everything that is necessary. You have been a great help, but you must listen to Mrs. Darcy. Do not worry. You do yourself no good pushing yourself so. See—here is Abigail, and she agrees."

"Please, mistress, let me attend you," begged Abigail. "It is late. Come upstairs and take your rest."

"I know you all mean well, but I shall not, not while—what was that?" Caroline turned around, staring out into the darkness. "I heard horses."

Their attention riveted, the women watched as a group of riders approached out of the gloom. As they came into the light of the lanterns, Caroline gasped in recognition and dashed forward, her shawl flying off her shoulders. "John! Oh, John!"

A moment later, a sobbing Caroline was wrapped in Buford's strong, dusty embrace.

THE EXHAUSTED ASSEMBLY MET IN SIR RICHARD'S STUDY, AND Mrs. Jenkinson remained above stairs with Sir Richard. Conspicuous by his absence was Mr. Evans.

"Where the devil is he?" demanded Buford.

Sergeant Gregory shrugged. "I last saw Evans at the village square just before we left to free the colonel."

Buford's eyes fell upon Anne. Her countenance was pale and downcast, her fingers twisting uncontrollably. By rights, the mistress of Rosings Park should have been in command of this gathering. However, the shock of Sir Richard's injuries had lain low more than his friend. Buford stepped into the void, sitting behind Richard's desk, but he was cautious. This was not his estate.

Buford continued. "Lady Anne, when we left Hunsford, the crowd had dispersed. However, I am not satisfied. Passions are still high. There is a great deal of fear and suspicion, and peace must be enforced. The constable's men are not adequate for the task. At the same time, we must see to the protection of Rosings House."

"We can send word to London for assistance," suggested Frost.

"No, that is the last thing we want," Buford declared. "Sir Richard shared Colonel Brandon's latest letter. He writes that the government there is frightened. We would have a regiment of soldiers descending upon us should London learn of this. Then, anything could happen."

Anne glanced up, furious. "They tried to kill my husband!"

"Forgive me. I am as distressed as you are, Anne, but these are your people. You know them. They had nothing to do with this."

"I can't believe those two villains were the only ones involved," said Gregory darkly. "They weren't much smarter than poor Cork. Someone else is behind this, mark my words."

"Then find him! As for me, I must return to Richard." Without another word, Anne rose from her chair and left the room.

"I had best go with her," offered Elizabeth.

"A moment if you please, Mrs. Darcy," Buford requested. "Mrs. Parks, will you accept orders from Mrs. Darcy or Lady Buford when your mistress is unavailable?"

"Aye, Sir John," said the housekeeper.

Elizabeth nodded. "Mrs. Parks, we shall only act in place of Lady Fitzwilliam if necessary. Otherwise, you are free to run the household as is your custom. As for me, I shall assist my cousin in caring for Sir Richard. That is my place."

Caroline nodded. "Of course. I shall help Mrs. Parks. Be sure to make use of Mrs. Jenkinson, Eliza. Pray make certain she gives Anne that draught!"

"I will, even if I have to give it to her myself."

"Very well." Buford turned to Gregory. "Our first priority is to inspect the defenses of the estate. After that, I shall return to Hunsford. I shall have Mr. Clarke and the other farmers help keep the peace until morning. Things should be better with the dawn."

"God willing," said Gregory.

LATER THAT NIGHT, MRS. JENKINSON SAT ALONE WITH SIR Richard, the exhausted valet, Joseph, having taken himself off to his bed. She gently replaced the compress on his forehead with a fresh one, all the time hoping this Mr. Macmillan of London was the miracle worker Lady Buford claimed. For herself, she had doubts.

Mrs. Jenkinson had little respect for the so-called "men of science." After all, it had not been the learned apothecaries, surgeons, or physicians that had cured her dear Anne but herself. She alone determined that cats, particularly Lady Catherine's series of pet cats, were the source of her charge's life-long illness. She never spoke of her discovery, for she knew no one would believe her. Instead, she had taken matters into her hands, rid Rosings of the fell beast, and saved her dear girl. Anne then recovered sufficiently to assume the ownership of the estate and marry her beloved Richard.

Mrs. Jenkinson dashed away the tears that threatened to fall. The grief she felt for Anne, whom she loved like a daughter, was great. All Anne's life had been a struggle. She lost her father at a young age. Lady Catherine's dominating personality overwhelmed any maternal instincts. She was more a school mistress than a mother. Anne's illness had almost robbed her of finding joy in marriage. Now, married and in her rightful place, when all should be right in the world, her husband is struck down.

*Was happiness so transitory? Why did dreadful things happen to Anne? What sins had she committed? Why was God so cruel?*

At that moment, the bedroom door opened. Mrs. Jenkinson expected it to be Mrs. Darcy returning, but to her shock, she found Lady Catherine de Bourgh standing just inside, leaning heavily on her walking stick.

Mrs. Jenkinson jumped to her feet. "Milady, it is so late. Here, pray sit. Anne has gone to her bed—"

Lady Catherine silenced her with a wave of her hand, her eyes fixed upon the unmoving figure in the bed. Her gaunt, pale face seemed to have aged a hundred years. "Will he live?" Her voice was low and hoarse.

"The apothecary has done all he can for the moment. He will know more once the swelling has gone down. A London physician has been sent for."

"Mr. Evans informed me of this outrage." The grand dame moved to Sir Richard's side. A trembling hand reached out. "My son...my son..." Never had Mrs. Jenkinson seen Lady Catherine so overcome. She snatched back her hand. "You will stay with him?"

"Of course, madam. Lady Fitzwilliam, Mrs. Darcy, and I shall attend him without fail."

"Good. I shall depend upon it!" With some of her former firmness, Lady Catherine commanded, "You will inform me at once should there be any change in his condition. At once, you understand!" She turned towards the door.

"Milady, are you to return to the dower house?" Mrs. Jenkinson called after her. "Surely, you would wish to remain close by. Shall I have Mrs. Parks arrange a room for you?"

"No, I have business that cannot be delayed. Do your duty, and I shall do mine."

It must had been due to Mrs. Jenkinson's exhaustion that she did not recall or report until much later Lady Catherine's mumbled coda: "They tried to kill my son. They will pay. They will *all* pay."

# Chapter 30

The next day, a carriage from London arrived at Rosings. However, it did not contain Mr. Macmillan. Emerging from it was a younger man, short and lanky, his curly black hair cradling his hat. After presenting his card, he was shown into the blue parlor while Lady Fitzwilliam was summoned. It was not long before she arrived, accompanied by Lady Catherine, Lady Buford, and Mrs. Darcy. They were announced by the butler.

"Ladies," the man said in a high, thin voice as he bowed. "I am Nathan Haddick. My master, Mr. Macmillan, sends his deep regrets. He is needed to treat several exceedingly serious cases in town and cannot be excused. He has sent me in his stead. Lady Fitzwilliam, may I be shown to Sir Richard's room?"

During his speech, the ladies took in his appearance. The man could not be more than thirty years of age. While well-dressed, his attire was not that of a wealthy and famous physician of long standing.

Lady Catherine frowned deeply. "Mr. Macmillan sent *you?* Why, you are but a boy! What experience have you?"

Mr. Haddick hardly blinked at the attack. "Milady, I have been apprenticed to Mr. Macmillan these dozen years. I have learned much at—"

Lady Catherine interrupted. "Did you attend Cambridge, or at least Oxford?"

Mr. Haddick's lips tightened. "No, milady."

"There, you see?" She gestured at the man with her cane. "Anne, you cannot have this…this *person* attend Richard. You must insist that Mr. Macmillan come at once!"

"Mr. Haddick!" cried Caroline as she stepped forward. "How delightful to see you again." She took his hands in hers. "Forgive me for not greeting you as I should."

"You know this gentleman?" asked Anne.

Caroline turned with a smile. "Oh, yes! He accompanied Mr. Macmillan many times to minister to Sir John. He has impressed me with his manners, knowledge, and attention." She turned back to the young man. "Mr. Haddick, how fares your good mother? Well, I hope?"

Mr. Haddick seemed lost for words for a moment. "My…my mother is well, Lady Buford. Thank you for asking. Has Sir John continued to improve?"

She smiled. "He has, thanks to your good care."

Mr. Haddick acknowledged Caroline's praise with a slight nod and returned his attention to Anne. "Lady Fitzwilliam, I should like to examine Sir Richard, if I may."

Anne quickly looked between an earnest Caroline and a furious Lady Catherine. "Of course. Right this way."

"Anne!" hissed her mother. "You cannot be serious!"

"Mother, enough! Mr. Haddick, pray accept my apologies."

He showed no reaction. "Think nothing of it, milady." The two left the room, with Lady Catherine following, continuing to express her displeasure.

Elizabeth looked at Caroline curiously. She had never witnessed such courtesy to a man like Mr. Haddick from her before. "I did not know you knew Mr. Haddick so well."

"Eliza!" Caroline snorted. "We are hardly acquainted."

Elizabeth frowned. "But you inquired about his mother."

Caroline waved a hand. "He had mentioned at some time or another that he lived with her."

"Then what was that performance about?"

"It was for Lady Catherine's benefit," Caroline declared spitefully. "I care nothing for Mr. Haddick, save that he assisted Mr. Macmillan treating my John. For that, I shall hear nothing ill about either of them!"

ANNE AND LADY CATHERINE SAT IN THE SMALL PARLOR OUTSIDE the master's chambers while Mr. Haddick conducted his examination of Richard with Mr. Lloyd attending him. Lady Catherine continued her abuse of Mr. Haddick, much to Anne's displeasure. Finally, the good men came out to give their diagnosis.

"My dear ladies, Sir Richard has suffered a severe concussion of the head," Mr. Haddick reported. "There is swelling on the brain, to be sure, but not to the extent that it must be relieved by bloodletting or leaches. Should his condition worsen, we shall reconsider that possibility. He is weak due to his captivity, no doubt. I should think he had little food or water. It is a wonder he has not fallen ill to fevers.

"Lady Fitzwilliam, it is important to keep him comfortable in a darkened room. You must get him to drink water. That is vital."

The apothecary took that moment to speak. "Yes, Mr. Haddick is absolutely correct! A man may live for a week or more without food, but he will expire within days without water! And I am impressed with Mr. Haddick's knowledge. He has learned much at the side of the renowned Mr. Macmillan!"

"Thank you, Mr. Lloyd," said Mr. Haddick evenly. "My dear ladies, Sir Richard's condition is serious but by no means hopeless. He has every chance of recovery, but it is in the hands of Providence."

"Thank you, Mr. Haddick," Anne managed. "Everything shall be done as you direct. Shall you stay and attend my husband?"

"Of course. Once I see to the young man who was injured, I

shall obtain a room in the inn."

"Nay, my good sir. You must stay here at Rosings."

"Anne!" cried Lady Catherine. "You do not mean—"

"Mrs. Parks, prepare a room for Mr. Haddick close to the family quarters so he may more easily attend my husband." She turned to Lady Catherine. "Did you wish to say something, Mother?"

The grand dame simply glared.

Buford and Gregory returned to the house in the late afternoon.

"All our efforts have so far resulted in nothing," the knight reported over the soup at dinner. "We have yet to find anyone who knows anything about Fitz's abduction. It appears the Shepardson brothers planned and executed this outrage by themselves, yet everyone who knows them says those two were incapable of such a thing. I can make neither heads nor tales of it."

Anne was taking her meals above stairs, keeping close to Richard, so Lady Catherine acted as hostess, sitting in Anne's place at the foot of the table. "It is your belief, I take it, Sir John, that these miscreants had assistance in Hunsford. That does not surprise me! The conspirators must be rooted out!"

"I beg your pardon, milady, but I did *not* say that," Buford responded impatiently. "What we have found is that the brothers had no friends in the village. Indeed, there was little surprise they were engaged in criminal activities. What we found was a general belief that a kidnapping was beyond their mental abilities."

Lady Catherine would not be appeased. "How can you say no one in Hunsford helped the villains when you acknowledge they must have received aid?"

Caroline could see her husband growing angry at Lady Catherine's tone. "Will you need to enlarge your search?"

Buford sighed tiredly. "I believe so, my dear. I foresee long days in the saddle for us."

"Why?" demanded Lady Catherine. "What you seek is in Hunsford, and Mr. Evans agrees with me!"

Buford stared hard at the old woman. "You have spoken to him, milady?"

"Yes," she declared proudly. "He keeps me apprised of events and happenings. At least *he* knows his duty to me!"

"His duty is to Sir Richard and Lady Fitzwilliam." Buford would have risen to his feet had not Caroline grasped his forearm.

"I am sure he is aware of that," interjected Elizabeth. Turning her face away from Lady Catherine, she sent a silent plea to the Bufords to pursue another subject of conversation. "Lady Catherine, I believe we are ready for the next course."

Later, after Lady Catherine returned to the dower house, a spontaneous "council of war" convened outside of Richard's bedroom. Joining the Bufords, Elizabeth, and Anne were Sergeant Gregory and Corporal Frost. Buford reported his findings to Anne, as well as Lady Catherine's surprising information about the Rosings steward.

"Allow me to understand you," asked a weary Anne. "You believe the villains had help but not from any of the people of Hunsford?"

"Yes," said Buford, and Gregory nodded in agreement.

"You say Mr. Evans has not helped with your investigation. In fact, you have not known where he has been or what he has been doing. Is that correct?" When the knight and the majordomo agreed, Anne continued. "Yet, he finds time to meet regularly with my mother."

Elizabeth was concerned about Anne. She was pale and drawn, with circles under her eyes. She seemed to shrink in her clothes, and there was a slight tremor to her hand. Her cousin had never been of a strong constitution, and Elizabeth was worried that the strain of caring for Richard and managing Rosings was taking a toll on Anne's health.

She asked Buford, "Could Mr. Evans be involved in the kidnapping?"

Buford shared a look between Gregory and Frost before speaking. "We thought of that, but it does not fit. For one thing, there is no connection between Evans and the Shepardsons. Adam worked in the house and stables, you see."

"Adam reported to me," said Gregory, "and he seemed to dislike Evans as much as he disliked the colonel. Besides, it appears Evans was mistreating the Johnsons."

"In what way?" Anne asked.

"Mrs. Johnson has been talking to me, milady. She claimed Evans was charging rent on their cottage. That is strictly against what I was told your father arranged for the Johnsons. But there is more. I cannot find any entry in the ledgers recording receipt of the rent."

"Are you suggesting Mr. Evans is stealing?"

"If Mrs. Johnson is telling the truth," said Gregory carefully, "it is hard to account for the discrepancy otherwise."

"That scoundrel!" Anne shakenly rose to her feet. "I shall dismiss him this instant! How dare he steal from my tenants!"

Gregory rushed to take Anne's arm. "Milady, you must not overdo! Pray be seated. There is no action to take now, in any case."

"What do you mean, Gregory?" Anne demanded, her de Bourgh fire in full evidence. "Is Mrs. Johnson lying?"

"No, milady. I believe her, but we shall need more than her word." He helped Anne back into her chair. "I cannot yet talk to Cork. He is insensible due to the laudanum given to him. Perhaps I may do so in the morning."

"Oh yes, Cork," said Elizabeth. "Do we know anything of his condition?"

"Mr. Haddick is currently resting," said Gregory, "but the maid who looks after Cork reports that he is sleeping quietly. There is great hope for his survival."

"Good." Anne closed her eyes. "We shall not forget what we owe to the Johnsons."

Elizabeth knew this meeting had to end soon for Anne's sake. "You will continue your investigations, will you not, Sir John?" At his nod, she turned to Sergeant Gregory. "And will you look into Mr. Evans's...activities?"

"Yes, madam."

"Then I believe we should retire." Elizabeth frowned at Anne. "You particularly, my dear."

"I shall not leave Richard," Anne stubbornly insisted.

"Just lie down for a time," Elizabeth suggested. "Mrs. Jenkinson or I shall let you know immediately of any change."

"No laudanum this time. Promise me!"

Elizabeth smiled. Anne's command signaled her capitulation. "Of course not, dearest."

"We shall retire, as well," Caroline announced as she and her husband rose.

The next day dawned cool and gray, just as far too many mornings had in England during the last two years. The gloomy atmosphere exactly matched the mood of the people of Hunsford. They went about their daily business, concern and suspicion in their breasts. Outrageous crimes had been committed by their own people, and they did not know whether more villainy was contemplated by their neighbors.

Soon, other matters would concern them.

It started as a low rumble, much like the thunder of a distant storm. The noise grew and grew ever louder. Only horses—many, many horses—could make that sound.

The reverberation was odd, for Hunsford was not on any of the main roads in Kent. The three thoroughfares went through Tunbridge to Tunbridge Wells, Maidstone to Ashford and Dover, and Chatham to Canterbury and Ramsgate. There was little traffic on the narrow road to Hunsford.

Louder and louder the noise became. The people knew this was not the mail coach. No, there was a mighty host approaching. Sure enough, coming around the bend, they appeared.

Tall, magnificent warhorses, two score or more, all jet-black, trotted in perfect unison. Upon their backs rode men as tall and strong as their mounts. The gloom of the day faded before the glory of their uniforms: bright scarlet jackets over grey overall trousers, topped with crested helmets adorned with black horsehair. Each man wore a heavy cavalry saber by his side. What little light there was gleamed from buckles and saddles. The host was led by two officers and a trooper holding aloft the standard.

These men were not parade ground dandies or amateur militiamen. Their scarred faces told the tale of countless skirmishes against the forces of the former tyrant. They were battle-hardened warriors—professional killers—prepared instantly to obey any order from their officers.

The Twelfth Dragoon Guards had come to Hunsford.

The villagers' concerns and suspicions now were superseded by new sentiments—fear and dread.

Once the horsemen reached the village green, an officer—a major, according to the flashes on his coat—raised a hand and called for a halt. He pointed to one of the numerous civilians watching in awe.

"You, there!" the major shouted. "Where may I find Mr. Hibbert?"

The man, gaping at the horsemen, slowly approached the intimidating cavalryman. "Mr. Hibbert? He'd be at his estate, m' lord, 'bout a mile down th' road." He pointed in the general direction.

The major coldly examined the area around the green. He gestured at a building. "Is that the assembly hall?" The man assured him it was, and the major then turned to his fellows.

"Lieutenant, have the troop dismount and rest the horses. Find a source of water and feed. Sergeant, find this Mr. Hibbert. Tell him Major Tilney is here in answer to his letter and desires to meet with him directly at the assembly hall."

The sergeant saluted and rode off.

Major Frederick Tilney descended from his horse, his tall, black Hessians kicking up a bit of dust from the road, ruining his batman's hard-won splendor. Throwing his shoulders back, Tilney and his lieutenant strode confidently into the hall to take possession of the building and, in effect, Hunsford itself.

As the windows of the mistress's sitting room faced the road, the ladies of Rosings Park had an excellent view of the soldiers riding past.

Elizabeth frowned. "I thought the soldiers were attending to the troubles in the north." *Helping my husband,* her thought continued silently.

"I think they are dragoons," remarked Caroline. "They are heavy cavalry—so says John. Are they going somewhere else?"

"No, not on our road," said Anne. "They must be for Hunsford. Somehow, London must have learned of the kidnapping."

"But who could have told them? Who has the influence to call the army here?" asked Caroline.

Anne's face darkened. "It only could have been Mother. She could have used her connection to the House of Matlock like a weapon—as a daughter, sister, and aunt of earls."

"Yes," mused Elizabeth. "With the government as uneasy as Colonel Brandon claims, such a request would receive particular notice, especially with Kent being at London's door."

"This is not well done," said Caroline. "The dragoons have a hard reputation."

Suddenly, the door to the hall opened. "I understand the soldiers are here. Excellent!"

The ladies turned to Mr. Evans, astonished that the steward was in the family wing. "What mean you by that, sir?" demanded Anne.

Instead of answering, Mr. Evans strode directly to the window. "They made good time. Now we shall set things to rights."

"Mr. Evans, I asked you a question," cried Anne, her rudeness inflamed by his.

Mr. Evans turned to her with a tolerant expression. "Forgive me, Lady Fitzwilliam. I was distracted." He bowed. "How may I be of service?"

Anne pointed out the window. "What do you know of that?"

"The soldiers? I asked for them. Rather, Lady Catherine and I asked for them by express. They are here to root out and arrest the malefactors."

Anne was astonished. "Without my permission?"

"My lady, you are occupied with Sir Richard." He gestured to Richard's bedroom door. "I did what needed to be done."

"How can the criminals be arrested if they are dead?" inquired Elizabeth, one eyebrow raised mockingly.

Her gesture was lost on Mr. Evans. "They are not all dead. Two are in this very house."

"Of whom are you speaking?"

"The Johnsons, of course."

"What?" cried Anne. "You would arrest the people who saved Richard?"

"Saved? Only to preserve their own necks." Mr. Evans sneered. "I am certain they were part of the kidnapping plan from the beginning."

"Carrying away the victim and being shot for the trouble by one's collaborators is a strange way of participating in a kidnapping," Elizabeth pointed out. "Would you not say?"

Mr. Evans frowned. "With respect, Mrs. Darcy, you should concern yourself with Sir Richard and the household. This is men's work."

All the women gasped. It had been some time since the mistress of Pemberley had been so directly insulted. So long in fact that

Elizabeth struggled with a response. Anne, however, had no such trouble.

"You will pack your trunks and leave Rosings this very day, sir," she ordered.

"Lady Fitzwilliam, you are overwrought—"

Anne took a step toward the steward, her eyes aflame. "Mr. Evans, you overstep! How dare you set foot into my chambers without my leave! Must I remind you *I* am the mistress of Rosings Park?" Her tone was a proud mixture of de Bourgh arrogance and Fitzwilliam authority. "You think we do not know of your misdeeds? You have charged the Johnsons rent in violation of the agreement established by my honored father. Where is that money, Mr. Evans? It has not been recorded. What have you done with it?"

Mr. Evans blanched. "Lady Fitzwilliam, forgive my intrusion. I only wanted a better look at the soldiers. I meant no disrespect. As for the Johnsons, I can explain."

"Oh, *do!*" Caroline broke in, not in the polite voice of Lady Buford, but as the sarcastic and superior Miss Bingley of the past. "Pray, tell us of your investigations into Sir Richard's more…*secret* activities. What was it? Oh, yes—assignations with unknown women in Tunbridge Wells, I believe."

"*What?*" cried Anne.

Caroline's eyes never left Mr. Evans. "That was your justification for not searching the estate, was it not? A waste of time—at least, that is what you told Sir John." She smiled maliciously. "Oh! Did you not know my husband shares *everything* with me? Well, Mr. Evans? Speak on. I am certain we ladies would be *delighted* to hear your reasoning."

"It…it is not unknown for a gentleman—" Mr. Evans began.

"Then you do not know Sir Richard," said Elizabeth. "What you claim is impossible."

"For Sir Richard, certainly, Eliza. It is inconceivable that *he* would act in such a way," a malevolent smile on Caroline's face again, "but not others. Pray, Mr. Evans, do *you* visit Tunbridge Wells often?"

"Enough of this!" Anne stood tall, her fists clenched at her side. "Mr. Evans, you are hereby dismissed without a character. You will return to your house accompanied by two footmen, who will search your rooms and belongings before you pack your trunks. You will leave Rosings by sunset today. You will contact our solicitor, Mr. Tucker, for wages owed, and we shall deduct anything missing from the estate's coffers, starting with what you stole from the Johnsons. If you are found on my lands ever again, you will be arrested for theft."

"You cannot dismiss me!" Mr. Evans insisted.

"I can and I do. Caroline, would you be so kind as to have Mrs. Parks attend me immediately? And have her bring my strongest footmen."

"I will not stand for this!" Mr. Evans thundered as Caroline left the room. "I will not be treated like a common criminal!"

"Then you shall be treated as an *un*common criminal," Elizabeth observed, arms crossed.

Mr. Evans flashed a look of loathing at Mrs. Darcy. "You wish me gone? I shall be gone within the hour!"

"Not yet, Evans." Sergeant Gregory stood at the sitting room door with Caroline by his side. "You'll do as the mistress commands."

"Sergeant Gregory!" cried Anne in relief. "You are not with Sir John!"

"Corporal Frost is with him, milady," the majordomo reported. "I was about to seek them out when the soldiers rode by. I thought to report it to you, but Lady Buford stopped me on the stairs and informed me of your wishes." He glared at Mr. Evans. "We can do this the easy way or the hard way, Evans. What's it to be?"

Mr. Evans puffed up the remnants of his pride. "You have been looking forward to this for some time, Gregory, I am sure."

"Believe what you want. Come along quietly now." Gregory extended a hand towards the hallway, indicating that Evans precede him.

The former steward of Rosings Park straightened his coat and calmly exited the room, sparing no one a look, Sergeant Gregory at his heels. Once they were out of sight, Anne collapsed in a chair.

"*Brava*, Anne!" exclaimed Caroline. "You did it! You got rid of that horrible man!"

"I did," Anne said breathlessly, a small smile dancing across her lips. "I dismissed him." She then blanched. "Oh, Lord, I dismissed the steward! What have I done?"

Elizabeth seized her hand. "What needed to be done, my dear. That man is a disgrace."

"But Lizzy," responded Anne wide-eyed, "I have no replacement. Richard is ill. Who will run Rosings now?"

"Certainly, Sergeant Gregory can manage things until Darcy returns. My husband will be here in a day or two, I am sure, and then he will see to things until Richard is well," Elizabeth said with more hope than conviction. "You must not worry. Richard is our first concern." She hugged her cousin. "Do you not wish to rest?"

The door to Richard's room opened. "Lady Fitzwilliam, I must insist that there be quiet while I treat Sir Richard," Mr. Haddick softly requested. "Loud voices do him no good."

"Of course," Anne acknowledged. She rose from the chair shakily. "May I sit with my husband while you attend him?"

"If you wish." The young man of medicine extended his arm. "Pray, allow me to assist you."

Anne took his arm with a grateful smile, and the two left the room. Elizabeth sat in a chair, her stomach roiling, as it usually did when she was upset while in her delicate condition.

Caroline returned to the window. "Are you well, Eliza?"

Elizabeth placed a hand to her midsection. "A passing unpleasantness. It is gone already."

"You are fortunate," Caroline said as she looked out. "Such episodes have me in my bed for half a day, at least." She turned away from the window. "I can see nothing more. I wonder whether

John is aware of the soldiers' arrival."

"Perhaps. We can request that Sergeant Gregory send a man—"
The sound of a large woman walking with a cane interrupted
Elizabeth's thought.

"What is going on?" cried Lady Catherine as she entered. "Why
is Mr. Evans being treated so disrespectfully? He was practically
forced marched past me just now. I must speak to my daughter!"

Elizabeth was on her feet. The last thing Anne needed to do
was to deal with her mother. "Lady Catherine, pray be seated. The
physician requests quiet during Richard's recovery."

"That...*boy*?" she sneered. "I shall speak as I please." Still, she
did moderate her tone as she took the chair indicated. "Is Anne in
my son's room? Have her brought to me immediately. She must be
informed of this travesty."

"Aunt Catherine, Anne was forced to dismiss Mr. Evans." Elizabeth hoped by using the more familiar address to placate the
old woman.

"*What?*"

"Aunt, please! Your voice carries. Yes, Anne dismissed Mr. Evans.
He was embezzling from the estate." Elizabeth slightly changed the
facts to suit Lady Catherine's temperament. There was no need for
her to know of Mr. Evans's salacious accusations against Richard's
character.

"No! It must be a falsehood."

"The facts are undeniable. Sergeant Gregory is searching his
rooms this very moment." Elizabeth knelt and took her hand. "It
was dreadfully shocking. When faced with the accusations, the
man was very rude to Anne."

"We witnessed it, milady," added Caroline.

"No!" Lady Catherine's expression changed from incredulity to
anger. "He—he was stealing? From my Anne? And he *insulted* her?"

"I am afraid so, Aunt."

Lady Catherine stared at Elizabeth. "You saw it." She turned to

Caroline. "You too? This cannot be borne! How dare he steal and abuse my daughter! The magistrate must be summoned at once."

Elizabeth squeezed the dowager's hand. "Anne has dismissed him without character, deducting what he stole from his wages. She feels that is a just punishment."

Lady Catherine glanced at Elizabeth. "My daughter is too kind to that…that *scoundrel*. All this time," the grand dame mumbled to herself, "all this time, he has been visiting me, complimenting me, consulting me, *charming* me! He told me I reminded him of his mother. Tricking me! All the while, scheming and thieving! I saw nothing. I should have seen it. I should have known it. That rogue, that villain! I am…I am—"

She stopped abruptly, her expression stony. Whether her ire was directed at Mr. Evans or herself, Elizabeth could not tell. Lady Catherine said nothing for over a minute.

"Dear aunt," said Elizabeth softly, "are you well?"

Elizabeth's words caught Lady Catherine's attention. She stared hard into her face at first, and then the dowager's eyes softened a bit. Was there a hint of affection in them?

The door to Richard's bedroom flew open. "Oh, Mrs. Darcy! Lady Catherine!" cried Mrs. Parks. "The crisis is upon the colonel! Come quickly! He might…he might…" The housekeeper broke down.

In an instant, Elizabeth was on her feet, tugging at Lady Catherine. "Come, Aunt. Come with me."

Lady Catherine paled. "M-my son!" Her eyes filled as she sat, still as death. Then her whole demeanor changed. With grim determination, the dowager dashed away her tears and rose to her feet. "I can waste no more time here. The soldiers came at my direction. It is time to wreak justice and retribution upon those who attacked my family. I must be off."

"But Aunt Catherine! Richard—you must come to Richard."

"There is nothing I can do for my son but avenge him! Hunsford will pay for what they have done!" She yanked her hand free and turned to Mrs. Parks. "Out of my way, woman! I have business in the village that can no longer be delayed!" With that, she stormed out of the room.

Elizabeth was frozen by indecision. Lady Catherine was sure to cause trouble, but Richard was at the turning point! She could not move or think.

Caroline was of one mind. "Eliza, go to Richard! Anne needs you! I shall see to Lady Catherine."

"But she will not listen."

"I will *make* her listen," Caroline declared. More softly, she said, "Eliza, your place is here. Leave Lady Catherine to me."

# Chapter 31

Caroline rushed down the stairs and found Lady Catherine in the hall putting on her gloves. "Lady Catherine, I think it best that you remain at Rosings and attend Anne. You should not go to Hunsford." Her tone, while respectful, brooked no opposition.

Lady Catherine seemed both shocked and offended by this pronouncement. "Is that so, madam? And who are you to tell me where I should and should not go?"

"I assure you I have only the best interests of Anne and Sir Richard in mind."

"Are you implying my leaving will harm them in some manner?"

"I believe further actions in the village will do no one good. You must remain—I insist upon it."

Lady Catherine's face flushed. "*You* insist? Upon my word, you give your opinion most freely! How dare you question me! It is not to be borne! I shall go where I will. My business is not a matter for you or anyone else to decide."

To Lady Catherine's surprise and her own, Caroline stepped between the dowager and the door, blocking the way. "In Anne's service, I shall do what I must. Pray, come into the parlor with me."

With that, Caroline took Lady Catherine by the elbow and all but dragged her into the adjoining room. Such was the grand lady's surprise at being so handled that she barely made a word of protest until the two of them were well inside.

"How dare you touch me, woman!" She flailed her walking stick like a weapon. "I shall see you—"

"*You* are the one who needs to see, milady," Caroline interrupted. "You need to see that your place is here with your daughter and son. You have done enough damage in the village."

"You accuse *me* of damage? The damage I see was done to my son—done by those ungrateful peasants, those criminals who struck down their better! A gentleman who was trying to help them! Well, the Crown has sent me soldiers, and I shall see that they do their duty. Justice shall be done in Hunsford!"

"Justice or revenge?" Caroline asked quietly.

"Call it what you will. I have no time for you. Step aside!"

"I shall not. Whatever it is you intend to do, you shall live to regret it. Heed my counsel or you will destroy Rosings."

Taken aback, the older woman could only sputter, "Destroy Rosings? What foolishness is this?"

"Lady Catherine, I am the daughter of a tradesman, as you take such pleasure in reminding me, but I have learned much from living at Buford Manor. A grand estate is nothing without its people. What is Rosings Park without farmhands and servants and tenants?"

"You presume to tell *me* how to run an estate?"

"Perhaps you have forgotten. I have been told you were once closely involved in the village. Nothing escaped your notice. You knew each family and shared your guidance freely with all. I understand your advice was always excellent.

"But a few years ago, you withdrew. You no longer give Hunsford the benefit of your counsel or presence. Anne took up that burden in your stead and did it against your will. That was long before the events of this week.

"The point I wish to make is this: at one time you cared about the village and its people, and that time has passed. Why? What has changed? Why did you, who so loved Hunsford, grow to hate it?"

During Caroline's discourse, Lady Catherine had turned her head towards the chimney piece, refusing to look at her companion. "What insolence! You care more about that scum than your friend's husband. It is due to your roots in trade, I suppose!"

"You think I care about Hunsford?" she retorted to the back of Lady Catherine's head. "As far as I am concerned, the whole of the village can go to the devil. But my thoughts are for Anne and Sir Richard. There would be no Rosings without Hunsford."

"Yes, and they show their gratitude by trying to kill my son!"

Caroline moved to face Lady Catherine fully. "No, milady, not *all* of Hunsford. I am told the malefactors are dead. The rest of the village is innocent of any crime. Further retribution is pointless and indeed wrong. It will harm more than the villagers. Heed my advice, I pray you."

"Who are you to advise me?" the older woman sneered. "A pretentious parvenu with no connections and little fortune. Married to an infamous libertine. Renowned for your disgraceful pursuit of my nephew. Yes, I know it all! And my daughter places someone like you in charge of my late husband's estate. You upstart! You never should have left the sphere in which you were born!"

"Well, Anne may do as she pleases, but *I* do not have to bear your appalling company a moment longer. I insist you get out of my way!" With that, Lady Catherine stormed towards the door.

"You know, you and I are much alike," Caroline said quietly.

Lady Catherine froze.

"I once thought as you do, believing that behaving in a superior manner proved that I was a superior creature. But we both know better, do we not? It is all playacting. Do you not grow weary of being an actress, milady?"

Lady Catherine looked scandalized. "An *actress*? How dare you!"

Caroline smirked. "You enjoy saying that, do you not? *How dare you!*" she mimicked Lady Catherine's outraged voice. "You are capable of achieving a level of indignation I was never able to master. You have my congratulations. The secret you hide must be considerably more painful than mine.

"Yes, I know all about hiding pain, milady. I also admit you are correct about my previous behavior. What a fool I made of myself pursuing Darcy! Thank heavens I did not succeed."

"You expect me to believe that?" Lady Catherine scoffed. "You rejoice in not securing one of the most eligible men in all England? I am not a simpleton."

Her opponent shrugged. "It matters little what you believe of me. But I shall tell you in hopes you might understand. A marriage between Darcy and me would have been a disaster. I know that now. I enjoy London society and all its diversions, but Darcy loathes town. He is only comfortable in the country, particularly at Pemberley.

"As for me, if I did not have my frequent trips to Cardiff, Glouces-ter, and Bath, I believe the tranquility of my excellent family's beautiful Welsh estate would drive me to distraction. Sir John knows this and humors me. No such diversions exist in Derbyshire. Had I married your nephew, I would have grown to hate one of the best men I have ever known."

Lady Catherine was unconvinced. "You still desire him, I see."

Caroline slowly shook her head. "You are wrong. I can admire Darcy without loving him. Eliza has been good for him, and I am pleased to call them both friends. I am not one to wear my heart on my sleeve, but I tell you I reserve my affections for my husband alone, and I would not trade him for anyone in the kingdom." She paused. "He makes me want to be a better person."

"If you are so happy in your marriage, what is this secret pain you speak of?"

"It is the pain of not living up to my own expectations." She saw Lady Catherine flinch. "Ah, you know it too. My parents, whom you despise, raised me to take my place among the First Circles of London. Do not laugh—there are more well-dowered daughters of tradesmen in the *ton* these days than you know.

"I desperately fought to leave my roots behind. Nothing was beneath me. I cut friends and insulted strangers to curry favor with my betters and lied through my teeth to all and sundry. More than once, I denied my own family history. My path to acceptance by marrying Darcy was ill-considered and foolish, and it brought me nothing but mortification and pain. I became a laughingstock to those I sought to impress. Darcy was clearly unattainable. My infamous treatment of Jane Bennet nearly caused an irreparable breach between my brother and me.

"As it is, Jane and Charles have forgiven me—not that I deserve it but because there is not a resentful bone in their bodies. Eliza and I are friends now, but I have forever destroyed any possibility of true intimacy between our families. I have done too much to deserve more. It was only after I gave up my father's dreams that I followed my own. And that led me to my present happiness. Still, my former behavior haunts me, and there are those in town who remember and will not forgive."

Caroline was pleased that Lady Catherine had ended her efforts to quit the conversation. Indeed, the old woman seemed spellbound by wariness and melancholy. Satisfied that she was correct in her assumptions, Caroline continued.

"I suspect your story is not very different from mine. You are the daughter of an earl, yet you settled for a mere baronet, and not a particularly prominent one. Your sister married one of the richest untitled men in Britain. How that must have rankled."

"Silence!" There was more distress than outrage in Lady Catherine's command.

Caroline ignored the outburst. "You are estranged from your family. You never visit town. What is it you hide from?" Her expression grew earnest. "Tell me. Perhaps I can help."

"You, help me?" Lady Catherine snarled. "I need no help! I-I have tarried long enough. I shall listen to no more of your nonsense."

"Is it nonsense to say you are abandoning your child? I am a mother too, and I say your place is not in Hunsford. Go to Anne. She needs you."

Again, Lady Catherine refused to meet her eyes. "No, she does not."

"How can you say this?"

Lady Catherine's reserve collapsed. "Because there is no hope!" The sudden change in the grand lady was enormous. The imperious dowager was gone; in her place was a mother already grieving a dead son. "You foolish woman, can you not see? Richard shall never awaken." A tear crept down Lady Catherine's wrinkled cheek. "It is only a matter of time before…"

Caroline reached out to Lady Catherine, but she recoiled. "There is only one thing I can do for Richard, and I go to do it. And as for you, you insolent, grasping, interfering—"

Just then, a frantic Mrs. Parks barged into the room. "Lady Catherine! Lady Buford! Come quickly! The colonel—the colonel!"

Lady Catherine gasped in agony. "Oh, God, is it all over?"

"Yes! I mean, no!" Mrs. Parks was almost incoherent. "Come above stairs, my lady! He is awake! The colonel is awake! He lives!"

Caroline's hand flew to her chest. "Truly? Thank heavens!" She turned her attention to Lady Catherine, who had gone ashen. "My lady, are you well?"

The older woman's hand shook as she leaned on her walking stick. "I-I—" Lady Catherine looked about the room.

Caroline placed a gentle hand on her shoulder. "May I assist you above stairs? Surely, you wish to see Sir Richard."

Never had Caroline seen Anne's mother so confused. "No, I can manage." She turned to Mrs. Parks. "You are not mistaken? Richard is awake?" Her voice was pathetically hopeful.

Mrs. Park's smile threatened to split her face. "Come with me, milady, and see this miracle for yourself!"

"Of course, I shall— No, wait. My appointment in the village."

"Do not concern yourself with that," said a low voice from the door. Caroline beheld Sir John there, a joyful gleam to his eye. "I shall go in your place. Go to your son, milady."

"Yes, I shall," she meekly nodded. "That is very good of you, Sir John." Lady Catherine gathered herself. "Mrs. Parks, pray accompany me to the sickroom." The housekeeper offered her arm, which was accepted immediately. Silently, the two left the parlor.

Caroline ran to her husband. "You have returned to the most wonderful news!" As she fell into his embrace, a thought occurred to her. She looked up. "When did you arrive?"

Buford did not answer but only smiled. Caroline, clearly suspicious, stepped back and narrowed her eyes.

"You were outside this room! How much did you overhear?"

Buford's grin grew. "You would not trade me for the Regent? I *am* flattered."

"John Buford! Oh, there shall be no living with you now!"

She could say no more as Buford swept her up and kissed her thoroughly.

"Now that we have established that," Buford said to his pleasantly flustered wife, "let us see Fitzwilliam before I leave to go to the village." He frowned. "Did you know there are soldiers in Hunsford?"

FITZWILLIAM THRASHED ABOUT THE BED, TERRIFYING ANNE. Her vision blurred by tears, she slipped out of the chair and knelt by the bed, grasping her husband's hand and whispering Richard's name over and over again, like a chant. She could hardly feel Elizabeth's hand on her shoulder.

Suddenly, Richard fell quiet. He did not appear to be breathing.

Anne laid her cheek on her husband's hand and sobbed. *Was this the end?*

Richard gasped. "Anne."

She started. It was Richard's voice! Anne raised her head and saw her husband's half-opened eyes staring at her. "Richard, Richard! I am here," she managed. Meanwhile, Mr. Haddick placed a hand at his neck while the other held a watch.

"Where...where am I?" Richard's voice was a low groan, full of pain.

"Home, my dearest. You are home in your room."

He grimaced. "Oh! My head...aches."

"I should say it does, Sir Richard," remarked Mr. Haddick. "Pray be still. It will hurt less."

Richard turned towards the physician, earning another groan. "I do not...think...we have been...introduced."

For the first time, Anne beheld a smile on the young doctor's face. "My name is Haddick, Sir Richard. I work with Mr. Macmillan. Pray, tell me how you feel."

Richard's lips quirked. "Like hell."

Anne could not help but giggle, and Elizabeth, behind her, laughed out loud. If Richard were well enough to make jokes, he would heal! Hope, reignited in her breast, raced like warm fire throughout her body.

A joyful Mrs. Parks was hopping in place with excitement. "Oh, I must tell everyone that the master is awake! My lady, may I?" Anne nodded and the housekeeper was out the door the next instant.

"Dark...it is so dark in here."

"Yes," Haddick answered. "You have suffered a concussion of the head. Light can be uncomfortable."

Richard started to roll his head, crying out in agony. "It was... dark there. Light...please."

"The drapes!" cried Anne.

"I shall see to it," Elizabeth said before she began opening the curtains.

"Only a small amount, Mrs. Darcy," advised Haddick. "We must not introduce too much light until we know more. Sir, how much do you remember of your captivity?"

"Dark room…pain…hungry." He twisted his head and groaned.

"Sir, you must lie as still as you can. It will make you rest easier." Haddick turned to Anne, who still held Richard's hand in hers. "Milady?" She reluctantly released it and reclaimed her chair, all the while assuring Richard that she would not leave his side. Haddick asked whether Richard remembered anything more.

"Talking to…crowd."

Anne frowned. "That was the speech in Hunsford. It was days ago."

"It is not unusual in cases like this for memories to be lost," said Haddick, just as the door opened to permit Lady Catherine and Mrs. Parks to enter. Anne rushed over to embrace her mother before walking her to a chair, assuring her that Richard had awakened.

"Yes, so I see." Lady Catherine's frightened gaze moved from Richard to Anne. "Richard will be well? Are you certain?"

Anne smiled brightly. "Yes, Mama. Mr. Haddick believes Richard shall make a full recovery."

"But, what is this I hear about his memory?" the grand dame demanded.

"As I was informing Lady Fitzwilliam," Haddick responded in a calm voice, "it is quite common in cases like this for there to be some loss of recent memories. Sir Richard's injuries should not impair his mental capacities in the future."

"Will you not bleed him?"

"That is not necessary, Lady Catherine. I have inspected the site of his injury, and there is limited swelling. Certainly, nothing that indicates any pressure on the brain. Bleeding would do nothing but weaken him, and Sir Richard needs all his strength to recover fully.

"Lady Fitzwilliam, I know he has just awakened, but rest is most advantageous at this time. I recommend dosing him—very lightly, mind—so that Sir Richard may sleep. He will be more comfortable. First, however, he requires nourishment."

As he was speaking, the Bufords entered.

"Pray, Mrs. Parks, have the cook send up some barley broth with a touch of meat. No bread—I think chewing would be painful. We shall review this tomorrow." He frowned at the now-packed bedroom. "Forgive me for pointing out that crowds are not what Sir Richard requires now."

Buford bowed. "Our concern for our friend must be our excuse, my good sir. We are pleased to find Sir Richard awake."

The patient scowled. "They are...talking of me...as though...I am not here. Blasted rude of them."

Buford grinned. "I am sure. Mr. Haddick, it is good to see you again. We shall take ourselves off and leave my friend in your care." He turned to Anne. "Lady Fitzwilliam, may I speak to you for a moment?"

*Hunsford*

"Leave?" said Major Tilney incredulously, leaning back in his chair. "We have just arrived. We cannot leave!"

"Damn it all!" cried Buford. "I tell you things are in hand! Why not leave, Tilney?"

The two men sat at a table in one corner of the assembly hall. Joining them were the magistrate Mr. Hibbert and Corporal Frost. The room was fairly dark as the few windows cast little light. A requisitioned candelabra at least allowed the attendants to see each other's faces.

The table was to be Major Tilney's *office* in Hunsford. The rest of the space was intended to house the non-commissioned officers of the Twelfth. The rest of the troop would be sheltered in tents. Major Tilney and the lieutenant were for more comfortable accommodations as befitted their rank.

Major Tilney frowned at his friend across the table. "Buford, you of all people know I cannot do anything without orders from Whitehall."

"And you know what fifty armed men can do to a small village!"

Buford took a breath and calmed down. Anne had authorized him to speak for her and Richard, and anger would be detrimental to his purpose. "Tilney, the constable says things are quiet in Hunsford now that the scoundrels are dead. We appreciate that London has sent you here to help keep the peace, but that task is done."

Mr. Hibbert used a handkerchief to wipe the nervous perspiration from his forehead. "Um, yes. The longer your troops are quartered here, the more likely there will be an incident. People were worried about the food stores before this all happened. Now with extra mouths to feed—"

Major Tilney waved him off. "You know the law. London will pay for what we take."

"Yes, at a paltry rate that will not cover half the loss," Buford pointed out. "And there is more at risk than money. Soldiers and civilians are a bad mix, especially when there are pretty girls about."

"Your men are no longer needed here," Mr. Hibbert reiterated. "Surely, you see that."

The officer held up his hands. "Sir, it does not matter what *I* see. All that matters is what my commanders see! *They* see a country in turmoil, and when the aunt of an earl demands protection—" Major Tilney paused. "Pray forgive my outburst. I know this situation is rife for disgraceful behavior. This is not the first troubles I have been ordered to quiet. But, until my troopers are needed elsewhere, here we must stay, whether I like it or not. Believe me, I would much prefer to be at Richmond with my wife." Major Tilney took a breath. "Buford, I shall threaten the men, warn my officers to be vigilant, and hope our stay is of short duration.

"As I said earlier, we are an advance party—I only have half a troop. My commander will use my report to decide whether to send in the rest of the squadron."

"Good Lord, Frederick!" cried Buford. "A squadron of heavy cavalry? That is another hundred troopers!"

"I know, Buford, I know."

"What would you have us do, Major?" asked Mr. Hibbert.

"Write to whomever you can in London and hope it makes a difference." Major Tilney shrugged, indicating the hopelessness of the circumstances.

"Major Tilney, I believe your wife's father, Sir Percival Blakeney, has great influence at court," suggested Mr. Hibbert.

Major Tilney sucked air between his teeth, clearly furious. Buford quickly jumped in.

"Mr. Hibbert, it would be highly irregular for the major to use his family connections for such a purpose." He knew that his old friend held the baronet in the highest regard, and for him to impose upon Sir Percy was unthinkable.

The magistrate deflated. "That is unfortunate. I am afraid I am at a loss to know what to do about the troops."

Strong steps approached the table. "Major," announced a sergeant, "this gentleman says he needs to join your meeting."

Buford turned and saw a familiar figure through the gloom. "Darcy! Well met!"

It was a very bedraggled Fitzwilliam Darcy that approached the table. His coat dusty and rumpled, his cravat askew, his chin in bad need of a shave, it was clear that he had not wasted a moment on the road from Derbyshire to Kent. However, his deep concern was evidenced by the gleam in his eye and the strength of his handshake.

"You know Richard has awakened? Mr. Haddick says he shall recover."

"Yes, I am aware of this wonderful news." Darcy smiled. "We stopped at Rosings, and Anne informed me of Richard's condition. Caroline told us of this important meeting, and Elizabeth suggested that I continue into the village."

Buford smirked. "Suggested or commanded?"

"*Strongly advocated,* I would say." He nodded at the officer at the table. "Major Tilney, well met. I take it there is an issue with the soldiers' presence here. How may I be of assistance?" He all but fell into the chair Corporal Frost pulled up. The others quickly related how matters stood in Hunsford.

"So, with the criminals dealt with," concluded Mr. Hibbert, "there is no need of the army to keep the peace."

"Yes, I understand," said Darcy as he wearily rubbed his forehead. "With all due respect, Major Tilney, troopers quartered in villages for any length of time are unwelcome guests at best. I am recently returned from the north and have seen it for myself. Things are still unsettled in Derbyshire, and much resentment remains." He sighed. "I can call on my late uncle's friends in the Lords, and I have contacts in the Commons as well. Surely, we can have your company recalled to barracks in short order. I shall write to London as soon as may be—this very day."

Major Tilney rubbed his jaw. "That might be enough. Thank you, sir."

"Mr. Darcy," Corporal Frost cut in, "if you would pardon me for saying so, you look right worn out. You can send your letters tomorrow."

At first, Darcy would not be moved, until Buford smiled. "I shall tell Lizzy about your obstinacy!"

Darcy pretended to be taken aback. "You would not dare."

Buford just grinned wider.

Darcy threw up his hands. "In the face of such opposition, I have no choice but to concede to your wise counsel, Mr. Frost." The others laughed lightly, and Darcy joined them. "But expresses shall be sent no later than noon tomorrow. Come, let us make our plans."

# Chapter 32

Darcy was as good as his word. Before the sun reached its zenith, a Dragoon trooper, courtesy of Major Tilney, dashed towards the capital with several letters in his pouch. Meanwhile, Mrs. Collins organized a large dinner for the body of Tilney's company. The intention was to entertain the soldiers while soothing the fears of the villagers.

Accomplishing all that could be done, Darcy continued his joyful reunion with his wife and children. He did not visit with Richard until the middle of the afternoon, and Elizabeth accompanied him. The pair entered the sickroom hand in hand, quite inseparable. After greeting their cousin and Anne, Darcy and Elizabeth made themselves comfortable in the remaining chairs that had been placed about the bedchamber.

"I still own a devil of a headache," Richard confessed to Darcy's inquiry about his health, "but I have suffered worse on campaign. Tell me how my mother and brother fare."

"Everyone is well. I shall not say the crisis did not frighten Andrew, but he found his footing soon enough. He is assisting Devonshire with his Grace's investigation."

"The duke? I am astonished. Andrew might grow into his seat after all."

"Richard!" admonished Anne.

Darcy chuckled. "I admit Lady Eugenie was helpful in…encouraging him."

"Pushed him out the door, most likely," Richard quipped.

"Otherwise," Darcy continued, "there were no troubles to speak of at Matlock, Ambervale, or Pemberley. The Bingleys are safe, though Charles received quite a scare."

"Indeed?"

"Mayfield was in a bit of an uproar. The tenants were sure the marchers were to fall upon them at any moment, and Charles was… unsure how to deal with matters."

Richard shook his head, which caused him to groan in pain.

Anne answered for him. "I am sure all has been set right now."

"As much as it can be. The general unhappiness remains. Conditions are bad, people are hungry, and there is no work to be had. Rumors abound everywhere about revolution, spies, and instigators. The government acted harshly, and the people are terrified there is worse to come."

Anne noticed Elizabeth nodding. "You are not surprised, Lizzy."

Elizabeth bestowed an affectionate glance at her husband. "Fitzwilliam and I spoke of this last night, and I share his concerns. We should think of returning to Pemberley."

"No, not now," Darcy responded in a tone that bespoke an unresolved disagreement. "I shall not have you or the children travel until I am certain of your doing so in safety. Our people know this and are content with our absence. Besides"—he turned to his cousins—"there are matters here that require our attention."

"I shall not say you are wrong, Darcy," Anne admitted.

"Anne!" complained Richard. "Oh…my head!"

"Anne needs us, Richard," Elizabeth said.

Darcy took his wife's hand. "We shall only act as your agents. You and Anne have my word on it."

Richard stared at the ceiling. "Damn this head! I have no choice but to accept your help."

"Can you relate what happened the night you were rescued?" Darcy asked carefully.

"I have begun to remember it." He turned to Anne. "Buford said something about Cork Johnson yesterday. Is he hurt?"

"Yes, my dear—hurt while saving you. Mr. Haddick attends him."

"Ah, Mr. Macmillan's assistant," Darcy murmured to himself. "An excellent physician. You are both in good hands."

"He prodded me enough yesterday," Richard grumbled. Returning to Darcy's question, he continued, "I do remember being held by the Shepardson brothers. Buford said they were killed during the rescue. I…I think that was a mistake."

"What?" said Anne. "Why do you say that?"

"There was at least one other involved." Richard looked at his cousin. "I think we need Buford and Gregory in here for this, Darcy."

"I believe they are in the library." Anne stood. "I shall have them sent up at once."

"Kendrick?" shouted Anne. "*He* was behind your kidnapping?"

Richard winced. "No, dear, at least not in the way you say."

"How did you learn of Mr. Kendrick's involvement, Richard?" asked Darcy.

Richard relaxed back into his pillows. "I spent most of my time propped up against one wall of the storage room. It was the exterior wall, you see. Kendrick and Adam Shepardson were arguing outside. I suppose they did not suspect I could overhear them."

"Or care, if they planned to kill you," added Buford. It earned a well-deserved outcry from the ladies in the room.

Richard nodded grimly. "Too right, Buford. That was one of their arguments."

Darcy pulled at his chin. "The Shepardsons were certainly after the ransom money. But Mr. Kendrick? What could he accomplish? Did he expect a share?"

"No, he wanted no part of the scheme." Richard turned to Anne. "It seems Kendrick was paying Shepardson to cause mischief about the estate. Shepardson was responsible for salting the kitchen garden at Kendrick's urging. The kidnapping was Shepardson's idea alone."

"That sounds right," said Sergeant Gregory. "A simpleton could've come up with a better plan. Adam Shepardson wasn't known for his wits, and Simon had even less."

"Shepardson was blackmailing Kendrick for his assistance," Richard went on. "He was to provide a wagon to carry me out of the district."

"I did not see a wagon at the cottage." Buford looked to Gregory and Frost, and both men shook their heads. "Perhaps Kendrick betrayed them."

"Or the wagon had not reached the cottage before you found me."

Buford shared a look with the others. "We did not find you, Fitz. Cork Johnson told us where you were, and he carried you out before we stormed the place."

"And got himself shot as payment." Richard's eyes were pained. "Will he live?"

Anne took her husband's hand. "Mr. Haddick extracted the bullet. He says Cork is recovering as well as can be expected."

"Mr. Haddick has had training as a surgeon," Darcy explained.

"I pray the boy recovers. He saved my life." Richard's face hardened. "So, what do we do about Kendrick?"

"I would be willing to call the bastard out on your behalf," Buford declared.

"John—no!" cried Caroline.

Buford scowled. "The scum deserves to be stuck like the pig he is." Both Anne and Caroline protested.

"Sir John," offered Elizabeth, "as pleasing as those sentiments are, I am certain we can concoct an equally satisfying means of securing justice for Richard without resorting to such methods." She turned her fine eyes to Darcy.

"Let us look at the evidence," Darcy began. "Frankly, all we have is hearsay."

Richard sputtered in protest and began to sit up.

"Richard, be still!" Darcy insisted. "I believe you, but your word is not enough to condemn the man. You know that. The only people who can corroborate what you overheard are dead."

"This boy, Cork, can he not help?" asked Caroline.

"No, my dear," Buford answered her. "Even if he could give testimony against Kendrick, no one would give credence to the word of a simpleton."

Darcy nodded. "Kendrick cannot be held responsible for the kidnapping or the damage about the estate."

"So, he walks free?" cried Richard, who grimaced at the effort.

A wicked smile grew on Darcy's lips. "No, we shall find another way. And I know just the man to help us do it."

THE NEXT NIGHT AT THE ASSEMBLY HALL, MRS. COLLINS'S dinner was a success. The troopers, unused to such hospitality (and well-watered wine), enjoyed themselves while on their best behavior. Anne did not want to attend, but she was persuaded that Lady Fitzwilliam's presence as hostess was required to ease the villagers' worries. Lady Catherine fumed at what she considered her demotion but sat quietly at the head table and held her complaints. At least she was seated next to the Darcys. Mrs. Darcy might be objectionable, but she was her niece by marriage—far superior to those grasping Bufords.

Sir John and Lady Buford occupied the opposite end of the table. Caroline suffered to sit next to the Collinses so her husband could share wine from Rosings's private stock and war stories with his good friend Frederick Tilney.

"I thought you would have left the army by now," Buford said.

"I had hoped to," Major Tilney admitted, "but the baronet and I thought it best that I put in a few more years before retiring. It is just as well. Father is pleased"—Tilney rolled his eyes—"and Whitehall needs me because of the troubles. I plan to put away my sword before the end of the year."

Buford cocked his head. "Why would Sir Percy advise extending your career? You told me you were to learn farming at his elbow. Has that changed?"

"Postponed, Buford, postponed. That is still the plan. With my promotion, it would be bad form to retire too soon."

Buford narrowed his eyes. "How *did* you earn that promotion? You never said."

A strange, guarded aspect arose in Frederick Tilney. "Services to the crown and all that while I was with the Blues." He downed his glass. "After all, someone has to look good on the parade ground."

Buford had a feeling that Tilney was not telling him everything but let the matter drop.

BACK AT ROSINGS, RICHARD LAY IN HIS BED, HIS HEAD ACHING and his pride smarting. He refused any more laudanum, for he wanted his head clear to think, to reflect on the weight of his failures.

For years, he was trained to do only one thing—to lead men into battle. He knew nothing about managing an estate, but he thought it would be a simple matter to learn. He had ridden without hesitation across muddy battlefields pockmarked by exploding cannonballs, right into the teeth of French bayonets. Rosings Park was only a farm—a large farm, to be sure, but a farm, nevertheless. All that was required was to lead by example and choose a loyal and talented subordinate.

That man was supposed to be Mr. Evans. The steward was so clearly a disaster that Anne had dismissed him without character when Richard was incapacitated. *She* could tell Evans was unfit for the position, something Richard had failed to recognize. He had been warned of his unsuitability—by Gregory, by Darcy—even by Mr. Collins, in a way. Richard had ignored them all and placed

Rosings in danger.

Anne trusted her husband to care for Rosings, and he had failed at the off.

His musings were not the only reason Richard did not want to sleep. Awake, he could escape his nightmares.

He had not told Buford the entire truth before about battlefield memories. He had them, of course, like any other soldier. He recalled many a time awakening from a dark dream in a cold sweat until he learned a trick from a fellow officer. "One could not rid oneself of such dreams," the man said, "one must control them—trap them—banish them to the furthest reaches of memory."

So, Richard created a place in his mind to put his battlefield nightmares, one that allowed him to lock those dark thoughts away. The place was likened to a trunk, and Richard had the only key.

The trick had worked very well for years—until the kidnapping. In the dank storeroom, in pain and fear, his *trunk* began to fall apart. His freed nightmares, like demons, invaded his sleep. His rescue did nothing to stand off visions of death and gore and horror. The only respite was found by staying awake. He allowed himself only an occasional catnap. Deep sleep was to be avoided.

The result for Richard Fitzwilliam was exhaustion and melancholy and, because of head pain, a peevish attitude. He did not talk but to complain and did not move except to use the necessary. Light bothered his eyes, and loud sounds hurt his ears. It was not surprising that even the most dedicated nurse would find such a patient tedious.

Such was the situation in which Anne's companion and Richard's valet found themselves. After being scolded for "reading too loud"—Sir Richard found the sound of page turning annoying—Mrs. Jenkinson took herself off to the sitting room just outside the master's chambers. Joseph had already withdrawn to the dressing room, to Richard's relief.

Now, in addition to his other complaints, Richard felt guilty, lonely, and maudlin. Lost in his melancholy thoughts, he did not hear the door to the hallway open.

"*Oh!*" a young child's voice exclaimed.

Richard beheld little Chloe Wickham peeking into the room.

"This is not Aunt Lizzy's room," the little girl said.

"No, child," Richard answered, "it is not. She is not at Rosings at the moment."

"Mrs. Nivens said she was gone, but I wanted to see." She suddenly turned, gave a light cry, and scampered in, closing the door behind her.

Richard frowned. "What is amiss?"

"Mrs. Nivens will catch me." Chloe moved to hide behind one of the chairs.

"I take it you escaped from the nursery?" At her nod, Richard added, "Is this something you do often?"

"No…yes…sometimes."

Richard laughed. "I think you do it quite regularly—oh!" He clutched his head with one hand.

"Are you hurt?" Worried eyes gazed at him.

"My head hurts like the devil," he managed, grimacing.

"Oh! Did you fall down?"

"No." He would not tell her the entirety of his misadventure. "Bad men did this to me."

Chloe cringed. "Are they coming here?"

He sighed. "Do not worry. They are—they shall not hurt anyone anymore."

The child nervously moved closer to the bed. "Were the bad men pirates? Uncle Darcy tells me pirate stories."

"No, they were not pirates."

She relaxed. "Good. I am scared of pirates."

"So am I." Richard watched with amazement as Chloe, showing remarkable ability for one so young, climbed onto his bed. "What are you doing?"

"When I feel bad," she paused as she finished her climb, "Aunt Lizzy sits with me." She made herself comfortable at the foot of the bed, propped up against a bed post. "Who sits with you?"

"Well, Mrs. Jenkinson, for one, but not on my bed. Should you not return to the nursery?"

"I want to wait up for Aunt Lizzy. Please, may I stay?"

Richard sighed. "Very well. But you must be quiet. It pains me to talk."

Chloe's eyes grew wide. "I shall be good, I promise."

Richard closed his eyes and tried to rest. He lay as still as he could, so as not to aggravate the pain in his head. Perhaps if he concentrated on pleasant thoughts, he could keep the nightmares at bay for a time.

He was pleased to see that Darcy's ward no longer feared him. It was not the little girl's fault who had fathered her. Miss Chloe, raised at the Darcys' expense, had all the advantages her father had enjoyed. But she had none of the disadvantages: a disinterested, spend-thrift mother, an overindulgent godfather, and a father unwilling or unable to discipline his son.

To be fair, George Wickham had been a good companion in his youth, always ready for an adventure, whether raiding the kitchen or starting a snowball fight. Perhaps if Wickham had a better mother, or if Uncle Darcy had not spoiled him, he would not have turned out wild and selfish. Maybe.

Surely Darcy and Elizabeth would not make those mistakes.

"Does your momma sit with you?" Apparently, Chloe could not be silent for more than three minutes at a time.

Eyes closed, Richard responded. "My mother is in Derbyshire."

"I live in Derby-sure when we go to Pemb-lee. I like Pemb-lee." She bounced a bit on the bed.

"Pray stop that."

"I am sorry," she cried. "May I stay?"

"Only if you do not bounce. My head, you see." Richard wondered why Mrs. Jenkinson remained unaware of Chloe's presence. Perhaps she was angry at him for snapping at her earlier. It would serve him right. "I like Pemberley, too. Why did you sneak out of the nursery?"

Chloe whined, "I want Aunt Lizzy to hug me good night."

"Unfortunately, I am told she and your uncle are with the others at a party in Hunsford. Surely, she will return in good time to perform her nightly duties."

"I like parties."

Her mind jumped from subject to subject. *Were all children like that?* "I like parties, as well. Now, I believe we must be quiet."

There was a pause. "Shall you hug me good night?"

Richard opened his eyes. "I beg your pardon?"

Chloe started to crawl towards him. "I want a hug good night."

Before Richard could decide the wisdom of that, Chloe had tucked herself by his side. Without thought, Richard's arm cuddled the child.

Chloe cooed. "You hug nice."

"Thank you." Richard returned to his musings over the child. It certainly seemed the Darcys were treating their ward as though she were their own. It was not commonly done, he knew. Distinction of blood, class, and rank had to be maintained. Lady Catherine would be outraged if she were made aware of it.

On the other hand, Miss Chloe was Mrs. Darcy's blood relation. There was little chance of the child's mother in far-away India reclaiming her anytime soon—if ever. Would parental kindness and care for the little girl truly upset the established order of Britain? Of course not.

The adoptions of nieces and nephews happened all the time. There was no Mrs. Wickham to counteract the Darcys' childrearing, and the girl was a sweet soul.

Richard hugged her firmly. *Yes, a sweet child, indeed. She deserves all the happiness in the world. I shall not say a word against her ever again.*

The door to the sitting room opened. "Sir Richard, pray excuse me," said an anxious Mrs. Jenkinson, "but we are looking for—why, here she is!" Her voice grew stern. "Chloe Wickham, what are you doing here?"

Chloe buried her face deep into Richard's side.

"She was looking for a good night hug," stated Richard evenly, "and I am providing it."

Mrs. Jenkinson was taken aback. "But…Mrs. Nivens is beside herself."

"Ah, well. Have her brought in." Richard glanced down at the squirming child. "Miss Chloe, I believe it is time for bed."

"I do not want to go," she cried.

"There, there. No tears, now." By then, Mrs. Nivens had arrived. "Here is your charge, my good lady. Pray do not scold her. I am happy for her visit."

"As you wish, sir. Come, Miss Chloe, it is time for bed." Chloe reluctantly allowed the nurse to pick her up. "Say good night to Sir Richard."

A sleepy Chloe turned to him. "Good night."

"Mrs. Nivens, you did not refer to me properly just now," Richard informed her with a grin. "*Cousin* Richard bids Miss Chloe a good night."

The girl's face lit up. "Good night, Cousin Richard!"

"Good night, my dear."

For some reason, Richard did not suffer nightmares that night.

# Chapter 33

The orders came in, recalling the Twelfth Dragoons to Horse Guards. Buford went into Hunsford on their day of departure to farewell Major Tilney. The two friends walked out of the assembly hall towards the amassed troopers mounted on their warhorses, the Twelfth's standard waving in the morning breeze.

"It has been too long, Frederick," said Buford. "We must have dinner with you and Mrs. Tilney when we are next in London."

"When will that be?"

"Before the Season, to be sure. Perhaps November?"

"Excellent! I should have put away my sword by then."

Buford patted Tilney on the back. "Cannot wait to be a farmer, eh?"

Major Tilney lost his good humor. "It is not just that. Buford, you have no idea how matters are in London. The government is terrified. They want this unrest stopped by whatever means necessary. We were fortunate this time, very fortunate."

He halted and turned to Buford, speaking in a low voice. "If conditions in the country do not improve soon, our luck will run out. They will be too many hungry and angry people at the wrong place, saying the wrong things. The government will act in a disproportionate manner, and some poor bugger will have to order his troopers to draw swords against our own people." His expression was distraught. "I do not wish to be that officer."

A stunned Buford could say nothing to that as Major Tilney mounted his horse. "Farewell, Buford, until we meet again." The Twelfth Dragoons moved out in columns of two, heading back to the capital, Buford watching as they rode away.

*July*

A FORTNIGHT LATER, THOMAS TUCKER WAS ANNOUNCED BY the butler at the library door.

"I have drawn up the papers you desired, Darcy," said the young solicitor, indicating the bag at his side. "Is Sir Richard recovered?"

"Not fully, Tucker," said Darcy as he shook his hand, "but his health is improving by the day. You made good time. Mary and Rosanne—they are well, I trust?"

A small smile cracked Tucker's usual serious demeanor. "They are in excellent health, Brother. Mary sends her warmest regards, and I have letters for the ladies."

"We shall meet with them once our business is completed. I am authorized by Anne to offer you a room for the night."

"And by me," added Richard as he slowly entered the library. "Well met, Tucker." He moved with great care to join the others.

Tucker placed his satchel on a table, took Richard's outstretched hand, and gripped his elbow with his other. "I am pleased to see you up and about, but should you not sit down?"

"He should," declared Darcy. "He also should have a footman assisting him."

"Careful, Cuz," said Richard as Tucker guided him to a chair. "I need no more scolding from you. Your days of managing Rosings are numbered." Richard made himself comfortable while the others found their seats.

"Here are the papers." Tucker opened his bag and handed Darcy the contents of his satchel.

Darcy began reading. "You are certain we shall succeed?"

"Without a doubt. He has mortgaged the place to the hilt. He will have no recourse but to pay or let it go."

"And he cannot pay if what we have learned is true," added Richard. "That is a vast amount of money, Darce. I must repay you."

Darcy raised a hand. "Do not concern yourself. I consider this outlay an investment. According to what Tucker proposes, I shall eventually recover what I extended and more besides. Save your funds for Rosings."

Richard rubbed his chin. "If it is as good an investment as all that, perhaps I should participate as well."

Darcy glanced at Tucker who nodded. "Very well. We shall speak again after our visit to Glendale Farm." He put the forms aside. "Pray keep your seats, gentlemen. I shall call for the ladies and refreshments."

### Glendale Farm

A WEEK LATER AT TWO IN THE AFTERNOON, DARCY'S WELL-sprung carriage made its way through the gates of Glendale Farm. With Darcy were Sir Richard, Sir John, Sergeant Gregory, and Corporal Frost. Both Darcy and Richard were taken aback at the condition of the fields. The crops were in an exceedingly bad way—short and scrubby with weeds everywhere. They beheld emaciated livestock, neglected tenant houses, ramshackle barns, and a dilapidated main house.

"Is he even trying to farm?" asked an appalled Richard. "I have never seen a place in such disarray."

Darcy took in the sight thoughtfully. "Yes," he said mostly to himself, "very bad, indeed. But with a bit of work and care, the improvements—and returns—should be substantial."

Richard shook his head. "I shall take your word for it, Cousin."

Darcy's attention returned to the others. "Gentlemen, you will recall our agreement on handling this matter."

"You mean *I* should remember," grumbled Richard.

Buford patted his shoulder. "Darcy is right, you know. This way is much more painful than calling him out."

Richard eyed his cousin. "Again, I shall have to rely on Darcy's word for it."

Minutes later, the carriage arrived at the manor house's entrance. No footmen or stable hand attended the visitors. Once the gentlemen presented themselves at the door, the butler refused entry, claiming his master was not available for visitors. Buford muttered about forcing their way in, and the two former cavalrymen had clubs, but Darcy had a better solution.

"Here is a note from Mr. Hibbert, magistrate for Hunsford, attesting to the importance of our demand to see Mr. Kendrick immediately. If that is insufficient for you, we can request the attendance of Mr. George Best and Mr. William Morland in short order."

The names of the justice of the peace and the high sheriff were enough to frighten the old man. The delegation was shown at once to the master's study. There, Reginald Kendrick was found slouched in a chair behind a desk strewn with papers and empty bottles. The place stank of cheap brandy.

"Farmingsworth!" Mr. Kendrick raged. "I said no visitors! Throw these interlopers out!"

Richard turned to Gregory and Frost. "Make certain we are not disturbed, will you?" The cudgel-wielding men nodded, escorted the butler out, and closed the door.

By now, Mr. Kendrick was on his feet. "Farmingsworth, I gave you an order! *Farmingsworth!*"

"Be seated, Kendrick," Richard growled. "The sooner you do, the sooner our business may be completed, and we can depart from your revolting presence."

"You dare invade my house and insult me?"

Richard walked to the desk and leaned over it, his fists planted on the dull and dirty wood. "Enough, Kendrick! I know all!" He barely held to his promise not to beat the man. "I heard you at the

Johnson cottage, talking to Adam Shepardson. I could hear every word. You have been behind our misfortunes at Rosings."

Mr. Kendrick blanched as he fell back into his chair.

"One hundred pounds. You offered Shepardson *one hundred pounds* to kill me."

"I-I do not know what you are talking about. Shepardson? I know no Shepardson. These are all lies."

Richard growled, "I should kill you for all you put my wife through."

"N-now, see here—"

Richard went on as though Mr. Kendrick had said nothing. "The only reason the sheriff is not here to take you to Newgate is your agents are dead and cannot testify against you. It is really too bad. I would like to see you hang."

"I had nothing to do with your abduction!" Mr. Kendrick turned to the others. "Gentleman, you must see that Fitzwilliam is mad!"

"I do not recall Sir Richard saying he was abducted," said Sir John calmly, swinging his cane about. "Do you, Darcy?"

"Nor do I," replied Darcy in that clipped manner of his.

"It is common knowledge!" Mr. Kendrick blustered.

"It is not. Not a single word appeared about the matter in the papers." Richard was now icy calm. "I shall not argue with the likes of you. I shall instead simply dispose of you in a rather unsatisfactory manner. Darcy?"

His cousin removed a paper from his pocket and placed it on the desk. "This is a list of your creditors in Kent. While extensive, I am certain it is not complete. You are almost £5,000 in debt, Mr. Kendrick, over twice your income."

"Shopkeepers," Mr. Kendrick spat. "What are they to me?"

The look of distaste on Darcy's face grew more severe. "I have bought up your debts. You now owe *me* £4,800, and unlike shopkeepers, I *can* take you to court."

"Debtor's prison, Kendrick," Richard said with a predatory

snarl. "It is King's Bench in Southwark for you. Who knows, you *might* survive it."

Darcy continued, "In addition, my men of business shall soon hold your mortgage. If you cannot pay me, I shall take possession of Glendale Farm. You will be hearing from my solicitor."

The obese man seemed to shrink in his chair. "Gentlemen, I-I beg you to reconsider! I am innocent of these accusations!" He pointed at Richard. "Always the Fitzwilliams have been my enemies! First, the earl stole Rosings from me, and now the son wants me dead! You must not listen to him!"

"You delude yourself, man," Darcy spat. "Sir Lewis bought Rosings Park upon his baronetcy. It was never part of the de Bourgh family holdings. It was never yours to inherit, and Sir Lewis could dispose of it as he wished. The court has made this clear, but you choose to ignore these facts."

Richard shook his head. "All this deviltry over land forever out of your reach. I shall waste no more time on a drunken fool." He backed from the desk and glanced about. "Come, my friends. It is time we departed this pigsty."

He and Darcy had taken a few steps towards the door when there was a loud crash accompanied by a shriek of pain. The two whirled about to see Buford, still standing next to the desk, brandishing his now-shattered cane.

"My hand!" Mr. Kendrick screamed. "He broke my hand!"

By now, Gregory and Frost had dashed into the room.

Buford jabbed what was left of his cane under Mr. Kendrick's fat chin. "You are fortunate it was not your head," the knight calmly stated before he glanced at his friends. "I saw the bastard reach into a drawer and pull a gun." He gestured toward a small pistol on the worn, filthy carpet. "I am afraid you owe me a new cane, Fitz." He prodded Kendrick again. "It is a pity I do not have my sword."

Gregory retrieved and unloaded the pistol, while Darcy grasped

Richard's arm. "Fitz, I know what you are thinking, but you must not—"

Richard shook him off. "Do not concern yourself. I shall not hang for the likes of him." Mr. Kendrick sat, moaning and cursing. "Let him rot in gaol."

Gregory tossed the harmless firearm onto the desk, and the party from Rosings left the decaying shell that was Glendale.

*Rosings*

CORPORAL FROST WAS IN THE DRESSING ROOM, LAYING OUT Sir John's clothes for dinner, when his employer called for his attendance in the bedroom. Upon entering, he was surprised to see not only a grim Sir John and Lady Buford, but a frightened Abigail Smith as well. Frost was immediately on his guard; there was no reason for Abigail to be in the master's bedroom unless…

*Unless they had been found out.*

Gritting his teeth, Frost assumed a position of attention, his mind working franticly. Surely, this was the end of his and Abigail's employment with the Bufords. He only hoped they would receive a recommendation, for if they were dismissed without a character, he had no idea how they would get by.

"Corporal Frost," said Sir John formally, "I thank you for your attendance. A matter of some importance has come to our notice."

*Damn it, this is my fault. I have been careless*, thought Frost. *Abby told me it was dangerous to carry on here, but I insisted. One of the other servants must have seen something.*

Sir John continued. "As you know, we Bufords do not tolerate fraternization between unmarried servants."

*I could return to the army, but the pay won't support the both of us. I won't abandon Abby, though. I won't!*

"Therefore, imagine our surprise and disappointment to learn that your friendship with my wife's personal maid had progressed to something quite unacceptable."

Abigail broke down in tears.

"Sir, you must not blame Miss Abigail. I accept full responsibility for my actions." *Perhaps we can immigrate to the Canadas, or America.*

Sir John frowned. "Oh? Did you force your attentions on—"

"No! Never!" cried Abigail. "He did nothing wrong!"

Frost turned to the sobbing maid. "Abby, no! This is my fault."

Abigail wrung her hands. "Lady Buford, I am so sorry for what we have done. I know I have disappointed you, but we could not help ourselves! We love each other! Please don't send us away! I-I'll work in the kitchens...anything!"

Lady Buford did something surprising—she took Abigail's hands while saying to her husband, "Enough of your folly, John!"

A wry grin grew on Sir John's face as he got to his feet. "I take it, Frost, you plan to do the honorable thing in this matter?"

"Yes, sir. We shall marry as soon as we are settled." *Where, I have no idea.*

"Good, good. We cannot have any objectionable behavior going on above stairs, now can we? Bad for discipline, you know. Do you have a situation in mind?"

"John!" cried Lady Buford.

Frost could not make out what Sir John was about. "I...I might have some ideas, sir, but nothing definite yet."

"Ah." Sir John smiled. "Well then, may I suggest remaining in our service?"

"What?" Frost was stunned.

Sir John laughed while Lady Buford turned to Abigail. "Sir John and I would like you and Corporal Frost to train to be our housekeeper and butler at the Dower House at Buford Manor. I know Frau Lippermann and Roberts currently have those positions. Roberts has talked of retiring soon and Frau Lippermann...well, she is not best placed as housekeeper, given her poor English. Would serving under them for a time until you know your duties be of interest? Mother Buford has already given her blessing."

Frost and Abigail stared at each other. Under-butler and assistant housekeeper would allow them to marry and stay in service with the Bufords!

Sir John tried to look stern. "You two would have to marry first, mind!"

Frost and Abigail smiled. "Of course, sir! We accept!"

Sir John patted Frost on the back. "Excellent! We shall have the banns read once we get back to Buford Manor. In the meantime, you shall continue with your current duties." The jubilation in Buford's voice grew somewhat serious. "I trust there will be no further carrying-on in the meantime?"

Abigail blushed while Frost sighed. "No, sir. I give you my word."

"Wonderful," said Lady Buford. Her smile disappeared as she gazed at her maid. "Abigail, is something troubling you?"

"Oh, no madam!" she responded. "You and the master have been too kind to us. But, what of Frau Lippermann? Is she to be discharged?"

"Your concern does you credit, Abigail, and only validates our decision for your future. Do not concern yourself over Frau Lippermann. She is happy here and will not return to Vienna. She will either remain with us in a new role, or she may decide to take a position at the manor. Frankly, I think she will be relieved at the change. She has difficulty with English, despite her hard work learning it.

"But enough of such matters. This is a cause for celebration!"

"Indeed!" Sir John handed a bottle of wine to Frost. "Open it, Davy, so that we may all drink a toast to you and Abigail! Hurry, man!"

Davy Frost, former corporal of light dragoons, valet to Sir John, and future butler of the Buford Dower House, grinned at his intended as he did the honors. Their future secure, life could not get better than this.

That night, Buford and Caroline lay intertwined in bed, Caroline absently caressing her husband's left shoulder. "You are so quiet."

"I am sorry, Caro. I was preoccupied."

"Have you any misgivings over Frost and Abigail?"

"No, none at all. It is a different matter altogether. Richard and I have been speaking, and he suggests I write to Lord Castlereagh or the Duke of York about a position in government."

"The Duke of York?" Caroline's voice became alarmed. "You wish to return to the army?"

"No!" Buford instantly returned. "We spoke of civilian staff work or perhaps diplomacy."

Caroline relaxed. "Oh, you frightened me. I could not bear it if you fought again."

"I said I would not. Besides, I am useless with this arm."

"I shall not have you say that again!" Caroline rose and looked down on Buford, her green eyes flashing. "You are not helpless! Think of Lord Nelson and what *he* did with one arm and one eye."

"Nelson is also dead."

"John! You promised me you would not fight again, and I mean to hold you to your vow."

"I jest with you, dearest! I shall never fight again. I promise."

"Wicked man!" Caroline settled back into his embrace. "Richard's idea has merit, though. You could prove invaluable with your gift of languages. What is your opinion?"

"It may mean travel overseas."

Caroline grew quiet for a time. "It would be an excellent opportunity," she said slowly. "You should pursue it."

"You would not find it hard to leave all your friends and come away with me?"

Caroline was incredulous. "You mean to take me with you?"

"Of course—you and the children."

"Oh, John! How you tease me, you horrible man! I thought you would go by yourself, as you did in Belgium."

Buford shuddered. His decision to send Caroline back to England during the Hundred Days Crisis, while well-intentioned, was the worst mistake of his life. It set in motion the series of misunderstandings that nearly led to disaster. Believing Caroline had forgotten him, a drunken, despondent Buford succumbed to the seduction of an old lover, the French spy, Countess Roxanne de Pontchartrain. But Caroline had remained true. Her letters from England had been misdirected, just as Fitzwilliam had always claimed.

During their courtship in 1814, Buford arrogantly subjected Caroline to small, secret tests to determine the extent of her transformation from a selfish, would-be member of the *ton* to a respectable young lady. She had never disappointed him, and he should have remembered that during his black days in Belgium. He had not, and so it was he who had failed the greatest test of all. Two years later, he still felt unworthy of Caroline's love and devotion.

Buford could never confess his fall to her, for the possibility of losing her affection and respect terrified him. He bore his injuries as penance for his sins and vowed to live the rest of his life being the faithful, loving husband and father his wife and children deserved.

"I shall never go away from you if I can help it," Buford told her. "I need you, Caro."

"My place is with you, wherever you go. I never want to be parted from you."

Buford kissed Caroline with all the love he had for her, and she responded in kind. Love soon turned to passion, and the two were lost for a time. They could not speak coherently until they found themselves in an embrace again, this time naked and spent.

Buford lay half dozing, flat on his back, while Caroline played with the hairs on his chest. "Johnny," she said hesitantly, "may I ask you something?"

"Of course."

"That…that woman in Vienna, Countess Pontchartrain—"

Buford thought his heart had stopped.

Caroline frowned. "Did you love her? I mean, before we met. Did you want to marry her?"

Buford wanted to scream a denial, but something told him there was more to this. "No, Caro, I did not," he said as calmly and carefully as he could. "Why do you wish to speak of her?"

"This talk of travel brought her to my mind. I-I always wondered, you know. She is very beautiful."

Buford knew he should not say empty, stupid things. Only truth would do—as much truth as he dared. He could not lose Caroline's love and trust and survive.

"The *comtesse* is very beautiful, that is true, but only on the outside. She was empty and wicked on the inside, and I never loved her. I was very foolish." *Beyond foolish*, he thought.

"She is much like my former friend, Annabella Norris, then," Caroline concluded.

"Yes. Caroline, you should know I loved none of them. I was the worst sort of man, only interested in my own pleasure. I never knew what love truly was until I met you. I never wanted to marry anyone except you." Buford looked into her eyes. "You have given me so much—you gave me Bea, and—" His hand caressed her belly. "You are well, both of you?"

Caroline gave him a small smile. "We are both well. You must not be upset over my illness in the morning. It was the same with Bea." She placed her hand over his. "What do you wish for?"

"I do not care." He smiled at her unbelieving look. "Truly. It does not signify whether the babe be a boy or girl."

"Men always want sons," Caroline insisted.

"I do not have an estate to pass down."

"He *will* be a boy. I am determined."

Buford chuckled. "If you say so, my dear." He grew serious. "Caro, I love you. You must know that."

She kissed him. "I depend upon it, sir." She changed the subject.

"Richard's idea—shall you act on it?"

"I have not fully decided, but it cannot hurt to write a letter to Wellington. He would know whether any positions are available."

"He will help you," Caroline said firmly, "especially after *I* write to his cousin, Lady Beatrice Wellesley."

"Caroline!"

She smiled impishly. "She is my friend. You cannot stop me."

# Chapter 34

The time for leaving had come. It was a bright, mild day when the various carriages were assembled outside the grand entrance to Rosings. Sergeant Gregory and Corporal Frost supervised the footmen packing the guests' belongings, while Mrs. Nivens and Mrs. Foley saw to their charges' things. A footman held Romeo as he strained against his leash.

Unexpectedly, Lady Catherine came down from the dower house to see the visitors off. The grand dame took her normal station outside the door, attended by Dawson and Mrs. Jenkinson. She condescended to shake each hand, even Lady Buford's, although it must be noted her eye was fixed on the shrubbery when Caroline took her hand. Surprisingly, Lady Catherine embraced Mrs. Darcy, declaring her a dear niece, and kissed both Bennet and Franny, though she ignored Chloe Wickham.

Sir Richard and Lady Fitzwilliam saw their friends off in a more informal manner. Anne kissed Darcy's and Buford's cheeks while Richard performed the same service to Elizabeth and Caroline.

Richard crouched to look little Chloe in the eyes, a grin on his face. "Farewell, Miss Wickham," he said formally, the name now rolling off his tongue as easily as any other. "I hope we shall meet again soon, Cousin Chloe. Be good to your aunt."

Chloe bit her lip, tried to curtsy, but instead threw her arms about his neck. "Goodbye, Cousin Richard!" she cried. Richard gave her a kiss.

Anne lost all composure as she said goodbye. She had grown up an only child, sickly and alone, but she found her sisters as an adult, and she embraced them both. "My heart is breaking! Say we shall meet again soon!"

"Such a silly thing to say, Anne," Caroline whispered in her ear. "Of course, we shall." She glanced at Anne's lavender dress, trimmed in black. "When it is proper, we shall make merry in London, I am determined!"

"Caroline is always right!" quipped Elizabeth.

"Eliza!" Caroline's frown lacked any censure.

Elizabeth laughed, and then held Anne's face with both hands. "My dear cousin, you must write me as often as may be."

"You must be certain to stay in good health," Anne replied with a deliberate look at Elizabeth's waist. "You too, Caroline."

"We shall." Elizabeth lowered her voice. "Your time will come, Anne, I know it."

"And Eliza is always right," added Caroline.

Anne kissed all the children farewell. Bennet and Chloe then ran over to Romeo, to the greyhound's obvious delight.

The gentlemen's parting was far more solemn. Richard embraced his brother-at-arms. "Buford, you have saved my bacon again. I do not know how I can—"

Buford brusquely cut him off. "Enough of that, Fitz. Why, if we stood here recounting the times we did good service for each other, we would be knee-deep in snow. Does your head still pain you?"

"I am well. The spells have passed. And you?"

"In a strange way, better than I have been in years." There was the old confidence, tinged with arrogance, in Sir John Buford's eye again. "I shall write to Wellington as soon as I return to London."

Richard smiled. "Safe travels, Brother." Buford gave a soldiery nod, and Richard turned to Darcy, who suffered to be embraced as well. "Permit me to trouble you for another list of candidates for steward," Richard sheepishly requested. "I promise not to be so pigheaded this time."

"I shall do better than that," Darcy declared. "There is a young man, Mr. Barksdale, at Pemberley who shows great promise. I would groom him for steward if Thompson were older. I shall send him down for you to interview."

Richard gave him a half smile. "If you recommend him, that is good enough for me. You are to Pemberley?"

"Not yet. I want to be assured the troubles up north are done before I bring Elizabeth and the children. We shall be in town, and I shall write to Mr. Barksdale." He glanced at the carriages. "I see all is ready."

"You never were one for long goodbyes, Darcy!" Richard pointed out with all good humor before embracing him again. "Thank you for everything, Cuz."

Darcy, embarrassed, only nodded. Within minutes the coaches were loaded and on their way, the ladies waving handkerchiefs as their carriages rolled down the gravel road. Anne and Richard held hands as they watched their friends depart.

"Anne! Richard!" cried Lady Catherine. "Pray recall you are in public!"

The puzzled pair turned to her. "I beg your pardon?" said Richard.

Lady Catherine gestured with her walking stick. "Such familiarity is unseemly! What will be next? Shall you ravish my daughter in the lane?"

The two looked at each other in confusion before remembering they were still hand in hand. Richard wore a grin as he raised Anne's hand slightly. "Ah! I suppose you refer to this particular situation. I am of your opinion, milady, but my wife is insistent."

"Indeed, I am, Mama." Anne's declaration was less certain than her husband's, her eyes moving between the two.

"You see? There is nothing for it." With that, Richard moved quickly and picked a surprised Anne up in his arms.

"Richard! What *are* you doing?" cried his aunt.

Anne's voice was lower. "Yes, Richard, what are you doing?"

"Saving us all from mortification!" With his lovely burden, he walked nonchalantly to the front steps. "You see, Lady Fitzwilliam is determined to be ravished this instant. As a dutiful husband, I must bow to her demands, but I shall protect our good name. As you so correctly observed, it would not do to perform this activity in the lane." He stopped before Lady Catherine. "Shall you come in for refreshment? Anne can call for tea in the parlor for you."

His dumbfounded mother-in-law, now aware of his teasing, shut her open mouth and scowled. "Never mind. I shall remove myself to the dower house. Dawson, attend me!"

Anne slipped her arms about Richard's neck. She asked calmly, "Shall I call for the barouche, Mama?"

Lady Catherine, her wrinkles folding into a smile, patted Anne's face affectionately. "I can manage the few steps to the house. Always have I been celebrated for my health and vigor. I shall see you at Wednesday dinner, my dear." She glared at Richard. "Certainly, this...*activity* shall be concluded by then."

Richard wore an innocent expression. "One never knows about such things, Aunt." He bowed as much as he could with his wife in his arms. "We wish you a good day." With that, the pair disappeared into Rosings Manor.

Mrs. Jenkinson's giggles were silenced by Lady Catherine's frown. "Mrs. Jenkinson, as my daughter and son will be...*occupied* for some time, you may accompany me to take tea. Dawson, let us be off."

The three ladies walked down the steps of the great house, observed by Sergeant Gregory and two footmen, one still holding Romeo's leash. Gregory laughed to himself.

"Red Fitz—always tweaking the lion's mane." Shaking his head, the three made their way to the servant's entrance.

Despite Richard's declaration, the pair did not go up to Anne's chambers. Instead, they ensconced themselves on the couch in Richard's study. There, Anne curled herself in her husband's lap, her head on his shoulder.

"Now, this is pleasant," drawled Richard, one arm supporting Anne while the other rested lightly on her knee. "Just an old, battered soldier and his best girl." He placed a light kiss on her forehead. "Are you well, my dear?"

She snuggled deeper into his embrace. "I am, Richard. I just wish to settle my feelings."

"Shall I get you something? Wine? Tea?"

She closed her eyes. "I need nothing but you."

Some little time passed before Richard spoke again. "Are you troubled, love? Will you tell me?"

Anne was silent so long that Richard thought she had either fallen asleep or refused his request. Just as he was about to ask again, she spoke in a soft voice.

"My thoughts are so muddled I can hardly make sense of them. So much has happened in just a few days. You lay insensible in your bed! I was so frightened!"

"Hush, Annie. I am well, I assure you."

"Pray allow me to finish, Richard. You are so dear to me I can no longer imagine my life without you. I only wish to keep you near me, safe and happy." She frowned. "But my Cousin Kendrick, that terrible, terrible man! Are you certain Darcy's plan will succeed?"

"His debts are extensive, and he has no hope of settling them. Mr. Hibbert will have him in hand soon if he has not already. Kendrick will never trouble us again."

"Gaol is too good for him!"

"We are of a like mind about that, love." He stroked her hair. "What else ails you?"

Something between a gasp and sob escaped her lips. "I love Lizzy and Caroline as my sisters, but...when I look at their happiness, their...

children." She wept. "Richard, I so want to give you a child! But what if I cannot? I do not wish to disappoint you, to lose your love."

"Impossible!" Richard cried, hugging her to his breast. "You cannot lose my love, Anne. Whether we are blessed with a dozen children or none, it does not matter. All I desire is you."

Anne's tears faded, and they sat in comforting silence for a while.

"Richard, what is to be done for Cork Johnson? We owe him a great deal."

"I have thought on that, dear, but I wished to speak to you before anything was done. He risked his life to save mine, even though his relations were Kendrick's agents."

"What does Mr. Haddick say of his recovery?"

"He will live and walk, but the other results of his wound are not known. Certainly, his shoulder will pain him for some time. We do not know whether he can work again."

"That does not matter!"

"Certainly not. He and his mother should not be made to return to that cabin. It was barely suitable before, and now it is completely unfit for man or beast. I thought of setting them up on the Home Farm, closer to the village."

Anne looked up, her eyes alight. "Yes, yes, that is what we shall do! And Cork will find work on the estate, if he is able, or be given an allowance if not."

"You are ahead of me again, Annie." He kissed her. "I am not surprised."

Just then there was a knock at the door. "Colonel," came Gregory's voice, "there's a message just come. Says it's urgent."

"Oh, what evil now?" cried Anne.

It was a stern Sir Richard that helped his wife to a seat on the sofa before crossing to the study's door. He opened it just enough to take the message from his majordomo and request him to stand by. After closing the door, he read the note. He was clearly surprised at the contents.

"Richard, what does it say?"

"Kendrick shall not be going to prison," he responded softly.

All of Anne's fears reignited. "*What?* Why not?"

Richard looked grimly at his wife. "It seems he decided to take matters into his own hands and ate a pistol ball."

It took Anne a moment to understand his meaning.

Stuffing the note into his pocket, Richard returned to Anne's side. "Kendrick shall never bother anyone again."

"*Good,*" Anne muttered into his coat.

# Epilogue

The Honorable Sir Richard Fitzwilliam was enjoying a lazy Sunday afternoon in his library, reading a book. It was his favorite time on the Sabbath, for it was quiet, very unlike services at the Hunsford church with Mr. Collins's droning sermons and Lady Catherine's monopolization of the conversation later at dinner. For a few short, precious hours, Richard was at peace. He was willing to share his sanctuary with a few favored guests, and two of those preferred companions now snoozed at his feet.

There had been changes at Rosings, as the master and mistress strived to place their own stamp on the manor, much of it focused on this very room. Richard and the new steward, Mr. Barksdale, had labored over the last year to restore the plantations to a fit state, pleasing the tenants and filling the estate's coffers.

However, the funds for redecorating the couple's favorite room came from an unexpected source. Reginald Kendrick had neglected to leave a will, and in a case of extreme irony, the courts determined that Lady Anne de Bourgh Fitzwilliam was his heir. Anne and Richard wasted no time in disposing of Glendale Farm. They paid off Kendrick's debts, including those Darcy bought, and renovated Rosings's library with the remaining funds.

The door opened without a knock. Richard did not look up to see who it was, for only one person in Rosings could enter any room in the house with impunity. In any case, his companions gave him fair warning—they were instantly on their feet, dashing to greet the intruder.

"Ah, Romeo, Juliet, you must not jump!" cried Lady Fitzwilliam. "Down, my loves, down! Romeo, I shall thank you to sit, sir!"

"Good luck to you, my dear."

Anne shot a glare at her husband as she walked over to a small sofa, purposely placed next to Richard's armchair. The warm afternoon sun fell most agreeably upon Anne's preferred seat and gave the location a secondary source of comfort. The two small white dogs eagerly jumped up and draped themselves over Anne's lap as she took up her needlepoint, Romeo's tail beating a rapid cadence on the armrest.

"I believe," Richard observed, "the reason we acquired a second Italian greyhound was for the express purpose of my having my own lap dog. It seems, however, that yours is to be favored over mine."

"Oh, dear, I am sorry," said Anne. "Here, take Juliet."

Richard held up a hand. "No, no. Far be it from me to disturb such a tender scene of domestic felicity. It is not their fault they like you best." For their part, the dogs seemed not at all guilty for their partiality.

"I am sorry, Richard," she said as she gently stroked the dogs.

"Do not be, sweetheart. Zounds, *I* like you best too. I cannot fault their taste."

Anne smiled, put on her spectacles, and returned to her handwork while Richard began reading again. The dogs settled down and slept. For three-quarters of an hour they relished the blessed silence, as only two people totally in harmony with one another can enjoy each other's company without sharing more than five words in all that time.

Unfortunately, all good things must pass. The pair's attention was caught by slow, heavy steps, accentuated by the sound of a cane against the floor. The dogs awoke and turned towards the door.

"Lord, make us truly thankful for what we are about to receive," murmured Richard as he set aside his book.

Anne's hushed admonishment was drowned out by the entrance of Cork Johnson. He looked slightly ridiculous in his livery: his chest too broad and his arms too long for his coat, and his head too large for his powdered wig.

"Lady Catherine de Bourgh," he announced with a slight bow, his serious words spoken in a surprisingly high voice for one so large.

Richard shook his head. He needed Sergeant-Major Gregory to have a footman's coat made to fit Cork properly. Mrs. Johnson was a seamstress, for heaven's sake!

Lady Catherine, a woolen wrap around her shoulders, gingerly made her way into the room, no small feat given the amount of space Cork occupied. Back bent, she relied more upon her ebony-painted walnut walking stick than before.

She frowned at her daughter. "What are those creatures doing here?" By now Cork had left, closing the door behind him.

Richard rose from his chair and walked over to his wife's mother, gently taking her free arm. "I believe you have met Romeo and Juliet before."

"Of course I have! There is nothing amiss with my memory! I wish to know why they are here! Animals in public rooms—it is not to be borne!"

"Mother," said Anne in a tired voice, for they had had this conversation many times, "there is nothing amiss with having pets in the family rooms. It is all the fashion in town."

Lady Catherine scowled as Richard seated her in an overstuffed chair, one reserved for her exclusive use. She plopped into it heavily. "I cannot like it. Not all things that are fashionable in London are proper! The next thing I know, you both will be attending parties at Carlton House!"

Anne rolled her eyes. "Hardly *that*, Mother."

"I do not approve of the behavior of the Regent and his friends. Such debauchery!" Lady Catherine continued. "And you, Richard! I shall have you know I have been celebrated for the keenness of my mind. You will remember it." She softened her reprimand by kissing his offered cheek. "Now, where is he? Where is my grandson?"

"He shall be sent for. No, Anne," Richard said to his wife, "remain seated. I shall see to it."

Richard stepped out of the library, making his escape, only to see Mrs. Jenkinson had anticipated him.

"I learned Lady Catherine had arrived and took the liberty of procuring this little man." She passed the small bundle wrapped in a blanket to Richard.

He allowed himself a moment to gaze lovingly at the precious burden before slowly returning to the library, careful not to awaken the baby, accompanied by Anne's former companion.

"Here you are, my dear aunt." He handed over the swaddled child to his grandmother. "Lewis Hugh Richard Fitzwilliam."

Lady Catherine peered at the baby, rocking him gently, a tender look upon her wrinkled face. "A fine name—a goodly name. A kingly name. Ah, yes, he indeed has the Fitzwilliam look about him. Did I not say so before? You have done well, Anne, my love. Very well, indeed."

Richard proudly regarded the little miracle in Lady Catherine's arms. Anne's pregnancy, fraught with danger, was as difficult as the Fitzwilliams had feared. There had been months when Anne never left her bed. Richard could not recall Anne's hours of pain during her labor without dread. And for all that, their boisterous boy was born hale and healthy, and Anne recovered from her laying-in exceedingly quickly.

There had been changes in his friends' lives, as well. In the last eighteen months, Elizabeth and Caroline had been safely delivered each of a son, and a few months ago, so had Mary Tucker.

But the greatest change had been in his own life. Richard now knew what it was to be a father. It was a feeling like no other—a mixture of wonder, pride, concern, and love. A love transcendent—different from, yet just as ardent, as that he held for his wife. He understood his own father better. Oh, how he missed the old lion! Not a day passed when he did not yearn to speak with him, to share these new and remarkable sentiments. The earl would have adored this child.

"Andrew, of course, shall be his godfather," he informed his aunt, "and Anne desires Lady Buford for his godmother."

"Not that horrid Buford woman!" cried the grand dame. "She was insufferably rude to me when last she was here!"

Anne would have none of it. "Caroline is a dear friend, Mama. We owe more to her and Sir John than we can ever repay."

"I am appalled you would take the side of a stranger over your own flesh and blood." Lady Catherine scowled at her daughter but found it failed to intimidate the young mother. In her ascendancy and marriage, Anne had found her strength. "Have it your way, then! I would wish you to think the better of it. Mrs. Darcy would be a superior choice."

Richard was taken aback by this declaration. "You would choose Elizabeth over Caroline?" He had known that Lady Catherine had condescended to visit Pemberley occasionally, despite the pollution it had suffered, and had been civil to Elizabeth during family gatherings, but this was beyond everything.

"Of course! The mistress of Pemberley is far above a mere knight's lady, especially one who has roots in *trade*."

"Mother…" Anne said dangerously.

Lady Catherine continued as though nothing had been said. "Besides, it would be a fine thing should Lewis and little Anne Francis Darcy wed."

Anne was incredulous. "*Franny?* Mother, she is but fifteen months older than Lewis! They are babies!"

Lady Catherine raised her chin. "Anne, it is not too soon to think of the future!"

Richard rolled his eyes. "And so, it begins again."

# THE END

# Suggested Readings

**Austen, Jane.** *Pride and Prejudice.*
— . *Sense and Sensibility.*
— . *Northanger Abbey.*
— . *Persuasion.*

**Caldwell, Jack.** *The Three Colonels: Jane Austen's Fighting Men.* Naperville: Sourcebooks Landmark, 2012.
— . *Mr. Darcy Came to Dinner – a Jane Austen farce.* Prairieville: White Soup Press, 2013.
— . *The Companion of His Future Life.* Prairieville: White Soup Press, 2014.
— . *The Last Adventure of the Scarlet Pimpernel.* Prairieville: White Soup Press, 2016.
— . *Persuaded to Sail.* Prairieville: White Soup Press, 2020.

# About the Author

J ack Caldwell is an author, amateur historian, professional economic developer, playwright, and like many Cajuns, a darn good cook.

Jack is the author of eleven Jane Austen-themed historical novels. *Pemberley Ranch* is a retelling of *Pride & Prejudice* set in Reconstruction Texas. *Mr. Darcy Came to Dinner* and *The Companion of His Future Life* are *Pride & Prejudice*-flavored farces.

The **JANE AUSTEN'S FIGHTING MEN SERIES** began with *The Three Colonels,* a sequel to *Pride and Prejudice* and *Sense and Sensibility. The Last Adventure of the Scarlet Pimpernel* is a mash-up of *Northanger Abbey* and *The Scarlet Pimpernel. Persuaded to Sail* is a sequel to *Persuasion. Rosings Park* is a sequel to *The Three Colonels.* The upcoming **Brother of the Bride** is a sequel to *Pride and Prejudice.*

In 2015, he released the first four books of a series of historical novels about New Orleans, titled **THE CRESCENT CITY SERIES**. *The Plains of Chalmette* begins the series, commemorating the Bicentennial of the Battle of New Orleans. Jack marked the tenth anniversary of Hurricane Katrina with three modern novels: *Bourbon Street Nights, Elysian Dreams,* and *Ruin and Renewal.*

When not writing or traveling with his wife, Barbara, Jack attempts to play golf. A devout convert to Roman Catholicism, Jack is married with three grown sons. Jack's blog postings—**The Cajun Cheesehead Chronicles**—appear regularly at **Austen Variations**. Web site: **Ramblings of a Cajun in Exile** –
https://cajuncheesehead.com
Blog: **Austen Variations** – http://austenvariations.com/
Facebook: https://www.facebook.com/pages/
Jack-Caldwell-author/132047236805555
Twitter: @JCaldwell25

## JANE AUSTEN'S FIGHTING MEN SERIES

The Three Colonels

The Last Adventure of the Scarlet Pimpernel

Persuaded to Sail

Rosings Park

Brother of the Bride
*Coming Soon!*


## THE CRESCENT CITY SERIES

The Plains of Chalmette:
*A Story of Crescent City*

Bourbon Street Nights:
*Volume One of Crescent City*

Elysian Dreams:
*Volume Two of Crescent City*

Ruin and Renewal:
*Volume Three of Crescent City*


## OTHER NOVELS BY JACK CALDWELL

Pemberley Ranch

Mr. Darcy Came to Dinner
*A Jane Austen Farce*

The Companion of His Future Life